Poor Naked Wretches

Rosemary Rowntree

Poor Naked Wretches

Copyright © Rosemary Rowntree 2025

The right of Rosemary Rowntree to be identified as author of this work has been asserted in accordance with the Copyright, Designs and Patents Act 1988.

All rights reserved. No part of this publication may be reproduced, stored in a retrieval system, or transmitted, in any form or by any means, electronic, mechanical, photocopying, recording or otherwise, without the prior permission of the copyright owner.

ISBN: 9798341005815

Cover photograph: Srdjan Randjelovic/Shutterstock

Also by Rosemary Rowntree:

When Good Men Die

Earthquake, Wind, and Fire

Poor Naked Wretches

Rosemary Rowntree

Chapter 1

Sally was the first to die.

Her morning hadn't started well. The temperature fell sharply overnight and she was bitterly cold, her sleep fitful. Aching and stiff, she made her way to the Hills Road Shelter, arriving shortly after it opened. She had expected to find Joe there, but there was no sign of him. She collected tea and toast and found herself a small table at the back. Putting her breakfast down, she shook off her rucksack and dumped it on the opposite chair. A moment later, one of the men whom she least liked came over to her table. A leer on his face, he was about to push her rucksack off onto the floor when she told him to leave her alone. Her voice was loud enough to attract the attention of the serving staff, and he decided to back off.

After half an hour, there was still no sign of Joe. She approached the counter and asked if he'd been seen. She was disappointed; he must have forgotten. She was angry too. She knew he had spent some time at Tommy's, the residential shelter, but had not stayed long. He'd promised to tell her why over breakfast, now that she'd been told there might be a place for her there soon.

She wandered around the city centre for a while then decided to walk along Tennis Court Road. The street was long, with no shops or cafés. Most of the buildings were probably associated with the university, although there were a few cottages with tiny gardens. Sally remembered he'd been sleeping there recently. Eventually she saw his rucksack and sleeping bag in the porch of a seldom used doorway. At first, she thought he might still be inside but looking closer she could see it was empty. Why had he left his stuff behind? Certainly, the sleeping bag was pretty worn, but even if he'd found himself a better one, why would he leave his rucksack? She was pondering this dilemma when she noticed a small, half empty, bottle of Scotch. She knew he liked a drop, although he rarely had enough money to buy any. He certainly wouldn't leave it behind voluntarily. She decided to take it. If she didn't find him, she would have it herself. If she didn't, someone else would, before his other stuff was swept up and thrown away.

After wandering aimlessly around the streets of Cambridge until she tired, she decided to use some of her rapidly dwindling cash to treat herself to a baguette and coffee in the Grafton Centre. When waiting staff made it clear she was outstaying her welcome, she moved on. Dusk began to fall. Not knowing what else to do, she returned to Tennis Court Road, hoping to find Joe. The doorway was empty. Further down the street there was still no sign of him. She found a sheltered corner and settled down for the night. She was still angry, and also depressed. Maybe his whisky would help relieve the tedium and discomfort of her life.

Her relief proved to be permanent. Which is not to say that her death was painless. She experienced diarrhoea, projectile vomiting, extreme pain and violent seizures. Soon she was struggling to breathe.

Sally's body was found early the following morning. The Control Centre arranged for an ambulance and police. Two uniformed constables were first on the scene. The woman who called it in refused to give her name and had disappeared. PC Taylor had seen the dead woman occasionally during the last few weeks and had spoken to her a couple of times. While waiting for the ambulance, he called Mary Canning, the most senior and experienced outreach worker in the city. He explained what they'd found. She was shocked and concerned. Sally was the last person she would have expected to die like this. She'd looked fit enough the previous day. On the strength of her feedback, and with a well-known tendency to cover his arse whenever possible, Taylor asked for someone from CID to attend. By the time DI Morton Harrison arrived, the paramedics had pronounced her dead.

At Parkside station an hour later, Morton was taking a mug of coffee from the machine. His boss, DCI James Upwood, approached, clearly on a similar mission, suggesting they shift to Upwood's office.

"So, Morton, what have we got?"

"No idea, Sir. An unexplained death for sure, but beyond that I haven't a clue." Upwood laughed. He was in a fairly relaxed mood. For once his team had no very serious case on the go. Some were trying to catch up on paperwork, others taking some well-earned time-off-in-lieu.

"I hope you don't mean that literally!"

"All I can tell you is that she was youngish, early thirties, we think. Reasonably well-nourished. Thought to be in decent health. She'd vomited, that was clear. And there was a small empty bottle of Scotch beside her." Morton took a sip of his coffee and grimaced. "Goes by the name of Sally Bremner. Hasn't been on the streets long. Taylor tells me he spoke to Mary Canning, the outreach worker. Sally tried her best to look after herself and was on a waiting list for a place at Tommy's. Could have got it in a week or two apparently. She wanted to get her life back on track. Shame. Quite good-looking, actually."

Upwood looked at him sharply. "Does that make a difference, Morton?"

Morton practically blushed, an unusual look for a man with his physique. A big man, former rugby player, his battered features and short, gingery blond hair tended to make him appear much less intelligent than he was. Suspects he interviewed underestimated him, something they would rarely do with his boss. "No. Of course not. Just can't see how someone like her ends up dead." He paused. Upwood abandoned his coffee. Really, it was undrinkable. Morton resumed. "The whole scenario seems hinky."

Upwood chuckled, good humour restored. "Define hinky."

It was Morton's turn to laugh. "Can't, Sir. It just doesn't seem right. How does an apparently fit and healthy young woman end up dead in the street?"

"Alcoholic poisoning?"

"Maybe. Mary said she wasn't a drinker, so maybe she couldn't handle it. We'll have to wait for the PM report. In the meantime, it's being treated as an unexplained death."

"Probably misadventure. No signs of foul play I take it?"

"No, none that I could see. It might be suicide, I suppose."

They were silent for a moment or two. Morton recalled that suicide was a touchy subject for his boss. He'd been torn off a strip more than once for what Upwood thought were inappropriate remarks. A case thought to be suicide but which turned out to be the murder of Katie Melhuish's partner. Upwood had subsequently become very close to Katie. And it wasn't so long ago that one of their colleagues had hanged himself either, after murdering his desperately ill mother. Altogether a touchy subject, then. As he rose to leave, he took a chance. Upwood didn't always take kindly to questions about his personal life. But he seemed in a decent enough mood today. "Katie come back yet, Sir?"

Upwood frowned. "No. And I haven't heard from her for a while. If I'm honest Morton, I'm worried about her."

Such an admission was uncharacteristic of him, but Morton decided not to press him further.

Chapter 2

It was Friday before Sally's PM report came through. Morton's sergeant, Debra Graf, had read it. "What does it tell us, Deb?"

"No signs of physical injury. No signs of drug abuse or chronic alcohol abuse, although she had drunk alcohol shortly before she died. Nothing unusual in the tox reports. Cause of death was acute respiratory failure. There was evidence of hypoxia."

"What does that mean, for heaven's sake?"

"Tissue damage caused by lack of oxygen, apparently."

"How might that happen?"

"I googled it. Lots of straightforward medical reasons. But also drugs like fentanyl, and poisons like cyanide, can cause it."

"Neither of which showed up in the tests, I take it."

"No. But I'm not sure if they usually test for those."

Debra sat quietly while Morton quickly scanned the report for himself. Like Morton, she, too, had been keen on sport and had played football competitively for nearly twenty years before injuries took their toll. Now she played bridge competitively. There was a tournament this coming weekend. She was looking forward to it. She suppressed a grin.

Before Morton could offer any further thoughts on Sally's PM, his phone rang. There was another body.

The dead man had been found in an alley off Johnson's Lane that led to the River Cam. This time Morton and Debra both attended. Neither could see any evidence of crime. The man, like Sally, had vomited, but there were no obvious signs of injury. Neither was there any obvious sign of drug abuse. In his case, too, there would be a post-mortem. They had to be as thorough as if it were a clear case of murder. They knew from experience, as well as their training, sometimes the most obvious looking case could turn out to be anything but. It was essential that they followed the correct procedures at the outset. Leaving Debra to supervise, he arranged for all the resources needed to examine the body and to secure the immediate vicinity.

Morton was troubled. This was the second unexplained death of a street sleeper in a matter of days. Both victims appeared to be less than forty years of age and even allowing for an unsatisfactory lifestyle, could have been expected to live longer.

Mary Canning also admitted concern to them. "What can you tell us about him, Mary?"

"Kevin Broome? Not a great deal." She looked weary although it was not yet midday. Maybe it was the nature of her role. "He didn't talk a lot, but we picked up bits and pieces over time."

"How long had he been sleeping rough?"

"About three years I should think. He was quite resourceful. He'd got himself a tent as well as sleeping kit and always packed it up in the morning and carried it around with him. I guess he was used to that. He had a medical discharge from the Army: PTSD. An all too familiar story. Seen too many of his mates blown to pieces by IEDs or taken out by snipers. Stuff like that can mess with your mind."

"Did he beg?"

"Not that we know of. But I think people saw his Help for Heroes wristband and gave him money."

"Drugs, alcohol?"

"Only a bit of weed from time to time perhaps. He did drink though."

"Did he have any particular mates?"

"No. A real loner. Most sleep close to the city centre. It's warmer and the shop doorways offer better protection. We advise them to. It's safer. Kevin didn't. He quite often slept on Jesus Green, which is close to where you found him. No one else does for obvious reasons."

Morton looked perplexed. "Sorry, you've lost me. Can you explain?"

"Generally, it's fine by day. But there's a gay cruising site near the lido, and the toilet block is used by street drinkers. They don't all necessarily sleep rough, but there are fights from time to time. You wouldn't want to sleep there unless you could look after yourself."

This was all news to them. Problems on the streets were not dealt with by their team and neither had served in uniform in the city.

"So, no mates. Anyone have a grudge against him that you know of?"

"No idea. I really don't think I can tell you anything else. No, sorry."

They thanked her. The PCSOs they'd spoken to couldn't add to what she had told them.

Back at Parkside they took stock. "So, what's your gut telling you Deb?"

"It's odd, I'll give you that. We've not had a prolonged cold spell. It's not likely to be hypothermia. You?"

"I don't like it. Kevin may have had psychological problems, but he seemed reasonably fit. It sounds as though he walked more than most, assuming he came into any of the shelters and soup kitchens for meals. Sally was even younger and had only been on the streets a few months."

"It's a bugger."

"My thoughts exactly. Where do we go from here?"

"No idea. I can't see any sensible line of investigation. I think we'll have to see what the PM report on Kevin has to say."

His phone rang. It was Mary Canning. "DI Harrison. There's something I ought to tell you. I should have remembered it when we were talking about Sally. Another street sleeper went missing about the same time she died. A guy they call Smokey Joe. We've not seen him for days." He thanked her and asked Debra to make some enquiries.

Later she went back to see him, a frown on her face. "You're not going to like this."

"Go on, make my day. It's Emma's birthday and we've got a babysitter."

She laughed. "You're OK. It'll keep till tomorrow. But I think we need to get a warrant to examine Smokey Joe's records at Addenbrooke's. He died there four days ago."

Upwood had left Parkside before the news of Joe's death reached him. It was unusual for him, but he had quit his office at a reasonable time, hoping to beat the Friday evening rush hour. As he closed the front door, he could see the light on his answerphone blinking. The phone sat purposely on his hall table so he wouldn't miss messages. He knew instinctively it was June, the mother of his late wife, Anne. June was practically the only person who used his landline, apart from cold callers. But for her, he'd probably have had it disconnected. He pressed the play button. "James, dear. It's June. Katie came to see me today. She's in a dreadful state, poor girl. You need to go and see her. I'll let her explain." He could hear the anxiety in her voice. Immediately he dialled June's number, only to hear her outgoing message. Friday. Their night for whist with friends. He decided against leaving a message.

It was weeks ago that Katie, a partner with a large accountancy firm, had been sent at short notice to Buenos Aires. Apart from a couple of brief messages, he'd not heard from her since. She'd been very upset after their last meeting. She'd pleaded with him to tell him what had happened to his wife and daughter. When he'd told her, Katie had been deeply shocked and said she needed time to come to terms with it. It was natural she would be upset. Anyone would. But for the life of him, he couldn't work out quite why she had taken the news so badly. Now she'd been to see June and Jeff, whom she had never met. Why?

Chapter 3

When Katie opened the door, Upwood was appalled. Her face was a kaleidoscope of purple, blue and yellow. Heaven knew what injuries were hidden by her dressing gown. It looked as though she had lost weight. Her eyes and hair were lifeless, and he guessed he had just woken her. "Dear God, Katie! What happened?" She stood aside so he could enter, closing the door gently behind her. He led her to the sitting area at the far end of the room. "Was it an accident?"

"No." She shuddered.

"What then?"

"I was mugged." Getting the words out was clearly an effort.

"Here or there? When did you get back?"

"It was there. I got back yesterday."

He looked at her, compassion written on his face. "When did you last eat?"

She almost laughed but didn't quite pull it off. "June gave me a sandwich at lunchtime."

"And before that?"

She shook her head. "I can't remember."

"Can I make you a coffee? Or would you rather have something stronger?"

"A whisky, please. I haven't had any painkillers for hours."

"Fine. I'll sort that and see if I can rustle up a light meal."

This time she did manage a brief laugh. "You'll be lucky. I haven't done any shopping since I got back."

Upwood was a decent, inventive cook. He needed to be as he enjoyed good food and lived on his own. He smiled at her. "You know me. Like a challenge."

In less time than she could have imagined, he called her to the dining table and offered her a plate with a modest portion of pea risotto. "What did you use? There was no stock."

"Water and white wine. The parmesan was well over date, but I reckon it'll be OK as crisps. Come on. Do the best you can. Then we should have a proper talk."

She didn't finish it, but she made a valiant effort. They did finish off the rest of the white wine, then took another Scotch back to the seating area.

"Feeling better?"

She gave him a weak smile. "A bit. June told you, I suppose."

"Only that you'd been to see her and that I should pay you a visit. Nothing else. Tell me what happened."

She sank into the sofa, letting out a heavy sigh. "I was attacked. It was about a week ago. Quite late. I was just coming out of the office and some guy rushed at me, punched me, knocked me to the ground and then kicked me repeatedly." She shuddered again at the memory.

"Did he rob you?"

"No." She paused, fiddling with the collar of her dressing gown. She couldn't look at him.

"Did you get a good look at your attacker?"

"No. He came at me from the side. Took me completely by surprise. The light was poor, and he was wearing dark clothes. I didn't see his face properly." She shrugged. "And he was wearing a hood."

"Of course. Bastard. Did you tell the police?"

"One of my colleagues came out of the office and chased him. He did. Call the police, I mean. But they never came to talk to me. I was taken to hospital, but they didn't keep me in."

Upwood decided to hold back from further questions about her attack. "Tell me about your posting. How did it go?"

Suddenly she burst into tears. He moved closer to her and gently drew her to him. Her sobbing on his chest broke his heart. Whatever had happened it had clearly shaken her to the core.

After a while she became calmer and raised her head. "It was a nightmare. A complete fucking nightmare."

Upwood was shocked. She never swore. "Tell me."

"I was told that I had to replace a partner who was on sick leave." She sat up, straight, anger lending her strength. "What a joke! They'd made him choose between rehab or resignation. He went for rehab. Cocaine. Although they didn't tell me any of that to start with. He had been running an M&A operation like mine. Five weeks ago, I found evidence of fraud in one of his recent projects. He'd seriously over-stated the benefits of an acquisition to his clients, the potential purchasers."

"What would he gain from that?"

"I suspect he was bribed by the other company to inflate its value." Her response was heavy with cynicism.

"Obvious, really, I suppose. What did you do?"

"I told the senior partner on site what I'd found. He looked into it and then the guy responsible was fired. Only then did they tell me about his cocaine habit. I don't know how they dealt with the client company. All hell broke loose. The atmosphere in the office was evil. Some of the staff were openly hostile to me. A week later I was attacked."

"And you think he was behind it?"

"I did do. Until I found the note."

Upwood stared at her. "What note?"

"He'd shoved it into my coat pocket. The guy who attacked me, I mean."

"Are you sure? Someone in the office might have done it. You said some were hostile."

"No. I'm fairly sure I felt him do it."

"What did it say?"

"There's nowhere I can't find you."

"In English?" He dreaded her answer. He knew what it would be.

"Of course. It was from MacKay."

"Christ. It's a bit of a stretch."

"The note was in English. I told you." She held out her glass for a refill. He wasn't sure it was a good idea: she hadn't had much to eat. But he rose, refreshed both their drinks and returned to the sofa.

"The attacker might have thought the message would be more threatening in your own language." Upwood was grasping at straws here.

"Maybe. But it's just up his street, isn't it? Another campaign of terror. And the longer he's in prison the more contact he has with career criminals who can arrange this sort of hit."

She'd clearly given it some thought, and she was right on both counts, he decided. It really was right up MacKay's street. After all, he'd blackmailed his nephew, forcing him to attack Katie to discourage her from investigating Mark's death. And made him send her threatening messages. He blamed her for the fact that he was serving a life sentence for murder. He'd had all the time in the world to plan this latest attack. Upwood decided to downplay it for the time being.

"June told you why I went to see her, I imagine."

"No, she said she'd let you explain."

It transpired that George, the husband of Katie's old friend Melanie, had told her that trolls were spreading rumours about Upwood. They were suggesting that the death of his infant daughter, Olivia, had not been natural, and that Anne's was not suicide. Upwood was seething but tried hard to control his feelings. Now was not the time to add to Katie's burdens.

When she'd finished telling him about her visit it was clear to him that, as usual, June had been fully supportive of him. He valued her love and friendship. She and her husband Jeff had been a tower of strength after Olivia and Anne had died, even though their loss was as great as his.

Katie slept much of the next two days and was feeling somewhat stronger by Sunday evening. Upwood had visited Waitrose in Trumpington and done a big enough shop to last her the best part of a week. He'd slept the previous couple of nights in her spare room but needed to return home in order to prepare for the week ahead. Katie had urged him to stay. She did not feel safe. It was a situation they'd been in before. In the end they agreed she would remain indoors. He would stay with her each evening until they could work out a longer-term solution.

Chapter 4

On Monday morning DS Mo Ramachandran and DC Margaret Starr were with Dr Chalmers, an intensive care specialist, trying to understand the records on Smokey Joe. Dr Chalmers confirmed that the paramedics had found him comatose and suffering breathing problems. They had intubated him and on arrival at the hospital he was taken straight to the resuscitation room.

There they assessed him as 3 on the Glasgow Coma Scale – the lowest score possible: no eye, verbal or motor response. Arterial blood gas tests gave results for a number of crucial factors, including pH, oxygen level, carbon dioxide level, lactate, bicarbonate and glucose. They concluded that he showed signs of both hypoxia: low levels of oxygen in the arterial blood; and metabolic acidosis: increased acidity in blood and tissue. The former could rapidly lead to brain damage. The latter could easily lead to death.

Chest X-rays showed no underlying pneumonia as a potential cause of the hypoxia. A CT scan of his head showed no obvious causes of his low score on the coma scales, such as an intracranial bleed, tumour or infection. Another scan ruled out a pulmonary embolism. Venous blood tests ruled out poisoning by paracetamol or aspirin. They did indicate poor kidney and liver function, although there was no evidence in his liver of a long-term problem with alcohol. The tests did show a moderately high level of alcohol in his blood, however.

As a precaution he was prescribed antibiotics. For a homeless person, and one who may well have aspirated some of his vomit, pneumonia was a definite risk, even if he did not present with its symptoms. Despite the medication, and following a brief rally and a return to consciousness, he did in fact develop pneumonia. Subsequent tests ruled out bacterial infections, such as TB, or viral infections such as flu, as causes. HIV was also discounted. He died.

But by the end of the meeting neither Mo nor Margaret felt they were any the wiser. Because Joe's death was sudden and the circumstances complicated, a post-mortem had been arranged. The results were not yet available, and it wasn't known if there would be an inquest.

Mo and Margaret left the doctor's office and made their way to the hospital café. They grabbed drinks and snacks and found a table in a quiet corner.

"So, what next, d'you reckon?"

Mo stirred his coffee. "Let's see if we can talk to any of the staff in the high dependency unit who looked after him. Maybe he gave someone a clue about how he became so ill."

Margaret sounded sceptical. "Is that likely?"

"Probably not. But let's try it as we're here."

Their request at the HDU was likely to be unwelcome. As usual they were operating at full capacity and were short staffed. Fortunately, the person in charge was sympathetic. She suggested that they talk to two of the nurses who had cared for him. Their luck was in; both were on duty. They were sent to the adjoining family room. Margaret thought that whoever had selected the Jeremy Kyle Show to watch on TV either suffered from an over-developed sense of irony or, more likely, was brain dead.

The young man who joined them a few minutes later looked nervous. "Will this take long? We're rushed off our feet." He slumped onto one of the moulded plastic chairs, all the room provided. Metal legs screeched on the hard floor as the chair shifted under his weight. A tall, lanky man, he was clearly uncomfortable.

"No, I'm sure it won't. We just want to ask a couple of questions about Joseph Walters."

"Go on then."

"We'd like you to tell us anything you can remember about what he told you."

"He didn't say much. Sounded confused. It was all I could do to get his name and birthdate."

"Is that it? Didn't he give you his brother's name?"

"Yeah. Not much help cos he had no phone number or address. That was it. I didn't get anything else out of him."

"Not even where his brother lived?"

The young man thought for a moment. "Yeah. Right. He probably did, like, now I come to think of it. Lynn, that's what he said. Confused me cos he said brother not sister. I thought he was right out of it. P'raps he meant King's Lynn."

Ten minutes later a young woman, whom Margaret guessed was Filipina, came in and introduced herself as Dolores. She had little to tell them apart from the fact that he had said, two or three times, whisky. She laughed, saying she'd told him she didn't have any. Mo and Margaret exchanged glances. He made a mental note to arrange for Joe's fingerprints to be taken.

It hadn't taken long to track down Joe's brother, Malcolm Walters. He didn't live in King's Lynn itself but in Clenchwarton, a small village to the west of the town. Malcolm was in his mid-fifties, with grey hair and a closely trimmed beard. He was dressed in dark camo joggers and top and a pair of scruffy trainers. A mutt growled at his heels.

"I don't know why you've come. I 'aven't seen Joe in years." His voice was as surly as the mutt.

"We're sorry for your loss, Mr Walters," offered Mo.

"Don't give me that garbage. You don't know me, and I doubt you knew 'im."

"He told the hospital that you were his next of kin. That's why we're here. May we come in, please?" The door opened straight into a cluttered living room. Walters let them pass but did not invite them to sit. "May we?"

"If you must." The mutt picked up his tone of voice and let out another low growl. Walters pushed him with his foot, an action just short of a kick, and the animal slunk out into a room at the back.

Mo resumed. "There will be arrangements to make in due course, so we imagine that will be your responsibility. There will be a post-mortem, but we don't know if there will be an inquest."

"So what 'appened then?" Walters remained standing, leaning on an old-fashioned tiled fireplace, and lit a cigarette.

"He was found in the street in Cambridge, in a coma. He was taken to hospital but died some days later. The cause of death was pneumonia."

Walters flicked his cigarette in the general direction of an ashtray, already overflowing. "Stupid bastard."

"What d'you mean, Mr Walters?"

"Stupid to get 'isself into that position. Losin' his job, divorce, losin' 'is 'ome."

"How did that happen?"

"God knows. Did better at school than I did. Got himself a half-way decent job. Then he started gambling, Mandy, 'is wife, said. No idea why. Internet gambling. Ran up huge debts. They 'ad constant rows about it. She threw 'im out and divorced 'im. He lost 'is job. Ended up on the streets. I tracked 'im down a few times and dragged 'im to people who could of helped. Shelters an' stuff. He didn't wanna know. He kept telling me to piss off. So I did. I decided it was 'is bed, like, and 'e'd 'ave to lie on it. It's not as though we'd been very close before."

"When did you last see him?"

"Must be four year ago. More. I tried to find 'im before that Christmas and 'ave one last go at getting the stupid bastard to sort 'isself out."

"So you've not seen him recently?"

"No."

"When were you last in Cambridge?"

"Cambridge? Probably not since that last time. Why, are you suggestin' I went in and bumped him off to protect the family reputation?" He laughed harshly. "We ain't got a rep to protect."

"What happened to his wife?"

"Mandy? Not sure. I did hear she'd shacked up with an old school friend and gone up north. She never wanted to clap eyes on 'im again, I know that much. Can't say I blame 'er, mind."

They left soon after. As Margaret said: "Not a happy family."

Chapter 5

A week later Morton and Debra had the post-mortem results for Kevin. They were no more useful than those for Sally – the cause of death was once more given as acute respiratory failure. Yet again, no clue as to what triggered it. The coroner had made it clear that an inquest would be necessary in both cases. Morton decided it was time to get his boss involved.

The last thing Upwood wanted to hear was that the deaths of three street sleepers were the result of unlawful killing. He knew, though, that following the inquest the coroner would have to determine the cause, and that the terms used to describe that cause were defined. Some of these could clearly be ruled out in these three cases: stillbirth, road traffic collision, industrial injury or disease, alcohol or drug abuse, for example. Some seemed unlikely; there were no signs to suggest that accident or misadventure had occurred in any of the cases.

"You really think they're all unlawful killings?"

"I do, Sir. Only because any other explanation seems implausible. We've already agreed that most of the causes the coroner can determine are not remotely relevant. Suicide? All three? And all in ways we can't establish? No chance. They certainly aren't lawful killings. So what are we left with?"

"Well, unlawful killings, or natural causes."

"They can't all be natural causes that can't be identified. It's too much of a coincidence. We have to be looking at unlawful killings. The only other option open to the coroner is an open verdict. Surely that leaves us in much the same position."

"Come off it Morton. What you're saying is that someone's bumped off three people in short order using some undetectable poison." He stared at his junior officer. "This is the stuff of tabloid fantasy. Or fiction."

Morton was tempted to say that they were much the same thing, but sensibly decided his boss would not be impressed with the idea.

"All three suffered from hypoxia. We're told that drugs like fentanyl, and poisons like cyanide, can cause it. No traces of those were found. But maybe there is an element or compound that causes it that the usual tests don't show."

"But they are hardly prime targets for an assassin using a mysterious poison. It's daft even to think of it."

They were silent for a minute or two. "Even if we believe they may be murders, what is there to investigate that we haven't already done?"

"Other than the fact that they all slept rough we've found few connections between them. Joe and Sally sometimes had breakfast at the same shelter. Kevin didn't go there. Neither Sally or Kevin had ever stayed at Tommy's the accommodation shelter. Joe did some years ago, apparently, but couldn't stick to their programme and he left after a couple of weeks.

"The pathologists found no puncture wounds, so it doesn't look as though they were injected. And they found no evidence of pill residue in their stomachs.

"There was little forensic evidence of any conceivable use. They did find a half bottle of cheap whisky in Sally's den, nearly empty. It didn't yield any clues other than Joe's smudged prints and some clearer prints of hers. We couldn't find any of Joe's stuff – it had probably been cleared off the street while he was in hospital. In the alley where we found Kevin there were several empty beer cans and various fast-food wrappers. One of the cans had his fingerprints on it, but interestingly, no others. Nothing else helpful. There are no CCTV cameras anywhere near where Kevin was found. There are some cameras in Tennis Court Road but they're on buildings for their own protection. None gives a view of the sites close to where Joe and Sally were found. Door to door enquiries have produced no statements of any value whatsoever."

"So what would you suggest we do?"

"I think we should talk to people on the streets again. Find out if anyone's been offering them food or drink. When interviews were done before, it was to find out if anyone had seen any suspicious activity near the three scenes in question. So far as I know, they weren't asked about any unusual interactions they may have had with anyone else."

"How many people are we talking about?"

"It's difficult to know. The shelters say there are as many as thirty. PCSOs don't think it's that high. But we get people coming into the city on a daily basis begging. It's not always easy to tell them apart. But if we go to the shelters that do breakfasts and suppers, we should catch up with a good few without having to trek round the streets at night."

"Who do you want to do it?"

"Margaret for one. She is probably the friendliest looking of us."

"Is she still partnered with Mo?"

"Generally. They seem to work well together."

"Anything else?"

"I want someone to look again at the food and drink wrappers to see if there's anything we've missed. I'm planning to get Debra to do that."

"OK. But don't spend too much time on it."

Morton bridled. "Why? Because the victims don't deserve it?"

"Damn it, Morton. Surely you know me better than that. No, it's just that the proposition that a serial killer would target rough sleepers sounds so unlikely. Never mind we have no evidence at all suggesting murder."

"How many serial killers do you know who target wind farm developers?"

Upwood glared at him. "OK. Point taken."

"And it won't play well in the press if we get another one and aren't seen to be taking it seriously."

This time Upwood winced. Cambridgeshire Constabulary in general, and he in particular, had taken a mauling from the media over the murder investigations earlier in the year. Morton was right. They had no choice. Apart from anything else, other people sleeping rough needed to believe they were safe.

DS Aamodin Ramachandran, known to his friends and colleagues as Mo, was potentially a more intimidating prospect than DC Margaret Starr. They decided she would tackle the day centre that served breakfast. He would tackle the one that served supper – some of their customers might be more difficult at that time of day.

Margaret arrived at 8.00 am just as the Hills Road Centre was opening. The supervisor, Elaine Harding, was expecting her. Margaret found herself in the lobby of an imposing Victorian building with only discreet signage on the outside. Elaine took her straight to the café where volunteers were already busy preparing for service. The centre offered hot and cold breakfasts, seven days a week. It also provided shower and laundry facilities as well as clothes lockers. There was a good range of support services, too, for people who wanted to get themselves back into a more self-sufficient lifestyle. Margaret asked her what she knew about Sally and Joe. Elaine told them what she could but had little to add to the accounts others had given them.

Elaine took Margaret over to another table where two men sat. One had a plate of beans on toast, the other just toast. Both had mugs of steaming tea. The supervisor introduced her and said she'd like to ask them a few questions about Joe and Sally. She then left Margaret to it.

The men were wary. Margaret addressed the older of the two first, as he was about Joe's age. He gave his name as Biker. No, he hadn't known Joe well. Joe was a bit of a loner.

He hadn't ever spoken to Sally, but he'd seen her around, in the shelter sometimes. He had no idea whether he'd seen either of them on the days they became ill. One day was much like the rest. The younger man, who declined to give a name, said he didn't know either of them. Neither had seen any unusual activity on the streets in recent weeks.

Margaret moved on to other tables and spoke to eight more people. None had any information of value to offer. One or two seemed uninterested. Others looked as though they were beginning to realise the streets were even less safe than they thought.

Mo tried his luck in the evening shelter. The only interesting news was that two of them claimed to have found cans of lager left beside their pitches a couple of weeks earlier. Both had drunk it and come to no harm. Neither could remember the brand. No, they had never known this happen before. Some people would hand out coffees or sandwiches, but handing out booze was unheard of.

Chapter 6

Upwood was mesmerised by the sparkling sea in front of him. Even though the moon was waning, the light was remarkable. Katie had been granted three months' sabbatical following her sick leave. She had arranged to borrow the apartment from her friend Monica and had begged him to join her. He was familiar with the area, and she was not, so it made very good sense that they went down together. After he left, she could stay on for a few weeks if she wanted to.

The apartment was in the Marina de la Marquesa, west of Estepona on Spain's notorious Costa del Sol. He loved the area and had spent a good deal of time birdwatching, especially in the area close to the strait. But that had generally been in spring or autumn. Now in late May, he had missed the main spring migration. However, the upside was that he might finally have the chance to see a Bonelli's Eagle, a rare species that so far had eluded him. He'd heard that a pair was nesting in Utrera Gorge.

When they arrived, they had an early meal on the pavement outside Mesón de la Torre, one of the oldest restaurants in the village. Its menu had probably changed little since it first opened, and it continued to offer a complimentary glass of Manzanilla with a saucer of nibbles when guests were seated. Their meal was leisurely and the service attentive.

When they returned to the apartment it was too early for bed, so they took nightcaps out onto their terrace. People were still walking and cycling along the paseo below them. Waves lapped gently on the shore. Upwood was in an unusually tranquil frame of mind. *"When the moonbeams kiss the sea..."*

"How very poetic, James."

"Well it is from a poem. Love's Philosophy, by Shelley. One of Anne's favourites. especially the second verse."

"Do you know the rest of it?"

"No. But I can look it up." He passed her his phone.

She laughed quietly. "Oh no, you're going to have to read it to me."

"Really?"

"Yep."

So he did:

> *"See the mountains kiss high heaven*
> *...And the waves clasp one another;*
> *No sister-flower would be forgiven*
> *...If it disdained its brother;*
> *And the sunlight clasps the earth*
> *...And the moonbeams kiss the sea:*
> *What is all this sweet work worth*
> *...If thou kiss not me?*

"Beautiful. And beautifully read. Makes me feel quite romantic."

It was he who needed a lie-in the following morning, much to Katie's amusement. She was on the terrace with toast and coffee when he came out, still in his bathrobe. Suddenly there was frantic screeching, and a small flock of green birds shot past.

"God in heaven! What was that?" Katie had her head in the newspaper and hadn't seen them.

"Monk Parakeets." He pulled out his pocket guide.

"You take that into the shower with you?" She was helpless with laughter.

"I'm not that daft. I picked it up from the living room when I came out. I like to keep it handy when I'm down here."

"Go on, then. Show me."

He did. It was a handsome, small bird with bright green plumage and a long tail. Very fast and very noisy.

"They're a bit of a menace, not native to Spain. They've not been on this stretch of coast long. Same with

Purple Gallinules. Years ago, we had to drive nearly to Cádiz, to see them. Now, on a good day, you can see them at Sotogrande."

"What are they like?"

"Here, look." It was a glossy bird whose plumage was almost iridescent. "They call it a Purple Swamphen now. No, don't ask! I don't know why. It annoys me the way birds are renamed." He chuckled. "There is one they should rename though: the Bearded Tit."

She was struggling to control her laughter again. "OK, I give in. Why?"

"It's not a tit. And it doesn't have a beard." He paused. "It has a moustache."

Her peal of laughter was simply joyous. "You're making it up."

"I'm not. Don't you remember? I pointed one out when we went to Minsmere."

"No. I wasn't on very good form that day." The reason for that trip was not one she was keen to recall. "The parakeets are noisy little buggers, aren't they?"

"Never mind, they've gone now. And the Blackbird has started singing again."

"Thank God there's something I recognise." Smiling, she held the paper out to him. They'd picked up a couple on their way to supper. "Did you read this one yesterday?" she asked.

"No. I read the other one. Found anything interesting?"

She handed it over. "See for yourself."

One year on, no solution to shocking murders...

A year ago, a prostitute had been found dead on waste ground close to the western end of the Estepona bypass. Apparently, the authorities did not know how she'd died. She was the fourth such case in twelve months. He went back inside for his iPad and searched for the newspaper's website. It took no more than a few minutes to find the reports of the earlier cases. All the women had been prostitutes with pitches on the A7, the coast road. None had shown signs of injury. None had died of drug or alcohol overdoses. Upwood was intrigued.

"Well. How very strange."

"There can't possibly be a connection. Can there?"

"I shouldn't think so for a moment. But I know someone who might be able to tell us a bit more."

"Who's that?"

"A former colleague. He might have some contacts. Do you mind if I give him a call?"

She shrugged. "You're only here for a week."

"I know. But aren't you interested too? You showed me the article, after all."

She laughed. "Go on, then."

He went in to make the call but came back almost immediately. "Voicemail. I left a message. Why don't you rustle up a picnic while I get dressed? I know a great spot not so far from here. It will give me a chance to show you some of the scenery."

He took her up to Casares, one of Andalucía's stunning white villages. Perched on the side of a mountain with its houses seemingly stacked haphazardly one atop another, it was dominated by a Moorish castle. He wanted to show her the Griffon Vultures, a colony of which roosted high in Sierra Crestellina behind the village. As soon as they had parked in his favourite viewing point, half a dozen floated across, hardly moving a muscle, drifting on the thermals. He reminded her of the damage done to these magnificent birds by the vast arrays of wind turbines close to the Strait of Gibraltar. Only then did she really understand why it made him so angry.

He then drove to the other side of the village and turned off-road. They ended up in a broad valley at a spot where the rivers Genal and Guadiaro met. The river was wide and rocky, and the water level low, chattering over the pebbles of the riverbed. They heard the chirps of Bee-eaters, the distinctive, repetitive call of a Cetti's Warbler and the rich melody of a Nightingale. Katie was thrilled by the Nightingale. "Surely they don't sing by day?" she asked. Upwood smiled. "They do. This one's probably a male, holding territory."

Just as they reached the apartment, Upwood's mobile rang.

"John, hi. Thanks for returning my call. How are you?"

Pleasantries concluded, Upwood explained his unofficial interest in the prostitute murders. His friend, former DI John Laidlaw, was intrigued to hear about the Cambridge cases. He had a golfing buddy, an officer in the Policía Nacional, whom he could talk to, off the record. Upwood gave him his email address.

Katie and Upwood walked into the port for another early supper. Their table was in a secluded corner and over the main course Upwood, encouraged by their love-making of the previous night, asked the question which had been troubling him for weeks.

"Why did you not keep in touch, Katie? I missed you." He reached across the table and let his hand fall on hers. "I worried about you."

She looked at him; her large brown eyes, tinged with violet, were extremely beautiful. But troubled. She sat back in her chair and took a large gulp of wine. "I thought I was pregnant."

"You what? But you were on the pill." Upwood kept his voice low, but he was seriously worried. Love her he did, but he couldn't cope with the prospect of another child.

"I was. But I'd not been on it long enough. I'd been going through a bad patch, getting broody, thinking of clocks ticking. I'd begun to wonder what it would be like to have a child with you." She looked up at him. He was speechless.

"That night I cooked you dinner at my flat? I was prepared to take a chance. And then when I missed my next period I began to panic. And when I missed the second one, I was absolutely terrified."

Upwood put the question as calmly as he knew how, his heart racing. "How far gone are you?"

She laughed hysterically. "I'm not. It was a false alarm. Apparently very high levels of stress can do that. But by the time I knew I was safe I was so ashamed of myself I didn't know what to say to you."

"Oh, good God. Blakeney. You'd missed a period by then?"

"No. But when you said that you could never ask another woman to carry your child, I realised how stupid I'd been. I had no right to risk conceiving a baby you wouldn't want." Finally, Upwood understood why she'd been so upset when he'd told her about Anne and their daughter.

Shortly after 6.00 am the following morning his mobile rang. It was Morton. "I hate to do this to you, boss. But can you get back? We've got another one."

The Bonelli's Eagles would have to wait.

Chapter 7

By ten, Upwood had boarded a flight to Stansted. By three he was at Parkside. The fact that he was supposed to be on leave, and that it was also a public holiday, mattered not. He'd called Morton when his plane landed and arranged that they meet as soon as he got in.

Neither was concerned about idle chat, they just nodded to each other. "What have we got?"

"Executive summary? Male, IC1, rough sleeper. About forty. Found in Mill Road Cemetery yesterday. No wounds or injuries. No evidence of recent drug abuse. He'd vomited."

"Just like the others by the sound of it. Talk me through it."

"A call came in to the control room at 4.30."

"Why so early? A bit early to walk the dog. It wouldn't even be light then."

Morton laughed. "You'll like this, Sir. Some anorak was out to hear the dawn chorus!"

Upwood laughed, too. "Just past its peak, but not as daft as it sounds, Morton. Some forty different species have been recorded there, including most of our best songbirds. Anyway, we digress. Carry on."

"He says he didn't touch the body. The deceased was still in his sleeping bag. Our anorak –"

"Name, Morton, for crying out loud!"

"Sorry, Sir. David Starling." He waited for a response, but Upwood was in no mood to humour him. Morton grinned. "Starling watched him, he says, for a couple of minutes and convinced himself the man was dead and called it in. Debra met me there about half five and we had a preliminary look. Uniformed officers secured the three entrances."

"Which are? I can't remember."

"Mill Road itself, via a long path leading to the south-west corner, Norfolk Road, leading to the north-west corner, and Gwydir Street on the east side."

"Don't know that last one."

"Not much used, I should think, apart from the locals. You have to go through a small industrial estate."

"How big is the cemetery?"

"Three and a half hectares."

"Come on, Morton. I don't do hectares."

"Just winding you up, Sir."

"Don't. You've ruined not just my beauty sleep this morning, but also my holiday."

Morton didn't miss a beat. "8.6 acres."

Upwood shot him a look. "Cheeky sod. What state's it in? I've not been there for years."

"A bit like an overgrown garden, I'd say. If you remember it has walls on all sides, then a path shaped like a broad bean runs round it." Marriage to Emma, an artist, had given Morton a tendency to describe things in colourful terms. "Here, look at the map. There's a clearing in the middle where there used to be a chapel, and paths which radiate out to the perimeter path. In some areas the grass is kept reasonably short. Some areas, especially around the edges, are quite wild."

"Where was the body found?"

Morton pointed to the map. "Here, in this clump of trees in the south-east corner. A couple of yards off the path."

"Was there anyone else in the cemetery at the time Starling found the body?"

"We don't think so. But the growth is quite thick in some parts so it's possible there's still someone in there. Certainly no-one has left since we secured the entrances."

"When will the PM be done, do we know?"

"Not before tomorrow. SOCOs are still on site. We are trying to secure CCTV where we can. Most of the units in the industrial estate have cameras, as do some retail units on Mill Road. But they are, as per, covering their own premises so there's not a very good field of view. Norfolk Street is mainly residential. There's one terrace of small shops and a scattering of individual ones. Unlikely to be a very good hunting ground."

"Have we found any useful evidence at the locus?"

"So far as I know, no. But it's very early. I asked if they'd found any food or drink containers nearby and they said no."

"Have we ID'd him yet?"

"No. We are going to get Jim Bligh, the senior PCSO, and Mary Canning to have a look at him later this afternoon. They might have some idea."

"Does Detective Superintendent Adams know about it?"

"Yes. I called her. If I hadn't done and she picked it up from the media, she would have gone ballistic." Morton had developed a good working relationship with Emily Adams earlier that year when charged with handling a very sensitive investigation involving both Katie and Upwood. Katie, who had recently returned from another long spell overseas, had received a number of malicious text messages, one of which threatened to expose her affair with a 'high ranking police officer'. Upwood was forced to admit to Emily that he had slept with Katie while his team were investigating the murder of her partner, Mark Campion. On the first occasion, she could easily have remained a suspect, although Upwood was adamant that by then she had been eliminated. Nonetheless, he had acted unprofessionally. Emily had been furious and relations between them became, to say the least, fraught. Morton had, fortunately, solved the issue quickly. Andrew MacKay, Mark Campion's killer, had blackmailed his nephew into sending the texts. Emily had been impressed with the way Morton had handled the matter. MacKay was still in Whitemoor, a Category A men's prison north of Cambridge, but Upwood knew he was still capable of causing serious trouble.

Upwood returned his attention to Morton. "Good call. She's aware of the other cases, but doubts they're all murders. I imagine she'll be much more concerned now. You've scheduled a briefing tomorrow?"

"Yes. 8.00 am."

"Good. Have the press picked up on it yet?"

"Of course. All it takes is a post on social media about the police presence and they're all over it. We've issued no statement yet. But tomorrow we're going to have to think very carefully about what we say. We can't keep the lid on this much longer."

Upwood was painfully aware of the fact. He intended to call it a day and advised Morton to do the same.

Detective Superintendent Adams chaired the press conference, flanked by Upwood and Morton. The room was packed and noisy. The statement she read was measured and short. Short, because they knew so little. She identified the victims, giving brief personal details. She explained that Sally's post-mortem showed no sign of injury, wound or disease and, while the cause of death was unusual, there was no indication that it was unnatural. She confirmed that the first three deaths appeared to take a similar form and it therefore might be anticipated that Pete's would follow a similar pattern. She did not state that they suspected the victims had been poisoned. However, it was implicit in the advice that people should not consume food or drink found in the city's streets. By this point, Upwood could feel the tensions rising in the room.

Finally, Emily finished her statement by making an appeal to the public for any information about sightings of the victims on the relevant days, and of anyone leaving items of food or drink in the street.

Then the floor erupted. Emily looked in vain for any familiar face that might be remotely sympathetic. There was none.

"Frank Cheshire, BBC Look East. Why have you withheld vital information since the first death nearly four weeks ago?"

"We had no reason to believe four weeks ago that any crime had been committed."

"Sheila Grant, Anglia News. It must have been evident to you after the discovery of Kevin Broome's body more than ten days ago that both he and Sally had been murdered. Why was no statement made then?"

"There was no clear evidence of crime in his case. There is no virtue in worrying the public unnecessarily."

Grant shot back. "But you may have been responsible for the latest death. You didn't warn people." Emily made no response.

Frank Cheshire rose to his feet again. "What poison is being used?"

"We do not know for certain that poison is being used."

"Clearly you do, otherwise you would not give the warning about food and drink. So what is it?"

"I repeat: we do not know for certain that poison is being used. It is entirely possible that all four deaths are from natural causes. Until we have the results of the post-mortem on Peter Johnson, and any further forensic tests which may be necessary, speculation is futile."

Reporters clamoured for her attention. They asked the same questions in as many different ways as they could find. She still could not give them any satisfactory answers. But she had given them a sensational story.

Once the questions became repetitive, it looked as though they would be able to wrap up. Just as Emily began to signal the close by shuffling her papers, a final question came. "Trevor Rix, Cambridge Herald. Is it true, DCI

Upwood, that you went on holiday after it was already apparent we have another serial killer at large in Cambridgeshire?"

There was no acceptable answer that he could give, so he did not attempt one. He did however give the reporter a withering look. Emily stood, gathered her papers, reminded them to appeal for witnesses and closed the meeting.

Emily, Upwood and Morton repaired to her office. They all felt shell-shocked. Although there had been initial ambiguities about the first of the deaths, the wind farm cases were obviously murder. They knew where the murders took place. They knew the causes of death. There was forensic evidence to be gathered. They knew how to find witnesses. The murderer had not been a stereotypical serial killer by any means, but he did have a motive for his actions. Now, with these cases, nothing was clear cut. And they certainly had not the least idea of any motive a killer might have.

"I think we have to assume we're looking at murder. And that some sort of poison is involved. Why would anyone trouble to use something so obscure it remains undetectable?"

"It buys the killer time," offered Upwood. She nodded.

"There's no need for contact with the victim so much lower chance of leaving forensic evidence on the body, or even in the immediate vicinity," offered Morton.

She nodded. "I think that would be true even if the poison were not so obscure. Nevertheless, both perfectly valid points. But how the hell is he doing it?"

Upwood answered. "I've spoken to the head of Hinchingbrooke lab. They don't have the capability to carry out tests any more sophisticated than those they have already done in Sally's case. He's suggested two commercial forensic science companies, experts on toxicology and the use of exotic plants in medicine. He's bitter about what's happening in forensic sciences. He says the service has been under-funded for years and has to compete with commercial firms. Morale is rock bottom."

"That's as maybe," responded Emily. "But it's no help to us at all." Her tone was acerbic. "Have you spoken to either of the two experts yet?"

"No. We've emailed them with a brief and asked them what samples they need. National news coverage might galvanise them into action. There will be kudos for whoever identifies what killed our victims."

Emily grimaced. "Let's hope so. I have a nasty feeling our killer is not finished with us yet."

Chapter 8

Trevor Rix returned to his office in a run-down nineteen sixties block out near the airport. Upwood annoyed him. It was more than refusing to answer his question. He hadn't expected him to. He just wanted to put him on the spot. That withering look was uncalled for. Just because he was wearing a suit. Rix couldn't wear a suit in his job. He was always on the go. Leather jacket over a tee shirt was more his style. Upwood was hiding something. Rix wasn't quite sure why he'd come to that conclusion, but his journalistic instinct was pretty sound. And there was something nagging away at the back of his mind. Something he'd read recently? He'd not long moved to the Herald from a newspaper in Norwich, so he didn't have first-hand knowledge of events in Cambridgeshire. But research was a strong point.

After he'd filed his copy following the press conference, he spent an hour re-reading every scrap of coverage of the recent killings. Nothing jolted his memory. He went back to his archive of the wind farm murders, including that of Jeremy Mallon. Strictly, it shouldn't be put in that category, but his murderer had attempted to attribute his death to the other killer. So somehow, Mallon's case was always associated with the others. Upwood had faced heavy criticism during the investigations, once because he had been spotted having lunch with a good-looking woman at a Michelin starred restaurant in Rutland. He was accused of neglecting his duties. The fact that Sir George Bland, who was then Chief Constable, was also heavily criticised didn't interest Rix. Bland had retired. But Upwood remained fair game.

It took another two hours for him to find what he was looking for. It wasn't in any of the articles published about the cases. It was in comments posted on those articles. Questions had been raised about Upwood's suitability for his job and even whether he had any right to remain a serving officer. Unpleasant though some of the messages were, none was libellous, since the allegations were phrased as questions. There were two in particular suggesting that he might have been responsible in some way for the deaths of his wife and baby daughter. He searched Google. Eventually he found a brief report, in the Gloucester Telegraph dated July 2003, of the verdict into the inquest held into the death of Upwood's wife. It was recorded as suicide following postpartum psychosis. An earlier article, no more than a single paragraph, recorded the verdict in the inquest into the death of their seven-month-old child. The verdict was natural causes. Anne Upwood had killed herself just three weeks after the verdict was given on her daughter's death.

There was nothing in either article to suggest that Upwood had in any way been responsible. And in 2003 there was no Facebook, no Twitter. Social media was still in its infancy, so there was no means of leaving comments on an article other than by letter or email. So where had the recent rumours come from? Rix needed to give this some thought. In the meantime, he made a note to apply to the Coroner's Officer for copies of the post-mortem reports and any depositions taken at the inquests, and copies of the verdicts.

Rix had no contacts in any of the media local to Gloucester, nor in the police. He did, though, know Bob Beatty who worked on one of the Birmingham papers. He called him.

"Blimey, Tricks! Haven't heard from you for ages. What are you after?"

Rix laughed. "Rumbled already! You're right, of course. I need a contact in Gloucester police or newspaper, and I haven't got any. I'm following up an old story, maybe a crime cover-up."

"Can you give me a bit more detail, mate, so I know who's gonna be best?"

"Not bloody likely, sunshine! If there's a story there, it's mine. But quid pro quo and all that. I think you owe me. The Drayton affair?"

"God, you've got a long memory. How long ago was that?"

"Doesn't matter. You still owe me. So who can you give me?"

"I'll have to check. I'll call you back, right?"

It was already after eight in the evening and Rix decided to call it a day. As usual he was the last to leave the office. Years ago, he supposed, there would have been staff working at night. These days, some of his colleagues hardly showed up at all – they could all pretty much work on the hoof. He set the alarm, locked up and went out to the car park at the back. He was mightily relieved to see that his pride and joy, a Ducati Multistrada 1200S was still there. Every time he went out, he was afraid some miserable scrote would have nicked it. He'd bought it new, only a few months before, and it had cost him as much as a small saloon car. But it was much more versatile, and he loved the fact that it offered him four different riding modes. With the variety of surfaces he had to cover, on some of which he might just as easily have been completely off-road, this was a bonus.

He travelled the twenty-four miles to his rented flat in Chatteris in just over half an hour. He'd tried a variety of different routes, eventually settling on one through Histon, then up the Twenty Pence Road (the history of which he kept telling himself he must research) to Wilburton. His journey took him past one of the most peculiar churches he had ever seen, with a tower and four pinnacles, like pineapples. They reminded him of those on the corners of King's College Chapel. The B roads were straight, if poor, but he knew every dip, speed bump and pothole. They took him over flat country, hedges either side, until the land opened up further north to fields with fewer boundaries. After Wilburton he was on A roads, although sometimes it was hard to tell the difference. They were all single carriageway and while the traffic was not heavy there were often tractors and agricultural vehicles to contend with. But riding was his passion. Out of the city he could let the bike rip, where overtaking was rarely a problem. He had gradually shaved minutes off his journey time.

It was an old fashioned flat, but it was cheap, which was good, its out-of-town location exactly what Rix wanted. He put his helmet on the Edwardian hall stand and glanced in its mirror. His face was always tanned because of his time outside. His brown hair, short on the sides and slicked back from his high forehead, was usually somewhat untidy. His eyes were brown under hooded lids, his eyebrows strong and arched. His smile was wide. Someone once said he looked a bit like a young Chris Packham.

After supper, he'd just stacked wet dishes on the drainer when his phone chirped. His contact in Birmingham, texting details of a reporter on one of the Gloucester papers. He was under way, he thought to himself. Upwood had underestimated Trevor Rix.

Chapter 9

Following the press conference, most media coverage was critical of their efforts, if much less brutal than during the wind farm murders. There were, though, plenty of thoroughly unpleasant messages on social media about rough sleepers. Certainly, there was some scare-mongering, but the feedback on social media was much more muted in relation to the investigation. Upwood came to the conclusion that the general public either did not feel personally at risk, which would be good, or that they frankly did not much care about the fate of rough sleepers. That thought hugely depressed him. Some street sleepers came from backgrounds that almost guaranteed a life of destitution and anti-social behaviour. Others led more normal lives until some event tipped them over the edge, one problem leading to another in an unstoppable domino effect. There but for the grace of God...

For those two days, large numbers of officers were seen on the streets. Others studied CCTV footage and several teams logged calls generated by appeals for information. All of it painstaking, repetitive work, and for the most part, unrewarding. Late Thursday afternoon Upwood and Morton put their heads together.

"Are we getting anywhere, boss?"

"Not very far, are we? When will we get the PM results on the Mill Lane case?"

"I'm told tomorrow. Not that I think it will get us any further forward. We need to pick up intelligence on the streets. Has Madam Adams made a decision on the forensic specialists yet?" Upwood over-looked Morton's use of this nickname. No other officer would dare use it in his presence. But Morton had earned some latitude and demonstrated high levels of loyalty and discretion.

"We haven't got the costings through yet. She's OK'd it in principle. She doesn't have much choice, frankly."

"How should we run the briefing tomorrow morning?"

"Have our team completed the background investigations on all four victims?"

"All bar the shouting."

"Then let's do as you suggest and see if we can identify similarities and differences between them. Then I'd like us to brainstorm motive and see if that generates a few ideas."

The mood in the incident room the next morning was subdued. Everyone was conscious that progress was painfully slow and there didn't appear to be any solid leads. Morton's handling of this briefing would test him and show Upwood how far he had developed in terms of the managerial element of his role.

Morton opened the meeting by stating its purpose: to examine the similarities and differences between the cases, then explore possible motive. The aim was to generate ideas that could be developed into constructive leads. They would start by looking at the information they had gathered on each of the victims, the outlines of which had already been logged and were visible on the display board. He invited Debra to tell them what she had learnt about Sally.

"Sally Bremner. She was thirty-two, married but separated. Her husband is thought to have been abusive and very controlling. When he was interviewed about her death he denied being involved. He has alibis for the forty-eight-hour period before she died. Her parents are dead and she has no brother or sister.

"Former neighbours confirm that she had not worked during the period that she shared her home with her husband and that she was very retiring. None counted her as a close friend. She is thought to have been sleeping on the streets since early January. Apart from Joe, she does not seem to have formed any bonds with any other rough sleeper. We have been unable to find any links between her and the other victims.

"She was not addicted to drink or drugs and apart from being moved on a few times, has not been in trouble. She has no criminal record. She was a bit under-nourished but otherwise in reasonably good health. She had got into the habit in recent months of having a decent breakfast at the Mill Road Centre, but her appearances at the other kitchens and shelters were more sporadic.

"And as you know there were no injuries or wounds of any kind on her body. That's about it."

"Thank you. I'll take Joe now, since he was the second to die. We know he was forty-eight years old, although he looked older. Long since divorced. His gambling addiction led to the divorce and the loss of his home. He's thought to have been sleeping rough for six years. His ex-wife has remarried and lives in Stockton-on-Tees. She, too, can account for her movements in the forty-eight hours before Joe was admitted to hospital. His father is dead, and his mother is in a care home, suffering from dementia. His brother lives in a village near King's Lynn and claims not to have seen him for four years. He acknowledges that they were not on good terms but seems to have no motive for murder. He cannot account satisfactorily for the relevant two-day period but does not appear to be a likely suspect. There are no apparent links between him and any of the other victims.

"Joe was a bit of a loner and had no close associates among the homeless community, although he was said to look out for Sally a bit. We have established no links with Kevin or Pete.

"He liked a drink when he could afford it, but his only addiction was tobacco, and he was often seen with roll-ups. He was under-nourished, under-weight and had a tendency to suffer from chest infections. He was not registered with a GP, though. He had no set pattern in terms of his use of any of the shelters or kitchens. He had some years ago stayed at Tommy's, the residential shelter, but had been unable to settle into a constructive regime. He left after a couple of weeks.

"Like Sally, there were no injuries or wounds, nor any disease which might have proved fatal."

"Thanks. Mo, what can you tell us about Kevin?"

"Thirty-nine years of age. Never married. Went straight into the army. B Company, 1st Battalion, Royal Anglian Regiment, which was involved in an intense firefight with the Taliban in Helmand Province in August 2007. Pete was badly injured and saw colleagues subjected to 'friendly fire'. His best friend was one of the three who were killed. Pete spent several weeks in the hospital at Camp Bastion before being flown back to England with Post Traumatic Stress Disorder. After his discharge he was found accommodation in a hostel but left after four weeks. His whereabouts for the next few months are not known. It's thought he might have been drifting. He's been on the city's streets for about three years. He was a loner and other homeless people gave him a bit of a wide berth because he could be volatile. He's had two ASBOs for being drunk and disorderly.

"His father's dead. His mother lives in Cottenham. She's an alcoholic. No siblings. He's still in reasonably good shape physically. We are told that he didn't beg, but people seemed to recognise him as a soldier badly damaged by his experiences. Perhaps it was because he looked the type and wore a Help for Heroes wristband. And they gave him money. So he didn't use the shelters that much but managed to find enough to eat and drink. And fund a mild drug habit, one that was apparently getting worse though.

"Nothing to indicate any connection with the other victims."

"Thanks. Margaret. Your turn. What can you tell us about Pete?"

"I'll tell you what I can, but we've not had much time. Name Peter Johnson. Age fifty-five. Thought to have been on the streets longer than the others. Going on seven years. He'd been in and out of psychiatric units in the region for more than twenty years. His most recent stay was in Fulbourn. He was in one of the acute wards for twelve weeks but was later moved back into the community. Since then, he's had a couple of ASBOs. He used to sleep in the city centre, but in the last couple of years he's been sleeping in more isolated sites, like the cemetery.

"We've failed to trace any relatives, or any contacts from his former life, although we are still looking. Another very sad case. No known links to any of the others."

When she'd finished, silence fell. These four brief case studies had shocked them all. For most, it was the first time they had really confronted the crises that drove people to homelessness or recognised that, for some, there would be no way to escape it.

Morton rose to address them. His motivational skills were improving, and they were certainly needed now. "Harrowing stories, all of them. Now it's our job to find out what happened, and if someone has been responsible for their deaths, to bring them to justice. If we don't do it, nobody will. And we can do it, I've no doubt. The cases may look insoluble, but we have the skills and experience to solve them, even if we have to come up with fresh ways of looking at problems. We'll still follow procedures, because in the end, it is usually dedication and hard work applied within a solid investigative strategy that produces results. So. Let's look at similarities and differences between the cases. Differences first."

"One woman and three men."

"Different age groups."

"Different triggers for becoming homeless."

"Different patterns in terms of addiction, or lack of them."

"They had different habits in terms of using the facilities for the homeless."

"Two had records, two didn't."

"No evidence of any links other than being on the streets."

The suggestions petered out.

"What about similarities?"

"They slept alone." Sniggers greeted this observation.

"This is not funny. Whoever that was should be ashamed. The point was perfectly clear. Some homeless people choose to sleep alongside one or more others, for safety. Our victims didn't do that. What does that tell us?"

"If someone had been watching them, he might have chosen them as targets, leaving drinks in places where he knew they would find them. Where there might not be any witnesses."

"Good thinking. What else?"

"None had a serious drink or drug problem."

"None seemed likely to drag themselves out of homelessness."

"Don't agree," argued someone else. "OK, maybe that's true for the men. But Sally might have stood a chance. We know she used the showers and laundry facilities much more frequently than the men. She might have made it. If she'd got into Tommy's, she'd have had a decent chance."

"None had any family willing or able to support them."

A few more suggestions came but both Morton and Upwood could sense the mood deteriorating again.

"OK. Let's leave that there for a while. Let's think about motive again. Why would anyone want to kill harmless, homeless street sleepers?"

"Been attacked by one."

"Forced into homelessness himself, dug himself out and despises those who can't."

"Someone who despises them for no particular reason."

"A Muslim who thinks begging is a sin."

"That's a bit of a simplification," retorted a colleague. "Islam says begging is acceptable in certain circumstances."

"Maybe. But that doesn't mean someone doesn't believe that begging is always a sin."

"Anyway, not all street sleepers beg."

"But lots of people think they do."

Morton had learnt from Upwood that, when trying to stimulate ideas, it was unhelpful to conduct any kind of evaluation of them in real time. "Let the suggestion stand. But let's not limit it to Muslims. There could be someone from any number of faiths who thinks begging is a sin. Any more ideas?"

"None of them had a dog."

Morton acknowledged this. "Good point." It was an astute observation. The killer would want to avoid the kind of disturbance a dog might make.

"Someone who hates the squalor, especially in such a beautiful city."

"Someone who thinks they're all criminals."

"Someone who thinks they're all illegals."

"Someone who thinks they're all gypsies."

"Someone who's afraid of them."

Morton sensed that they were losing momentum again. "Any more ideas? No? Well, that's a good list; we can keep adding to it as ideas come to us. But let's see if we can generate any leads from this last list. Let's look for anyone assaulted by a homeless person. Let's check with the shelters, case studies in the Big Issue and other publications. Let's see if we can find someone who has escaped homelessness and thinks everyone else should be able to. And let's explore social media sites to see if we can identify anyone who might fit any of the other profiles. If we can't identify a few people worth interviewing, I shall be surprised."

Chapter 10

The Corporate Comms people had done a good job. By Monday they had managed to pull together leaders of the council's service for homeless people, all the major charities and Streetfood, the student organisation providing food and drink to people living rough.

Upwood welcomed them all and thanked them for coming. When he asked if they had all seen or heard reports following the press conference, all confirmed that they had. "Ladies and gentlemen, the question we need to discuss with you is that of the provision of food and drink on the streets. For some of you, this is not an issue, because you provide food and drink in your shelters. But for others it is. We have to consider asking you to stop providing food and drink directly to people on the street. Given that we are asking them not to accept such offerings, it would be illogical to encourage you to continue."

"But it's virtually all we do," responded Seb Foulks on behalf of Streetfood. "Surely if we continue our regular rounds and deliver stuff to people we've seen before, there shouldn't be a problem?"

Upwood thought there would but invited responses from the others there. Mary Canning was one of the first. "I think there is, sadly. Playing devil's advocate for a moment, it's not impossible someone has joined your organisation in order to build trust with the homeless and create an opportunity to kill them. It would be good cover."

"You can't accuse us of harbouring a killer like this. We're out there in our own time, usually two or three together, and we pay for the food we deliver. Sandwiches, bananas, satsumas, all the stuff they like that's easy to eat. You know we do."

"I do. You do a brilliant job. And I know you also distribute blankets and so on. But if someone wanted to infiltrate your group, I suspect it wouldn't be too difficult. What do you say, Chief Inspector?"

"You're right, Mary, I'm afraid. The university alone has more than twenty thousand students. The chances of there not being a bad apple there are low. But the idea that the killer may have infiltrated Streetfood, or any of the shelters providing food and drink, is not my primary concern. I suspect the person responsible for these unlawful deaths is working alone. We can't be sure, but it's likely. I believe we need to tell those on the streets not to accept any food or drink. Suggesting a 'don't take sweets from strangers' approach is just too nuanced for them."

Jerry Basset from Tommy's had a suggestion to make. "How would it be if your members worked with us and the other shelters for a time? We could perhaps advertise evening meals even for those not staying with us, if we had more people to volunteer. And preferably more food donations. Is that a possibility?"

"Maybe. I'd have to talk to the rest of the committee about it."

"Maybe your people could be part of the solution to getting such a message across, too. You see your mission as engaging with the street sleepers as much as providing them with food and drink, don't you?"

"What concerns me," said a representative of the Hills Road Shelter "is that if we tell people not to give food or drink to the homeless, some will offer cash. And more of those on the streets will ask for money. It's not what we should be encouraging. We know that often it goes on drink and drugs."

"We will have to try to get that message across to the general public, but it won't be easy."

The discussion continued for another half hour. Upwood left, thanking them again for their time, leaving the media officer thrashing out a draft statement that those at the meeting could take back to their committees to discuss. The aim was to agree and publish a statement by the end of the week.

That evening, Mo had taken pizzas to Margaret's flat in Fen Causeway. They were both excited by their involvement in the case, but worried about it. When actively involved in the investigation into the wind farm murders, they had been fascinated by the forensic evidence. Once a likely motive had been worked out, there were people whom they could identify as potential suspects. The fact that there had been two killers and two entirely different motives, just made it more interesting. This time there was nothing to go on.

After clearing up, they returned to the living room to finish their wine. Margaret sensed that he was uncharacteristically uncomfortable and kept quiet. Eventually he plucked up courage.

"Mags. I've won a raffle prize."

She burst out laughing.

"What's so funny?"

"You look like a naughty schoolboy. What is it for heaven's sake?"

"Two nights' dinner, bed and breakfast in any one of half a dozen boutique hotels." He paused and looked at her. "For two people."

She blushed. "Oh."

"Will you come with me? Please?"

She looked away. Now it was she who was uncomfortable. She had resisted Mo's early advances and told him that her husband had brutally raped her six years ago. Twice. The first time she'd become pregnant. The second time, eight weeks later, she had lost the baby. She would never have another child. She had not slept with a man since, although her surgeons had told her there was no reason why she could not enjoy sex in the future. Mo had been shocked and very supportive. While she was now happy to kiss him, not just be kissed, they had gone no further.

"You trust me, right? You know I'd never hurt you?"

She nodded dumbly. "I'm not sure I can do it." Her lips trembled.

"You what?"

She shuddered. "It was always my job to arouse Luuk. If he couldn't get hard it was always my fault."

"Oh Christ."

"And because it was my fault, he would beat me." Tears were now rolling gently down her cheeks.

He stared at her, speechless.

"It happened gradually. He couldn't get hard on our wedding night. He said it was because he'd drunk too much. He didn't try again for a while. Then he asked if he could hit me with his belt, to excite him."

"And you agreed?"

"Yes. I loved him. I knew he loved me. But he'd obviously got a problem. When he did get hard, he wasn't very big." She laughed nervously. "Not that I'd slept with anyone else. But it was obvious. And it must have angered him even more because he was such a good-looking man. I felt sorry for him. But the belt didn't help. And he got more and more angry. I tried to avoid sex. Then he tried some new pill off the internet. And raped me." She sobbed, unable to control the tears.

She had given Mo only brief details before. What she was telling him now chilled him to the bone. He got up to fetch some tissues and returned, sitting down beside her on the sofa.

"Then you left him, right?"

"I had to. I was terrified at the way the violence was escalating. He always apologised afterwards. Bought me flowers. Told me how much he loved me."

"Classic. Oh, sweetheart." He didn't dare put his arm round her; didn't know how she'd react. Instead, he reached for her hand and squeezed it gently. "You told me he'd got you pregnant. Why weren't you taking precautions? You wouldn't tell me when I asked you before."

"I thought if I got pregnant, he'd feel more of a man, and he'd be kinder to me." She burst into tears again.

He watched her anguish, and his heart went out to her. "When he raped you the second time, why did you ever let him through the door?" Why did he ask? He knew what the answer would be.

"He could be very charming. Very persuasive."

He waited a moment, before the most difficult question of all. "Given what you've said, how did he manage to rape you so badly?"

"They said he used a weapon. A bottle or something. I didn't want to know." She turned to him and buried her face in his shoulder.

When she had calmed down somewhat, he raised her face. "Can I get you a coffee? Some brandy?"

She looked up at him and offered another weak smile. "Both, please."

A few minutes later he came back with the drinks. They didn't usually touch spirits during the week, but they both needed it tonight. They sat quietly for a while.

"I'm sorry, sweetheart. I should never have suggested it." Disappointment was written across his face.

"But the question was bound to come up. We both know that. It was only a matter of time." There was courage in her smile now.

"I don't want to hurt you, Mags. You know that. I want us to make love. Together. But I'll wait as long as you like." In truth, Mo wasn't sure whether he felt able to wait indefinitely. He was very fond of her. Fonder of her than other women who had been more than happy to sleep with him. But he needed to know. Could they ever have a physical relationship that would satisfy them both?

"When is it?"

Mo's heart quickened. "They've given us until the end of June. After that I guess they're too busy." There was a long pause. Mo waited anxiously.

"Are we going to be able to take time off with this case on the go?"

"I'm sure of it. You know how the DCI keeps banging on about resilience. Our only problem might be getting off at the same time, but I'm sure I can swing it with Morton."

She looked up, suddenly alarmed. "You wouldn't tell him we're going away together? Please?"

"No. Course not. I'll think of something. So you'll come?"

She laughed nervously again. "Let me sleep on it, OK?"

Chapter 11

Upwood left shortly after the meeting closed, taking the opportunity of a reasonably early night. There would come a time, sooner rather than later he hoped, when the investigation would put them all under real pressure. Then, early nights would be at a premium.

After supper he went into his study and logged on to his laptop. It seemed slow to boot. It was five years old. Probably virtually obsolete. He didn't relish the idea of replacing it. No doubt the operating system would be different. Would his application software run on it, or would he have to upgrade? He couldn't bear the thought.

As usual there were a few personal emails in his inbox, but they were, except one, all from vendors such as Amazon, utility companies and his bank. They could wait. What did interest him was the email from his friend and former colleague, John Laidlaw, about the cases in Spain.

He read it through carefully. He fetched himself a small shot of whisky and read it again. Then he phoned Katie. "Hi. How are you doing?"

"Hi. OK. No bruising left now. And I'm topping up my tan nicely."

"Have you been swimming?"

"You must be joking. The water's much too cold. But I have been walking on the paseo every day."

"Good weather?"

"Do you need to ask?"

"Probably not. Still no rain here. Even some quite big rivers have dried up."

"I know. I've been watching the news. You'd expect droughts in Spain rather than England. How's work going?"

"In terms of results, not well. But it's not for lack of effort. It's just very difficult to crack. But you remember I spoke to my retired colleague in Estepona? I've just had a very interesting email from him. To cut a long story short he says the local forces believe an obscure poison was involved. He hints that they have some ideas about where it might have come from. There's a suggestion of Russian involvement."

"Really? How likely is that?"

"Well, there are plenty of Russians on the coast. A lot are thought to be behind organised crime, including drugs of course. And prostitution. It's thought maybe there was a battle going on between two opposing gangs."

"I can see how that might work. But if that's what's been happening, I can't see any likely connection to your cases. Prostitutes are an asset for the guys that run them. Rough sleepers are, if you'll forgive the expression, more of a liability. No one earns money by putting them on the street, nor by taking them off it."

"Astute as ever, my darling. I agree. But it's their ideas about possible poisons that I want to explore. And John says his contact is prepared to say more, but doesn't want the information conveyed to me by email. So, I'm going to ask Emily if I can take a couple of days out to come down and talk to him: John says he'd be willing to meet, unofficially."

"So would you be working or on leave?"

"A bit of both. But at least I'd get to see you again and make sure your recovery is still on track."

"Well best of luck. I'd love you to come down, but what if the press pick up on it?"

"I plan to tell Emily that if she agrees, no one else at Parkside should know I'm going. Leaks are all too easy, even if they're innocent."

"Well good luck. Let me know."

"I will. I'll say goodnight, if that's OK. There's some research I want to do."

"Fine. Night."

"Love you."

It was early afternoon the next day before Upwood was able to see Emily. He had forwarded John Laidlaw's message about the prostitute killings in Spain so that she had a chance to think about the issue before they met.

He was glad to see there was coffee for both of them when he entered her office. Perhaps she would give him enough time to make a decent case for his proposal.

"Good afternoon, James. Come and sit down." She remained seated, dressed as usual in a dark skirted suit with a pale, plain shirt. An elegant woman, with fair hair and blonde highlights, she was still attractive and looked younger than her fifty-three years. When she did smile, she seemed younger still. Smiling was not her default mode, but today she looked decidedly amused.

"I have to hand it to you, your attempt to justify taking leave in the middle of a serious investigation like this is impressively creative."

"That's not what I'm doing, Emily." This time he felt comfortable using her first name. Having worked together for some years, she was one of the few who knew the full details of his background.

"Oh, I think so. The chances of there being any connection between the killer in Spain and the one we have here are vanishingly small."

"I'm not necessarily saying they're connected. But there are some interesting features about both sets of murders."

"And you're convinced ours are murders?"

"They have to be. You said so yourself after the press conference. And I'm sure we'll get the proof. I wish we could expedite the special forensic tests on the blood, urine and tissue samples. I shall be very surprised if that doesn't tell us something."

"So tell me what you think the common features are."

"Firstly, there is no obvious motive for the deaths. The cause of death is so far unknown, although all victims had shown signs of vomiting and died from what was attributed to either acute respiratory failure or asphyxiation.

"No violence was used against any of the victims. This is, as you know, unusual in the case of prostitutes who are murdered, when sexual violence is often involved.

"In every case, the bodies were found in the place where the death is believed to have occurred, even though those sites were visible to passing pedestrians or people in passing vehicles.

"All the victims were vulnerable and at risk by virtue of their place in society."

"But there were no signs of scene setting, or the taking of trophies which might have suggested psychopathy?"

"No, certainly no scene setting. And no trophy taking so far as we know, although I can't rule it out. That may be why no DNA traces recovered have yet proved to be of any forensic value. There may have been no physical contact between the killers and their victims at all. I don't really know whether there's any connection between the two sets of cases. It's not likely, but not impossible. But with John Laidlaw's help, I would like to hear from the Policía Nacional officer about their theories of poisoning. It's not so much what the poison may be, it's where it may have been sourced and how it might have been administered. And the possibility of a Russian involvement, and possibly organised crime as well, is interesting. Although in fairness I can't see the relevance of that to our cases. John says his contact will not put anything in writing, although he is willing to help."

"So a visit would be entirely unofficial? Why couldn't the Spanish officer tell your friend and have him pass it on?"

"Emily, that's a daft question. No officer from any force is likely to discuss those sorts of details with someone who is not himself a serving officer."

"No. Of course, you're right. But is it good use of your time?"

"I don't see why not. We have dozens of people still going through CCTV, and more on the streets also trying to track the movements of our victims in the period before their deaths. We've got people sifting through social media and so on looking for possible leads. You know we had the media strategy meeting a couple of days ago? There is a huge amount of work going on, but Morton's got it well under control. Corporate Comms tells me that the council and the charities have all agreed on a way of responding to the situation and we have also agreed on a joint statement with them."

"How long would you need?"

"I could go down tomorrow and come back on Monday."

"Why so long?"

"I'd like to see where they found the bodies as well."

"Not just an excuse for an extra day in the sun, then?"

"Perish the thought."

"What if the press pick it up? They'll crucify you. They'll crucify all of us."

"I thought I'd go out of Heathrow rather than Stansted. Much less likely to be spotted. I can get a flight with BA into Gibraltar. And I suggest that no one is told about the trip. I'll book my own flights and won't put them through expenses. And I can stay with John, so I don't need an hotel." This last was true, not that Upwood had any intention of staying with his old friend.

"Well. I think it's a wild goose chase. But I won't stop you."

"Thank you." He rose.

"You were in Spain on holiday when we called you back?"

"Yes. It's good for birdwatching."

"Really? Is Katie into birdwatching as well?" Her question was loaded with sarcasm.

His face flushed with anger. "I've told you before, Emily. I will not discuss my relationship with Katie with you."

She snapped shut the folder in front of her. "Let me know what you find out. If anything."

Upwood was furious. He thought she would have left the subject of Katie alone, especially after a major row earlier in the year when she had tried to ban Upwood from seeing her. He had accused her of jealousy: an idea that sprang into his mind spontaneously. Her response had suggested he was right. The situation embarrassed them both, although neither had spoken of the matter since. It was obvious the problem persisted, one he could do without.

By nine that evening he was in Gibraltar, having already decided that he would leave that evening if Emily gave the go-ahead. Katie was waiting to meet him.

"God, Katie. You look tons better!"

"I feel it, although I'm beginning to get a bit bored. So Madam Adams let you out to play?"

He laughed. "After a fashion."

"Does she know I'm still here?"

"I think she does, bugger it. How she found out, I don't know."

"Morton knew. You said you'd told him the night you had a drink with him. Someone may have overheard you."

"Possible, I suppose. I swear the pubs close to the station might as well be bugged. Are we walking over the border?"

"Yes. I could have brought the car over; the queues weren't too bad. Just didn't want to take a chance."

"Fine by me."

Less than an hour later they were sitting at a pavement table of Mesón de la Torre, sipping their Manzanilla, savouring the hint of chamomile, whence came its name. As usual, the restaurant was busy, favoured predominately by locals and resident expats. Tourists gravitated towards the restaurants with sea views. The view from this restaurant was of the village, with its narrow streets, simple cottages and small but elegant church. As a consequence, the atmosphere was more personal than in many of the restaurants in the marina, which they both liked.

Upwood's mobile signalled an incoming message. It was John Laidlaw, confirming that his contact, Francisco Garrido, would meet them on Sunday at 11.00 am at John's home in Estepona.

Chapter 12

Mo's mobile rang early on Saturday morning. It was Margaret.

"Hi, sweetheart. You're early."

"I thought perhaps we should go into work this weekend, earn some brownie points."

Mo was surprised. Then he wondered whether she might think they could wangle a weekend off if they put in extra time. He didn't want to ask her over the phone. "Why not? There's plenty we can get on with. Good idea. See you there."

By nine they were both at their desks. Morton had tasked them with searching mainstream media sites. This was within their competence since it meant using regular search engines, neither being familiar with the dark web.

They opted to search not just for news and features about street sleepers, but also for any active and vicious bloggers responding to those articles. If they found any worth further investigation, they could pass the details to the IT specialists who might then be able to identify them.

Mo started a general search on Google. Even using its filters to define the parameters as tightly as he could, and fixing the date range for the previous two years, it was an enormous task. Google returned 189 sites on the first run, and even more when the excluded results were added. Not all sites were relevant, but many were. They made depressing reading; the comments posted in response even more depressing. It would be too easy to assume that the writers were ill-educated people because of the poor grammar, syntax, spelling and punctuation. But the fact was, Mo reflected, many of these posts were badly written, expressing views which, if not extreme, were strongly worded. It soon became clear, too, that a small number of people were regular contributors to subjects relating to the homeless, street sleepers and beggars. Many acknowledged the difficulty of differentiating between those three categories, even allowing for the possibility of overlap between them. What shocked Mo even more was reading articles which expressed ideas he found unacceptable, written by people who were themselves part of the city's establishment. The very first such was published in January 2010 and cited a letter sent to the City Council by the Bursar of Disraeli College, supporting plans to secure the grounds of Round Church. He complained of vagrants contaminating the gardens. His comments provoked outrage, but many bloggers supported his views.

They worked steadily through the morning, taking it in turns to fetch mugs of coffee from the machine. At midday, they decided on a sandwich at one of the local cafés.

The bustle and chatter of the café were welcome after the incident room. True, there had been others working there, but in the main they too were working keyboards, not phones. The constant rattle as they pecked away created an atmosphere of tension. It was almost a relief when someone's mobile did ring.

They carried sandwiches and cold drinks to a table by the window. Mo took a large bite and began chewing hungrily. Margaret was distracted and sipped her smoothie. Neither felt like discussing their findings in public, so they had finished within fifteen minutes.

"Shall we go for a walk before we go back? Some fresh air would do us good."

"OK. Where?"

"Why don't we go to Mill Road Cemetery? It's not far. Can't be more than half a mile. I've seen plenty of pitches in the city centre. I'd like to see where Pete was found."

Their route took them in via the entrance off Mill Road. They turned right on the perimeter path. It was an odd but strangely comforting place. Established in the middle of the nineteenth century, it was designed to serve thirteen parishes, each having a designated area. In 1949 it finally closed for new burials. Now many of the headstones were leaning or hidden under shrubbery. Some tombs had collapsed. Although it was maintained, it did not have the manicured look of a war grave cemetery, the arrangement of the graves much more haphazard. Trees and shrubs provided good cover, and as the gates were never locked Pete could come and go at will. There were public toilets open until eight in the evening. There were no lights. They could see that for someone like Pete, who preferred solitude, the cemetery was a good site.

All the materials found at his pitch had been removed for forensic examination and there were no remnants of tape to show them exactly where he had been found. There were enough signs of activity in one corner, though, for them to make an educated guess. They completed their circuit and returned to Parkside the way they had come.

They continued working until early evening. From articles and letters, Mo had identified three other people who had spoken in condemnatory terms about rough sleepers. Margaret had found three more, although she could not identify them because they all used nicknames when commenting on articles.

Neither could face preparing a meal, nor stomach another take-away, so they walked to the Queen Anne Terrace car park and jumped into his car.

"Where are we going?"

"The Queen's Head."

"Not the one that our serial killer used? In Chilton?"

"Lord, no. In Newton, south of Cambridge. Fabulous log fire in winter. Really good beer. The menu's very simple, and their soup is legendary. It makes a good change from city pubs."

"Sounds good."

They enjoyed their meal and the old-fashioned feel of the place. People said it hadn't changed in a hundred years, and they could believe it. Because the meal was simple, they finished soon after eight and headed back to Margaret's flat.

Mo put the kettle on for coffee while Margaret booted up her laptop. He brought two mugs into the living room and put them down on the coffee table. He put a hand on each of her shoulders and kissed the top of her head.

"Have you decided, sweetheart?"

She stood and turned towards him and put her arms round his neck. "Yes. Yes, I'll come." Tears glistened in her eyes.

Chapter 13

Rix was glad that he was travelling cross country on a Sunday. There were fewer lorries. His journey to Worcester would take over two hours. He was also glad the man he was meeting lived there rather than Gloucester; it saved him fifty miles on the day. He would have been quite pleased if the guy had offered to meet him halfway, but as he was the one who wanted help, he was in no position to ask.

They had agreed to meet in a pub on the northern edge of the city, close to the junction with the M5. Mike Fraser was about his age, perhaps a little older, but not much. Fraser was shorter, fatter and blond. A sharp look in his eyes suggested he was no soft touch. Fraser ordered a beer and so did Rix, except his was non-alcoholic. He had learnt very early on that beer and bikes don't mix. They gave their food orders and took their drinks out to the garden.

"So what brings you half way across England to talk to me?"

"Did Bob tell you I'm based in Cambridge? Working with the Herald. We seem to have our second serial killer in a year. The SIO is a chap called Upwood who used to be based in Gloucester. I heard his wife and child died there. I was interested."

Fraser supped his beer. "You've done some research, I take it?"

"Yup. But there's not a lot to find. A couple of very brief reports in the Gloucester Telegraph. The inquest on the child returned a verdict of natural causes. His wife committed suicide. She'd been suffering from postpartum psychosis. I wondered if there was more to it than that."

"What, like she smothered the child when she was deranged?" Fraser studied the other man's face, but Rix was a good poker player.

"Maybe. What was going round on the jungle drums?"

"Not a lot. The police will have looked hard to see if the child's death was natural and will have looked at both parents for sure. They have to, you know that. People were asking whether she might have done it. But it was more like they were looking for a story than anything else."

"And him?"

"I can't really remember, if I'm honest."

"And what about her death?"

"That looked pretty clear cut from what I remember. I did attend her inquest. She'd been sectioned for a while following the birth and developed a habit of self-harming. She used to cut herself, in places where her husband couldn't easily spot it."

"But surely he'd have seen – they shared the same bed presumably?"

"Latterly they didn't. She would wander about in the night, hallucinating sometimes. They had separate bedrooms."

"And how did she die?"

"Overdose of the meds she was on. Then slit her wrists in the bath."

"Was there ever any doubt about it?"

"None expressed publicly. But there were one or two conspiracy theorists who thought he might have bumped her off for killing their child. Or simply couldn't face being shackled to someone who was completely barking."

"What do you think?"

"I don't. It's an old story. Died a death. Got other stuff to worry about."

"Is there anyone you know who was involved in the cases?"

"What? Police?"

"Yes. Someone who might be prepared to talk."

Fraser laughed. "You don't want much do you? No one I know would touch this topic with a barge pole."

"Was Upwood reckoned to be a good copper?"

"Yeah, I think so. He's been promoted since then, hasn't he?"

"Yup. DCI now."

"And what's his rep in Cambridge?"

"I think the jury's out at the moment. Had a good run until earlier this year. Had a lot of bad press over the serial killings, but in fairness to the bloke there were two killers with different agendas, so it wasn't easy. But he's made no headway at all on the recent cases so far as I can see. They don't even know how the victims died. And he's been caught out taking time off again when the public think he should be working his investigation harder."

"You chasing this idea in your own time?"

"Yes."

"Thought so. Not sure it's got legs."

Rix laughed. "You're probably right."

Their burgers arrived. Fraser had a side of fries. Rix did not. And that may have accounted for the fact that their physiques were different. They chatted idly over their food about the parlous state of print media and speculated over their futures. Both were young and more than competent with keyboards and smart phones. Either could survive a switch to an entirely digital format. In their own ways, though, they were a bit old fashioned. Both had a fondness for the printed word.

Rix left soon after they'd finished their meal. It was obvious that Fraser had no more to tell him. He could be back home by half five, bung a load of washing on and nip out to the pub. He reached home just in time. Clouds had been building up all day as an area of low pressure spread eastwards. Rix felt as though storms were chasing him and as he parked his bike in the car port the first rain drops began to fall. He abandoned his plan to go to the pub and was idly watching the sports results on TV, can of beer in his hand, when his mobile rang. It was Fraser.

"I've just remembered. Bloke I knew retired from the police about five years ago. I think he was forced out and wasn't going to get a full pension. Right pissed off about it he was. He might be prepared to talk. At a price."

"Sounds promising. D'you know how to get hold of him?"

"No. I can only give you his name. After that you're on your own."

"OK. What's he called?"

"George Muspratt."

"Spell?"

"M U S P R A T T."

"Thanks, mate. I'll give it a go."

"Well, good luck." He paused. "By the way, Bob referred to you as Tricks. Is that right?"

"Call yourself an investigative journalist?" He laughed and ended the call. Now all he had to do was to track down George Muspratt.

Chapter 14

Upwood followed John Laidlaw's advice and picked up a taxi at the rank outside the marina. The drive to Estepona was easy, but parking anywhere near John's home in the old part of town would be a nightmare. Streets were narrow and many were one-way. One wrong turn could lead you well away from where you wanted to be. And the old town was so beautiful with its low houses painted white, geraniums ablaze on every window ledge. There were small squares with orange trees, and others Upwood could not identify with tightly manicured canopies of evergreen leaves. They looked just like the trees he had drawn as a child. It was picture postcard perfect. Much better to take a taxi so he could enjoy the ride.

He arrived just before eleven. He hadn't seen John recently, although they had kept in touch sporadically. They'd met once or twice when Upwood had been in the area on birdwatching trips, but John was not a birder. Tapas and a few drinks reminiscing was about the extent of their meetings. Upwood was shocked to see how John had aged. He was only a few years older than Upwood himself and despite playing golf a couple of times a week, he had put on a lot of weight, which he did not carry well. Upwood assumed that because many of the local courses were hilly, John used a buggy. If that were so, then perhaps he wasn't actually getting much exercise at all. Not that he was an expert. He had no time for golf in either sense of the expression. For him golf courses were simply good places to watch birds. He'd once seen a large flock of Yellow Wagtails, on passage on a local course whose fairways and greens were irrigated daily.

"John, how are you? Good to see you."

"Christ, James. However long has it been? Four years? Five? You haven't changed a scrap."

"Nor have you," responded Upwood untruthfully. "Thanks for setting this up. I really appreciate it."

"Come in. Paco will be here soon, I'm sure. I thought we'd sit in the inner courtyard."

The courtyard was a riot of colour, every shade of red, orange, purple and pink that geraniums can produce. There were fuchsias, petunias and other plants that Upwood could not begin to recognise. There were large pots on the ground and dozens hanging on the walls, some of them nearly as high as the eaves. Geckos, some tiny, scampered up and down the walls looking for their next meal. A small fountain played in the corner, helping to keep the air in the courtyard moist, and providing a gentle background noise.

"It's magnificent, John. I've never seen it look so good. It's as good as anything I've seen in Córdoba. How on earth do you maintain it?" Upwood was impressed, but the effect was overwhelming in a relatively small space. A definite case of sensory overload.

John laughed, a deep laugh that spoke of heavy smoking over too many years. "The great thing about having so many is you can't see the irrigation pipes. It's a micro system. I just kept adding to it over the years. It's all automatic. All I have to do is change the battery in the control unit every now and then, and I change the times and frequency of the watering programme a couple of times a year. Easy."

They heard a knock at the door and John went back in to greet his friend before bringing him out to the courtyard.

"James, meet Francisco Garrido, of the Policía Nacional here in Estepona. Paco this is James Upwood, Detective Chief Inspector in Cambridge."

"Buenos días, Francisco. Sorry, apart from ordering beer and a meal, that is about as much Spanish as I know." He laughed. This was not strictly true, but he certainly was a long way short of fluent.

"Paco, please. I am 'appy to meet you. I speak a little English, but if we 'ave problems, John will 'elp us, no es verdad?"

John beamed. "Of course. Now sit down and I'll get some coffee."

"The patio is magnifico, no?"

"It is. Like Córdoba. La Fiesta de los Patios."

"Sí. Is good. You go?"

"Yes, in 2006. Wonderful. A beautiful city."

"Is true. Estepona is beautiful, too, I think."

John returned, handed them small cups of café solo and sat down with them. After a few minutes of small talk Upwood thanked Paco for agreeing to meet him. He asked if he would like to hear more about their cases. Paco was keen to learn more than John had been able to tell him, so Upwood gave a summary of what they knew so far, adding that they suspected an unusual poison was being used.

Paco then described their own cases, with John chipping in from time to time to help with translations. All the victims were prostitutes, all, it was thought, being run by the same pimp. This was a man well-known to the police locally although they had not managed to convict him of any offences since his teens. He was a local man and, while his operation had not reduced in size, it was thought that his fortunes were declining because of competition from an east European outfit which had established a number of brothels in the area. Their theory was that the east Europeans were trying to force the local pimp out of the market and had deliberately targeted those of his prostitutes who solicited along the main road.

The women who had been killed were of different nationalities. One was Spanish, one was from Ecuador, one from Colombia and the most recent was from the Dominican Republic. Each had worked from a regular pitch on the A7 west of Estepona, typically at a junction with a minor road or track leading inland. All of them exhibited symptoms similar to the Cambridge cases. The toxicology test results had been inconclusive.

The Policía Nacional believed that the east European outfit was controlled by a Russian mafia group. Upwood did not ignore the possibility but wondered if such a group would use an obscure poison. "Surely they'd be more likely to take the girls out with an AK47? Why poison?"

"Take out? What is this?"

"Sorry, kill."

Paco sighed. "Sí. Claro. Is good question. Is not their technique. I 'ave a problem with this idea."

"What do you think happened?"

"I hear, how you say, rumours? We 'ave many Russians here. Some, they have much money. Much, much money."

"Millionaires?"

"Sí. They come since twenty, thirty years. They come with money. They make more money buying 'ouses and washing the money. There is one we know. He dead now. But 'is wife still 'ere. She here from twenty years. Más. More. She 'as son. Is top man now. You know the Keen'a'an family?"

Upwood had to think for a minute. "Kinahan. Yes. Major organised crime group. Weren't they busted last year? A big operation?"

"Sí. Ver' big. But we 'ad to let go. Is fiasco."

"Why mention them?"

"Ah. Sí. Is good question also. Daniel, the son with most age, is good friend with the Russian boy. We see them at the most expensive nightclubs. And they are in England too."

"Sure. But they're an Irish family. I can't think there's any connection with my cases. And I doubt they're involved in yours either. They'd not be bothered by a local pimp. Bigger fish to fry."

"Qué?"

"Not important enough to worry about."

Paco laughed. They returned to the family who might be responsible for the prostitute murders. Paco's account became more complicated and John had to work harder at translation. Eventually Upwood gathered that the widow, who lived in a huge villa on the edge of town, set in acres of grounds, conducted a private clinic practising homeopathy. It wasn't a business; she had no need of extra income. More, it was a hobby she indulged in, catering to wealthy friends. But apparently there were rumours that you could obtain highly specialised substances from her, at a price. Not run of the mill recreational drugs, but something much more exotic. They had no proof, and no means that they could see to obtain it.

There wasn't much more to add. Upwood promised to let Paco know if they managed to identify any substance that may have caused the death of the Cambridge victims. He thanked him warmly: Paco had given him a few ideas to follow up when he got back.

There was a decidedly sceptical look on Emily's face when they met on Monday. "So, James. Was your little jaunt of any value at all?"

"Good morning, Emily. Yes, I think so. For me the interesting feature in both sets of murders is that they occur in the open, potentially in view of anyone passing by. There is the risk therefore that the killer will be seen. But by providing the poison in what looks like an unopened and harmless container, the killer can leave the site knowing that it might be hours, even days, before his victim drinks the contents. That makes finding him through witness statements much harder. And provided he avoids physical contact with the victim, and spends only a moment or two in his or her vicinity, there's a good chance there will be no usable DNA evidence. In fact, it's quite possible the killer never meets his victims, simply leaving spiked drinks where he knows they will be found."

"But you could achieve the same effect by using a poison more easily available, surely? Why use something apparently untraceable?"

"Maybe because the killer knows how to get hold of it. Maybe he has a secure source. No need to look elsewhere in that case."

She scowled. "And how likely is that?"

"I don't know. But one lead I want to follow up is the Russian widow who practices homeopathy in that part of Spain. She's the widow of a man thought to have mafia links. It is rumoured that she can supply exotic drugs, not the routine recreational kind. And the Russians have form in terms of using unusual poisons. And her son is now apparently running the family business: organised crime."

"Preposterous! How can that possibly be good use of your time? And anyway, how can you follow that up when they're neither Brits nor on British soil?"

"Obliquely."

"And what the hell's that supposed to mean?"

"I'm not sure I can explain, yet. I'm still working on it. But I'm hoping to persuade the local police to see if they can set up a sting, perhaps send someone to her as a potential customer."

"Why on earth would they do that?"

"They've had four murders, too, don't forget."

She shrugged. "Well, all I can say is that I'm glad the cost of your trip did not come out of our purse. It sounds a complete waste of time to me." She looked at him pointedly. "You do realise there will have to be a Major Crime Review, don't you? It's more than four weeks since the first incident."

"I know that. But it wasn't until we found the second body that we gave serious consideration to the likelihood that the deaths were not natural causes. That was three weeks ago."

"I'm quite capable of counting, James. You know perfectly well that a review might have been ordered before now. Thank your lucky stars I've been able to fend it off this long."

"So has a decision been taken?"

"I'm expecting to hear shortly."

"Who will head the review team?"

"I think it's likely to be someone from Herts or Beds."

He nodded. Probably better that way. He did not want a review. He knew the policy was that they should be conducted in a spirit of co-operation but in his experience the reality was often rather different.

He decided not to tell her about the potential gang warfare between the two prostitute rackets. It would only muddy the waters. There was evidently nothing of the sort happening in Cambridge. However, he would, unofficially, talk to a contact in a local security company which had more dealings with Russian oligarchs than he had had. Emily would no doubt consider that a waste of time, too. Never mind the reviewing officer.

Chapter 15

The incident room was full again for the briefing on Monday morning. Morton began by giving them a summary of the post-mortem results on Pete. There were no surprises. All the indicators were that he had died in the same way as Sally, Joe and Kevin. This time, however, there was no physical evidence suggestive of murder by poisoning since the crime scene team had been unable to find any can or bottle showing puncture wounds. They all knew that a can or bottle could be picked up in one place and its contents consumed elsewhere. They did not know when the drinks had been consumed. Nor did they know how long the poison took to take effect. Morton was painfully aware as he summarised these points, that the unknowns outnumbered the knowns - not encouraging. He knew how Donald Rumsfeld felt.

He then confirmed that they had found no record of any death of a rough sleeper elsewhere in the country with circumstances similar to those of their cases. The killer was breaking new ground in England.

He was able to tell the team that a member of the public had called on Friday morning reporting the finding of a can of Red Bull. The man had been taking a shortcut from Bridge Street through the yard of Round Church. There, sleeping on the bench in the corner of the churchyard, was a young man, his few possessions in plastic carrier bags alongside him. On the arm of the bench was the Red Bull. The pedestrian had recalled the warnings given by the media and stopped to look. He decided to wake the man. He was groggy, but turned and sat up, still in his sleeping bag. When asked, he said he had no idea where the can came from. His name was Freddie. He couldn't recall what time he had fallen asleep the previous evening, but thought it was unlikely to be much later than eleven thirty. Although the streets were less busy at night, there were still pedestrians going in and out of the various nearby pubs.

Subsequent examination of the Red Bull can found at Round Church showed that it had, indeed, been tampered with. Morton reminded them that the whisky bottle, the contents of which were thought to have killed Sally and Joe, had a puncture hole obscured by a sticker. The beer can found with Kevin's fingerprints on it had a puncture hole that had either not been covered or had lost its cover. The Red Bull can had been punctured very carefully in the middle, presumably when the can was on its side, making a hole through the eye of one of the bulls. (This discovery prompted the inevitable jokes about the killer having a sense of humour.) The hole had then been plugged with a black sealant, rendering it almost invisible. There were no fingerprints on the can; the man finding it had had the good sense not to touch it, and had made sure Freddie did not either. The contents were now being analysed.

Some discussion ensued, during which mention was made once more of the fact that two cans of beer had been found elsewhere in the city and their contents drunk without ill health or death. Mary Canning, outreach worker, had recently reported that conversations between her colleagues and folk on the street had picked up several more cases, although none very recently.

So what did this mean? Was the killer trying to lull potential victims into a false sense of security? Did his handling of the contaminated cans indicate that he was refining his methods, and if so, why? The only conclusion they could come to was that by using different products, he was trying to make his tampering more difficult to spot. This wasn't a very encouraging thought either.

CCTV footage was now being examined to see if any trace could be found of the person who deposited the can. They were searching coverage during the period from ten o'clock in the evening until the time the pedestrian found the can. They considered the possibility that the pedestrian had himself left the can because he was simply an attention seeker. But they discounted the idea, since tampering of the drinks containers had not been publicised.

Morton had little more to say and invited contributions from the team. Mo reported that he and Margaret had worked, voluntarily, over the weekend. Between them, they had identified four people whose real names were known, either in newspaper articles or letters, who made highly unpleasant remarks about rough sleepers and beggars. They had also found a further twelve people using nicknames when commenting online on published articles.

"One of the people whose letter to the council was leaked, the Bursar of Disraeli College, bears looking at. The college is one of the smaller, newer ones, and has a reputation for being more radical than most. It is an independent college within the university, and is a registered charity with its own governing body. The Bursar is one of the top management team, responsible for many of the financial and administrative functions. His name is Charles Mancini. His name crops up in responses to comments made about his letter, but dry up about three months after the row broke out. Disraeli's Principal and Governing Body distanced themselves from his remarks. He is highly educated and could well have the skills to plan and execute killings of this kind.

"Of the other three we can identify, one is a student who has been active in several campaigns, including anti-hunting and animal liberation. We think she's worth a look, as well. Another is a former president of the Civic Society, who we don't see as a likely suspect. And there is another woman who describes herself as a Friend of the Cambridge University Botanic Garden. We're open-minded about her. Margaret can tell you about the bloggers she's found."

"Thanks, Mo. I imagine what you've found is only the tip of the iceberg?"

"I'm sure of it."

"I'm sure you're right. We may need to put more people onto this while you begin to interview those you have found. Margaret?"

"Well, as Mo said, the ones I've found we can't identify. I imagine we'll need a warrant to access the websites where their messages have been posted in order to get hold of their IP addresses. The specialists will have to see if they can track the users from that. But some are writing very nasty stuff. I can't remember who suggested the idea about begging being a sin in Islam, but one of the writers does seem to think that all street sleepers are beggars, and that begging is always a sin. Another says that they're all gypsies. I think we should definitely try and track down this lot. The posts are fairly illiterate, but that doesn't make the writers stupid. Some people who write this bilge deliberately write in that style to make themselves harder to identify."

"Good point. I'd not thought of that, but I can see it makes sense. Track down the four you've identified. Interview them all. Even if your Civic Society member can be ruled out, don't ignore the possibility that he?she? has friends with similar views that we might want to know about. And Margaret, let me see your material and I'll organise the necessary warrants. I'll allocate other members of the team to carry on where you've left off.

"Debra, you're doing a similar exercise with the special interest media? Big Issue, student mags and so on?"

"Yes, I'm on it."

"OK, everyone, crack on. There's plenty to go at."

Mo and Margaret easily found Disraeli College on the Madingley Road. The main building was an imposing Victorian structure in red brick, well hidden by mature trees. Behind it were several other large, modern blocks. They parked and made their way into reception.

"Good morning. We're here to see Charles Mancini. We have an appointment at eleven o'clock."

"Your names please?"

They held out their warrant cards. "Ah, yes. Of course. I'll see if he's available. Please take a seat."

She made a call then nodded at them. A moment later Charles Mancini came down the stairs to their right, surprisingly quickly and lightly. He was a man in his mid-fifties, of medium build, slightly olive skin tones and with a very well-dressed head of silver hair brushed back from his forehead.

"Good morning. Shall we go to our meeting room? It's just down the corridor here." He strode off without waiting for an answer, opened the door and stood back to let them through. Margaret went in first. She was to describe her impression later as like going through an airport security scanner, so thoroughly did he examine her from head to toe.

"What can I do for you? It's a very busy time of year. Dammit, it's always a busy time of year. And why didn't you tell my secretary why you wanted to see me?"

"To be honest, sir, it was none of her business."

"If it's college business then it is."

"I don't think it is."

"Then why are we meeting here, in college hours?"

"It's convenient. And you might not want us to turn up at home and worry your family. And we didn't think you'd want to come across town to Parkside."

"Just what the hell is going on here, officer?"

"We'd like to talk about street sleepers and your views on them."

Mancini's laugh could have alarmed the local foxes. "Are you mad? I suppose you've seen the letter that was leaked last year. Don't you think they contaminate our streets? Do you really want to see them sleeping in that little churchyard, leaving their litter and needles?"

"One nearly died there last Thursday. Did you know that?"

"Well, that proves my point, doesn't it? The public shouldn't have to walk by so close to vermin like that."

"Why are you so opposed to people sleeping on the street?"

"Because they're too idle to do a proper day's work. Too bloody idle to better themselves. I hate the fact that they expect us to look after them."

"Even though some of them have been the victims of violence, or of war? Or they're ill?"

"I don't bloody care. Ship them off somewhere else. Keep them off our streets. Our college takes in a lot of foreign students. They pay good money to come here. If Cambridge gets a reputation for being the rough sleeping capital of the shires, they are going to stop coming."

"Do you know others who share your views?"

"Of course I do. They don't necessarily have the guts to speak up about the problem, though."

"But you're happy to do so?"

"Look, I wrote that letter to the council supporting plans to repair the wall round the church and reinstate the railings. Others did the same. I didn't send it to the newspapers. But I stand by what I said."

"Do you use social media?"

For the first time Mancini seemed less confident. "No. Not really."

"Yes or no? It's a simple enough question." Margaret wasn't prepared to see him duck it.

"I have done. I don't now."

"Why? It's a good way to get your views across."

"Waste of time. I got fed up with the garbage that other people post."

"Can you tell us what your role involves, Mr Mancini?"

"What on earth has that to do with rough sleepers?"

"It's not a big deal, is it? We'd like to know."

Back on familiar territory, Mancini relaxed again. "I'm in charge of finance, IT, HR and administration for the college. I manage everything other than the academic and research activity. It's a broader role than in some other colleges as we are relatively small."

They thanked him and took their leave.

"Snake oil merchant."

"What?"

"Slimy. Arrogant bastard."

Mo thought perhaps she hadn't warmed to him.

Chapter 16

Upwood found what he was looking for easily enough with sat nav. He preferred maps, but recognised that technology had its uses, particularly if you were trying to find a specific site in a sprawling technology park. His target was Sandton & Pell, a discreet but highly regarded security company. He had met its CEO some years before at a seminar held in the city, bringing together delegates from the police and other statutory forces, as well as leaders of organisations which felt threatened by security issues, or, like Sandton & Pell, tried to protect them.

Frank Pell came out to reception to meet him. He was taller than Upwood by several inches, lean and wary looking, mid-fifties with very short hair. A pair of rimless glasses gave him a rather earnest look. He shook hands. "Good to see you again, Chief Inspector. I gather you want to pick my brains?"

"Good morning, Mr Pell. Yes, I do. I'm not quite sure whether I'm doing it officially either."

Pell raised an eyebrow. "Interesting. Come. We'll go into one of the interview rooms. Nearer than my office."

A tray of coffee was waiting for them, a welcome sight to Upwood.

"Did I read somewhere that the firm had changed its focus from what it was originally?"

"You may well have done. My partner and I are both ex-military as you probably know. We started in all the usual stuff: close protection, personal security, dealing with kidnaps, hostage resolution, that sort of thing. Some of that is tricky in countries where it's illegal to carry weapons. We moved into business security in a wider range of fields. But business is global and that meant we needed a truly global reach, like Control Risks, and Kroll have. We decided we didn't want to do that and began increasingly to specialise in corporate security of a more technical nature. More coffee?"

Upwood thanked him but declined. Was Pell being just a little defensive in describing what had clearly been a fairly major shift in their business model? Or was Upwood, as usual, seeing problems where perhaps none existed?

"So what's your main focus now?"

"We handle work in the fields of due diligence, anti-corruption, fraud investigation, and particularly cyber-security. That's why we are based here, now. A lot of the biotech and life sciences companies are involved in research that is commercially highly sensitive. They are targets for people who want to short circuit their own R&D. Or simply to shut down a competitor. But tell me, how do you think I can help?"

"I don't know that I do, but I'm not sure where else to go."

"Well, that's honest, at least." He laughed. "So, what's the problem?"

"I'm keen to learn what I can about Russian involvement in organised crime in the UK and Spain. Especially in relation to drugs."

Pell raised his eyebrow again. "And you think I can help. Why?"

"Perhaps you've had Russian clients. Or more likely clients who were at risk from Russians, state sponsored or otherwise."

"We did do some close protection work for two oligarchs, but that was years ago. To the best of my knowledge, neither was engaged in criminal activity in the UK."

"But maybe via third parties still in Russia?"

"It's possible, I suppose. But the nature of close protection work doesn't give you much access into their business dealings."

"What about clients threatened by Russian interests?"

"That's a different matter, of course. But in the main it's the cyber threats we're looking at. Not organised crime like drugs and prostitution. We do sometimes have to investigate money laundering, but again, I don't recall any cases that suggested a Russian involvement. Hacking yes. But then we are involved in protecting firms from hacking, data recovery and so on. We are not pursuing the perpetrators if they are based offshore. That's not our job. If they're based in the UK, we'll work with the police where we can. But why aren't you talking to SOCA about this? Isn't this their field?"

Upwood laughed. "Yes, but I'm not sure the problem I'm looking at comes under their definition of serious and organised crime."

"It sounds to me as though you're chasing shadows, Chief Inspector."

"You're probably right. I'm sorry. I've wasted your time."

Pell shook his head dismissively. "You mentioned Spain. Why?"

"It's been suggested that Russian crime syndicates may be behind similar crimes there to those we are investigating here."

Pell gave him a sceptical look. "I'm sorry I can't help."

Upwood was frustrated as he made his way back to Parkside. He'd achieved absolutely nothing. And he couldn't think of a way to raise the issue with SOCA officially. There was no way they would see the recent killings in Cambridge as being a product of the kind of serious and organised crimes they handled.

Mo had taken the lead in their interview with Charles Mancini. Margaret would take the lead with Frances Matthews. It had not taken long to find her as a Google search threw up a number of references, including her page on the Cambridge Veterinary School site. She had gained a BSc in Biomedical Sciences and more recently an MPhil in Haematology. Needless to say, when she explained the nature of her research neither Margaret nor Mo understood a single word of it. Their impression, however, was that she had medical knowledge, which might be significant.

She was charming. At forty-two years old she had found the career path she loved late in life. Of medium height, she was slim, with rather unorthodox good looks. Her hair was prematurely grey, long and in need of brushing. She had rather bushy eyebrows which, had they been better groomed, might have been fashionable. Fashion was clearly not her strong point. But she did have an infectious smile. And a decidedly cut-glass accent, product of a good school no doubt.

"Thank you for seeing us, Frances. It's OK if we call you by your first name? Good. We are looking into the deaths of people who have been sleeping on the street."

There was no longer a smile on Frances' face. "You think I'm involved in that?"

"We're not suggesting that for a moment. But you have gone on record as being unsympathetic towards street sleepers."

"I don't have much sympathy, frankly. They've no self-respect. Most of them could pull themselves together if they made the effort. It's the ones with dogs that most annoy me. Did you know there are only two rooms in shelters in the city that will allow dogs? So they're nearly all denied access to residential support where they could be helped back on their feet. And their poor sodding dogs have to sleep outside as well. It should be a criminal offence."

"Have you had any personal contact with people on the streets?"

"Yes, I have as it happens. I volunteered years ago in the Hills Road Shelter, helping with breakfasts. It was a thoroughly unpleasant experience. A lot of them smelled.

They all said they had no money, but they could always find or steal enough for their booze and fags. They just made no effort at all. I've no time for them."

"Do you have friends who feel the same way?"

"Some, not all. Some are constantly bleating on about poverty and how government cuts are driving people onto the streets. People need to take more responsibility for their lives."

"You're anti blood sports, too? Am I right?"

"Yes. And I support animal rights. I am at vet school, you know."

"Both movements have a history of direct action. Have you ever taken part?"

"I've demonstrated. I've not attacked anyone at Huntingdon Life Sciences, if that's what you're driving at. I've done no criminal damage."

"Do you condone the efforts of those who do?"

"No." She sounded defensive.

"Have you taken direct action over street sleepers?"

"Have I killed them do you mean? Certainly not. How dare you even suggest it?"

"I am not suggesting it, Frances. Direct action can take many forms."

"Well, the answer's still no."

"How would you deal with the problem?"

"Make sleeping on the street illegal. Make keeping dogs on the street illegal. Make it mandatory that they spend at least three months in a shelter undergoing rehabilitation programmes. Send the fruitcakes back into secure units." She stared at them defiantly.

"If you convict them of crimes they'll end up in prison. They won't be able to afford fines. And what if they refuse to go into the shelters?"

"I don't know. But what's being done at the moment isn't solving the problem."

"Do you know anyone who might be prepared to take direct action against them?"

"You honestly think I'd tell you if I did? You're not real. Now unless you have anything sensible to say I suggest you leave me alone."

When they were back in their car, Mo turned to his colleague. "What do think?"

"I wouldn't put it past her. Who knows, she might even have the relevant knowledge. I think she's more likely than Mancini. But I'm not sure I'd rule him out either."

Chapter 17

When Debra reached her desk the next morning, she saw that Margaret had beaten her to it. "You're in early again. How long have you been here?"

"Only half an hour or so. Are you OK? You look a bit pale."

"Not feeling brill, if I'm honest. I think I might have a bit of a virus."

"Ought you to be here?"

"Yeah, I'm OK. I'm sure it's not infectious, whatever it is. What are you up to?"

"Trying to find out more about the four people we found who hate rough sleepers. How are you getting on researching the other sources?"

"I haven't found much, to be honest. I've been looking at magazines and online forums. A lot of them are student oriented. So plenty of mouthy criticism but nearly all in favour of supporting them and bringing down the government. One or two leads might be promising but I've still got a lot to do."

They both settled down to work. After twenty minutes or so, Margaret vaguely noticed Debra leave the room. A few minutes later she decided she'd go to the loo and then get herself another coffee. She heard the sound of retching as soon as she went through the door. "Debra? Is that you? Are you OK?"

She heard more retching. Then a weak voice, undoubtedly Debra's, said, "I'm OK. I'll be fine in a minute."

"OK, if you say so. I'll come back in a bit." She went out, fetched a coffee for herself and a mug of cold water for Debra and took the drinks back to their desks. Then she went back to find her colleague.

Debra had emerged from her cubicle and was now at a hand basin, splashing her face with water. She looked up nervously as Margaret came in. "You won't tell anyone, will you?"

"Why should I?"

"No reason. But you know how some of the men like to pick on any sign of weakness."

"Don't worry so. Why don't you go home? You look as though you could do with a lie down."

"I'll be fine. Honestly."

Two hours later, and after three more trips to the loo, Debra gave in and left for the day.

Margaret carried on her research. She didn't find much that was recent on Mancini, other than a fine for speeding. However, eight years previously he had been charged with a Section 4 offence under the Public Order Act. He had used threatening behaviour to a vagrant who was urinating in the street. The charge might have been more serious since his victim insisted Mancini had also accused him of being a Roma, turning it into a potential, racially aggravated crime. Mancini had avoided this escalation of the charge because although there were witnesses to his threatening behaviour, no one had been able to hear what either man had said.

Matthews was also interesting. She had said that she hadn't attacked anyone from Huntingdon Life Sciences, but five years ago she had been interviewed under caution about acts of vandalism in relation to one of their suppliers. No charges had been preferred due to insufficient evidence. She had also been interviewed after saboteurs had harassed hunt members, but camcorder images of the incident were so poor that no positive ID could be made.

Mo came in just after lunch. "I've got an appointment with our Civic Society lady. Coming?"

"Yeah, good. I'm getting bogged down here."

The Civic Society lady was The Honourable Harriet Houndsworth, daughter of the 19th Baron Netherfield, whose title dated back to the fourteenth century.

When they found her home in Brookside on the map, they realised they must have passed it countless times. They could walk there easily from Parkside. The street ran parallel to Trumpington Road but was set back behind a park and a stretch of water known as Hobson's Conduit. She lived in what looked to be a five-storey house, if you counted from the basement to the dormer windows at the top. They rang her doorbell. After what seemed like an age, she answered, but kept the chain on and asked to see their ID. When she was satisfied that she knew who they were, she let them in and led them into an over-crowded sitting room. She was a tall woman of slim build and looked as though her entire wardrobe came from Marks & Spencer. Her hair was all one length, cut to her chin, with a thick white fringe. Nonetheless she had a certain presence. Whether the house was Victorian or Edwardian, Margaret did not know, but she guessed the former. There were elaborate plaster cornices and a ceiling rose; it looked as though the fireplace was original. She guessed the house was probably worth £1 million (she was wrong, it was worth nearly twice that), but if this room was anything to go by it probably needed a six-figure sum spent on it. A six-figure sum the owner probably couldn't find.

"I am sorry. I don't like to be rude. But we are always being told to be careful, aren't we? And I do think it's good advice, don't you agree? It's such a dangerous world. I do admire you young people taking up jobs like yours. You must put yourself at risk all the time. May I get you tea?"

They both declined, and it rapidly dawned on them that Harriet Houndsworth did not have an off switch. They did accept her invitation to take a seat and ended up side by side on a vintage Knoll sofa that had probably needed re-upholstering at least a decade ago. Margaret leant briefly against the arm and quickly straightened again as she felt it begin to move.

"Now do tell me how I can help you."

"We're looking into the deaths of four homeless people. We understand that you don't like them very much."

"I feel sorry for them. Of course I do. There's nothing I can do for them though." Try downsizing and giving your money to a homeless charity, thought Margaret. "But I'm frightened of them."

"Why is that?"

"I was attacked by one in the street here a few years ago. Maybe he was on drugs, I don't know. But he was violent. He grabbed my handbag. I wear it on a strap over my shoulder. It's safer. Except of course when he grabbed it, he pulled me over. So perhaps it isn't safer, if you think about it. I crashed onto the pavement. Then he dragged the bag over my head and ran off. I couldn't get up straight away. When I did, he was nowhere to be seen. The police told me they found my bag in the bushes in the park there. My purse had gone of course. Not that I carry much money. But I had to cancel my cards and order new ones. A frightful nuisance."

"Were you injured?"

"No, just a few bruises. But it did frighten me. And they never caught him of course. I really don't think people like that should be out on the streets attacking people all the time."

There was no point in telling her that rough sleepers were much more susceptible to violent crime than the general public, at least ten or fifteen times more likely to be victims, depending on which figures you looked at.

"You wrote a letter to the local paper last year. Why was that?"

"Well, I'd read that there was a debate about whether to put railings up at Round Church. A beautiful little church. 12th Century. Modelled on the Holy Sepulchre in Jerusalem. I don't suppose you know that, do you? Well, you might," she said, looking at Margaret. Mo resisted the temptation to tell her he had attended a Church of England school, sensing it would be a waste of time. "I supported the idea. Putting up railings, I mean. It's dreadful to think that beggars are fouling that little churchyard and using it as a latrine. Absolutely frightful. Ghastly. I really do think they should all be taken off the streets. Some of them should be in asylums, I'm quite sure."

There was no point in trying to tell her that not all homeless people were beggars either. Her ideas were as entrenched, if different, as those of some long-term homeless themselves.

Margaret was still surreptitiously studying the room. It really was a time warp. Dull oils and duller watercolours on the walls, faded photos of an earlier generation in tarnished silver frames on the side table. "Do you have television?"

"No. I have better things to do with my time. I listen to the wireless. I do so like Book at Bedtime, don't you?"

Margaret dared not look at Mo. "What about a computer?"

"Certainly not."

"How did you write your letter to the paper?" As soon as she'd asked the question, she realised how stupid it was.

"Are you quite mad, my dear? By hand. How else does one write a letter?"

Margaret mumbled an apology, trying not to giggle. "Are you still a member of the Civic Society?"

"No. It no longer exists."

"How do you spend your time?"

"Petit point. I win prizes."

Mo and Margaret both looked baffled. Peas? She grew peas?

The old woman pointed at the cushion on the chair beside their sofa. Finally, they understood.

They put a few more questions to her, thanked her and left. Once safely away from her front door they burst out laughing. Was she a killer? Unlikely, was their conclusion.

Chapter 18

Upwood once again left the station at a civilised hour. He was restless, his day having been less productive than it should have been. Scores of people were still working tirelessly, examining CCTV and talking to potential witnesses. He knew that they were gradually building up some sort of timelines for the activities of their four victims during the two days before they were thought to have consumed the spiked drinks. But the progress wasn't fast enough. Based on the feedback from his team, he had decided that Mancini and Matthews should be brought in and questioned under caution. They were also going to bring in the botanist on the same basis. They needed to exert some pressure. Somebody had to know something that would help them. At least they'd now been given the go ahead for much needed extra tests on fluid and tissue samples. He hoped they would deal with them urgently.

He'd been optimistic that his meeting with Pell would be more useful. Once home, he went straight to his conference file in the study, where he kept delegate lists. These were always a source of potentially useful contacts. He found the one he wanted, that for the seminar he and Pell had both attended. There was one good contact, forgotten as their paths had not crossed since. It was Will Bailey, a member of the International Department, based in London. For some reason Upwood could no longer recall, Bailey had given him his email address. He sat down at his computer and sent off a short message, asking if they could have a brief, unofficial chat. He hoped the guy hadn't changed his email address. Fifteen minutes passed without it bouncing back, so he'd have to wait and see.

He went out into the kitchen and started preparing an early supper. He'd not been to the shops lately and knew there was nothing in the freezer to tempt him. In his fridge he found three eggs and half a packet of rather dry looking bacon. Omelette it was, then. As he was assembling the ingredients on the counter, his phone rang with a number he did not recognise.

"James? James Upwood? You asked me to call you."

"Will, thank you. It's a bit of a liberty, but I could really do with some advice. I've got an investigation going on into the deaths of four homeless people and I've got bugger all to go on. The first one was more than three weeks ago. We still don't know for certain how they were killed, but we think there is some kind of unusual poison involved. By chance I have learned of four unexplained deaths in similar circumstances in southern Spain. Unofficially, the Policía Nacional think that drugs from a Russian source might be involved. They think it's likely that gang warfare between two prostitute runners is behind their cases. Nothing like that's involved with ours, but there are other similarities. I can't see any justification for suggesting SOCA look at our cases. But I wondered. Is there anything you can tell me that could help me follow up a Russian poison connection?"

Bailey laughed. "Christ, mate, you are desperate. Dunno. It's not something I've been involved with. You want me to sniff around?"

"Anything you can tell me would be much appreciated."

"Might cost you a pint."

"No problem. Seriously, anything at all you can tell me would be great."

"Give me a day or three."

"Of course. Thanks, Will."

After supper Upwood returned to his study and began researching again for information about homeopathy and poisons. The problem was that all homeopathy products carried a poisonous element but in such minutely small traces as to be almost undetectable. The idea that you might overdose on one seemed laughable.

His research into poisons was not much more illuminating. He'd already been down this route before and got nowhere. All the poisons much loved by Agatha Christie, in weed killers, insecticides and other compounds, had long since disappeared from the shelves. He had not realised that she was so knowledgeable about poisons, or that she was a trained pharmacist. After two hours his head was reeling. He had learned nothing of use.

He decided to call Katie to cheer himself up.

"Hi, James. Another bad day at the office?"

He laughed. "You could say that. We're making very slow progress. Any minute now I'm expecting to hear there will be a Major Crime Review."

"Is that a bad thing?"

"It depends. Mainly on who leads it."

"What does it involve?"

"Another senior officer, probably with a support team sitting alongside us. They'll probably set up another HOLMES system parallel to ours and examine every decision, every action we've taken, to see if we've missed anything in the investigation."

"Is it the sort of thing the IPCC does?"

"No, not at all. They investigate complaints. The Crime Review team are concerned about the quality of the investigative process."

"Is it an adversarial process?"

"Christ, I hope not. It's not supposed to be. But it depends on who leads it. If they appoint someone I've pissed off at some stage, it will be a real pain in the arse. And it will slow us down."

"Might it be helpful?"

"If it is, fine. But it's not going to identify what poison's been used, and I doubt it will tell us who administered it. We'll get there eventually, but it's so slow. Random killings are always the worst. Especially when there's more than one. Most murder victims know their killers, and motive is then usually fairly easy to determine. Our only chance in this case is to find something on CCTV that leads us to a solution. It's a massive job. Anyway, enough of this. What have you been up to?"

She'd driven to Estación San Roque and then taken the train to Ronda.

"So you saw all the storks nesting on top of the pylons?"

"I did. Even I could recognise them. It was a great day out. I've decided I like trains. No chance you can get down here again soon, I suppose?"

"Not a snowball's, my darling."

Chapter 19

Debra was late in to work. She did not look well. Margaret decided not to comment on it immediately. But after Debra had left the room for longish intervals three times, she felt she had to. The next time Debra went out, Margaret followed her. She was in the loo again.

"Deb, you're still not well. Have you seen a doctor?"

"No. Don't fuss."

"Well, honestly, I think you should."

"I told you. It's a virus. There's nothing you can take for that."

"But you don't know that's what it is."

"Just shut it, will you? It's bad enough feeling grotty without you nagging me." Now she understood how Tom had felt earlier this year. She'd been nagging him to see a doctor, although with the benefit of hindsight she should have done it sooner and more vigorously. She still felt guilty that he'd hanged himself after being diagnosed with cancer. He'd suffocated his elderly mother first. She'd been dependent on him and had dementia. Debra ended up rehoming his cat.

"Sorry. Don't get your knickers in a twist. Just trying to help."

"I know. But pack it in, please."

Margaret left her to it.

Later she went for a coffee. Morton was standing at the machine, cursing because he'd pressed the wrong button and got soup. "What's up with Deb, Margaret, do you know? She's not her normal self and I can't get any sense out of her."

"Just a virus so far as I know. No big deal."

"Sure?"

"Yes." She wasn't, but she wasn't about to drop Debra in it. Not yet, anyway.

Maud Fowler, Friend of the Cambridge University Botanic Garden, was outraged when officers called on her and asked her to go with them voluntarily to Parkside to help with their enquiries. She ran a garden centre on High Ditch Road in Fen Ditton, a few miles from the city centre.

"You can't just expect me to drop everything at a moment's notice. I've got a business to run."

The business, if truth be told, was not that large. Following a good deal of persuasion, and when it was obvious that one way or another she would have to comply, she agreed. Her Deputy Manager would have to hold the fort until she returned.

She was still seething when Mo and Margaret finally managed to get to the interview room where she was waiting. The rules of engagement were explained to her. She was not under arrest and was free to leave at any time, but she was entitled to free legal advice if she wanted it.

"No. Just get on with it, will you? I can't imagine for one minute that I'm going to be able to help you, but fire away." Forty years of age, she was tall and athletic in appearance with short brown hair and blonde highlights. She had the bluest eyes Margaret had ever seen. Contacts maybe? Fowler wore jeans that were distressed through hard wear rather than fashion, and a striped cotton shirt. She sat with legs crossed and her hands folded in her lap. Her look was intelligent but confrontational.

Mo took the lead. "Thank you, Miss Fowler. We have told you that we are investigating the deaths of four homeless people in the city. We believe that on occasion you have made your views on the problem of street sleepers known, am I right?"

"Yes. I imagine you wouldn't be talking to me otherwise. The paper published my letter last year. After the debate blew up about railings at Round Church. I am entitled to my views. We do still have freedom of speech in this country I take it?" She uncrossed her legs, then crossed them the other way.

"Tell us your views on the subject please."

"I think it's a disgrace. We have over five million visitors a year to the city. They bring in about half a billion pounds. What impression do those visitors get when they see these vagrants on the street? They're dirty. They're often drunk, or on drugs. And as for the dogs some of them have, they should be put down. The mess these people make beggars belief. It's not just the natural environment we have to protect. It's the built environment, too."

"What do you think should be done?"

"Some of them should definitely be locked up. Some should be dried out. Bung them in a bloody great hostel. I don't know. That's not my problem. I'm a gardener, not a politician." She uncrossed her legs. This time her booted feet were both on the floor.

"Did you have any training as a gardener?"

"What the hell's that got to do with anything?"

"Please answer the question."

"I have an MSc in the biodiversity and taxonomy of plants from Edinburgh. Before that I did my BSc at UEA."

"UEA?"

"University of East Anglia."

"Did your studies include the medicinal use of herbs and plants?"

"Yes."

"And their toxins?"

"Of course. You need to know what you're handling."

"Environmental science is not what you're doing now. Why switch?"

"I caught malaria in Belize. It's not considered a high-risk country, but I still caught it. I decided that field work in countries where malaria was a problem would not be a good idea. I also wanted to be my own boss."

Mo had a shrewd suspicion she was not much of a team player. "Did you ever talk to any of the homeless people you saw on the streets?"

"No. Why would I?"

"Have you ever taken direct action in support of a cause?"

"I joined a picket when I was at Uni. We were protesting about the proposed development of a site on the edge of Therfield Heath in Royston. The heath is known for its pasque flowers and orchids. Development of that site would have been vandalism."

"Is that all?"

"Yes."

They already knew she'd been charged with affray under the Public Order Act for the incident, her first offence. She'd pleaded not guilty but was convicted, receiving fifty hours' community service. Three of the four people they'd interviewed had already been involved with the police and held unpleasant if not extreme views. Currently, Fowler was just as much under suspicion as Mancini and Matthews. Any of them might have relevant knowledge. They all felt strongly about the subject. Two had experience of direct action. All were intelligent, and fit enough, to have carried out these attacks.

Was one of them their killer?

Chapter 20

Upwood led the morning briefing, the last of the week. The senior members of his team looked jaded, and he could understand it. They were nearly five weeks into this investigation and still had no real leads. Fortunately, the media were not maintaining the barrage of criticism that had plagued his last major investigation. He knew they would need to hold another press conference soon, although he was afraid there would be little concrete information he could provide.

    He adopted an approach similar to one they had used before. Morton would summarise any new information on Joe, Debra would do so for Sally, Mo would take Kevin and also Freddie, and Margaret would take Pete.

    Morton began. "It proved relatively straightforward to track Joe's habits because he'd been on the streets for some time. He varied his routine occasionally but recently he had been using a pitch in Regent Street, close to John Lewis, and then returning to Tennis Court Road at night. Occasionally, as we know, he would go to the Hills Road Shelter for a cooked breakfast, but apart from Sally he didn't mix with the others. None of the others we've interviewed remember seeing anyone giving him food or drink, but it's been more than a month since he was last on the street, so it's not really surprising. He used to be a Big Issue seller but stopped more than a year ago."

    Upwood looked round the room for Debra but could not see her. "Is Debra in? Has anyone seen her this morning?" People looked around the room as though she might suddenly materialise, then shook their heads. "OK, Mo, tell us what you've found out about Kevin."

    "Also known as Kit, short for kitbag, which he always carried. It was a large one, capable of holding his tent and other stuff. He had a small army pension which is why he didn't need to beg. It provided just enough that he could feed himself. The donations he sometimes received are probably how he funded a growing drug problem. He generally spent his days at the market, and one or two of the stall holders would give him perishable food at the end of the day. At night he normally slept out in Jesus Green or in streets or passageways nearby. He apparently used the public toilets on Jesus Green for his ablutions. Brave man. There is just one cubicle and a long urinal, like a trough. It doesn't appear to have been renovated for decades. Tiling is damaged and there is a lot of graffiti. Drug users as well as street drinkers use the building, and as already reported, the area is a gay cruising site. I checked the PM report. They found no evidence to suggest that he was gay.

"We've spoken to Freddie who was sleeping at Round Church when the Red Bull can was found. He's twenty-seven and has been out of work for six months following an accident on a building site. He had lived with his parents until they split up and neither could provide him with a home. He's only been on the street for three weeks and is still learning the ropes, as it were, and hasn't a regular pitch by day. He says he's tried the market but got warned off by someone whom we presume, from his description, was Kevin. Says he was very aggressive. And the stall holders weren't very friendly, suggesting he should get himself a job rather than scrounge. Kevin's wristband does seem to have won him sympathy with the stall holders. Freddie'd been sleeping at Round Church for about a week, but now he's using Petty Cury. The arcaded shop fronts near the entrance to Lion Yard provide good cover. Mary Canning's been talking to Tommy's to see if they can provide him with accommodation and resettlement support before he becomes too entrenched on the streets."

"Thank you. Let's hope Freddie can be salvaged. Margaret, what news of Pete?"

"Apparently he'd been sleeping at Mill Road Cemetery for a while. A number of householders had seen him going backwards and forwards along Norfolk Street. Then we've got CCTV images of him going into the Grafton Centre via Burleigh Street. He varied his pitches around the centre. One of the coffee shops gave him tea and toast in the morning quite often. The manager thought Pete probably had psychiatric problems and was sympathetic as his father had suffered too. That's about it."

Upwood then introduced Nick Spacey, recently drafted in from Hinchingbrooke, to head up what was now a sizeable team of people working on CCTV images. "Nick, your turn. We've heard a couple of references to what your team has found. What more can you tell us?"

"Morning everyone. Well, as you've gathered, we've picked up several sightings for our five subjects, not so many for Joe and Sally because of the timings. But we've also picked up a number of sightings of other people who may be of interest. I'll take them in reverse order.

"Freddie is seen lying and then sleeping on his bench on the night in question. Over a period of hours, dozens of people pass him, either via the pavement on Round Church Street or on Round Church Street itself. The bench is too far from the Bridge Street pavement to make putting a can down on the arm of the bench a practicable proposition, but it might be possible from Round Church Street. And of course, if someone is in the churchyard it can be done. There are two large notice boards, each as wide as the bench, joined together at right angles. They provide partial screening of the bench from the street. We've seen someone standing close to the bench just a few minutes before midnight. Because of the screens we can only see part of his torso. He's wearing a dark hooded jacket. Then a minute or two later we pick up someone wearing a similar jacket cycling up Bridge Street towards Magdalene Bridge. We get a brief look at his face as he turns right into Thompsons Lane. After that we lose him." He pointed at a picture on the white board of someone wearing a dark jacket, and dark trousers, possibly sweatpants. "There are no distinctive markings on the clothing that can be seen. When he turns the corner, he raises his head and his hood slips back. We get a brief view of his face and in particular the right side. The eyes and right ear are just visible. We are unable to tell the length of his hair. We estimate him to be five feet nine tall, slightly built and fairly young. We are still looking to see if we can find him anywhere near our victims in the relevant periods. As you know, despite what fiction writers tell us, our ability to enhance these images is limited.

"We also have footage of two others that might be of interest. One guy bumps into Pete at the Grafton Centre. We can't tell from the film, but it's possible that the third party was able to slip something into Pete's rucksack. We've seen the same person bump into someone else at the Centre. We'll get you the best still shots we can later today.

"The other one is a woman, seen having a lively conversation with Kevin on Market Hill. Again, we'll get you stills as soon as. We've drafted in more people, as I'm sure you've been told. But there's still a massive amount of footage to review."

"Nick, thank you. That's encouraging. We may need to get images out to the media to see if anyone can identify them. Now, Stephanie, how are we doing with the social media trolls?"

DC Stephanie Mungo, also temporarily moved across from Hinchingbrooke, was a short, plump woman, just short of middle age, with mousy hair and rather prominent teeth. She did, however, have a lovely smile. "A lot of work for not much by way of results. When the newspaper's website administrator gave us the addresses from which the messages had come, we found that three were via email, three from Facebook and four from Twitter. We've been able to identify those using email and Facebook. The three on Twitter are using nicknames. We haven't applied for a warrant to Twitter. The cost is prohibitive, they notify the user of the enquiry and they almost always deny the request on the grounds that it is 'overly broad'. They just won't co-operate. There may be other ways to identify them, but it will take time.

"Of those we've identified we can eliminate one. She actually lives in Peterborough, although she used to live in Cambridge. She doesn't drive and looks after a disabled son. Details are in HOLMES, as they are for the other five. One is Amanda Hillyer. She also has a Facebook account, so we know she is twenty-four years of age, single and lives in Cambridge. Darren Bateley. He's twenty-nine, unemployed and on JSA. Also on Facebook. Then we have Mick Brenson, Polly Parfit and Tina Barnet. We're still researching them. They're the only ones we can give you for now, but we're still working on it."

Upwood was clearing his desk when his mobile rang. It was Will Bailey from SOCA.

"Glad I caught you. I'm off to Miami tomorrow for a couple of weeks."

"Nice for some." Upwood laughed. "Did you manage to find anything useful?"

"No. Not really. We've had our suspicions about a number of unexpected deaths among the Russian expat community in recent years, but we've not managed to find any definitive evidence of poisoning. Plenty of other criminal activity that we are pursuing, but not, as I say, poisoning. But I did have a thought. Have you heard of super recognisers?"

Chapter 21

It was almost seven in the evening when Mo and Margaret took the turning off the A14 towards St Ives and the Hemingfords. Marsh Lane was a surprise. They might have expected boggy ground. What they saw, once the high hawthorn hedge on the left-hand side petered out, was an enormous lake, dotted with islands covered in dead and dying trees, more dying trees standing in the water. It was an apocalyptic scene, an impression reinforced by the curious atmospheric conditions. The weather had been very unsettled during the last few days. Now the sky was dark grey, tinged with purple and yellow. Rain could not be far away. Weather in England always had the last laugh. That day the powers that be had declared their part of the country a drought region.

Tosedale Manor was a Georgian country house hotel with only sixteen bedrooms. Set in four acres, it was at the end of a long drive lined with lime trees. Their bedroom was huge with wood panelled walls and heavy drapes at the windows. A sofa stood at the foot of the bed and there were high-backed wing chairs either side of a round occasional table on which stood an arrangement of cream roses, pale pink peonies and dark astrantias.

Mo had booked dinner for eight o'clock, so they unpacked and made their way to the bar. Margaret ordered asparagus, goat cheese and fig salad, followed by line-caught wild seabass, tomato tagliatelle, palourde clams, miso broth, and crayfish. Mo ordered crab and leek tart followed by grilled swordfish with broad bean sauce and gremolata. On the recommendation of their waiter, he ordered a Chenin Blanc to drink with their meal.

The dining room was already nearly full when they went through. Candles shone on every table and there was a gentle hum of conversation. "Cheers, sweetheart. You look lovely tonight. Did I tell you that?"

She laughed. "Yes. That's the third time. But it's fine. As long as the repetition doesn't indicate early onset dementia."

"Seriously, that colour suits you so well. You should wear it more often." Her dress was a rich shade of burgundy which set off her deep blonde hair beautifully.

"Not quite the thing for work though."

"Perhaps not."

Their first courses were small and exquisitely presented. Mo's tart was garnished with tiny fresh viola flowers, much to his surprise. His main course surprised him, too. "Have they dyed these broad beans, do you think?"

"Idiot! They've shelled them."

"What? By hand?"

"Of course. How else would you do it?"

"Mad. Perhaps that's why it's one of the most expensive dishes on the menu."

They declined puddings but opted for espresso coffees. Soon after nine thirty they had climbed the wide, shallow stairs up to the first floor and reached their room. Mo opened the door and allowed Margaret to go in first. She gasped in pleasure. Apart from dim lamps on the bedside tables, the only illumination came from tea lights in heavy crystal holders dotted around the room. She was enchanted.

"How on earth did you manage that? It's stunning."

"I upgraded us to the honeymoon suite."

"I don't deserve this."

He kissed her. "Oh, but you do." He kissed her again then led her to one of the wing chairs. Alongside the table there was now an ice bucket with another bottle of Chenin, uncorked, and two wine glasses.

"I could get used to this."

"Please don't. Not on our salaries." He poured wine for them both.

"What was the raffle? You said it was a prize."

"You won't believe it. I entered it months ago and forgot all about it. It was one of those where the tickets are on sale for ages. The ultimate irony. It was to raise funds for Tommy's."

"The homeless shelter?"

"Yep."

"Heavens. So here we are in the lap of luxury and they're on the street. It doesn't seem right." She sipped her wine, deep in thought.

"Hey! Lighten up. They did raise more than eight thousand pounds so it's not all bad."

She kicked off her shoes. He hadn't seen her wear kitten heels before. And she'd applied her make up with more care than usual.

"You look stunning, do you know that?"

She giggled.

He put his glass down and rose from his chair. He bent down and kissed her on the lips and then went to the bathroom. She gazed out of the windows. Lamps had come on down the sides of the drive but even through the rain it looked magical. The bathroom door opened, the light still on behind him. Apart from a colourful sarong he was naked.

She giggled again. "You look stunning, d'you know that?" He did. He had a magnificent body and was proud of it. His dark skin glowed in the soft lighting. He had the most elegant feet she had ever seen on a man.

He smiled, pulled the door to, and walked towards her. He held out his hand, drew her up and kissed her again. He slid one hand round her shoulder and found the tag for the zip. Slowly he pulled it down and slipped the dress off her shoulders. She stepped out of it, and he laid it on the sofa.

"Gorgeous." Her breasts needed little support, which was just as well, as the red lace bra was about as flimsy as he'd ever seen. As were her panties. He pulled her towards him, hands caressing her body. She shivered slightly. "Cold, sweetheart? Or are you a bit nervous?"

"A bit of both, probably," she mumbled.

"Don't be nervous. I want us to be able to do this again, understand?" He kissed her gently and slowly she responded. He released her bra and slipped the straps off her shoulders, then removed it and dropped it on top of her dress. He eased her panties off. "You are gorgeous. Just like the Rokeby Venus. Only with lighter hair."

She laughed nervously. "But…"

"I love your butt. If you were going to say it's too fat, don't. It's plump. I like plump. Plump is good. Plump is peachy." His hands held her bottom. "Doesn't that feel good? And your breasts are perfect. Pert and pretty, just the way I like them." He cupped them in his hands and gently squeezed her. Her nipples were hard. He kissed her again.

He drew back a little, and with his left hand took hold of the fabric bunched into his waist and pulled it loose. His sarong slipped to the floor.

Margaret woke the following morning to find Mo shaking her gently. His hair was wet, and he had obviously showered. He was wearing one of the robes supplied by the hotel. "Morning, sweetheart. Quick shower? Breakfast in ten."

She sat up. "I can't possibly be ready that fast."

"Don't panic. I've ordered room service. Go on, scoot."

When she emerged from the bathroom wearing the other robe, breakfast had already been laid on the table. She joined him as he raised the covers on the dishes revealing scrambled egg and smoked salmon. There were glasses of orange juice and a half bottle of Champagne stood in a fresh ice bucket.

When they'd finished, he raised his glass to her. "So. Moment of truth. Did you enjoy it?"

"Fabulous! Really creamy, just the way I like it."

He thought about it for a moment and then burst out laughing. "Muppet! Last night, I meant."

She tucked her feet up underneath her on the chair as colour rose in her cheeks. "I had no idea it could be like that," she said softly. "No idea."

He laughed gently. "I didn't really need to ask. I could tell. The expression on your face was a joy to see."

She cast him a slightly troubled look. "Why did you take so long, at the beginning?"

"I had to be sure you really wanted me to go all the way."

"Would you have stopped if I hadn't encouraged you?"

"I hope so. I don't know. But when you put your arms round me and pulled me down it was just the sweetest moment. And it was easy, wasn't it? You were ready. And after that it just got better and better."

They both turned to look out of the window as lightening flashed. Thunder clapped almost immediately as a summer storm broke. Mo smiled at her, rose, and hung the 'do not disturb' sign on the door.

The telephone woke them at five in the afternoon. Mo answered it as Margaret headed for the bathroom. There was a huge grin on his face when she came out.

"Who was it?"

"Reception. They've only one table left for dinner. Did we want it or did we want room service again?"

They collapsed in peals of laughter.

Chapter 22

It hadn't taken Rix long to locate George Muspratt. There were only eight listed in Gloucestershire. This time Rix's journey was over a hundred and forty miles. He'd started very early, which may have been a mistake as overnight temperatures were unusually low, and in some places there had been an air frost. The weather had been evil throughout. Even in full helmet and leathers, the strong wind chilled him and made the trip extremely uncomfortable.

He hadn't known quite what to expect. The man he was meeting had given his address as Tirley Park. It turned out to be a site holding a couple of dozen residential caravans. Mobile homes? He didn't know what to call them. The site was nice enough, on the banks of the Severn, but looked rather neglected. The caravans had obviously been there many years and Rix wondered how much longer they would last.

Number 19 was at the far end of the park. Like the others on site, its plot was clearly demarcated and held not just the living accommodation, but also a single prefab garage. He knocked on the door. It opened to reveal a man who was even shorter and fatter than Mike Fraser had been.

"You Rix?"

"Yes, Trevor Rix. You're George Muspratt?"

"I am. Come on in. Bloody cold out there. Thought it was meant to be summer."

"Thanks. Nice and warm in here."

"Not surprising. I've had to put the heating on. Should be outside in a deck chair. Tea? Coffee?"

"Black coffee please."

"It's only instant."

"Is there any other sort?"

Muspratt laughed. "Not in my cupboard that's for sure." He filled the kettle from a sink in the kitchen area of the main living room.

"Yours is an unusual name."

"Muspratt. Ay. Local to Gloucestershire and Wiltshire mainly. That's about as much as I know. I looked it up in the library once, but I were none the wiser. Bloody nuisance it is. No one ever knows how to spell it. Try speaking to an Indian call centre with a name like mine and see how you get on."

He made the coffees and took the mugs over to the gas fire. Easy chairs stood on either side.

"Right then, take it. And tell me why you've ridden halfway across the sodding country in this weather to talk to me."

"I'm a journalist with the Cambridge Telegraph. James Upwood. Former DI at Gloucester is now a DCI at Cambridge."

"I know. I saw the bugger on the news earlier this year. Headed up the wind farm murders investigation."

"That's right. I'm thinking of doing a biographical piece on him. High profile local copper with an interesting back story."

He waited. Eventually Muspratt responded. "Well?"

"Mike Fraser suggested you might be able to help fill in some of the background."

"Always was an interfering bastard. Expecting me to tell you the inside story, are you?"

"I don't know what to expect, George, if I'm honest. But you agreed to see me. And unless you've got a particularly vicious streak, I can't think you invited me down here if you didn't think you had something interesting to say."

"It's about the death of his babby and his wife I suppose?"

"There must be a story there."

"There was some local coverage at the time."

"Not a lot that I've been able to find online."

"There were rumours. I don't think the papers dared print 'em."

"What were they?"

"What you'd expect, really. That he'd killed her for some reason or other. Or killed the babby and that's what drove her mad. Take your pick. Everyone loves a good conspiracy theory."

"What did you think?"

Muspratt looked at him, a serious expression on his face. "Something and nothing I allus thought."

"How did you rate him?"

Muspratt glared at him. "'E were a right bastard. I'd be there now if it weren't for 'im."

"What happened?"

"Made me resign or face disciplinary action. Said I were a dinosaur. I mean. Come off it. If the lasses can't take a bit of banter, they shouldn't join the force." The leer on his face suggested to Rix that there was probably more than banter involved. And of course, to Muspratt it had been the force, not the service.

"Is there anything at all you can tell me about the two deaths?"

Muspratt told him more or less what Fraser had said, clearly not wanting to be too specific.

"You must know more than that. I got that much from Mike."

"Well, you'll not hear it from me. It's more than my pension's worth. And that's less than it should be, thanks to that pillock Upwood. Anyway, it's not as though I worked closely with 'im." He glared at Rix again.

"But?"

"Talk to the landlord of my old pub: The Red Lion in Quedgeley it used to be. Owned by one of the big breweries now. The group's given it a new name. No idea what it is now. I reckon 'e heard something."

"Did he say what?"

"I ain't goin' to tell you. You'll 'ave to ask him yerself."

"Can you tell me his name?"

"Stephen Gerrard."

"Are you winding me up?"

Muspratt laughed. "No. It's Stephen with a ph, not a v. It's as much as he can do to watch the bloody game, never mind play it."

It was obvious Rix would get nothing else from Muspratt. All Rix had to do was find Stephen with a ph Gerrard.

He left Muspratt and made his way to the pub in Tirley and ordered a Becks Blue. It didn't take him long to track Gerrard down to the pub now known as the Mangel Wurzel. Gerrard was too busy to speak to him but said that Rix could call back late afternoon.

That suited Rix well. He could ride home, dry out and change into something more comfortable and call him then.

Thankfully, the journey home was not quite as bad as the journey down, but it still took more than two and a half hours. He had thought of going straight to Quedgeley but decided against it. Thank heavens Gerrard had said they could talk on the phone. Rix wasn't expecting the landlord to have first-hand knowledge of the Upwood cases. But publicans always knew the gossip.

So it proved. Gerrard told him that a couple of years before, one of his customers, who was rather the worse for wear at the time, had told him that Upwood's alibi for his wife's death didn't hold water. He wouldn't say more over the phone, and he dropped hints that his information was probably worth a few quid. If Rix wanted to call in next Sunday, he'd be prepared to tell him the customer's name.

Rix was excited. Maybe his story had legs after all.

Chapter 23

Upwood went up to see Detective Superintendent Emily Adams as soon as she was free on Monday morning. He had spent a good deal of time thinking about the suggestion made to him by Will Bailey of SOCA and wanted to bounce some ideas around with her. As usual she was wearing a dark suit, today with a lime green shirt, a much brighter colour than she normally wore. He hoped it reflected her mood.

"Do, please, tell me we are making some progress, James."

"Some, but it's slow. We have seen three people close to, or interacting with, our victims on CCTV. We issued images to the media with a view to identifying them. We have also identified five of the people who have posted messages that are antagonistic towards the homeless. They are being investigated and will be interviewed. Of the four people whom we have interviewed already, those who wrote to the paper last year when the Round Church debate blew up, three may well be of interest. They have all been charged before for crimes against the person. We have conducted preliminary interviews with them, and I propose we bring them in for interview under caution. Our problem with all these interviews is that, with the exception of the last intended victim who did not drink the Red Bull left for him, we have no idea yet when and where the drinks may have been left. It means that we don't know what periods of time we are checking for alibis."

"So unless, for example, you can establish that a suspect was nowhere near Cambridge in the forty-eight hours or so before the death of a victim, we can't eliminate them."

"That's right. And even then, we have to consider that there may be more than one person involved."

"Not two murderers again, James. Don't even go there." She sighed heavily.

"We can't rule it out. Someone may have started it and a copycat got in on the act. Or two or more people might be working together."

"We never had cases like this before you moved here, d'you know that?"

"Coincidence, Emily. Look. I want to try a new approach. A contact of mine, a guy in SOCA–"

"I've not authorised you to call them in," she said sharply.

"I haven't. It was an informal, off the record chat, with someone called Will Bailey whom I once met at a seminar. He suggested we use super recognisers."

"What on earth are they?"

"People who have an innate ability to recall almost every face they have ever seen, even if it was only an image. He gave me contact details for someone at Greenwich University who is doing research in this area. Apparently, some experts at Harvard published a paper on the subject a couple of years ago. Now Greenwich are researching the subject here. They have been talking to the Met about it since April. Someone there is very keen on the idea because he has noticed a number of officers have a much better record of identifying suspects when their images are published, two in particular. Bailey has spoken to both of them, off the record and explained why it was we were having to examine such a huge volume of CCTV footage. Both confirmed that super recognisers would be much more effective than most officers. Greenwich would be willing to lend us a couple as part of their research programme."

"But even if they are so highly skilled, they won't know who they're looking for."

"I've discussed that with the guy from the Met. We agree that it is likely our murderer has committed other crimes. As you know, it's not common for someone with an unblemished record to go straight to murder, much less become a serial killer. So the idea is that our secondees be given the chance to look at photos of all those charged, even if not convicted, of crimes against the person, in Cambridge."

"Over what period? It sounds impossible."

"I think it's doable. I went through the stats for last year over the weekend. Here, look." He passed her a copy of a spreadsheet he'd prepared and kept one himself. "In all there were some nineteen thousand crimes reported. If you count anti-social behaviour, public order offences, robbery, theft, and violence and sexual offences, there were approximately nine thousand and forty cases, almost exactly half the total. Taking all crime categories into account only eight hundred and fifty offences resulted in police or court action. If we halve that number to take account only of the categories we're looking at, there are perhaps only four hundred and twenty-five sets of photos they will need to look at."

"But you can't assume that the man we are looking for will have offended last year."

"No, of course. But even if they go back five years, I am told it's doable. Once they've seen the images of our suspects there's a good chance they'll spot them on our database. We can select the photos we want from the metadata."

"It sounds extraordinary. And how much is this going to cost for heaven's sake?"

"Nothing. The university will fund it as part of their research programme."

"Extraordinary. There's nothing to lose then, I suppose."

"I think it's certainly worth a try. After all, three of the four people we've interviewed so far have been charged with offences of the type I think our murderer may have committed before starting on this spree."

"You classify these murders as spree killings?"

"I used the word loosely. How long does a cooling off period between murders have to be before you call them serial killings? I suppose I said that because of the apparently random nature of the crimes. They don't seem to have needed the level of planning that we'd typically expect from a serial killer. I'm not sure the label matters terribly. I just want to catch whoever's responsible before he kills again."

"Do you think he will?"

"No reason why not. There are still plenty of targets out there. They certainly won't have been watching TV or reading the papers and seen the warnings we've put out."

"The PCSOs and outreach people will have been warning them, surely?"

"Of course. But who knows whether they've spoken to them all? Or even whether those they've spoken to have understood the risk or even recalled the conversation. Remember some of these are damaged people. It's why these cases make me so angry. Why murder the most vulnerable adults in our society?"

"I have no more answer to that than you, James. It sickens me too. In a city like ours. One of the most civilised you would think. It really is shocking."

By the end of the day two of their suspects had almost certainly been eliminated from their enquiries. Polly Parfit was so obese that she was definitely not the cyclist on CCTV close to Freddie's bench in the Round Church grounds. If she ever ventured further than the local chippy, the officers interviewing her would have been very surprised. Tina Barnet had been on holiday in Majorca for the first two weeks in May when Joe and Sally had died. Of those they'd identified it was two down, three to go.

The last straw for Upwood was a call from Emily just as he was leaving. She confirmed that there was to be a Major Crime Review. It would be led by a DI from Norfolk Constabulary, someone whom Upwood did not know. "Why a DI, Emily? He's supposed to be at least of similar rank."

"Apparently it's thought it will be a good career opportunity for him."

"But the policy specifically discourages such an appointment."

"I know that perfectly well, James." Her irritation was clear. "But it's not my decision. It's completely out of my hands."

"Do you know anything about him?"

"I'm told he's very thorough. Tenacious."

"Oh good. I am pleased." Upwood could do sarcasm just as well as Emily.

Chapter 24

At the following morning's briefing, Upwood explained to the team why the super recognisers would be joining them and what their role would be. He sensed a certain scepticism but no hostility, for which he was thankful. He guessed they would mostly take the view that any extra hands were welcome.

Response to the news that there was to be a Major Crime Review was more troubling. Some seemed to take it as a personal criticism of their own roles in the investigation, so Upwood took time to explain the way in which the review team would operate. Try as he might, he could not convince all of them that this was a positive development, and he explained again that the process was not intended to be adversarial. He urged them to be polite in any encounters. Antagonising the review team members would be unhelpful.

When the meeting broke up Upwood called Morton over. "Debra's not here again. What's the problem?"

"She's sent in self-certification saying she has a virus."

"She'll need a medical certificate soon presumably?"

"I suppose so. I can't remember how long she's been off."

"Look into it. We really could do with her back on the case."

Mo and Margaret spent much of the rest of the day interviewing Mancini and Matthews. To say that neither was happy to be interviewed under caution was an understatement.

Mancini was first. He had brought a solicitor with him, Colin Parker, whom their suspect in the wind farm murders had instructed when facing charges. A tall man, he was well-dressed, well-groomed and wearing a strong aftershave. Mo remembered that Upwood had complained about it after having conducted his interview. After only a few minutes in the room with Mancini, Mo could see why.

After completing the formalities, Mo began by asking Mancini to tell him about the incident eight years previously which led to his Public Order charge. Parker immediately challenged him as to the relevance.

"It is wholly relevant, Mr Parker. The incident involved aggressive behaviour by your client towards someone on the street. Someone has been showing extremely aggressive behaviour to street sleepers recently as I'm sure you are well aware. Mr Mancini, please tell us what happened."

"I protest. It was eight years ago, for heaven's sake. It was the vagrant who started it. I should never have been charged. You must have all this on record. Why don't you just look it up instead of wasting my time?"

"Why do you think he was a vagrant?"

"He had an old bike with several plastic bags rammed with stuff. He was scruffy."

"That doesn't necessarily make him a vagrant."

"Why have a bike if he's not moving from place to place?"

"Why does his lifestyle give you a problem?"

"You think urinating in a public place is acceptable?"

"Is that what he was doing?"

"Yes. When I told him not to, he turned round and pissed over my shoes. That's why I got angry."

"From the evidence given at court, he denies this. Did you invent that as a reason for abusing him?"

"Don't be ridiculous. I've far better things to do with my time."

"Neither of the witnesses saw him urinating. Nor did CCTV footage show it. But it did show you using abusive behaviour. Why was that?"

"I've told you. He pissed on my shoes. It was disgusting. I had to throw them away."

"The shoes were not found in your household rubbish bin, were they? Where did you dispose of them?"

"I don't recall. It's too long ago."

"You said at the trial you couldn't recall, but that was only three months after the incident took place. Why could you not recall then?"

"When people get angry, as I was, I suspect emotion interferes with the ability to remember every detail."

"Can we please move on, Sergeant?" Parker seemed no more impressed with his client's answers to some of these questions than Mo was.

"Is this incident why you are opposed to street sleepers now?"

Parker put a cautionary hand on his client's arm.

"I've never approved of them. But it's the beggars I dislike most."

"The court was told you accused the man of being a Roma. Did you?"

"No. And there was no evidence that I had done so either."

"Where were you on Monday 2nd May?"

"I imagine I was at college."

"All day?"

"It's where I usually am."

"Even on a bank holiday?"

"It's a good time to catch up on admin."

Mo asked him about his movements on Tuesday 3rd May and Tuesday 17th May and received the same answers. When asked about Sunday 29th May, Mancini had to think for a moment. "Was that the bank holiday weekend? I was in Yorkshire all weekend, with my wife."

"When did you return?"

"Sometime early evening on Monday."

They would have to check, but if verified, it was highly unlikely that he was responsible for Pete's death, or implicated in the other cases. No one wanted to believe that they had two killers on the go again.

Frances Matthews did not want a solicitor. Like Mancini, she was annoyed to have her old cases raised. "That first incident was five years ago."

"Indeed it was. And we do understand that no charges were preferred. But you don't deny having been a member of SHAC, Stop Huntingdon Animal Cruelty?"

"No," she answered grudgingly.

"And they are still active in what many describe as a ruthless and sustained campaign." In fact, since 1999 it had been responsible for many acts of vandalism, intimidation and violence, not only in the UK but overseas. In 2005, the FBI's counter-terrorism division referred to SHAC's activities in America as domestic terrorist threats. SHAC members had made false allegations of child abuse, sent hoax bombs, and delivered sanitary towels allegedly contaminated with the Aids virus, to try to traumatise staff. In the UK the CEO of Huntingdon Life Sciences had suffered a violent physical attack.

"Is that a question?"

"Are you still a member?"

"No."

"When did you resign?"

"After I was investigated."

"Do you still support SHAC's activities?"

"No comment." Matthews may not have had a solicitor with her but she'd either taken advice or watched too many police procedurals on television.

"Tell us about the incident at the Cambridgeshire Hunt meet."

"I was interviewed about suspected sabotage activity at a meet near St Neots. I wasn't charged. You must have all this in your records."

"Do you belong to the Hunt Saboteurs Association?"

"No."

"Have you ever been a member?"

"No comment."

"Do you support their activities?"

"No comment."

Mo then proceeded to ask her about her movements on the days that interested them.

"Monday 2nd May was a bank holiday. I went rambling with a friend in the dales. I wanted to be as far away as possible from all that royal wedding crap. Parasites, all of them."

For the late spring bank holiday weekend, she had been in Amsterdam, returning on the Monday evening. The other days she had been working.

She was allowed to leave. Mo and Margaret were dispirited. They would have been happy to see either of them in the frame. "Spoilt middle class radical who'd rather have a republic than the monarchy." Margaret didn't like her any more than snake oil merchant Mancini.

Mo went round to Margaret's flat in Fen Causeway before returning home.

"Sweetheart, I've told Morton we should be split up."

There was a very worried look on her face. "How did he take it?"

"He was fine, really. He thanked me for suggesting it. I think he knew we were getting close."

"You didn't tell him we were away at the weekend, did you?"

"No, but I'm sure he suspected."

"Why?"

He laughed. "As the mother of a school friend used to say, 'You look like the cat who got the cream'."

Margaret blushed. "What do you mean?"

"Just that. There's something about you. Like you've just hit the jackpot but don't want anyone to know."

She giggled. "You're kidding me."

"The weekend was good for you, wasn't it? You've been missing out all these years."

She giggled again but nodded. "It's made a difference, that's for sure. But what's Morton going to do?"

"Pair you with Debra when she gets back, I suspect. She's had no regular partner since Tom died. Morton thinks it's time she had one."

"And you?"

"Not sure. Maybe get one of the two from Hinchingbrooke to move across permanently."

"I know it's the right thing to do, but we do work well together."

He winked at her. "We'll just have to play well together instead."

Chapter 25

Joan Keiller and Dirk Ravencroft arrived the following morning after checking into their guest house. Their sponsors, Greenwich University, had decided that they would be more effective if they immersed themselves in Cambridge. Their accommodation had been chosen because rooms were equipped with microwaves and kettles. They would therefore fund their own meals as they would at home. For a booking expected to be for a month, the arrangement was almost cost neutral.

Joan was forty-three years old, an experienced PCSO whose record of identifying even poor police mug shots of people seen previously had been recognised as exceptional. Dirk had been identified as having a similar skill. He had retired after twenty years as a custody officer based at Paddington Green and was talented at spotting people who had passed through his hands on previous occasions. For both of them, it was their first experience of trying to apply their skills outside London's metropolitan area. Although pleased to be given the opportunity, they were naturally anxious. Would their skills apply here, when they lacked the years of experience in dealing with, or seeing, some of the same people more than once?

Upwood welcomed them. "We're delighted to have you both with us. The crimes we are dealing with are very unusual. We have four victims whom we believe were unlawfully killed, probably by the administration of poison, although we are waiting for further forensic tests results before we can be certain. There is a fifth person whom we believe was an intended victim. Apart from the most casual of interactions, there is no discernible link between them. We do not know the motive for these attacks. We do not know, in any of the four fatal cases, where or when the poison was acquired. Nor do we know where or when it was consumed. We do have CCTV footage that we believe shows the deposition of a contaminated drink close to the fifth subject. We have not found DNA traces that suggest the identity of the perpetrator.

"Our current line of enquiry is identifying people who have displayed behaviour antagonistic towards street sleepers, and those who have previously been charged with crimes against the person. We believe lower levels of crime in this category may be a precursor to these recent crimes.

"What we would like you to do is study still images of suspects, like those of the man seen near our fifth subject, and photos of others identified through letters and social media, and then work your way through the database of those charged with previous crimes."

"How many individuals will that be, Sir?" Dirk looked sceptical.

"We analysed our crime statistics for Cambridge. We believe there are approximately four hundred such cases a year."

"Is that just for Cambridge? Surely the person responsible could live outside the city?"

Upwood smiled ruefully. "You're right of course. But we have to start somewhere."

She raised another question. "How far do we have to go back?"

"I can't tell you. My intuition tells me not that far. If the recent crimes are an escalation of earlier ones, I don't think there will be a gap of more than a few years. So how do you feel about it now you that have more background?"

Joan and Dirk looked at each other. "It's going to be difficult." They answered together and laughed. "We'll just have to give it our best shot," Dirk added.

Mo and Margaret were back in Interview Room 2 facing Maud Fowler. Fowler had already been interviewed under caution but had not been asked about her movements on the relevant days. Her botanical knowledge, coupled with her conviction for affray, made her a viable suspect.

When questioned about her movements she insisted she was working each of the days in question, including Sundays and bank holidays: that's when people like to visit garden centres.

"When do you have days off?"

"Not very often. It's tough making a living."

"But you can't work seven days a week every week, surely?"

"I tend to in the summer. I can take more time off in winter."

"What time do you close the garden centre?"

"Four on Sundays, three in winter, and seven o'clock every other day."

"Do you always lock up?"

"Almost invariably. And that doesn't necessarily mean I go home. I often have paperwork to do."

Her alibis would have to be checked. But there were no grounds to detain her, however unpleasant her letter about homeless people.

Amanda Hillyer was next to be interviewed under caution. She declined the offer of free legal representation. With no previous contact with Cambridgeshire Constabulary, she was fairly confident she didn't need it. Twenty-four years old, five feet two, slim and single, she had been found on a public Facebook page complaining several times about homeless people in general and beggars in particular. As was often the case, the mangled English in her posts was even worse than her spoken English. She worked in one of the cafés close to the Grafton Centre.

"Miss Hillyer, you've posted several messages online and commented on others making clear your dislike of homeless people. Can you tell us why that is?"

"I don't like 'em. It's not a crime, is it?"

"Why don't you like them?"

"They're filthy. We often have to clear them out of the doorway in the morning."

"How often?"

"Goes in phases, dunnit? Sometimes it's every day for a bit. Then they bugger off somewhere else."

"Is there anything else that troubles you?"

"I don't like the way they scrounge. Always trying to get us to give 'em free drinks and food."

"Do you not have any sympathy for their circumstances?"

"No. They're either drunk or high."

"Has anyone ever threatened you in any way?"

"I feel threatened."

"It's not the same, is it? Has anyone used threatening behaviour towards you?"

"I hate the way they call out to me."

"What do they say?"

"You know…"

"No, I don't. Tell me."

"Asking me if I've got the time. If I've got anything for them. They're all the same."

Her prejudice was clear to see, the behaviours described by no means typical of the homeless. As Mo and Margaret spent more time on the investigation, they were confident of the fact. Her dislike of homeless people was deep-rooted, if perhaps ill-founded. The interview got them nowhere. Apart from, perhaps, confirming the fact that homeless people were likely to choose doorways that offered some shelter as a place to sleep.

When asked to account for her movements, she had difficulty remembering what she'd been doing. She was not the sharpest knife in the box. Eventually they established that she did have an alibi for the most recent bank holiday weekend. Provided that it could be verified, it was unlikely that she had been behind Pete's death. She too was sent away.

DI Sam Whiskin of Norfolk Constabulary was standing at the window looking down over Parker's Piece when Upwood returned to his office after a meeting with the forensic management team. "You have a nice view, Sir," he said, turning round. Taller than Upwood by a good couple of inches, he was smartly dressed in dark blue suit, white shirt and tie. His beard was short but full, his hair short with a spiky cut on the forehead that, for some reason he could not explain, Upwood did not like. Except later when he did think about it, he thought it showed a degree of vanity of the kind he eschewed.

"Good morning. You are DI Whiskin, I take it?" He gestured for the man to sit down.

"I am. I am happy for you to call me Sam, as we're going to work together."

In the most polite tone he could muster, Upwood replied, "Better if we keep it formal, I think. I and my team are more than happy to co-operate with you and your colleagues, but undue informality is not the norm here."

"I understand, Sir. That's fine with me."

"Can I offer you some coffee?"

"No, thank you. I'm good." This last was an expression Upwood hated. Not only was it a misuse of the English language but somehow it also conveyed a rather smug, patronising air. "Have you had cases subject to a Major Crime Review before, Chief Inspector?"

"Of course."

"So are you familiar with the procedure?"

"Fully."

"Are there any questions you want to ask me about our work here?"

"Not at the moment. Perhaps just one. How many of these reviews have you conducted?"

"This will be my second."

Oh, good grief. An ambitious, arrogant, younger officer, undoubtedly with less experience than Upwood. And how had Emily described him? Tenacious. This was going to be a real pain in the arse.

Chapter 26

By Thursday the call centre team had processed the responses for information about the people shown on CCTV in the Round Church grounds near Freddie's bench, the man seen bumping into Pete and one other in the Grafton Centre, and a man seen apparently talking to Kevin on Market Hill. However flimsy the content of some of the calls, they had all been logged and taken seriously.

No one had offered a name for the Round Church figure. Most of the names suggested for the other two men had already been eliminated. But eight of those named had records on the PNC. One, Smith, had been convicted of drunk and disorderly behaviour; another, Jones, for drink driving; another, Black for drug dealing; Warner, for affray at football matches; two, Montague and Falconer, had been convicted of driving offences; another, Elliot, for drug possession and finally one for a sex offence.

This last person was soon eliminated when it was realised that he had only been released from Littlehey Prison on 31st May. He could not, therefore, have been responsible for any of the four deaths.

Morton was with Upwood for a meeting late on Friday evening to review the results.

"So tell me what we've learnt about the seven on the PNC that are still in the frame."

"Smith. Twenty-eight. Convicted three times for drunk and disorderly. Not very intelligent. We don't think him capable of crimes this sophisticated, frankly."

"Alibis?"

"Weak. He seems to spend most of his time in the Dobblers, often at the pool table."

"That's the one near the Mill Road Cemetery, isn't it? A Charles Wells pub?"

"Yes. He's not very popular there and he's been told that if he causes trouble, they won't hesitate to call us. It's ironic, when we spoke to the landlady, she told us that one of the meanings of Dobbler is said to be "a person with low standards who lacks motivation", which seems to describe Smith pretty well."

"In or out?"

"We can't rule him out yet. But I don't think he's our man. Jones is much the same. Thirty-two. Used to be a forklift driver till he lost his licence. Favours the White Swan on Mill Road. They have five screens and are well known for their sports coverage. They also stay open till 2.00 am. Jones was done for drink driving after France beat England in the final of the Six Nations in March last year. Currently unemployed. They have live music on a Tuesday. The pub is further out on Mill Road, the other side of the city from where Kevin was found. Witnesses confirm he was in The Earl of Beaconsfield on the evening when Kevin probably acquired his can. And like Smith, he's not really the type for this sort of crime."

Upwood laughed. "Think yourself a profiler now, Morton?"

"Don't be daft. You know what I mean."

"But still in contention?"

"Can't eliminate him yet. But I'm fairly sure he's not the man we're looking for."

"Who's next?"

"Black. Twenty-six years of age. Convicted of supplying cannabis. Right down the bottom of the food chain. Got two years. Also a user. No alibis. Again, he's not right for it, but we'll keep him in the frame for now.

"Warner is forty-seven years of age. He's a courier. He was convicted of affray after fights broke out at Carrow Road when Norwich were beaten 7-1 by Colchester. It was the Canaries' biggest ever defeat and the fans weren't pleased. Judging by his appearance he's a man who likes his pie and a pint, but he doesn't look like a credible suspect. He does have a firm alibi for the Tennis Court Road cases, so we can eliminate him for now.

"We've got two who were convicted of driving offences, Montague and Falconer.

Montague is fifty-three years of age. He was convicted for doing forty-three in a thirty mile an hour zone. He's a surgeon at Addenbrooke's and said he was called in for an emergency operation for a patient following an RTC. He was given six points but not disqualified because of his need to be on call at unsocial hours."

"Does he have the right kind of medical training for our crimes?"

"I don't know. He's an orthopaedic surgeon which isn't very relevant. Whether his medical training would have covered obscure poisons I don't know. We are checking to see if we can establish what his curriculum might have been. We are also checking out his alibi for the last bank holiday weekend. So in for now, but I think he'll be eliminated.

"Falconer was convicted of dangerous driving in 2009. He was on a motor bike and overtook between two vehicles on the A14. The vehicle in the outside lane took evasive action and hit the central barrier. Falconer himself was injured and now has limited movement in his left arm. Could he have done it? Unlikely in the extreme I should think. We're still checking his alibis.

"Finally, Elliot. Convicted three years ago for class A drug possession. He looked promising at one stage, but we've had to rule him out. He was in hospital for two weeks in May following a case of sepsis."

"Is that it?"

"It is for now."

"Realistically, who have we got in the frame?"

"Maud Fowler, botanist, convicted of affray. If the alibi she gave us for one event checks out then she drops off the radar, too.

"Amanda Hillyer, café worker. We've got one alibi to check for her, as well.

"Finally, there's Darren Bateley. He's one of those who posted unpleasant material online and has a caution for spraying graffiti targeting beggars near the Bus Depot in Emmanuel Street. We haven't managed to interview him yet."

"It's not looking good." Upwood frowned.

"How are you getting on with Withnail?" A smile hovered on Morton's lips.

"What on earth are you talking about?"

Morton laughed. *"We want them here and we want them now!* I keep forgetting. You're not much of a film buff, are you? *Withnail & I.* That scene was one of the defining moments of the film. Classic."

Upwood laughed. He didn't know the film. But whoever had come up with that nickname for him was spot on. "For God's sake don't let him hear you call him that. He's just looking for some way to shaft us. And for God's sake don't…"

The door opened. Whiskin put his head round. "Not interrupting, am I?"

Chapter 27

"Morning Katie. How's it going?" Upwood was glad to find her in. He had felt thoroughly depressed after leaving Parkside the previous evening. Usually more than happy with his own company, today he needed to talk to someone who was on his side.

"James, how lovely. I didn't phone because I know how immersed you get in these big cases. I didn't want to distract you."

"Katie, darling, you can distract me anytime, you know that. Sometimes I positively need distracting. Anyway, what have you been up to?"

"Playing the tourist, still. I caught one of the local buses down to La Línea and walked over the border into Gibraltar."

"You didn't drive?"

"Couldn't be arsed. Anyway, on the bus, I could see more of the scenery. I enjoyed it. I'm not sure I liked Gibraltar all that much. The shops in Main Street seem to cater only for tourists. Tacky, mostly. I couldn't find any decent shops. And the Marks & Sparks is a bit minimal. It's a franchise apparently."

"Was it busy?"

"Marks or Gib?"

"Gibraltar."

"Heaving. There was a cruise liner in port. The *Azura*. It was massive. Towered over the dock and everything alongside. I looked it up when I got back. It carries over three thousand passengers and more than twelve hundred crew. I think they were all in Main Street. It was bedlam."

"It's bedlam here, too. May Week's just started." He paused. "They wouldn't let the whole crew off," he said drily.

"No, I know. But there certainly were crew there, stocking up on duty frees."

"Did you do any sightseeing while you were there?"

"Yes. I took one of the taxis and did a standard Rock Tour. The history of the tunnels was interesting. I'd rather be here though. Gib is definitely too crowded for me. So, what's new?"

Upwood told her about the super recognisers. She was fascinated but sceptical.

"If they don't prove useful, the guy heading the Major Crime Review will hang me out to dry."

"Oh Lord, has that started?"

"Yes."

"And?"

"He's a complete prick."

"Who is he?"

"A DI from Norfolk. Rejoices in the name of Whiskin."

She giggled. "He sounds like half an ice cream."

"What?"

"Baskin-Robbins. American ice cream."

"Grief. Don't you start. He'd been given a nickname before his first day was done."

"What is it?"

"Withnail."

"As in Withnail & I?"

"You know it?"

"It's a classic. A cult film, from the late eighties if I remember correctly. It's said to be one of the funniest British films ever. I take it you don't know it."

"No. It passed me by. Or maybe I passed it."

"Watch the trailer on YouTube. You'll get the general idea. So why do they call him that?"

"Something about wanting it and wanting it now?"

She collapsed in laughter. "Oh God, I remember that. There are just so many good lines. *Don't threaten me with a dead fish.*"

He began laughing. "Is it still available?"

"Bound to be. Get it on Amazon. I don't think there's ever been a version other than the original. Richard E Grant was in it. His first film. Get it, will you? We can watch it when I get home."

"Have you decided how much longer to stay there?"

"No. Probably not much longer."

"Why? Your friend said you could stay as long as you like. And you've three months sabbatical."

"I've been here about three weeks. In truth, I'm bored."

"But you're not thinking of going back to work early, are you?"

"No, not really. But I've got too much time on my hands. Too much time to think. And I'm not sure I want to go back to my old job."

"I'm not with you, my darling. What's the problem?" As soon as he'd put the question, he knew what answer she'd give.

"Because when I'm back, MacKay will find me again."

"You don't surely believe that?" But she did. Of course she did. Why wouldn't she? He did, for sure.

"Yes. He's got years yet before he'll be considered for parole, even if they do consider him. I think he enjoys having a project on slow burn. Planning new ways to frighten me gives him something to live for. Can we stop him, James?"

He groaned. "I honestly don't think we can. For a start, I don't think there's a cat in hell's chance we could prove he was responsible for your attack in Buenos Aires. We have no grounds for opening an investigation into it. It's a complete non-starter."

"But what if there's another incident when I get back to England?"

"That would be a different matter entirely."

"Would Madam Adams agree to an investigation?"

"Katie, darling. How can I possibly answer that? It would depend on the circumstances."

"I s'pose so." She sighed. "So what's Withnail like?"

Upwood laughed, glad she was moving onto safer territory. "I told you. A complete prick. He's only a DI, and Norfolk think it will be good career development for him. The policy specifically discourages an appointment when the review team leader is junior to the SIO of the case he is reviewing, and when it is for career development. He's years younger than me and hasn't got half my experience. And he's a prick."

"That's the third time you've said that. How's he managed to get under your skin so quickly?"

"The first time I met him he was waiting for me in my office, standing behind my desk and looking out of the window."

"Ouch."

"Last evening Morton and I were reviewing the case and Withnail barged in without knocking."

"Double ouch. Have you spoken to him about that?"

"No," He said grimly. "But I will. Very politely of course."

Katie giggled again.

"You don't seem very sympathetic."

"You don't need sympathy. I have every confidence that you will skewer him with great finesse. Elegance even."

"Just so long as he doesn't skewer me first."

"So you think he doesn't rate your decision to bring in these people, what d'you call them? Super identifiers?"

"Super recognisers. No. He thinks it's misdirection on my part so that he and his team don't look at the rest of the investigation properly."

"How long has he been on the case?"
"Wednesday."
"You're right. He's a prick."

Before starting preparations for supper that night, Upwood went to his study to check his emails. He knew that he could do it from the comfort of his armchair, on his iPad or even on his phone. But he preferred to run email on his laptop. That way he could keep a degree of separation between admin and down time.

There was the usual assortment of messages that, if not actually junk, didn't need reading and through habit, he deleted them. The only one of interest was from his friend John Laidlaw, the retired DI living in Estepona.

Hi James,

Thought you'd like to know there's been another death reported. Prostitute again, on the same stretch of road. First for over 12 mths. That's 5 now. Not much in the papers about it yet. If Paco can give me any gen worth passing on, I'll let you know.

Cheers John

The following morning, Katie was checking her emails when her mobile rang.

"Katie, good morning! It's Frank. Frank Pell."

"Frank. How good of you to call me so soon." In truth, Katie's email to Frank had been a bit of a long shot, and if she'd been entirely sober the previous evening, she might not have sent it at all.

"So, you are thinking of a career change?"

"I am. And you did say if ever I was interested, you'd like to talk to me. Is that still the case? It's a couple of years ago, after all."

"Yes. Very interested to talk. Can we meet?"

"It's a bit complicated. I'm in Spain at the moment, on a sabbatical. But I could come back."

"Where abouts in Spain?"

"Between Málaga and Gibraltar. Why do you ask?"

"Cos I'm coming to Madrid soon. Your old stamping ground if I remember correctly? Perhaps we could meet there? More discreet than your coming to the office if we decide not to pursue the idea?"

Chapter 28

Rix skimmed Google News as he munched his toast. He'd risen early but had not decided when to leave. The weather was still unsettled and there was a chance of strong south-westerly winds. He was probably going to have another unpleasant ride across country.

As soon as he'd cleared away, he decided he might just as well make a move. Sod's law said that if there was bad weather about, he'd hit it. In the end, his journey down to Gloucester, at least, was relatively straightforward. He'd arrived soon after eleven, Stephen with a ph Gerrard having said that once service started there would be no chance to talk to him before late afternoon. Rix parked his bike, locked his helmet away and went into the garden. The pub looked to be old enough to have been called Mangel Wurzel the first time round. Why the owners chose to change the name from a perfectly normal Red Lion to the name of a root vegetable was beyond him. Anyway, shouldn't it either be one word or hyphenated? He didn't approve of changing pub names. History was lost. It was one issue on which he and Upwood might have agreed.

He was checking his phone for messages when Gerrard came out with a tray of coffee.

"Morning. Trevor Rix, I take it. Good ride?"

"Hi. Bit blowy, but not too bad. It stayed dry."

"It'll rain before the day's out." He sat down and pulled out a packet of cigarettes, offering one to Rix, who shook his head.

Gerrard lit up, inhaled deeply and waited.

"So tell me, Mr Gerrard. You said a customer told you DI Upwood's alibi for his wife's death 'didn't hold water'. That was the phrase you used."

"Yes. I probably shouldn't have told you."

"Well, you did, and I'd like to know more. I've agreed I'll make it worth your while. And you know we gentlemen of the press never reveal our sources."

Gerrard laughed, a laugh that quickly developed into a thick cough. He looked at Rix. Spiky hair, thin face, arched eyebrows, pronounced Adam's apple, and biking leathers. He certainly didn't look like a gentleman. "That's as maybe. But if the punters think I'm gossiping about them, telling tales out of turn, it'll be bad for business. You got any idea how hard it is to make money in this game, son?"

"Strangely enough I do. I did an in-depth article of the problems facing the licensed trade for my last paper. I know it's tough. And that's why I appreciate you making time to see me. But I'm not local to here. Your customers won't know what gets published in Cambridge." He knew jolly well they would, if this story was as big as he thought it was. "Anyway, why would anyone suspect you of being the source?"

"I just can't take the chance."

"If you won't tell me who he is, can't you at least give me a clue about what he told you."

Gerrard took another deep drag on his cigarette. Rix reckoned the landlord's job would be less tough if he took better care of himself but kept this thought to himself.

Rix knew from experience that open-ended questions were the most useful. But Gerrard was clearly trying to avoid answering. He was going to have to pull these teeth one by one the hard way.

"I told you on the phone. He was in 'is cups and told me the copper's alibi didn't hold water."

"Alibi for what exactly?"

"The time of his wife's death."

"How did the subject crop up?"

"Can't rightly remember. Might have been something about police corruption in the paper. Summat like that."

"How did he know the alibi was dodgy?"

"Somebody told 'im, I reckon."

"Was it the person who provided Upwood with an alibi?"

Gerrard could see what Rix was doing. He should have told the guy to stay away. He should tell him to piss off now. But he admired the young man's persistence. He'd looked him up on Google during the week while he was trying to decide whether to go ahead with the meeting or not. He'd been impressed with what he'd read, both by and about him.

"No."

"Related to that person?"

"It's not bloody *Twenty Questions*, lad."

Rix laughed. "It is if I have to carry on like this. Make it easier for yourself and just tell me."

Gerrard wheezed. "No, mate. You'll have to work for it, I reckon."

"So, related or not?"

"No."

"A witness to whatever activity constituted Upwood's alibi."

Dammit, the lad was good. "No."

"Saw Upwood where he shouldn't have been?"

"I'm saying no more."

"No point in stopping there, Mr Gerrard. We're getting close, aren't we?"

Gerrard shook his head and stubbed out his cigarette. He stirred two spoonfuls of sugar into his cup and put the spoon down, drinking half the coffee in one go.

Rix picked up his own coffee. Sometimes you had to know when to push, and sometimes you had to know when to ease off. He thought easing off was called for. They sat there and a Robin sang an urgent sounding song from high up in one of the apple trees in the pub garden.

"Was I right? Upwood was where he shouldn't have been?"

Gerrard shook his head. "I shouldn't be having this conversation with you."

"So who was it saw Upwood where he shouldn't have been?"

Gerrard played with the teaspoon in his saucer.

"A neighbour of Upwood's?"

"No." Gerrard shook his head firmly, giving Rix some confidence in that answer.

"His partner?"

"What, you mean his wife?"

"No. The officer he normally worked with."

Gerrard stared at him sullenly. "No."

Rix was struggling now. "A neighbour of that partner?"

"I'm not giving you her name."

Rix inwardly sighed a breath of relief.

"Where did she live?"

Gerrard knew he was fighting a losing battle. "Not sure. Something Mews maybe. That's it. You'll have to make do with that."

Rix tried teasing further details from the landlord but this time he clammed up. Still, what he'd got was worth paying for. Just as well, he stood no chance of claiming these payments on expenses unless and until his editor gave his backing to the story.

After Gerrard had gone back inside to take care of his business, Rix stayed in the garden a while. He soon discovered that there was only one street with Mews in its title, and perhaps not unreasonably, it looked a small one. It seemed as though he would be doing door to doors this afternoon.

It took him all afternoon, but one householder did recall that there had been a policewoman living in the street a few years ago and was able to point the house out. A woman who lived next door did remember seeing Upwood drop off her neighbour on the day in question, sometime in the middle of the afternoon. She didn't know who it was at the time, but when his picture appeared in the paper the next day following his wife's death, she recognised him. The story had provoked considerable local interest. No, she didn't know the policewoman's name, sorry.

Rix rang the bell on the house identified as being that where the policewoman had lived. The current householder had been there four years. She and her husband had bought the house when the previous owners divorced. She was able to give Rix their names but had no idea what had happened to them. Rix was confident he'd be able to track them down. Perhaps Upwood was having an affair. Is that what drove his wife to despair? Or was it another reason that made Upwood want to get rid of his wife?

Chapter 29

One of Pell's characteristics was his ability to move quickly, a quality Katie admired in him. He was due at a conference on Tuesday but came down a day early so they could meet at his hotel.

"So. Katie. Tell me why you are thinking of changing direction."

"I just think it's time. I've been with the firm fifteen years. I'm a partner now, but I don't think there is much more I can realistically achieve there. But can you tell me what kind of role you have in mind for me?" She was keen to avoid tackling the complications before she'd decided if there was any future with his firm.

"I think on our due diligence team. Do you remember that conversation we had after you'd submitted your report? You explained one of your methodologies. It really got me thinking. I and the rest of the board had been quite keen on that acquisition and in lots of ways it made sense. But in hindsight, we were seeing what we wanted to see. It was the way you pointed out the risks and adverse consequences that made the difference."

"I'm sure you realised what they were. But perhaps you were not giving them sufficient consideration. Using the Kepner Tregoe Decision Analysis approach forces you to do so."

"I was impressed and I'm sure we could use it more in our work. We certainly gave much more thought to the issues you raised, so called off the acquisition."

"You made the right decision, I'm sure. The culture of the other company was completely different. It would have given you serious problems in the long term."

They talked for more than an hour and by the end of their discussion both had reached the conclusion that there was real mileage in the idea that Katie should join them.

"You said there were complications. Is there something in your contract which would frustrate your joining us?"

"No. No. Nothing like that. I don't know quite how to explain. You'll probably think it's all a bit far-fetched."

"Try me. If we're going to work together, we'll need to trust each other."

"Right. Yes. I know that." She paused again.

"Well?"

"OK. I'm the subject of a campaign of harassment, violent harassment."

"Good Lord. Why?" It was not what he was expecting. How to wriggle out of restrictive covenants, possibly, but not this.

"My partner was murdered more than four years ago. His killer received a twenty-year sentence and is now in Whitemoor. He blames me for his prosecution."

"Was it your evidence that convicted him?"

"No. It's more that the police were initially inclined to treat his death as suicide. Eventually they realised his death was suspicious, but the case went cold. It was largely my pushing them, and finding potentially incriminating evidence, that persuaded them to examine the case more closely."

"So what happened?"

"MacKay, that's his name, realised that I had stumbled over information he wanted kept secret. He blackmailed a nephew into trying to push me in front of a tube train." She gave a rather nervous laugh. "The nephew's heart wasn't in it, fortunately, and I only fell onto the platform. So here I am."

"Good Lord. You said a campaign. There's more?"

"A series of text messages threatening actions which would have compromised me and others." She didn't go into detail, didn't want to raise the subject of her affair with Upwood.

"Is that it?"

"No. I was badly beaten up recently in Buenos Aires."

Pell was becoming a little sceptical. "Local thugs, surely?"

"No. They left a note on me. In English, saying that he could find me anywhere. It's MacKay. I know it is."

Pell was quiet for a moment. He didn't know quite how to respond, nor what the implications might be if they hired her. "How can you be so sure?"

"Well, I don't make enemies on the whole. And he does have a real grudge against me. We know it was his nephew who sent the malicious texts, he admitted it. We're confident it was he who tried to push me under the train, but can't prove it. MacKay is a bully. The police are confident he is making concerted efforts to intimidate me." This was stretching the truth somewhat. But Pell didn't need to know that in this context Upwood represented the police.

"Can he be stopped?"

"Unlikely. The police can't pursue the attack in Buenos Aires. It's outside their jurisdiction. And even if they could, the chances of proving he was behind it are slim."

Pell thought again for a while. "And is he succeeding? In intimidating you, I mean?" He felt entitled to ask this question. If she was unduly anxious, it could well affect her behaviour and performance.

"I was nervous, I admit. Now I'm just angry. I will not let the bastard ruin my life. He did enough damage when he killed Mark. I do not plan to let him make me feel a victim too. As long as the police remain confident he won't try to arrange anything more serious than he has already done – and their psychologist shares that view – then I'm fine." She looked him straight in the eye and hoped to goodness she sounded convincing.

"I applaud your frankness, Katie, but why have you told me all this?"

She had the grace to laugh. "To explain why I would not want you to approach my senior partner for a reference if you make me an offer!"

"Because he won't give you a good one?"

"No, no, nothing like that. But he's a very good networker. The day after MacKay was convicted, I heard him on the phone. 'It's a bad business', he said. 'And he was in my Lodge.' And MacKay is also a chartered accountant. I think it's through his network that he found out I'd been sent to Buenos Aires."

"It would be unusual…"

"I know. But you do at least have first-hand knowledge of my work, as do some of your colleagues. And I'd be happy to have you ask a couple of recent clients for a reference."

Katie kept quiet for a while. She hadn't said that she thought MacKay would be quite capable of trying to make trouble for her with her employer, whoever that might be. But if Pell believed what she had told him, he could probably work that out for himself and assess any reputational risk to the firm.

"We've a lot to think about. Why don't you go back to the coast? I'll talk with my senior colleagues when I get back after the conference and we'll talk then. How does that sound?"

"Absolutely fine. Perfectly sensible."

Chapter 30

Debra returned to work on Monday morning and sat silently through the briefing. She could see that a tremendous amount of work had been done while she had been away, but also that they had very little to show for it. She also sensed that morale was low. When learning there was a Major Crime Review under way, she was not surprised. The super recognisers, on the other hand, interested her. Although tedious in some ways, the work she had done reviewing CCTV footage in the Mallon murder case had been quite satisfying. She had become more adept at recognising individual characteristics such as general impression of size and shape (the meaning of jizz, one of Upwood's birdwatching terms) and also body language. The idea that super recognisers might not be so good at that (and certainly would not have total recall of every car they had ever seen, for example) fascinated her. Their skill related only to faces.

After the briefing ended, Morton led her to Upwood's office, knowing it was free. "Glad to see you back, Debra. How are you now?"

"I'm fine. Just a virus."

"Well let's hope you're over it. We really need to be at full strength. I should like you and Margaret to work together for the time being. Are you OK with that?"

She wasn't, in fact, but knew admitting it would go against her. Tom's death had upset her more than her colleagues. It wasn't that they didn't care. The fact that no one really knew how to deal with it, and the fact that at the time they were still investigating the wind farm murders, meant that most of them immersed themselves in work. It was just their way of dealing with it.

For her, his death was much more troubling. Knowing as she did now that the annoying habit he'd developed in recent months of needing to pee at inconvenient times was a symptom of prostate cancer made her feel guilty. She kept telling herself that she shouldn't, but it didn't help. Nor did the fact that she'd accepted Tom's cat and rehomed him. He was a nice enough cat. Now, though, every time she saw him, she thought of Tom when she should be moving on. It didn't help, either, that her partner, George, seemed to be developing an allergy to her pet. She kept asking herself whether she shouldn't try to find the cat a new home, but continually put off a decision. If word went round at Parkside that she'd done so, she didn't think it would go down very well.

"Debra?"

"Sorry, Morton. My mind wandered for a moment. Yes, that's OK. She's a good officer. Any special reason?"

"I just think it would be good for you to have a regular partner again. And of course she's up to speed with everything."

"OK. So the next action is to interview this Bateley guy?"

"Yes. He's being brought in this afternoon. That will give you time to catch up and see what we already know about him."

Debra returned to the interview room to look for Margaret. "You're with me now. That OK with you?"

"Absolutely fine. It will make a nice change." Her tone of voice was not altogether convincing, and Debra had a shrewd suspicion that Margaret wasn't any more pleased about the arrangement than she was.

Bateley had not been keen on going to Parkside, but knew the system well enough to understand that little was gained by refusing. He had declined the offer of legal representation. On Job Seeker's Allowance, he could not afford his own solicitor. His previous experience of duty solicitors had not given him much confidence in the arrangement. He trusted himself to handle the situation.

Debra would make sure the formalities were conducted properly, then Margaret would conduct the interview as agreed. Deb would only chip in if she thought there was a line of questioning to pursue that Margaret had not followed.

"Mr Bateley, you know we are questioning you as part of our investigation into the unexplained deaths of four homeless people. As DS Graf has said, we are not treating you as a suspect, but we are aware that your views on homeless people are unfavourable. We should be glad if you would tell us why."

"Because they are a waste of space. They should make more of an effort and sort themselves out."

"You do realise that for some of them that's very hard to do?"

"If they've been on the streets a long time, I suppose it is. But they shouldn't let it go on that long. They are a drain on resources."

"Whose resources?"

"Ours. We pay our taxes. Ultimately, it's our money that's spent on them."

"Most of that comes from charities though, like Tommy's and the Mill Road Shelter."

"But most of their funding comes from the council. Well over half a million a year."

"It could be said that we are funding you, too, Mr Bateley. How long have you been on Job Seeker's Allowance?"

Bateley scowled. "That's a bit below the belt."

"How long?"

"Five months."

"That's how long ago you were cautioned, isn't it?"

"OK. OK. I lost my job because of that. It was stupid. But I get so fed up with them. There was one on Emmanuel Street. Used to sleep on the pavement opposite the bus stop where I got off in the morning to go to work. It shouldn't be allowed."

"Tell us why you were cautioned."

"Must I? It's all on record, surely?"

"We'd like to hear it from you."

"It was a dare. Someone from work. He said if I was so annoyed about it I should do something to demonstrate it. He bet me fifty quid I wouldn't have the guts. He kept winding me up."

"How did you respond?"

"Got a can of paint and sprayed a message on the door of one of the toilets they use, the one behind the taxi rank, next to the bus depot."

"Saying what?"

"Beggars fuck off."

No points for originality, thought Margaret, and from what she recalled of the photos, he didn't score highly on artistic merit either.

"And you were identified from CCTV footage, I understand?"

"Yes. I was an idiot. I'd done a recce but there was one camera I'd missed."

"And your employers dismissed you?"

"For bringing the college into disrepute. Honestly. It wasn't as though I was wearing a jacket with the college name on it. And I didn't deal with the public."

"What was your job, Mr Bateley?"

"I worked in the library at Emmanuel College."

"Did that not involve dealing with people?"

"Yes, but college staff and students."

"They're not members of the public?"

"Don't be pedantic. You know what I mean."

"Are you actively looking for work now?"

"Of course. I told you. I don't believe people should scrounge."

"On Facebook you are still posting unpleasant messages to that effect, aren't you?"

"I'm entitled to my views. It's a free country. Lots of people agree with me."

Margaret moved on to ask about his movements for each of the days before their victims were targeted. He had no real alibi for any of them. In the end, with no grounds on which to detain him, they allowed him to leave. Margaret was inclined to believe him innocent. Debra was less certain. They agreed that he was intelligent, and smarter than some of the others they'd interviewed. On the other hand, continuing to post offensive material about the homeless while embarking on a killing spree didn't seem like the cleverest idea in the world.

After Bateley had gone, Margaret looked at her colleague. "How much weight have you lost Deb? You don't really look fit enough to be back."

"Don't start nagging again Margaret, please. I'm back, OK? The virus just knocked a bit of the stuffing out of me, that's all."

Margaret was not convinced, but if Debra wouldn't discuss it there was not much she could do.

When they returned to the incident room, there was, for once, a bit of a buzz. Joan, one of the super recognisers, had identified the person who had bumped into Pete in the Grafton Centre. She had seen his face amongst the mug shots they'd been going through of those charged with public order offences. He was someone who had been convicted of theft – a pick pocket. He may not be the person responsible for the deaths, but her identification now vindicated the decision to bring them in.

Upwood, for one, was relieved to know this as he made his way home. Withnail had been a real pain in the arse again during the day, making sarcastic comments about the policing methods at Parkside. Maybe he'd be a bit more circumspect. One could always hope.

Chapter 31

Upwood was even more encouraged the following morning when word reached him that Dirk, Joan's colleague from Greenwich, had recognised Maud Fowler as the woman apparently having an altercation with Kevin on Market Hill. He asked Mo and Margaret to join him in watching the footage.

"Do you recognise her?"

Mo was the first to answer. "I can't honestly say I do. Roughly the same size and build, I guess."

"But her hair's the same. I might not have picked her out if I'd been reviewing it first, but I think Dirk's right," Margaret chipped in. "And the boots. Look. They're the same ones she wore before. What are they called? They're Irish, I think. Leather drawstrings at the top. The sort of thing you see on sale at country shows."

Upwood and Mo shook their heads, neither an expert on women's footwear.

They replayed the scene. Kevin had been sitting on one of the benches outside the Guildhall on Market Hill, his kitbag on the ground beside him. Fowler, assuming it was indeed she, stopped and appeared to speak to him. He shook his head. She spoke again. This time he jumped to his feet and waved a fist at her. She reached into her shopping bag and waved a can at him, taunting him. He grabbed it and pushed her away. The argument lasted no more than a minute. There was only ever going to be one outcome; Fowler dashed across the road and melted quickly into the people thronging the stalls in the central market. Kevin grinned and dropped the can into his rucksack. None of them would ever know it was the second can he'd acquired that day.

"Bring her in again. Today." Upwood would be very interested to hear how she talked her way out of that one.

Despite the new pairings, Upwood agreed with Morton that it made sense for Mo and Margaret to interview her again. Mo and his new partner, Stephanie Mungo from Hinchingbrooke, had had little chance to work together, since she spent most of her time analysing CCTV footage. They'd established no real rapport and had undertaken no interviews together. Margaret had been with Mo on both the previous interviews with Fowler.

When officers arrived at the garden centre to bring her in for a third time, Maud Fowler was even angrier than before. She only conceded to go voluntarily after the threat of arrest.

Once more she was interviewed under caution. Last interviewed on Wednesday 15th June, some four weeks after Kevin's body had been found, she'd been asked about her movements on Tuesday 17th May and also in the early hours of 18th May. She had said then that she'd been working both days, starting before eight in the morning and finishing after seven in the evening.

Mo and Margaret had agreed their strategy.

"Do you keep an eye on the news, Miss Fowler?" Margaret began.

Fowler turned her attention to Margaret, the look on her face wary. "Up to a point."

"How do you follow it? Newspaper? TV? Radio? Social media?"

"TV at night if I'm not too tired. iPad most days."

"What events do you recall from the last month or so?"

"Are you serious? I've got better things to do with my time than play games with you."

"Please answer the question."

Fowler fidgeted in her seat. "Royal wedding. What a load of crap. The media just couldn't leave it alone. Osama bin Laden. Volcano in Iceland. The Arab Spring grinding on.

I don't pay much attention. Nothing I can do to change the world."

"But you'd like to change things where you can?"

"How d'you mean?"

"Therfield. We discussed that before."

Fowler simply nodded.

"And we know you'd like to see homeless people off the streets in Cambridge."

This drew no response.

"Do you follow local news?"

"Up to a point." The same answer she had given to an earlier question.

"And where does the point come?"

"Environmental issues are the only ones that interest me."

"And you include the homeless people in that category?"

"Yes. I explained all that before."

At this point Margaret glanced at Mo, signalling him to take over the questions.

"Why did you lie to us about your movements on Tuesday 17th May?"

Fowler's face flushed. "I am not in the habit of lying, Sergeant." She folded her arms.

"You told us that you had been at work all day that day. We know that is untrue. Why did you lie?"

"I told you what I believe to be the truth."

"We have video footage of you having an argument with one of the four homeless victims in Market Hill."

"You must be mistaken."

"We are not, I assure you. The images are unusually clear. Time stamped 17th May at 15.03. Both you and Kevin Broome can be identified beyond any doubt. You are even wearing the same boots as when we first met. And you are clearly having an argument."

As he hadn't asked a question, Fowler was again bright enough, or experienced enough, not to try to fill a gap.

"What was the argument about?"

Fowler again remained silent.

"Miss Fowler, I'm sure you know how this works. You are under caution. Failure to answer may harm your defence in the future."

She snorted with laughter.

"Bollocks. There's nothing you can charge me with."

"Wasting police time? Could get you six months inside…"

Fowler fidgeted, keeping quiet.

"Why did you let Mr Broome take a can of beer from you?"

She laughed again. "Told him the sooner he drank himself to death the better."

"Why did you not tell us of this incident before?"

"Why the hell should I?"

"Following the press conference on 31st May there's been a lot of local coverage advising people not to accept drinks or food on the streets. This is your third interview since then."

"I didn't attend the press conference, Sergeant." She was becoming more sarcastic by the minute.

Mo could sense Margaret bristling beside him.

"But you've said you follow local news. And even if you don't follow it that closely, we made it clear at our first meeting on 9th June that we were investigating the deaths of four homeless people. In your second interview, on 15th June, we asked you about your movements on specific days. You told us that you had been at work on 17th May. Now, by your own admission, and as evidenced by the video footage we have of you, that is clearly a lie."

"An oversight. As I told you, I am not in the habit of lying."

"Your assistant also told us you did not leave the garden centre that day. Was she under instruction from you?"

"For God's sake. When you work in a business that trades seven days a week you have no idea what day it is most of the time, never mind the date. I go to the market two or three times a month. I don't put it in my diary. It's just not important. I don't suppose she gave it a thought either. We're talking about a visit to the market that took place four weeks before that interview, more or less."

They continued to question her for a while, but finally, once more, had to release her.

"What d'you think, Mo?"

"She's probably got the knowledge about poisons; she hates rough sleepers. She's cocky. She's been through the system and is bright enough to be forensically aware. I wouldn't rule her out. What about you?"

"Yeah. But if you look at that video very closely, I think you'd have to agree she wasn't wearing gloves when she let Kevin take that can from her."

He thought about it for a moment. "And there were no prints but his on the dodgy can we found near him. Bugger. You're not just a pretty face, are you?"

Mo and Margaret were having an early supper in their favourite Italian. Neither had any inclination to discuss the case. In any event, doing so in a public environment was never easy.

"How's it going with Deb?"

"OK. Not sure she's very keen on the idea. Think she'd rather be on her own. She's grumpy. And I still don't think she's well."

"Why d'you say that?"

"She was being very sick quite a few times before she went off. She's lost a fair bit of weight. And she says it's a virus."

"So?"

"I'm no expert, but it doesn't sound like a virus to me."

"Did she see a doctor?"

"No idea. No way of knowing."

Margaret was grappling with some particularly uncooperative pasta in her usual Spaghetti Aglio Olio when Mo's mobile began to vibrate. He grabbed it from the table just before it lurched over the edge. Either it was work related or he did not recognise the caller.

"Ramachandran," he heard. He frowned and looked up at Margaret, then hastily looked away. "What..." He listened for a moment, again looking briefly at Margaret.

She could see his temple throbbing, a sheen breaking out on his forehead. She felt her own pulse quicken. Had someone seen them at Hemingford? Someone trying to stir up trouble?

"What the fuck..." Mo stabbed at the screen and slammed the phone back on the table.

She toyed with her food, too anxious to ask him. They ate in silence for several minutes until she could stand the suspense no longer.

"What was that about?"

"Nothing," he barked.

"Tell me about it. Please."

"It's nothing to do with you. Mind your own business."

She was shocked. He had never raised his voice to her, never been rude to her. Someone had upset him badly. So badly that he left her to make her own way home after the meal and didn't even kiss her goodnight. She was frightened now. For the first time in her life she thought she'd found herself in a good relationship. Now she was terrified that Mo might, like her former husband, have a dark side.

Chapter 32

It was seven weeks since the attack on Smokey Joe. The investigation had all but stalled and Withnail had submitted his findings. Upwood was furious. While Whiskin had been unable to identify any obvious errors or omissions in Upwood's command of the case, he had nonetheless littered his report with snide observations about some aspects of the investigation, including the deployment of resources. He was especially withering about Upwood's laissez faire attitude to Debra, whom he judged not fit to be on the case. He also criticised the SIO for allowing Mo and Margaret to continue working together when it was entirely obvious they were having an affair. He commended Mo for suggesting they be parted professionally but made it clear that Morton or Upwood should have taken the initiative much sooner.

Emily had not been entirely sympathetic to Upwood. In truth she wasn't too worried about Mo and Margaret. While she did not see much of them, her general impression was that they were both professional officers and she knew they had both made good contributions to the resolution of the wind farm murders. She was, however, concerned about DS Graf. And she was still annoyed that Upwood had ignored her instruction some months earlier to tackle Debra about her affair with the former ACC.

"So you believe that DS Graf has been making a good contribution since this case began?"

"Reasonable, given her health issues."

"Which are what, exactly?"

"A virus she says."

"How many days has she had off?"

"Eleven."

"What did her doctor say?"

"I don't believe she consulted one."

"But she's required to if she's off that long."

"It wasn't in one spell. It was a few days, followed by odd days."

"What were her symptoms?"

"Vomiting, mainly, I think. Weight loss. Fatigue."

"I think we should send her to a doctor of our choosing."

"That's a bit heavy handed, Ma'am, surely?"

"Look at the girl, James. Does she look well?"

He couldn't answer her. He knew she was right.

"Get it sorted. I'm not looking to discipline her, and I dare say you've cut her a bit of slack because of her reaction to Tom's death. But she needs to be fit to do her job. If she's not, she puts herself at risk, and others."

Upwood left her office, returned to his own, and called for Debra's file.

Later that day Upwood had more good news from the super recognisers, this time from Joan again. She had recognised the cyclist whom they thought had left a can of Red Bull next to Freddie in the yard of Round Church.

Much to everyone's astonishment, she demonstrated that the cyclist was not a man but a woman: Alex Barron. Some were sceptical till she showed them an enlargement of one of the old photos on file and of the still taken from the CCTV footage from Round Church. It showed the subject's right profile, her shoulder length hair tucked behind her ear. "It's the ear lobes," Joan explained. "You can change your eyebrows, your nose and your lips. You can pad your cheeks. But ears are a dead giveaway." As soon as she'd pointed it out it was clear to everyone what she had found.

In the video footage taken near Round Church there had been a brief shot of her, face on, although her hair and part of her face were obscured by the hood of her jacket. As she turned into Thompsons Lane her right profile could be seen. In this, when enlarged, a simple ring could be seen in her ear lobe, but given she was riding a man's bike, it was insufficient evidence to dissuade those who had first looked at the footage that she was a man.

Joan had recognised her as someone convicted of threatening behaviour some three years previously. Margaret was asked to look into the case and report back at the evening's briefing.

Her report was not very illuminating. She had apparently been drinking one night in a city centre pub that had a live music performance. She was alone. One of a group of three men had told her to push off. "We don't want your sort in here." She told him in no uncertain terms to get lost, whereupon his mates started yelling at her. The situation became a bit rowdy and a beer bottle was smashed; it was said she'd waved it at the men. At this point two off-duty PCs intervened and arrested her for threatening behaviour. When she was interviewed, her solicitor had read a prepared statement saying that she was well educated, without a blot on her character and that she felt intimidated by three burly aggressive men when she was alone in a strange pub. She stated that it was not she but the landlord who had broken the beer bottle and that happened after the PCs had restrained her, an allegation that was strongly denied by all the witnesses for the prosecution. She did not speak at the trial. With the evidence of the landlord, himself a former police sergeant, the three men and the two PCs, and with no evidence to back up her allegation, she was found guilty and fined. What Margaret had also learnt from one of the PCs, now retired, is that the man who first accosted Alex was his wife's nephew, and that he and his mates were regulars at the pub. His theory was that it suited the landlord to blame Alex, but had no idea whether her account of the smashing of the bottle was true. In any event, as the landlord had served her the beer, which she had drunk from the bottle, both their prints were on it. He had no idea what had been behind the original taunt. Too posh, a hooker, a lesbian? He didn't know, but remarked simply that "she weren't very feminine looking". He did offer the view that it was a pub patronised more by men than either couples or women. All interesting stuff but neither Upwood nor Morton knew whether this incident shed any useful light on recent proceedings.

Nevertheless, instructions were given to investigate her background, track her down and bring her in for interview.

Upwood had looked through Debra's file. Her record was good and there was very little there to help him prepare for a meeting with her, bar the fact that her next of kin was noted as being George Watson, who was shown to be living at the same address.

She entered his office a minute or two after five, feeling slightly apprehensive. She had no idea why she had been called to see her DCI.

"Hello, Debra, come and sit down."

Upwood was behind his desk, so she had no option but to sit facing him. The meeting was clearly going to be formal. She settled into the chair, her hands in her lap.

"How are you? I gather you've not been too well lately."

"Fine, thank you, Sir."

"We're concerned about you. You've had sick leave recently, which is not like you. Your attendance record has generally been excellent."

"Just a virus. Nothing to worry about."

"And your doctor has confirmed that?"

She was gripping the ends of the arms of her chair. "Not necessary."

He frowned. "But the policy says you should provide a certificate if you're off that long."

She gripped the arms of the chair more tightly. "I didn't have more than five days off at a time."

"We think you should see a doctor. We propose to send you to Dr Standing, the one we use here at Parkside."

"I don't want to go."

"Then I'm afraid I'm going to instruct you to."

"I am not ill."

"You may think you're not. But you have been. And frankly you don't look well."

"I am not ill. Sir."

Upwood threw his pen across the desk. "Dammit, Debra. How can you tell? As Detective Superintendent Adams said to me earlier, you need to be fit in this job, otherwise you put yourself and others at risk."

"I repeat, Sir. I. Am. Not. Ill."

"For heaven's sake. Why would you risk disciplinary action over an issue like this? What is your problem?"

"I don't have a problem, Sir. If you must know, I'm pregnant."

Upwood sank back into his chair, the wind taken out of his sails.

"George must be thrilled," was the best response he could come up with.

"She is, Sir."

"George…?"

"Georgina."

Upwood was struggling for a response. "Oh. IVF. Good for you."

"No."

"No." It wasn't even a question. Upwood had never been in discussion with a junior colleague about anything like this before. He was not enjoying it.

And then the penny dropped. Christ Almighty.

"Assistant Chief Constable John Clarke." This wasn't a question either.

Debra had the grace to look embarrassed as well as shocked.

"I won't deny it. But I think you should know that I haven't told anyone else and don't propose to."

"Does he know?"

"No, of course not. And I don't propose to tell him either. He might not like knowing that I allowed him to shag me simply because I thought he was decent breeding stock."

Upwood winced. He couldn't believe his ears. Her coarseness shocked him. And the idea that Clarke was good breeding stock was one he had real trouble with.

"I'll make no demands on him. George has an extremely well-paid job. That's why we decided I should go for it. Well, that and the fact that I'm bi. She isn't. You might as well know, too. If all goes well I do not plan to return to work following maternity leave." Now Debra was in this unreal situation, she decided she might as well make her DCI as uncomfortable as possible. Judging by his body language, she was succeeding.

Upwood closed the meeting as quickly as he decently could. He had to think about this. And a large whisky would definitely help. He drove home, his mind in a whirl. Suddenly her behaviour when he put his arm round her to comfort her after finding Tom's body became much clearer. She might be bi, but it was all too obvious now that she was more comfortable with women. What on earth he was going to do about the situation he had not the least idea. And what Emily's response would be, he dreaded to think.

Chapter 33

At the following evening's briefing Morton was keen to hear the results of the actions issued earlier in relation to Alex Barron. Was she only a person of interest or was she a viable suspect?

Stephanie Mungo had been researching her status.

"I'm struggling, to be honest. I can't find an NI number for her, she's not filed any tax returns so far as I can see, and she's got no driving licence. She's not in the NHS system. It's like she doesn't exist."

"But she must have existed when she was charged before. What did we have on her then?"

"An address. A passport. That's all."

"Is she still at the same address?"

"No. Hasn't been since soon after she was charged."

"Was she working then?"

"Apparently not. No visible means of support. The thinking was that she had someone to support her, but she wasn't giving him – or her – away."

"Has anyone been round to her old address?"

"Yes, me," answered Margaret. "A single guy rents it now. It's an apartment in a smart block in Brooklands Avenue, on the far side of the Botanic Gardens from here. Not cheap. If she wasn't working and had no one to support her, she must have had a private income."

"Or an illegal one," offered Mo.

The room fell silent for a moment as the rest of the team digested the proposition.

"I did have one idea that may be worth following up. I've not had time to do it today. I contacted Royal Mail. For twelve months after she left, she had her mail re-directed. To another quite classy place. A duplex apartment in one of those blocks on Riverside. Overlooking the Cam."

"There's a surprise," someone muttered.

Morton was mildly annoyed but couldn't see who it was. "Is she still there?"

"Don't know for sure but almost certainly not. Records show it's owned by a company in London. They don't use letting agents and won't give us any information without a warrant. That's as far as I got today. Thought perhaps we should get round there and see if any neighbours recognise her. Sir?"

"Good idea. Do it, please. Who else has anything to bring to the party?"

Mo answered. "I went back through the old case file and managed to track down some of the witnesses. There was live music on that night and so far as they could tell, she was on her own. None of them I've spoken to have seen her since, or so they say. It's the same landlord and he reckons she's not been in again."

"Anything else?"

"The bike. It's an unusual one. For one thing, it's a bloke's. And it's expensive. A racing bike. It's an odd sort of bike to see in the city. I'm going to see if I can track down the retailer."

"Why?" came a query from one of the junior officers.

"Why what?"

"Why's it an odd choice?"

Mo laughed. "Well, it's got drop handlebars. Typically, you ride them leaning forward with your head down. Not a brilliant position when you're riding around busy streets, I wouldn't have thought. Although I suppose it means your face is caught on camera less frequently." Mo didn't look wildly confident that focusing on the bike might get them very far, but they had so little to go on that Morton nodded to him.

Morton elicited nuggets of feedback from one or two others, but all in all it was not a very inspiring haul. Margaret's lead seemed the most promising, but they'd have to wait until the following day to see if she could take them closer to Barron.

The news she brought them the following evening discouraged them all. Barron had apparently left Riverside after a year or so. None of her neighbours or the local shopkeeper had any idea where she'd gone. Royal Mail had no record of mail redirection.

They decided to issue a photo of her, asking the public to let them have any information they had on her. They would say she was thought to have been a witness to a recent incident. Upwood was not sanguine. The photo was several years old and it was entirely likely she had changed her appearance since then. It was all they had: the stills extracted from the CCTV footage were too poor to use in the media. At the last minute, it was decided that they would not use the photo. As Morton pointed out, the latest footage of her showed that her appearance had changed – she no longer wore her hair long so far as they could see. Apart from which, if they used the file photo, she would know that she had been identified. Instead, they agreed to use an E-FIT picture based on the images they had: it might be good enough for members of the public to recognise her but anonymous enough that she would assume she had not been recognised.

Upwood was depressed when he got home that night. Again. The case seemed to be going nowhere. And he was missing Katie dreadfully. He decided to ring her.

Her mobile rang out to voicemail and he looked at it ruefully. He sipped at his whisky and wondered what to do. He couldn't be bothered to cook. No one provided home delivery where he lived. He had more or less decided to go down to the pub, something he rarely did on his own, when she rang back.

"Hello gorgeous!"

He laughed. "That's my line, surely?"

She giggled. Then smothered a small burp.

"You've obviously started before me."

"Well we are an hour ahead don't forget." She giggled again.

"Are you OK to talk? You are on your own?"

"Yes. Am now. Had a late lunch with Monica and her boyfriend."

"Monica?"

"Her father owns the apartment?"

"Course. Sorry. Are they staying there, too?"

"No, thank God. They're on her boyfriend's gin palace in the port. Going up the coast and then over to Palma."

"So's he's loaded like her father."

"Looks like it. How the other half live, eh?"

"Not my scene, Katie, you know that. It's not really yours either is it?"

"No. But it was nice to see her again."

"Where did you go for lunch?"

"Arroyo Hondo. Hadn't been there before. Nice."

"I know it. Up on the Casares road. Good menu del día as I recall."

"It is. But Rafa chose from the main menu. All the most expensive dishes as far as I could see. Bit of a show off. Anyway. Nuff of that. What's new with you?"

"Not a lot. The case is grinding on very slowly. We've identified one possible suspect. Or rather, Joan, one of our super recognisers, has. But she's covering her traces really well."

"Joan?"

"Don't be daft. The suspect. You carried on drinking after you got home, didn't you?"

"Don't sound so censorious, James." She burped again and smothered a giggle. "I'm bored. Bored out of my tiny skull."

"Still concerned about coming back to Cambridge?"

There was a long pause. "Yes. No. Not really." Another pause. "A bit."

He knew she was dissembling. "Shall I come over this weekend?"

"Can you? That would be brilliant."

"It'll have to be a flying visit. Friday evening to Sunday evening."

"That's fine. That's wonderful. It'll cheer me up no end. Let me know what flight you're on and I'll come and pick you up."

"I'll do that. I'd better ring off, my darling. I'm expecting a call from Emily. And I'm not looking forward to it."

It was gone nine in the evening before Emily phoned. Her tone was frosty, which was not encouraging, given the news he had for her.

"Thank you for getting back to me, Ma'am."

Emily's senses were now on high alert. Upwood normally only called her that in front of junior officers or when he was getting a bollocking.

"I've spoken to Debra. She is not ill. She's pregnant."

"And is that cause for celebration? Or is she likely to terminate it?"

"She won't terminate. She and her partner made a conscious decision to have a child."

"Well. That's presumably good news, then."

"Maybe. But there is a potential problem."

"What? With the pregnancy?"

"No, with the father."

"But you said they wanted a child?" She was getting frustrated. It was like getting blood out of a stone.

"They do, but her partner's a woman."

"So? For God's sake, James, what's all the fuss about? They used IVF presumably?"

"No."

"Spit it out, for crying out loud."

"The father is John Clarke."

He could hear her intake of breath. "Jesus Christ. Was he a willing partner to this?"

"He knows nothing about it, she says. As far as he's concerned, she is unable to have children, so he used no protection."

"Is she going to tell him?"

"She says not. Her partner has a very well-paid job. She wants nothing more to do with him."

"This is a nightmare scenario."

He gave her a moment or two to consider the matter. "It doesn't have to be. I am satisfied she won't ask him for support. She's also said that if all goes well, she won't return to work following maternity leave."

"But what happens if she and her partner split? She might be very glad of support then."

"There's nothing we can do. It's not our job to tell him. And just so you know, if she does return to work for any reason, I will not have her on my team. Clarke may have been a dick but the way she played him was unforgiveable. I can't tolerate that level of immorality in an officer."

"I'm inclined to agree. Her behaviour is shocking. We'll have to worry about that if the problem eventuates." They sat in silence for a moment or two. "Did she volunteer the information?"

"No. I guessed. Her body language told me I was right, and she admitted it."

"Dear God. We'll have to think about it. I'm not sure saying nothing is an option. You know that John Clarke and his wife have no children?"

"No. No reason why I should."

"Maybe he'd like a child."

"Even if he does, it's still not our business to break Debra's confidence."

"I'm not sure I agree with you. Let's sleep on it. In the meantime, tell no one."

This last instruction annoyed Upwood more than she would have anticipated. He found it deeply insulting. And the thought that out of some misguided idealism, or sense of duty, she should expose the affair worried him deeply. It gave him another sleepless night.

Chapter 34

Since the call on his mobile the previous Tuesday, Mo had been by turns upset and angry. He was glad that he was no longer partnered with Margaret as he had no idea how to behave with her. Fortunately, their paths had barely crossed. He'd spent the whole of Saturday trying to decide whether he should meet the caller. He'd texted him for clarification. In response, he'd been told again, that only if they met would he be given more information. Reluctantly, he decided that he had no option but to do as he was told. He could not have such vile accusations haunt him.

Having decided to meet, he worried about whether to tell someone. Standard police procedures were of course, that no officer should knowingly attend a scene alone when there was the prospect of violence. But there would be none, surely? In any case, this was not police business. The writer either wanted him to know the truth, or was trying to wind him up. He didn't want to tell a friend or colleague and be made to look a fool.

The message had given the postcode for the King Charles pub on London Road, Baldock, and told him to be there at nine thirty that evening. It wasn't a place he knew, but he checked and found he could be there in about forty-five minutes. It would be dusk at nine-thirty, so he decided to aim for half an hour early. At that time of night, the pub would be busy, plenty of cars in the car park, easy to spot the person he was going to meet.

London Road was the old main road out of the centre of Baldock, used by those joining the A1 heading towards London. As he drove through the outskirts of the town, the scenery became more rural. He saw a pub on the left, the George IV, and knew he was close to his destination. But any relief he felt turned sour, the King Charles pub was not only shut, it was boarded up, the one derelict car in the car park abandoned. He cursed himself for not having researched it properly. He should have known; he might be entering a trap. At least he was here early, only now the prospect of waiting for half an hour with no witness to their exchange was no longer an advantage. He was anxious. Should he abandon the whole idea? Assume it was some malicious prank? Or should he wait it out, now he'd come this far?

There were times like now when Mo wished he smoked. Anything to pass the time. He was tempted to play around on his phone but knew that would take his eye off the ball. There might be a steady stream of traffic on the road, but the pub's car park was at the back, so while he could hear it, he could not see it. All he saw for now was a cat stalking across the yard, ignoring him to explore the ground around the wheelie bins. Mo had no idea how long the pub had been closed but he suspected the cat was going to be out of luck tonight. It apparently shared his view and slunk off into the bushes at the back.

Beyond the traffic on London Road, he heard the distant hum of traffic on the A1, a few snatches of bird song in between. What sang at night? Nightingales? Surely not? A Blackbird maybe. Or a Thrush? The brief phrases were quite melodic. He gave up guessing, fascinated instead by a steady stream of bats flying from under the eaves of the pub. They should have rich pickings, he thought. There were certainly enough damned insects about, enough to encourage him back into his car after a few minutes.

By quarter to ten he decided to call it a day, royally pissed off. He'd been sent a thoroughly unpleasant message, been worried about it for days, and now he'd been stood up. He was about to turn the ignition key, when he heard a car decelerate. Moments later it appeared at the entrance, turned in, reversed and parked in the opposite corner, close to the wheelie bins.

Mo flashed his lights. No response. As he got out of his car, the driver of the other car emerged. By now there was little ambient light. The sun had long sunk behind the horizon. Shrubs and trees on three sides meant visibility was poor. Mo could only tell the other guy was tall and dressed similarly in dark clothes.

The other driver stayed close to his car, forcing Mo to approach him.

"Well, well. It's the pillock from Parkside. Up for a bit of fun are you?"

It was then Mo knew he'd made a major error of judgment.

"Who are you?"

"Not much of a detective, are you? She wasn't raped. I told you that. She's just a prick-tease, know what I mean?"

"Bastard. Who the hell are you?"

"Not told you much, has she? Certainly not the truth."

"I don't believe you. Why should I?"

"You're here, aren't you? You must have thought there was something in it otherwise you wouldn't have come. How long did she make you wait before she let you fuck her? Months, I bet. Like I said, she's a prick-tease."

"You bastard. What d'you want?"

Suddenly the other man lunged at him and Mo saw the flash of steel. He feinted to the left and managed to parry the blow, but his assailant had already recovered his position, threatening him again. Mo hadn't engaged in any martial arts since he'd left university, deeply regretting it now. They danced around each other for a minute or two, the other man occasionally lunging at Mo with the knife, which to Mo looked vicious, all of six inches long. He tried to kick it out of his assailant's hand but failed, almost losing his balance in the process. The other man sensed an advantage and threw himself at Mo, jabbing with his knife. He knocked Mo off his feet and they both fell heavily against the pub door. Immediately a sensor alarm kicked off, wailing like a banshee. Mo's assailant picked himself up, sprinted the couple of yards to his car, started it, threw it into gear and shot out of the car park. Mo was oblivious. He had blacked out when his head connected with the door, with no idea that he was bleeding from two knife wounds.

The security company retained by the pub's owners was alerted. Not only were there sensor alarms on the doors and windows, but there was a camera high up under the eaves, scanning the back door and its surrounds. They could see a body slumped against the door.

"Probably a wino," one of the operatives said.

"Wind it back a couple of minutes," his supervisor said. "Let's see what we've got."

Even with the rather poor resolution of the footage, they saw the knife, called the emergency services: police and ambulance.

Mo did not regain consciousness. Following assessments at the Lister Hospital at Stevenage and surgery to remove his ruptured spleen, he was put into an induced coma. He had been carrying his warrant card, however, and so, after a series of phone calls around Cambridgeshire Constabulary, word finally reached Upwood.

Upwood was furious, livid that another of his officers had managed to get himself into such an appalling situation. What the hell had he been doing in Baldock, in the car park of a boarded-up pub late at night?

Chapter 35

For the first time in weeks, the weather on Sunday morning was fine. Rix was relieved. He'd had several uncomfortable rides down to the west country on his Ducati. It handled well, even on poor road surfaces, but blustery winds and rain had several times given him bad journeys. Today he set off in a thoroughly good mood. Not only was the weather fine but he was confident he was getting very close to finding out whether or not he had a good story, one good enough to secure him a job with one of the national newspapers. He grinned to himself.

Since his last visit to the west country, he'd done a lot of research, trying to find the couple who'd lived in the Mews, John and Pat Hembry. He'd found no trace in Gloucestershire of Pat Hembry. He considered widening his search to neighbouring counties but decided to focus on her husband. She might have remarried, in any event. Apart from which, he told himself, if she were still a serving officer she would be very reluctant indeed to discuss the case with a journalist, especially if it might prejudice her own career. And if these two reasons weren't enough, it was, after all, her husband who had told the publican of the Mangel Wurzel that Upwood's alibi did not stand up. This alone made it worthwhile for Rix to track him down.

Rix arrived in Welland Road, Keynsham just after eleven o'clock. The house was one of a number of well-kept, semi-detached properties overlooking the town's cricket ground. When he rang the bell, he heard a dog barking and a child crying. He had not made an appointment since he was fairly sure that Hembry would have refused to see him. He was hoping to take him by surprise. He did.

Hembry was at home, looking after a young child. His new wife had gone to Sainsbury's, the nearest of the larger supermarkets. When Rix introduced himself, Hembry tried to close the door, but Rix stuck his foot in it.

"I don't want to make trouble for you, Mr Hembry, really I don't. But I think you can help me with some research I'm doing. And there's no reason why I should disclose my source if you are able to give me any useful information. And of course, I'll make it worth your while."

It was this last observation that swayed Hembry. At least if he let the man into the house he could shut the door. That way he could keep the dog in and maybe quieten the child. Reluctantly he showed Rix into the front room. It had been fairly recently decorated, although Rix would have paid good money to avoid the effect achieved. A fake dado rail ran around the room and different patterned wallpaper covered the walls above and below it. The curtains were also patterned but mercifully, from the reporter's point of view, they had been hung, incorrectly as he understood matters of décor, with the pattern showing to the outside. He perched on the edge of the sofa, which was piled high with magazines and newspapers. The child, a boy, if the colour of the clothes were anything to go by, was probably less than twelve months old and lay grizzling in a carry cot beside Hembry's chair. Rix only hoped he could get the information he needed quickly and escape.

"What do you want to know? Upwood, you say?"

"Yes. I'm working on a feature. He's a DCI in Cambridge now and has handled some very high-profile cases. So it's a human interest story I'm working on."

"What on earth makes you think I can tell you anything useful?"

"Your former wife used to be his partner, I understand."

"That was a long time ago. You'd be better off talking to her."

Rix was not keen to disclose that he had not yet found her, nor in turn admit she might have powerful reasons for not wanting to talk to him.

"How long were they partners?"

"Christ, I don't know. Two years? Three? Until he took compassionate leave."

"Why was that, do you know?"

"You can't have done much research if you don't know the answer to that, mate. His baby died and then his wife topped herself."

"I read that in the papers. Must have been terrible for him."

"S'pose so."

"What do you think happened?"

Hembry looked at him, beginning to understand where Rix was coming from.

"No idea, mate. I just went on what was in the papers."

"Your wife must have had a pretty good insight, I suppose."

"Maybe. She didn't tell me much. She knew the rules. She kept to them."

"She and Upwood were on duty the day his wife died, I believe."

Hembry did not respond.

"On surveillance, I'm told. Watching comings and goings at an industrial site on Stephenson Drive."

"If you say so."

"But I gather she didn't complete her shift."

"Who the hell told you that?"

"I don't disclose my sources Mr Hembry. If you want me to observe that rule with you, you can't expect me to break someone else's confidence."

Hembry looked at him sullenly. "What if she didn't?"

"She may have had a perfectly good reason to come home early that afternoon. Did Upwood follow her into the house?"

The householder glared at him. "I'm not saying she did come home early. I wasn't there. How the hell would I know?"

"Because she told you? Because a neighbour told you?"

"No. I wasn't there. I didn't see it. If I didn't see it, it didn't happen as far as I'm concerned."

Rix knew he was lying but wasn't confident he could get the man to admit what he knew.

"You're divorced, I take it?"

"What the hell's that got to do with anything?" Colour had flooded Hembry's cheeks.

"Amicably?"

"Sod the fuck off. I've got nothing to say to you."

"Why let me in then? The thought you might get paid for some useful information? Unless you were going to make something up. My guess is that you do know something. What is it? Surely you could use a couple of hundred pounds?"

The man visibly wavered. "Bugger off. I know nowt. Get out of my house." He had risen from his chair now. Rix decided he would learn no more and made to leave.

"Where can I find your ex-wife, Mr Hembry?"

"No idea. Get out. Now."

Rix was an optimist by nature, and relentless. Hembry's behaviour and body language suggested strongly that he did know something but, perhaps from loyalty to his former wife, was reluctant to say. This only made Rix more determined. It was annoying, though. He wasn't sure if his story was strong enough to get past his editor yet, but decided to give it a try.

Chapter 36

"We can't possibly publish this, lad."

His editor's opening salvo was less than encouraging.

"Why not?"

"It's all supposition. Not enough facts."

"As far as I'm concerned it is a fact. He had no alibi for his wife's death."

"But you have no proof. Is the neighbour prepared to testify that she saw Upwood drop his colleague off at home that day?"

"I haven't asked her. That's not our job. But the behaviour of John Hembry, her then husband, convinces me the story is true."

"You want it to be true. You want your byline on a sensational story. It's not worth it if the story's not true."

Rix was stung by this rejection, even if he knew there was an element of truth in his editor's opinion. Of course he wanted the kudos of a major story. Of course he wanted a reputation like Woodward and Bernstein. Not that bringing down Upwood would be quite the same order of magnitude as bringing down Nixon. But nonetheless, it had the capacity to be a great story.

"But if I'm right, and a paper in Gloucester publishes it, we'll be kicking ourselves."

"If we do publish and we're wrong we'll have all the powers that be kicking us to kingdom come. You know how hard I've worked to get the top brass in Cambridgeshire Constabulary on side. Particularly since the wind farm murders. We've scooped other media several times this year as a result. And Upwood is popular with the public. We of the fourth estate may have given him a hard time during the wind farm investigations, but your idea is a different matter altogether. We could lose readership. And God knows we can ill afford to do that." He scowled at Rix.

"But what about all the rumours in the west country press? No smoke and all that."

"Don't be daft, son. We all love a conspiracy theory. You know what the trolls are like as well as me. We never landed on the moon, remember? And the earth really is flat after all. Come on grow up. Anyway, you know how this stuff works. It's no good having just enough material for one story. You need a good opener to whet the readers' appetites and then strong follow ups. That's not what you've got."

"But…"

"No. I'm not touching it. Not unless you can give me something more concrete."

Rix left the office in a thoroughly bad mood. How many days had he spent on his investigation? He dreaded to think. He decided to push off home. It was nearly time and he knew he wouldn't settle to anything now.

The ride home cleared his mind, as it often did. He loved it once he was outside the city and could open up his engine. Weaving in and out of the traffic on the poor country roads demanded intense concentration. It's why he couldn't live in the city. He needed this separation from the day's toils. If he did choose to think about work when he got home it was work of his choosing, not whatever mundane task he might have had in hand when he left the office. He decided he had no choice but to track down Hembry's wife.

Chapter 37

Upwood had slept badly. His flight back from Gibraltar had been cancelled because of strong winds. He and the other passengers had been bussed to Málaga, a tedious process because of the need to recross the border. The delay cost him more than four hours and by the time he reached home he was shattered. Going down on Friday evening, even if he had left a tad early, and returning forty-eight hours later didn't make for the most relaxing of weekends, never mind the delay. Katie had been in a rather strange mood, too. In the end he decided it was anxiety. She knew she couldn't put off her return to England much longer. It was two months since she was attacked in Argentina, and she'd been given three months' sabbatical. Soon she would need to come home and prepare herself for a return to work.

They'd discussed it on Saturday evening, over a late supper in the port. It soon became clear that she was reluctant to return to her old firm. The reasons weren't entirely rational. She was well respected there, as evidenced by their allowing her the sabbatical. So far as he knew, she got on perfectly well with her colleagues, with the possible exception of a few in Buenos Aires. And as a partner, not only was she on a good salary, but stood to share in year-end profits. In many respects it was a post many would envy. In the end, he came to the conclusion it was simply a way of putting the past behind her, making a fresh start. And he certainly couldn't criticise her for that.

But when she told him about her meeting with Pell, he was astonished. "You didn't tell me you were going to approach him. How did that come about?"

"I didn't want to distract you if it came to nothing. I headed a team handling a project for his firm a couple of years ago. He told me that if ever I was thinking of making a career change, I should get in touch. So I did."

"I know him slightly. In fact, I saw him only about three weeks ago." He laughed. "I was desperate. Tried to pick his brains about Russian organised crime. I think he thought I was barking! Anyway, he couldn't tell me anything useful. If I hadn't previously met him at some seminar or other, I don't think I would have had the nerve to approach him. So, is there a real possibility of a job with them?"

"I think so. I hope so. He's going to call me after he's discussed it with his top management team."

"It sounds promising. And the work? What would that be?"

"Not unlike what I do now in a way, due diligence. One field of work that's opening up is with clients who are concerned they may have problems that their accountants are not picking up. So there's an element of auditing the auditors."

"Poacher turned gamekeeper?" He chuckled.

"Well I can understand it. More and more we see the bigger firms, mine included, criticised for failing to do their job properly. It's not just that, though, the role would be a bit broader."

"Enough to interest you?"

"I think so. And they have a trading partnership with another boutique operation in Madrid, so my Spanish and knowledge of the Spanish business world would be of real value to them."

"More and more interesting. I'll keep my fingers crossed."

Upwood reached his office at Parkside a little later than usual on the Monday morning. He was in poor spirits over lack of progress on the homeless murders. While with Katie, he'd phoned his friend John Laidlaw for anything of interest concerning the recent prostitute murder on the A7. All Laidlaw could tell him was that the case had all the hallmarks of the others, but that the Policía Nacional were equally stumped. Accordingly, Upwood approached his day in a depressed frame of mind.

By mid-morning his mood was no better; he had waded through endless paperwork and dozens of emails, most of which were of no conceivable interest or use. He was just about to go out to the general office to see what was going on when his phone rang.

"Mr Upwood? Frank Pell. You came to see me not long ago."

Upwood was startled. Had he had some thoughts about the issues they'd discussed after all, or was it something to do with Katie?

"Of course, Mr Pell. What can I do for you?"

"I would have called you before, but I've been in Madrid on a conference. You released a picture. Someone you want to eliminate from your enquiries. Isn't that how you put it?" He chuckled.

"Do you know her, sir?"

"Yes, I do, after a fashion. Why don't you come over and I'll tell you what I know?"

Upwood didn't hesitate. Not only would it get him out of the station but perhaps it was the lead they needed.

He reached the Sandton & Pell office a few minutes before eleven-thirty and was shown into a small meeting room close to reception. Pell joined him almost immediately and poured them both coffee from a tray on the sideboard.

"So, what can you tell me? I'm all ears."

Pell sat down and laughed. "I'm not sure it will be very useful to you, but that's for you to decide. I met her at a conference…" He laughed again as he saw the expression on Upwood's face. "I don't just swan around all the time, Chief Inspector, conferences are a good way of keeping up to date with new developments, and networking. Networking is vital in our business. And I was a speaker on this one as it happens."

Upwood smiled and nodded. "Go on."

"She was a delegate, not affiliated to any organisation. She approached me and said that she thought she could be useful to us and offered to show me proof of how she'd hacked into a number of high-profile organisations."

"Does that sort of thing happen often?"

"What, the hacking? Or the approaches?"

"Both I suppose."

"Occasionally. Amateur hackers, if they are good enough, can be recruited by companies to strengthen their own IT departments. Or by organisations like ours."

"Did you follow it up?"

"Not immediately. I didn't altogether take to her, if I'm honest. There was something very slightly confrontational in her approach. She was somewhat androgynous in her appearance, too. Not that she could do much about that I suppose."

Upwood strongly suspected that hair styles and make up could make a difference but kept quiet. "So what happened?" Upwood was beginning to find Pell's slow drip approach to the dissemination of his information tiresome.

"She emailed me. Via our heavily encrypted intranet email system." He paused for the implications to sink in.

"Embarrassing."

"Deeply worrying, more like. Naturally I had to see her. After I'd given our own IT department a bollocking and told them to find out how the hell she'd done it."

"What did she have to say for herself?"

"She was bored. Not short of money. Wanted intellectual stimulation."

"Did she bring a CV?"

Pell laughed again. "No. I don't think she wanted employment, perhaps a consultancy project. And in any event, she said she wanted to be judged on her abilities, not her background."

"Did you go along with that?"

"At first. Frankly, if she'd just been lucky or devious – she might have bribed a former employee – but not as good as she said she was, her background was irrelevant. If she was good, we'd investigate her background later. Vet her thoroughly. And we'd do that for someone undertaking a consultancy project of that kind."

"So what did you do, give her a test?"

"A battery of tests, technical and psychometric. She aced the technical tests. She scored just about the highest marks we'd ever seen."

"But not, I gather the psychometric tests."

"No. The occupational psychologist we use had concerns. Alex, that was her name, had poor interpersonal skills. That's not unusual, some of our technical people are not party animals, to say the least. No, it was more than that. He detected a heightened level of amorality, bordering on immorality, and a propensity for risk-taking that he found unusual and worrying."

"Did you take her on?"

"Certainly not. Anti-social we can deal with. The other characteristics were a real concern for us. And if I'm honest, I'm not even sure she wanted an assignment. I think she was just getting a huge kick out of the whole business."

"How did she take the news?"

"We wrote to her, so we didn't see it first-hand."

"But you did get some response." It was not a question.

Pell looked at Upwood sharply, beginning to realise, if he had not known before, that this was a man who did not miss much.

"First she threatened to expose the fact that she'd hacked our systems."

"How did you respond to that?"

"We thanked her for drawing the weakness to our attention and sent her a cheque for twenty thousand pounds."

His hands were flat on the desk. He looked down at them. The look, to Upwood's mind, was one of embarrassment. Or defeat?

"Is that normal?"

"It's not unusual. Hackers like to show off their talents, but they still have to put bread on the table, and they often don't have regular jobs, or any jobs at all, come to that."

"Did she contact you again?"

"She started stalking me."

"Good heavens. Physically or electronically?"

"Physically. She must have followed me home one day because a few times I saw her hanging around. She made it entirely obvious that she was watching me."

"What did she hope to gain, d'you suppose?"

"No idea. But I was a para. If she thought she'd intimidate me, she was wide of the mark."

"Did you report it?"

"No."

Upwood was not surprised. Pell and his colleagues would be subject to ridicule if it ever got out that their own security had been breached and their CEO was being stalked.

"How did you deal with it?"

"One of our security team spoke to her. And then we stalked her for a bit. She got the message."

"What did he say to her?"

"You'd have to ask him, Chief Inspector. I imagine he would have told her that hacking a security company wasn't a very clever thing to do."

"When was this?"

"About a year ago. A bit more perhaps. It was winter."

"Have you heard from or seen her since?"

"No, thank heavens."

"Any more security breaches?"

"No, thank heavens."

"At least none that you know about." Upwood smiled dryly.

Pell's smile was glacial. "Quite so, Chief Inspector. Oh. By the way. She never presented the cheque."

Upwood left, in thoughtful mood. He had not, of course, mentioned Katie to Pell and there was nothing in the man's behaviour that suggested she had mentioned him to Pell. Best let sleeping dogs lie for now.

Chapter 38

Upwood was at his desk later that afternoon when Morton came in. He sat down heavily.

"I've no idea what's been going on with Mo, Sir. Frankly I'm worried about it."

"Is he still in a coma?"

"They won't bring him out for another day or so, they say. Needs a bit more time to start the healing process."

"When will we be able to talk to him?"

"Not sure. Maybe Wednesday? But there's been another development. You know we pored over the CCTV stuff the pub's security company sent us. Didn't see much except for the fact that they were fighting. The camera only covers the area close to the back door but there are grainy images of the assailant's car coming into and leaving the car park. We think it's a Ford Mondeo, Mark IV - it's the current configuration of the front light cluster."

"That's not going to get us very far. It's a very popular car."

"But what is interesting is that at approximately ten-fifteen that night, a Mondeo crashed into the back of a big artic on the hard shoulder of the A1M south of Stevenage, near the Knebworth golf course. The driver was killed."

"How does that help us?"

"The local guys told us paramedics couldn't immediately see why the accident might have killed him."

Upwood was getting irritated now. "So?"

"Apparently he'd suffered blunt force trauma to the back of his head. The injury is not likely to have been caused by the accident."

"How d'you know all this? It's Hertfordshire's problem, not ours."

"A mate of mine's a fire fighter. They had to cut him out."

"You think he might be Mo's attacker?"

"It's got to be worth investigating. If it is, we might learn something from his mobile."

"They didn't find Mo's mobile, did they?"

"No."

"Might his attacker have grabbed it?"

"It's possible. The CCTV footage doesn't cover all the action."

"What about Mondeo man's phone?"

"No idea. Herts will have that and they may not want to release it to us."

"Better look into it. The sooner we can sort this out the better. Have the press picked up on it?"

"Of course. Need you ask? But they don't have Mo's name or the fact that he is one of us."

"How long will that last?"

"Lord knows. But there was a big fire in Baldock that night, so that seems to be dominating the local news for now."

"Casualties?"

"Sadly, yes. One of the fire crew. Slates flew off as the roof trusses burned. He suffered severe head injuries. He'll live, they say."

"Thank heavens. But maybe it will be enough for Mo's incident to sink without trace."

"Let's hope so."

"Presumably Margaret knows?"

"Yes. She's at the Lister now. I've given her a few days compassionate leave. His parents are expected later on."

"Mo and Margaret are that close, are they?"

"Yes, from what he told me originally. They've both been pretty discreet about it, although the affair is common knowledge."

Upwood had to acknowledge that. It hadn't taken Withnail long to pick up on it either.

"By the way. I went out to the science park this morning to meet a chap called Frank Pell, CEO of Sandton & Pell, the security company. He told me he'd met Alex Barron a couple of times." Upwood explained what he'd learned.

"Can you have someone follow up a few things? I'd like to speak to their internal security guy, the one who spoke to Alex Barron and engaged in some stalking of his own. And we need to know what address or other contact details she gave them. I also want details of the conference Pell spoke at when he says she first approached him."

"And perhaps we should examine the email she first sent Pell?"

"Good idea. Maybe our tech people can find out how she sent it."

"If Sandton & Pell don't know that, they're not up to much, Sir."

"True." Upwood laughed. "Are we making progress on any other fronts?"

"No, frankly. Joan and Dirk are still trawling through photos from records, but they've come up with no other leads than Alex Barron so far. I'm not sure they're going to. Perhaps we should curtail their project. It was always a bit of a long shot." He paused for a moment. "Do you think this Barron woman might be of interest?"

"From what Pell said, she sounds like a sociopath to say the least."

"Sociopath or psychopath?"

"Not sure I could tell on the little he told me, although her criminal case sounds compatible with sociopathy. I'm no expert, though."

"We associate psychopathy with serial killers. Do sociopaths kill?"

"Apparently yes, but not necessarily in the same way."

"Have you called in the behavioural expert we used last time?"

"No. And I should have done. I'd better make sure Emily agrees – she doesn't come cheap."

"Sir. Something else is troubling me."

Upwood looked at his colleague. Morton was not easily troubled. He was one of the most equable people he knew. No doubt having a happy and stable marriage and a young daughter he doted on might have something to do with it.

"It's Debra."

Upwood mentally groaned.

"She's been unwell, you know. You spoke to her, I think. Did she shed any light on it?"

"She's had one or two issues to deal with I think."

"Like being pregnant?"

Upwood looked at him sharply. "Has she told you that?"

"No. But I reckon she's showing. Four months I reckon. And morning sickness doesn't just happen in the morning, you know."

Upwood threw his head back and laughed. "Fancy yourself a midwife, Morton?"

"She's a similar build to Emma. And it would explain the mood swings too."

"Well if she is, she'll tell us in her own good time, Morton, and it's nothing for you to worry about."

"It's all very well saying that, Sir. But she could be going on maternity leave in ten weeks or so time. And how soon will Mo be fit to come back? We could be looking at a resourcing problem before long."

"Well let's not panic yet. We'll just have to keep an eye on it."

"If you say so. Any idea when we're going to get the results back from the lab about the tissue samples?"

"No. Soon I hope."

"And what about the PM results on Pete? Have we got those yet?"

"Yes, arrived this morning. Acute respiratory failure is about all I can get from it, a bit like the others."

"So are we ready to go ahead with the inquests now?"

"Yes, arrangements are in hand for Sally, Kevin and Pete."

"Not Smokey Joe?"

"The decision by the hospital at the time was that it wasn't necessary. I'm not sure it would tell us much more than the other three anyway. Remember, Joe ingested the same whisky as Sally. Both their prints were on the bottle."

"So how long will it take for the inquests?"

"A good month I should think. We need to have the tests results before then in any case."

The test results came back sooner than Upwood had anticipated. Samples from Sally, Kevin and Pete all tested positive for a toxin derived from a plant called *Gelsemium elegans*. On first reading, Upwood was none the wiser. The only fact that caught his eye was an observation in the covering email that the poison was one favoured by, inter alia, the Russian criminal classes.

Chapter 39

Detective Superintendent Adams was waiting for Upwood in her office. He had called her late the previous evening when he had properly assimilated the contents of the lab report on the plant toxin and had carried out his own research on-line.

"Good morning, James. This sounds intriguing."

"Morning, Emily." Her tone of voice and the tray with coffee and biscuits encouraged this familiarity. "It does indeed. But whether it will make our work any easier I very much doubt."

"Tell me what you know. Tell me about the poison, first. I've not come across it before."

"None of us has. I haven't been able to find any confirmed case of its use in the UK. I'll come back to that though, since you asked about the poison itself." He reached for a couple of biscuits and sipped his coffee.

"*Gelsemium elegans* is one of three plants of the same genus, found in Southeast Asia. It's a vine and its form and structure are similar to some non-toxic Chinese herbal remedies. It's been traditionally used to relax the nervous system to treat various types of pain including headache, and pain associated with inflammatory conditions. That's why most deaths are, in that region at least, from accidental ingestion of lethal doses. Its use has also been recorded in suicide and homicide. Again, I'm talking about Asia. Because of its use in suicide, it's often known as 'heartbreak grass'. Extracts from the plant are used in homeopathic medicines, although these are of course in minutely small doses.

"When taken in toxic doses it can kill quickly – within thirty minutes in some cases, and certainly within an hour. From details of the few reported cases, we know that it acts a bit like strychnine. It acts on the brain and causes seizures and convulsions; it can paralyse the spinal cord and its related organs, including the lungs. Death is usually attributed to asphyxia or acute respiratory failure."

"It sounds like our cases, although we're going to have to rely wholly on expert advice – this is completely outside our knowledge or experience. What else do we know?"

"You mean apart from the fact it is thought to be used by Russian and Chinese criminal gangs to dispose of some of their enemies? Or that it is thought to have been used by state assassins?"

"James. For crying out loud! We've had this conversation before. No state sponsored assassin or mafioso is likely to be running around Cambridge killing our street sleepers. What would be the point?"

"None that I can see, I grant you. But perhaps our killer has links to such people. After all, we have to ask ourselves where this poison comes from."

Emily sighed deeply. "Why do you attract all the most bizarre crimes, James? Cambridge was a relatively civilised and normal city before your arrival."

He kept quiet. There was no remotely sensible answer to her question.

"I come back to the key issue, Emily. Where is our killer getting his poison? That's one of the key lines of enquiry we are going to have to pursue."

"And how on earth do you propose to do that?"

"I've one or two ideas, but I need to develop them a bit before I initiate action."

"And will you run those ideas past me when you're ready?"

"If they lead to actions you should know about, of course."

Why was Emily not remotely reassured by his reply?

Upwood returned to his office and phoned his friend John Laidlaw in Estepona.

"James, good morning old son. How goes it?"

"Curiouser and curiouser, John."

"Blimey, mate, don't go all literary on me. Can't cope with that. What's going on?"

"We've found what poison was used in three of our homeless murders. *Gelsemium elegans*."

"And what's that when it's at home?" Laidlaw sounded suitably sceptical.

Upwood was sure he heard the distinctive sound of a beer glass being put down on the metal table in his friend's inner courtyard. Could he also hear the swifts screaming overhead? He told him what he had learned about the toxin and its use.

"Pass it on to Paco, will you? Perhaps it's a lead that will help them. Have the national police made any progress?"

"No. It's the old story, mate. If it's a prossie they're not that bothered. I'm not even sure they're that bothered if a turf war breaks out between a couple of pimps. I've heard nothing about the cases recently. I think they are still licking their wounds after the fallout from Operation Shovel."

Upwood was familiar with the problem and it both worried and annoyed him. The presumption too many people made was that prostitutes chose their lifestyle. In his experience it was rarely the case. Women were often trafficked, 'broken in' by their captors – raped and forced to become addicted to drugs – and then put in a brothel or out on the street. In truth, they were, in the main, even more likely than street sleepers to be victims, whether of criminals or society. Upwood decided not to pursue the point. Laidlaw was, after all, known to be a dinosaur even before he retired. He'd probably become more, not less, entrenched in his views since then. But prejudice of this sort was too often a barrier to solving cases that were capable of being solved. He just hoped that the forces locally were not as laissez faire as Laidlaw had suggested.

"You told me you thought they had plans to investigate the Russian woman who was familiar with plants and possible poisons."

"Ah. Yes. True. I haven't spoken to Paco about that since he first raised it. Do you want me to have a word?"

"Please. It seems this poison is known in Russia, much more than it is in western Europe. Maybe she knows something about it. Anything you can find out about her would be of interest."

"I'll see what I can do, mate. But don't hold yer breath. If they've got anything going, they'll want to keep it well under wraps."

"Do what you can. I'll take you out for a good meal next time I'm down."

"Aye, and when will that be? Three or four years' time no doubt."

"Could be quite soon. My friend Katie will have to get back to England before long. If I can snatch another weekend with her first, I will."

That evening Upwood phoned Katie. He hadn't spoken to her since his return from Spain at the weekend. He'd arrived home so late on the Sunday night he'd simply sent her a quick text to confirm his safe arrival. Her response had been 'xx', nothing more.

He told her that tests had shown three of his victims had died from a plant-based toxin almost unheard of in England, although it was used in Russia. She was intrigued. She knew that there was a Russian presence on the coast, and he had mentioned the interesting sounding, very rich, widow of a Russian oligarch who lived outside Estepona.

"Is there anything I can do to help?"

"I don't think so, my darling. I don't want you getting mixed up in the Costa del Sol's underworld."

"I wasn't planning anything very ambitious, you mutt, but I could perhaps do a bit of research online.

Sometimes you can pick up quite interesting snippets from blogs on the expat papers."

"Fine. As long as that's all you do. Any more thoughts on when you're coming back? I thought perhaps there might be time for one more quick trip before then."

"It'll have to be at the end of the month, so if you do come, better make it in the next couple of weeks."

"Is that OK with you?"

She laughed. "Of course. You know how bored I am."

Chapter 40

Upwood's experience with psychologists was limited to say the least. The kind of crimes they had in Cambridge did not normally require such specialist input. He had consulted one some months ago, when Katie was on the receiving end of harassing text messages. It wasn't that her feedback hadn't been relevant – she summed up MacKay's motivation well enough – but she had come across as a bit of a light-weight. Emily had agreed that the expense was justified again this time and since Anna Klein was the designated specialist, he'd had little option but to consult her once more. Fortunately, she'd been able to respond very quickly and had been working her way through the files since Monday evening.

"Anna, good to see you again. Come and sit down."

She was a tall, rather austere looking woman in her forties. She favoured skirted suits, as did Emily Adams, but while Emily managed to look elegant and even stylish, Anna managed to look like the rather dowdy academic Upwood suspected her to be. Her one concession to good looks, if it might be put that way, was to sport a rather dramatic shade of deep purple nail polish. Upwood found it mildly disturbing.

"James, very good to see you again, too. And a much more interesting case, or should I say series of cases, this time." She sat down and reached for the cup of coffee that Upwood passed her across the desk.

"You've studied the files on the murders, and also the information we have on Alex Barron, I think. Can you start with the murders?"

"Very interesting as I say. In a sense I'm having to go on what we haven't got, as much as what we have got."

Upwood thought about it for only a moment before acknowledging the truth. "So what are your thoughts?"

"The killer, and I'm assuming there is only one this time..."

"I certainly hope so. I think we have to assume that. A copycat is extremely unlikely and I can't seriously imagine two people acting in concert."

"I hope you're right. Let's work on that assumption to start with and I'll revisit the question later, if necessary. So, assuming it is one killer, we can infer that he – I'll say he for convenience, but don't rule out the possibility that it's a woman – is intelligent and resourceful. He is using a toxin not well-known, indeed almost unheard of in the UK. That suggests a sophisticated level of research, not only into the poison itself, but also means of administration. It may also suggest access to sources of the toxin which are not widely available in the UK. The killer may be foreign or have overseas connections.

"He is likely to be well-funded. Procurement of such obscure toxins is likely to be expensive. He has thought through his killing strategy carefully. He leaves no fingerprints on the bottles or cans of drink he uses and depositing them as he does means that he has no contact with the individuals who pick them up. So there is, as we know, no forensic evidence that's been found so far. This strategy is clever because whoever picks up the drinks may consume them at any time thereafter and in some place distant from the place where they were deposited."

Upwood resisted the temptation to comment or intervene. Much of what Anna was saying was already clear to them, and some was little more than common sense. He knew, though, that she must be allowed to offer her views unchallenged at this stage.

"He has also been very successful in avoiding visual detection, with the possible exception of the Round Church incident. He is dressing and moving around in such a way as not to draw attention to himself. It is likely that he is doing so on foot some, if not all, the time, and on bike some of the time, hardly remarkable behaviour in a city like Cambridge full of students and visitors."

"The fact that he cannot control who picks up the drinks suggests that he has no personal connection to the people he has killed. His motive therefore is unclear to say the least. It is as if he is working to some private agenda that may not make much sense to us."

She paused for a few moments and drank her coffee.

"Have you come across a case like this before?"

She frowned. "No. I haven't. I've done some research, and I've not come across any historical case like this in the UK or USA. I'm not sure about Europe. It's not so easy to get the right kind of information. But my contacts at Quantico have certainly not come across a case like this. The only comparator, and it's by no means a good one, is Steve Wright, the Suffolk Strangler. And the only similarity is the apparent lack of motive. In almost every other respect they are different."

Upwood sighed. Emily was right. Weird cases followed him the same way Morton believed bad luck dogged Katie.

"What can you tell us about the background or personality of the killer?"

"Probably from a high-achieving family, probably with tertiary education, organised but capable of adapting. I say that because the basic MO has stayed the same, but the vehicle for the poison has changed, suggesting the killer is minimising the risk of detection. Probably IT literate, unless he has a readily accessible source of a poison known to him through family or criminal association. I say that because if he doesn't have such connections, it is likely he has to use the dark web to source the poison. If he's foreign, then I'm guessing he is of Russian or Asian extraction, based on the choice of poison. Fit. Because of the way he moves around the city. Probably not overweight or with unusual physical characteristics that would make him stand out."

"Age?"

"Probably 25-40. But that's an educated guess."

"Is he a sociopath or psychopath?"

"Difficult to say. It is likely that there are some of the markers of anti-social personality disorder. He's cunning, and shows lack of remorse, evidenced by his repetition of his behaviour; emotional shallowness, callousness and lack of empathy, shown by the disregard of the deeply unpleasant manner of death.

"But there aren't some of the signs that are often associated with psychopaths. There is no ritual element to the killings. No gratuitous violence. No display of the bodies. No taking of trophies, so far as we know. There is no obvious hatred of the victims. If he despises them, it's in an abstract kind of way."

They sat and thought for a while. Anna consulted her notes.

"Shall I offer a few thoughts on Alex Barron?"

Upwood nodded.

"She's got a very controlling personality based on what the file says Pell told you, because she seems to have told him very little about herself. Either that or he's holding back for some reason. Evidently highly intelligent if she did as well as she did in the tests – and managed to hack into the company's systems. Poor social skills, from what Pell says, and a risk-taker. Evidently well off if she didn't present Pell's cheque."

"Or she didn't want us to find out where she banked."

Anna acknowledged the possibility. "That would fit in with her controlling behaviour certainly. Margaret's report on her threatening behaviour case was interesting. Firstly, unusual but not unheard of for a woman to go into a pub with that sort of reputation. That she decided to drink there suggests she might be very self-assured or possibly not socially aware enough to pick up the vibes sooner. And presumably something about her appearance or behaviour annoyed her aggressors. Her giving a prepared statement at interview, but answering no questions, and refusing to speak at the hearing, are again indicative of a controlling nature."

Upwood mulled this over. "I'm inclined to think that the evidence was so heavily stacked against her, fairly or otherwise, her solicitor had probably advised her to keep quiet."

"You may be right. She appears to have gone to some trouble to hide her tracks since then. I think I'm right and you don't know where she is now?"

"Correct. The address she gave Pell is that she gave when she was arrested, and we know she hasn't lived there for several years. We know where she moved to, or at least we know to what address she had her mail redirected, but we've lost her after that."

"And the super recogniser – Joan was it – is sure it is her near Round Church?"

"Yes. And I trust her. She and Dirk have both proved to have exceptional talent."

"We don't know nearly enough about her. Would Pell talk to me d'you think? I've a feeling there's a great deal more he could tell us."

Chapter 41

Morton arrived at the Lister Hospital late on Wednesday morning and was directed to the main tower block. He knew visiting hours did not start until 11.00 am, so there had been no point in arriving earlier. He made his way to the High Dependency Unit where Mo was held. And held proved to be the operative word. Morton was stunned and annoyed to find that a uniformed officer was sitting outside Mo's room, and it wasn't one he recognised.

The officer stood. "Who are you?"

Morton introduced himself and showed his warrant card.

"I can't let you in, mate. Family only."

"But he's one of my team."

"Don't care, mate. Not my problem. Patient's not at all well, so it's family only. And then he's ours. The crime was committed on our patch, not yours."

"But he's a witness at best," Morton replied, for once showing signs of anger.

"We don't know that, mate. He may have started it for all we know." The officer's smile was smug, not far short of a sneer. "You'll have to wait until we've finished with him. And that's assuming we don't bang him up for GBH or summat else."

Morton was stumped. "Is Margaret Starr in there now?"

"That's for me to know, not you. I should clear off if I were you."

Now Morton was furious. He left the unit and went out onto the landing where he leant against the rail in front of the windows. Well, the HDU was on the fourth floor. He thought about phoning Upwood but decided against it. Even if his boss wanted to put pressure on his colleagues in Herts Constabulary it was perhaps too soon to do it. There was every chance that Mo was still not yet in a fit state to be questioned, other than at the most superficial level. He considered his options. He tried calling Margaret's mobile, but it went to voicemail, as it would if she were with Mo. Use of mobile phones was actively discouraged in units which were heavily dependent on high tech equipment. Or maybe she was driving. He sent her a brief text asking her to call him when she could. Should he wait and see if she left soon or just come out to go to the café? He decided against it. She might be in there hours. He drove back to Parkside in a dark mood. He only hoped Debra was making more progress at Sandton & Pell. They'd decided she should tackle the CEO first and then arrange for Anna to go in, provided, of course, that Pell was willing to talk to her.

Debra had not spent much time with Pell since there wasn't much more he could tell her, bar details of the conference where he'd first met Barron, and rather hazy details of her stalking him. He did, though, give her a photo he'd taken of her opposite his home at the time. The security man whom Pell had asked to speak to Barron and tail her had since left the company, but she had managed to obtain an email address for him. Thin pickings.

When she'd told Pell that they would like him to spend some time with their psychologist he'd seemed very reluctant. She'd had to remind him that not only was it murder they were investigating, but the murder of four people. He resigned himself to writing off a large part of the day.

Morton had called for a briefing meeting late that afternoon. There was a sense that they were losing momentum. He wanted to use the meeting to galvanise everyone back into action.

Debra spoke first. She confirmed that Pell had given her details of the relevant conference, held in Manchester in January 2010. She had managed to speak to the conference organisers who had, albeit unwillingly, emailed her a delegate list. Alex Barron's name was on the list. Further enquiries had elicited the information that her fee had been paid by a company, although she was shown on the delegate list as being freelance. The same company had owned the property in Riverside where it was thought she had been living, the address to which she had moved, they believed, after her arrest and subsequent conviction.

Her enquiries into the security man had drawn a blank. It had taken her ages to track him down. He was currently working in Syria and refused to answer any questions about his employment with Sandton & Pell, citing the non-disclosure agreement which bound him. Debra's troubled impression was that the agreement was only signed on leaving the company. In her experience, that usually suggested some sort of cover up. Morton did not seem to think this was particularly significant.

"Pell didn't give you much by way of personal details for her. Did you manage to learn something from HR?"

Debra snorted. "A bit up their own arses."

A look from Morton indicated he was not impressed by her observation. "I asked you what you learnt, Debra."

"Sorry. They didn't have much. Barron had approached Pell directly and they didn't like that. She hadn't produced a CV. All they had for her was the Riverside address. And a mobile number that is no longer active. If it ever was."

"Another judgemental comment, Debra. Can you justify it?"

She sighed. "No, not really. HR hadn't had any need to phone her, so we don't know whether the number was false, the phone died, or she destroyed it. Or lost it."

"What else did you learn?"

"Not a lot. She did not provide an NI number. Apparently, she said if she were to work for Sandton & Pell it would be through a service company."

"Is that usual?"

"It's not unheard of, they said. She was not prepared to give them the details unless the company offered her work."

"Anything else?"

"They had a copy of a letter on file, sent to Barron by the accounts department in May 2010, reminding her to present her cheque before it was too late. It came back 'return to sender' apparently."

None of Morton's other officers, nor Joan or Dirk, had anything remotely useful to report.

Stephanie Mungo, who had first been tasked with finding out everything there was to know about Alex Barron, had been digging deeper. The results were disheartening. They still had no NI number, tax reference number, NHS number or any record of her on Council Tax or other municipal records. She had failed to find any record of her graduating from a UK university. Was she not university educated? Anna had thought so. Might she have studied overseas?

"It gets worse, Sir. Her passport expired in September 2008 and has not been renewed. None of the mobile phone operators has a record of an account with a woman of her name. If she has a burner, there's not much we can do. None of the major banks has any record of an account with her. It's as if she doesn't exist." She sat down, with an air of failure.

"What does that tell you, Stephanie?"

"She must have changed her identity."

Groans spread round the room.

"But she hasn't done it by deed poll. I checked."

Morton frowned. "So, she really is flying under the radar."

Anna, who had been observing, now offered her view. "This is evidence of a very controlling personality, and perhaps of criminal tendency."

Morton, like his boss, and many others in the police service, for that matter, was not wildly impressed with psychologists and thought her observation added little value.

"Stephanie, am I right in thinking that the only connection we seem to have right now for her is the company that owned the property in Riverside?"

"Yes, I'm afraid so."

"What do we know about it?"

"Not a lot, but I was planning to look into it."

"Do, please. As quickly as you can. Anna, have you learned anything today that might help us?"

"I spoke to Mr Pell first. He described her appearance. It's in my report. I won't dwell on that as she may well have changed the way she looks. He confirmed that her interpersonal skills were not good. It took some teasing out of him, but his answers were, in the end, quite instructive. She rarely made eye contact with him. Her facial expression was hard to read. She showed little enthusiasm, but he formed the impression that she was pleased with herself for having hacked into their systems. He said that she sometimes was very slow to answer his questions, and when she did, she did so incompletely. After a while he worked out that she couldn't handle multi-part questions. Only once he disciplined himself to ask only simple, straightforward questions did he get much sense from her. He says some of the answers she gave, particularly in relation to her background, were evasive. He described the questions she put to him as 'very direct'. She also spent the whole meeting at their offices fiddling with her key ring."

"What did he mean, her questions were very direct?"

"He couldn't explain. He couldn't remember any specific questions. But he clearly had a strong sense that she asked the kind of questions that other interviewees wouldn't ask. The kind of questions he would not expect to be put to him."

"Is that it?"

"From Mr Pell, yes."

"And did you draw any conclusions from this?"

"Clearly, she shows consistently that she is secretive, either by nature or by design. It occurred to me, though, that she may not be suffering from an anti-social personality disorder, she might be on the autism spectrum. Maybe it's both, though. Her response to her arrest and prosecution would also be consistent with such a finding."

Morton took a deep breath. He thought he could get his mind around the idea of sociopathy or psychopathy. "What would the implications be if she were on the autism spectrum?"

"I'm not sure it would make much difference to whether or when you find her. It might make interviewing her difficult. I won't take your time with that now. I'll try to help when you're ready to talk to her. I did find out a little more though, from the tests she did."

"Good. What can you tell us?"

"Fortunately, the tests were conducted on computer and the results were stored. Interestingly, Pell had said that HR would have the summary results and the report from their occupational psychologist, but not the actual test papers. But HR said they do keep the papers. Well, they're electronic of course, but you know what I mean: the questions and answers. They keep them for a number of years apparently, in case people apply again. It can happen when someone first applies soon after leaving university maybe, but then again later when they have some relevant experience to bring. Sometimes comparing results can be instructive."

"But they wouldn't administer the same tests over and over, surely? People would get used to them."

"No, they would use a battery of psychometric tests. The technical ones certainly change, as technology develops. But the psychometric tests all look for the same personality traits. I didn't learn much from the technical tests. It's not my field. But I am assured she did uncommonly well. But the psychometric tests were interesting. Pell had said that the results were indicative of someone with the propensity to take risks, with an amoral or immoral personality. He suggested that she might have tried to rig the results."

"Could she do that? I thought it was almost impossible to do. Don't they ask the same question lots of different ways to stop you cheating?"

"That's the idea. But very clever people can cheat. I went back to Pell after I'd examined them, and the report from the occupational psychologist who'd marked the tests. The psychologist was rather ambiguous in his report. But Pell said that while the psychologist had been deliberately oblique in his written report, he'd told him at their meeting he thought she was deeply disturbed. Pell says he warned him against hiring her."

Chapter 42

Upwood and Morton were staring at their glasses. Each had a beer, although neither felt much like drinking. Ordinarily they would have stayed in the office to talk but both felt the need to escape. Their chosen venue was one they knew was not frequented by their colleagues, the Red Bull on Barton Road. It was a cool evening, and they were the only customers sitting in the garden.

"So what's the problem. Why can't we get to see him?"

"There was a real jobsworth sitting outside his room. Wouldn't allow me in. Said that as the incident took place on their patch, he wasn't letting me in."

"Even though he knew Mo's one of ours?"

"Yep. And I couldn't persuade him otherwise. Suggested that Mo might face charges."

"Oh Christ. Surely not?"

"I've no idea. We haven't got much to go on. The CCTV footage we've seen, as you know, doesn't show us who started the fight. By the time they're in range of the camera we know that the other man is wielding a knife, but we don't know what happened first. What is worrying is that a mate of mine at Herts HQ told me unofficially that the Mondeo man who died on the A1M that night is a Dutch man who used to be married to Margaret."

"God Almighty, it gets worse. Have you spoken to her?"

"Briefly. On the phone. She didn't want to speak about it at all. She was very emotional. Mo is barely conscious most of the time. The medics won't let anyone speak to him for more than a few minutes. And of course, his parents are there too. So Margaret doesn't know very much. At least, that's what she says. I didn't ask her if she knew about her ex-husband. And she didn't volunteer it. Someone in Herts may have told her of course. I want to go and see her. She sounds very frightened, and I don't think it's just the fact that he's so ill."

"Did she know he was going to Baldock?"

"No. She claims to know nothing about it. But she's not telling the whole truth, I think."

"So Mo goes alone, without telling anyone. Whether he instigates the meeting or not we don't know."

"We don't for sure. But I reckon the fact that they didn't find Mo's mobile at the scene suggests the other guy took it before he fled."

"Could be. There's no way Mo would have gone out without his phone. So, let's assume Margaret's ex-husband instigated the meeting. Why would he do that? What do we know about him?"

"You know Margaret was based at Hertford, of course, before she transferred to us. Luuk Jansen also worked for Herts Constabulary and was based at HQ in Welwyn Garden City. He left some months before Margaret transferred. Apparently, she'd been on sick leave for quite some time. I haven't managed to find out much more so far, but I don't think Jansen stayed with the police. And if he's still in the UK he's keeping a low profile. It sounds like it would be a common name, but it's not. I can't find anyone on social media that looks like him. Sorry, I don't mean physically looks like him. I mean the profiles aren't right. You know what I mean." Morton was flattering Upwood somewhat, given that the DCI was no fan of social media, but his boss got the general idea.

"Did your chum have any more information that might shed light on the background to all this?"

"I'm sure he did. But he certainly wasn't sharing it. And I got the distinct impression that going through official channels is not going to work. Is there someone you know you can lean on?"

"Not for something like this."

"Madam Adams?"

"Maybe. I'll ask her."

"Can we get Mo's mobile phone records?"

"We can try. But no doubt the provider will be as difficult as possible."

"But at least we might be able to establish whether Jansen phoned or texted Mo, or vice versa."

"Hardly, since we don't know Jansen's number."

"But if there were calls or messages via a Dutch provider we'd know."

"Sure. But it's not likely, is it? He'd have an English burner?"

"Yeah, I know. But I think it's worth a try. It's likely Jansen would only have contacted him once or twice so calls from an unknown number should be easy to identify."

"Go for it by all means. But can't we encourage Margaret to ask a couple of pertinent questions for us?"

"What are we trying to achieve here? It's not our case. Plod has made that abundantly clear."

"I'd just like some comfort that Mo did not initiate a meeting at which the other party was given an injury from which he subsequently died."

"But he died in the road accident."

"Yes, but if your original source is right, he may have sustained a head injury during the fight. Maybe he had concussion and wasn't fit to drive. Maybe that's why he drove into the back of the truck."

"Shit. I know you're right. I can't say I hadn't thought of that. But hearing you say it makes me feel very uncomfortable."

"Join the clan, Morton. Join the clan."

After a light meal at home, Upwood plucked up courage to phone his boss. This was another call he wasn't looking forward to.

"James. Why the call at home?"

"It's tricky. Walls have ears and all that."

She sat up straighter in her armchair. She'd just managed to lose herself in a novel she'd finally got round to reading. She took a small sip of her brandy and soda. She had the distinct impression that James was not calling with good news.

"It's Mo, Emily."

"He's not had a relapse, has he?"

"No. Nothing like that. At least as far as I know."

He proceeded to relay to her the little Morton had been able to tell him, and the substance of the conversation they'd had.

"So we think Jansen and Mo were fighting about something in Margaret's past?"

"Based on what we know it's difficult to put any other construction on it. Do you know anything about her history?"

"No. There's no reason why I should. She came on to your team from uniform, didn't she?"

"Yes. She was a PC."

"There you are. No reason why I'd know."

"Could you find out? All we know is that she seems to have been on sick leave for some time before she moved out of Hertford. Is there any way you can find out more about Jansen from Herts?"

"If it's really important I can probably find out more about Margaret. Finding out more about Jansen will be more difficult. They won't want to involve us in their case."

"But you'll try? Mo's a good officer. I don't want to lose him. And I don't want to lose Margaret either, come to that. Especially given Debra's pregnancy."

The moment he'd mentioned Debra, he regretted it. It was red rag to a bull with Emily. He could hear a heavy sigh at the other end of the line.

"I'll see what I can do. But I'm not very hopeful."

Upwood wasn't at all in a hopeful mood either. Their only suspect in the homeless murders seemed to have vanished into thin air. One of his best officers was pregnant, with the real possibility that she might not return from maternity leave, if her partner was as well-heeled as she'd said. Two others were out of commission, one of them facing a long convalescence, and possibly criminal charges. The immediate future looked bleak to say the least.

Chapter 43

Upwood spent most of the following day catching up on paperwork and administration. They were the bane of his life. Sometimes he wished he'd never accepted the promotion. Too little of his time these days was spent actively involved in investigations and he missed it. Now, too often, he had to enjoy the active side of case work vicariously, which didn't give him the same kind of satisfaction. He decided to attend Morton's evening briefing.

Stephanie was explaining what she'd learned about the company that owned, or had owned, the house on Riverside.

"The company is called Bletchly Holdings Ltd, formed in 2002, registered office a firm of solicitors, Grey, Hamilton and Fitch. One of the two directors listed is Edward Hamilton, partner in the law firm. Their website describes him as specialising in corporate law. The other director is Paul Ford, an accountant. His firm, Ford & Harrison, is listed as accountant to Bletchly. Both are shareholders but the majority of the shares appear to be owned by another company, one headquartered in Liechtenstein. Their bankers are Handelsbanken in London, and Landhardt & Partners, Zurich. The company's purpose is described as general trading and the provision of services. They are registered for VAT but have filed no annual accounts in the last three years. Accounts for earlier years do show property as being one of the asset classes."

Morton frowned. His team had been fidgeting while Stephanie relayed her findings. It was difficult to see how the information she had unearthed so diligently was going to help them at all.

"So, the company is British but owned by one incorporated in Liechtenstein. Their British bank is owned by a Swedish outfit. And their other bank is Swiss. And either they've stopped trading, or are very late filing their accounts. Did you draw any conclusions from all of this Stephanie?"

A predictable question she thought. "Not much, except the impression that the British company is probably a front for something, and the fact that they seem determined to make it moderately difficult to find out anything about it."

Upwood, sitting at the back, thought it a fair answer.

"Did you find anything at all connecting Alex Barron to the company?"

"No. But for what it's worth, Handelsbanken have a branch in Cambridge. She has to have access to money from somewhere. But if she has an account there, I bet it's not in the name we know her by."

"She may not have a personal account. What if she is a signatory on the company account? And I doubt a niche operation like Handelsbanken has its own ATMs. First Direct doesn't."

"No, but they deal exclusively by phone and online. Anyway, they piggyback on HSBC."

"Even so. Check. You'll probably find that Handelsbanken cards are issued by one of the major players, like Visa, and can be used in any cash dispenser."

Everyone seemed to be succumbing to gloom.

Morton was right. They soon discovered that Handelsbanken cards were issued by Mastercard. Using them at ATMs in the city would be no problem at all. So maybe the bank's presence in Cambridge was a red herring.

Upwood arrived at his home in Dry Drayton earlier than usual, leaving Parkside as soon as the briefing had drawn to a close. He picked up his mail as he let himself in, annoyed to see that of the half dozen or so items, all but one were catalogues or direct marketing material. Typical. He threw them onto the counter and reached into one of the cupboards for a glass and the whisky. He was all too aware that this had become a nightly ritual, and much as he rationalised it, he knew it wasn't too clever. Nonetheless, he poured himself a decent measure, added some mineral water from the fridge and took it through to his living room. He slumped into his chair and took a couple of mouthfuls of Scotch, staring idly at the picture of Wicken Fen. It was his favourite. The artist had captured the spirit of that mere perfectly; water like glass reflecting a sky so pale it was almost translucent. No birds or animals could be seen in the picture, but Upwood knew that the reeds would be alive with all kinds of creatures. Just looking at the picture helped him relax.

The shrill sound of the landline broke his reverie, and he reached out for the handset on the table next to his chair. He recognised the number as Spanish, but knew it was not Katie. She always called his mobile. John Laidlaw? Possibly. It was neither. It was Francisco Garrido, Paco, of Spain's Policía Nacional.

"James, 'ow are you?"

"I'm fine, Paco. Qué tal?"

"Good, my friend. Todo bien. Thank you for the informacíon you give me from John. I 'ave some for you. Can you come?"

"To Estepona? Sure, I was thinking I would come tomorrow evening. Is that OK?"

Paco was clearly pleased and explained where they should meet on the Saturday morning.

They rang off and Upwood immediately called Katie.

"Hi. I hope you don't have plans for the weekend. Can I come down?"

"Of course, that's great. How long can you stay?"

"It'll be a flying visit like last time. John's police chum has just called me. Apparently he has information for me."

"And he can't send it by email?"

"Evidently not. And clearly doesn't want to talk about it over the phone."

"Sounds intriguing."

"I hope it's worthwhile. That last two-nighter was exhausting."

She broke into peals of laughter. "Did I wear you out?"

"No. Don't be daft. It's just a lot of travelling only to have such a short time there."

"You're going soft in your old age, James. Some people commute every week."

"Rather them than me, that's all I can say. And less of the old age if you please. What have you been up to?"

"I've done a bit of online research, like we discussed. Not very fruitful. I'll tell you about it when you get here. Will you be on the same flight?"

"I will if I can get a seat."

"And if you can't?"

"Plan B."

"Which is?"

"No idea. I'll think of something if push comes to shove. Even if it means flying to Málaga. Would you mind collecting me from there if necessary?"

"No problem. It's only about an hour, after all. And there's not much traffic on the peaje. The toll's too expensive in the summer for most people. Worth every cent if you ask me. I find the coast road really hard work. Maybe when they finally open the tunnel through San Pedro it will make a difference."

"It's due next year, I think. About time too."

After he'd ended the call, he went straight online. He was in luck. It looked as though he'd got one of the last remaining seats on the BA flight out of Heathrow into Gibraltar. Another trip he dare not charge to expenses.

Chapter 44

Upwood left the office early on Friday afternoon, careful to avoid Emily. Heathrow was heaving as usual and while many in his departure lounge were dressed for vacation, he could see that Katie was right. There was more than a handful of suits, even if ties had been loosened, or removed. Or never worn in the first place. And yes. There was one with a perma-tan wearing an immaculate shirt with double cuffs and cufflinks. Upwood idly thought he looked a bit like Kilroy-Silk. Didn't he own a property down there somewhere? Gaucín? Jimena? Upwood knew little of the man and cared less. The passenger wore no tie, despite the cufflinks. And by the look of him, it was deliberate. It was an affectation Upwood couldn't stand, and he realised, not for the first time, that he was becoming more and more intolerant.

His flight landed on time. Katie was, as usual, waiting in the Arrivals area, having left the car on the other side of the border. She had decided that they'd eat in that evening and had prepared plates of bellota ham and chorizo as well as some particularly good, wafer-thin, home-cooked ham from the English Butcher. They ate slowly and lightly–it was too late for a heavy meal.

"So, tell me, what brings you down? What did Paco have to say?"

"I told you, not a lot. But the fact that he called me himself suggests he's got something important to tell me, and that he wants it off the record. Have you managed to find out anything useful?"

"I'm not sure. I found old articles in one of the local papers reporting development plans submitted by the man I think was probably the husband of the woman living outside Estepona. He was Ivan Baranov. She is Oksana Baranova. He was evidently a big player. There were reports of residential development, mainly upmarket villas, in San

Pedro, Estepona and Sotogrande. And then a few years ago he drops off the radar."

"When he died?"

"Maybe. Just no other reference to him that I can find. I did read something which suggested a son might be running the business now. Then it goes really quiet."

"When was that?"

"Early 2006, I think. That's about it, I'm afraid. Apart from a few highly generalised articles about Russian oligarchs moving onto the coast and suggestions that a number were involved in organised crime. I got distracted for quite a long time by reports about various members of the Kinahan family – Irish – who have links to this area. The father, Christy – wait for it: 'The Dapper Don' – Kinahan was convicted of drug offences in the 1980s. It is said he learned both Spanish and Russian in prison. I haven't found any links to the Baranov family. But that's not to say there aren't any. I gave up eventually."

"I'm not surprised. It was good of you to take the time. Thank you. Let's see what Paco says tomorrow."

Upwood met Paco on the site of the Sabinillas Sunday market. Early on Saturday there were only a few vehicles there, probably those who moved from market to market during the week and wanted to be in good time for the following day. The site was huge and the corner in which they had agreed to meet was some distance from the road. It was little more than a lane, which Upwood knew led up to the Roman Oasis, a popular restaurant open for only a few short months each summer. There was enough activity on site to avoid their being conspicuous. Not so much that anyone would be able to recognise them.

Paco joined Upwood in Katie's hire car. "Hola, amigo. Qué tal?"

"Bien, Paco, gracias. Y usted?"

"Sí. Cómo siempre. Todo bien."

Upwood decided Paco could count himself lucky if all was always well in his world. It certainly didn't seem to be in his own.

"Thank you for the informacíon about el tóxico. Is not one we know."

"Can you test for it in samples from the women who were killed?"

"I do not know. Maybe we do not 'ave the right samples. They try, for sure." He looked frustrated and unhappy and Upwood had the impression that Paco was not hopeful of a good outcome.

"I 'ave news for you. Is possible is not ver' important. We 'ave someone who works in the 'ouse of the Russian woman. Una limpiadora."

"Ah. Cleaner. She is a police officer?"

"She is civil."

"Civilian. But works for the Policía Nacional?"

"Sí. Es verdad. 'Er name is María."

Upwood doubted Paco would have given him her real name but let it pass. It probably was not important to him.

"And the Russian lady. Is this Señora Baranova?"

"Sí. Is true. 'Ow you know this?"

Upwood just smiled and shook his head. He could hardly tell him Katie had discovered her name.

"She 'as a daughter. Is called Saskia. She live in England. In Cambridge."

Upwood stared at him. "What else do you know?"

"Ver' little. Señora Baranova, she not like the preguntas."

"Questions?" Upwood guessed.

"Sí. She tell María she is there to work, not to talk. But María see photograph in the bedroom of Sra Baranova. She think it is Saskia. She take a photo on her móvil." Paco pulled out his own mobile and showed Upwood.

It wasn't the best quality in the world, but it wasn't bad. It looked like Alex. Clearly taken in Cambridge, alongside a young man of about the same age. The brother perhaps? Upwood was stunned. "Do you know his name?"

"María not sure. Perhaps is Felix or similar?"

Paco had nothing more of substance to tell him, except that they could find no record of a Spanish passport for Saskia. Upwood knew that Alex Barron had held a British passport when she was convicted. He gave Paco only the briefest details about her, stressing that there was no certainty it was the same woman, saying that she was a person of interest in their cases. In truth, for Upwood she had already been upgraded to suspect. Finding her seemed to be the problem.

Chapter 45

After Upwood's meeting in the morning they'd spent a quiet day, with a light supper at Mesón de la Torre. They'd chosen to eat fairly early, as he had promised to meet John for lunch on Sunday before his return to England. As they walked along the paseo towards the old village the sea sparkled like a tray of diamond chips being gently rolled around. The breeze was too light for any sailors and the small fishing fleet was safely tucked up in port. Upwood had become used to the sound of their engines as they made their way across the bay just before dawn. He found it a soothing sound and he enjoyed knowing that fishermen still plied their trade in such small craft. Now there was a good buzz, with couples and families strolling through the village, and tables in the restaurant slowly filling up. It was an environment in which both felt comfortable. Katie felt safe.

"I've booked my return flight."

Her observation caught him unaware.

"Good. Well done. When?"

"A couple of weeks. The 16th."

"Saturday."

"Yes. Can you meet me at Stansted?"

"No reason why not, as things stand. Text me the flight details, then I'll have them to hand. You've told your boss you're going back to work?"

"Not yet."

"But you'll have to, surely. You've been away a long time. They'll have arrangements to make."

She looked at him. Those wide brown eyes tinged with violet never failed to melt his heart.

"Sandton & Pell have made me an offer."

"Congratulations. That's brilliant! A good one?" He raised his aperitif glass to hers.

"Good enough. The pay's about the same but they're not big on bonuses or profit share. But I've a decent amount of capital and no mortgage. So their salary is more than adequate. And I'm really excited about working in a different environment. Not so many stuffed shirts. And fewer Freemasons, I suspect."

He laughed. "When do you start?"

"I don't know. My senior partner might be a bit iffy as I've just had three months off. I'll have to discuss it with him when I get back."

"Well, I wish you all the luck in the world with that. I'm pleased for you. Sandton & Pell have a good reputation. And I quite like the idea of your working for a security company."

"So do I, funnily enough!"

At an unfashionably early noon on Sunday, Upwood and Laidlaw settled down at the chiringuito. Close to Estepona, it was one Upwood did not know. He was disappointed to find that, even though it claimed to have been there more than thirty years, it had been rebuilt further up the beach to conform with recent regulations. As a result, it looked indistinguishable from most of the others. Concrete and glass. No doubt the old structure had been wood and much more characterful. The fact that the waiting staff seemed to know many of the customers well, however, was definitely a redeeming feature. They chose a mixed salad to start, followed by a selection of fish dishes: boquerones, puntallitas, gambas and something else Laidlaw had chosen that Upwood did not recognise. No matter, the food was excellent, and the tinto verano was refreshing.

"So have you spoken to Paco?"

"Yes. I saw him yesterday."

Laidlaw looked disappointed to have been left out of the loop. Clearly Paco was meeting Upwood unofficially, so why couldn't he have joined in?

"What did he have to say?"

"Not a lot, in truth. I got the distinct impression that they were not familiar with the poison and hadn't learned a great deal about it."

"So no links to their cases?"

"Not that he told me about. I don't think they know."

"And did he have any information for you?"

Upwood decided that discretion was the better part of valour. He knew his friend was highly sociable and enjoyed his drink. He could not afford to compromise either his investigation or that of the Policía Nacional.

"They think the Russian widow has links with England."

Laidlaw grunted. "Not rocket science, is it? They lived in England before they moved here."

"Of course. May be nothing in it."

"So why was he so keen that you come down?"

"Did I give that impression? I didn't mean to. I was coming down anyway and happened to mention it to him."

Laidlaw looked neither convinced nor impressed. He knew Paco well enough to know that he would not have telephoned Upwood just to pass the time of day. He also knew Upwood well enough to suspect that if he didn't want to tell him more, he wouldn't.

Chapter 46

Upwood collared Morton as soon as he arrived at Parkside on Monday morning. The flight from Gibraltar had been on time and he'd arrived home at a reasonable hour, slept well and now felt reasonably fresh. Morton, in contrast, looked rather the worse for wear.

"Minda's not still teething surely? How old is she now, more than a year?"

"She's about thirteen months. And yes, she's still teething. Just a bad night that's all. Usually she's no trouble now."

As Upwood's daughter had died in infancy, he had no idea about childhood development. Katie had said he'd have made a good father, but he doubted it. He'd never know now.

"I've learnt something useful over the weekend. Do you remember my mentioning ages ago that there had been a series of unexplained deaths on the Costa del Sol? Prostitutes who died at the roadside. Spanish national police were unable to determine cause of death."

"Vaguely. I didn't pay much attention because it didn't seem very relevant. Is it?"

"I don't know yet. But the police there have been keeping an eye on a very wealthy woman, widow of an oligarch rumoured to have been involved with organised crime. They believe she has access to exotic drugs. *Gelsemium elegans* is believed to be a drug of choice for Russian assassins."

Morton burst out laughing. "But no-one assassinates prostitutes for heaven's sake. Or street-sleepers come to that."

"There is a suggestion that the prostitutes are run by a criminal gang and that they are the victims of gang-warfare."

Morton considered this proposition. "OK. Fair enough. That I can understand. But our victims?"

"Clearly not the same. We've no idea why they are being killed as you know."

"So why on earth is this relevant?"

"The Spanish police told me the Russian widow went to Spain with her husband and daughter from England, having left Russia in the late 1970s."

"That's a bit early, isn't it? I thought the main exodus was ten years later at least?"

"Maybe. I'm not an expert. I'm just telling you what I know. Anyway, I gather that after her husband died, her son took over his father's operations. We think his name maybe Felix. He has been mentioned in the same newspaper articles as the Kinahan family, although I don't know if they are actually linked in anyway."

"I've heard of them. Irish. Keiron Fallon was involved with them, wasn't he? I remember my dad telling me about it. He liked the odd flutter."

"Right. Yes, the Kinahans were thought to be big in race-fixing amongst other things. The case against Fallon was dismissed if I remember rightly. The Kinahans are on the Costa del Sol now and their operations are much more extensive. They are thought to be the largest OCG in Europe. There was a huge operation to bust them last year. A fiasco. Christy Kinahan senior and his two sons, along with dozens of others, were arrested. They've since been released. Operation Shovel. Look it up in your spare time. Interesting, but of no concern to us so far as I can see.

"Anyway, the Russian widow. Her name is Oksana Baranova. I have just learnt that her daughter lives in Cambridge. And is called Saskia."

"OK. Cambridge is interesting. It might just be a coincidence of course. Saskia? Why is that significant?"

"It's a Slavic form of Sasha, another diminutive of Alexandra."

"Ah. That is more interesting. Do we know if Alex Barron has any Russian connections?"

"How about Oksana Baranova?"

"Do we know that?"

"No. But we sure as hell need to find out."

"Have you discussed this with Madam Adams?"

"What, the latest information? No."

"Don't you think you should? She'll go ballistic if you open up the investigation without warning her. You might be taking the lid off Pandora's box."

Upwood knew he was right. He should do it before initiating such a radical new line of enquiry.

His boss kept him waiting outside her office for more than ten minutes. He toyed with the idea of telling her secretary that the meeting wasn't important. He could see her another time. After all, there were steps they could take to investigate Alex/Saskia without setting any hares running. Well, not many. Before he'd finally made up his mind, her door opened.

Emily was predictably furious when he explained the reason for his visit. Furious that Upwood had gone down to Spain again without telling her. Even the fact that he'd told no one and had not charged it to expenses did not pacify her. She was particularly angry that he was again pursuing what she thought were the most tenuous links to organised crime.

"Can you imagine what will happen when the press find out you're exploring links to the Russian mafia? We'll be a complete laughing stock. This is the third time you've raised this question. You're becoming obsessed. It's got to stop." She glared at him.

"It's a valid line of enquiry, Ma'am. A young woman born in England whose name is remarkably similar to the daughter of a Russian widow known to have links to organised crime. A widow who has knowledge of obscure substances through her practice of homeopathy. Her daughter is said to live in Cambridge. Alex Barron is already a person of interest. How can I ignore it? In any event, we don't need to make it known even to the team that we are looking at the organised crime aspect. What we do need to do is research much deeper into Alex Barron's history. Not least because she has completely dropped off the UK radar since at least three years ago, apart from her contact with Sandton & Pell. And then she gave an out-of-date address and a phone number which is no longer valid. Her UK passport expired in 2008 and was not renewed. She may have adopted the name Saskia Baranova for all we know."

"She's hardly likely to do that in England, is she? It would draw attention to herself. If she is criminally inclined, she'd want to keep a low profile."

Upwood was mildly encouraged by these questions. It indicated that finally Emily was beginning to give some credence to his theory about Alex. "True. But if she does have links to organised crime, getting hold of a new identity is hardly going to be a problem for her. And we must see if there is any record of Saskia Baranova here."

Emily fiddled with her fountain pen, her lips pursed, and brow furrowed.

"Fine. Get the team digging into these two women," she waved a hand at him when it was evident he was about to interrupt her, "but do not, I repeat do not, share your concerns about the mafia with the team."

He nodded.

"Does Morton know?"

"Of course. I need to be able to discuss ideas with someone else."

She raised an eyebrow. Her eyes flashed.

"Apart from you, Ma'am."

"Oh, sod off, James. Do what you have to do. But for God's sake be careful."

He didn't like to ask her whether she was thinking about reprisals from criminal gangs.

Chapter 47

Rix still hadn't located Pat Hembry. He rose early the following morning and decided he would have to carry out more research online. Before deciding to concentrate his efforts on John Hembry, Rix had searched not just Google in general, but local papers in Gloucestershire. There had been several references to her in the context of cases she'd been involved in, but none in recent years. He widened his search to journals published in and around Bristol and Bath. He was rapidly coming to the conclusion that she'd reverted to her maiden name, married again, or left the police service. It took little time to discover that her maiden name was Childs, and her middle name, Anne. Armed with this information he searched again. This time he was in luck. He found three references to Pat Childs, a member of Avon and Somerset Constabulary, based in Wells. Was she the woman he sought? There was only one way to find out.

The journey took him more than four hours by car. The bike would have been quicker, but it was no good for the kind of surveillance he had to undertake. Traffic was heavy. It was still peak holiday period and from the time he left the M5 to the time he arrived in Wells he had seen, and generally passed, more caravans than he ever wanted to see in a lifetime. Once he'd checked into his B&B he headed west along the Glastonbury Road. The police station was an imposing brick building, the architecture of which reminded him of RAF bases around Cambridgeshire. Built in 1950, it seemed much too large to house what Rix knew to be a relatively small establishment of police and civilian personnel. Keeping the building under observation until he could spot Sgt Childs, now back in uniform, was not going to be straightforward. Glastonbury Road had no parking, with a bus stop immediately opposite the station. His only hope was the site of the old Cow & Gate factory, long since closed, still awaiting redevelopment. If he could park there, it shouldn't be too difficult to watch people coming and going. There was only one drive leading from the main road to the site.

He toyed with the idea of going into the station, but was unable to think of a credible reason for asking about her shift times. So, armed with a couple of packs of sandwiches, two cans of Coke and a compact pair of binoculars, he tucked his car onto a corner of the old site and settled down for what he expected to be a long wait. He wished she had shown up on the electoral roll. He had been completely out of luck trying to find a home address for her.

There was little traffic in and out of the site. Occasionally a marked car would arrive or leave, usually with two occupants. None was Pat Childs. Not until after eight in the evening did an unmarked car appear from behind the main building and approach the main road. Quickly checking through his bins, he confirmed that it was a woman, and unless he was much mistaken, it was Pat Childs. She had changed somewhat, but not a great deal, from the photograph in one of the Gloucester papers from a few years ago. She turned left into the traffic heading back towards the city. Rix followed, after allowing a couple of cars to catch her up, before merging easily into the light traffic.

He tracked her without too much difficulty up Strawberry Way and along Portway. It seemed she was heading for Wookey. He followed her into the village, past the Ring o' Bells into North Road. After a couple of minutes she pulled into a small, gravelled bay and parked. He parked close by.

Her cottage was an old stone building, low with a tiled roof. Plants with showy dark pink flowers forced their way out of the crack where its walls met the road surface, lending warmth to what might otherwise have been an austere frontage.

He gave her a couple of minutes before knocking on the door. She opened it cautiously, as though not used to visitors. He beamed at her. "Kiss me quick!"

Her face flushed scarlet. "What the hell do you mean?"

Rix laughed. "Red Valerian. I've just remembered. It's what my Gran used to call it. I do apologise, I didn't mean to be rude. May I start again?" His smile was so engaging that her stance softened somewhat. He offered his National Press Card and introduced himself.

"Ms Childs? I'm Trevor Rix, journalist with the Cambridge Herald. I wonder if you could spare me a few moments of your time?"

"How do you know who I am? How do you know where I live?" Now her tone was bordering on hostile.

He gave her his most winning smile. He knew she was a few years older than him, probably ten years or so. He aimed to disarm her. Boyish good looks helped him, he knew.

"Just basic research, Ms Childs. I understand you were one of the last officers to work closely with James Upwood before he moved to Cambridge. I don't know if you're aware but he's a DCI now, and very highly regarded. My paper has been running a series of profiles of key figures in the city and we're doing one on him. I was hoping you might be able to share one or two anecdotes – we like to make our subjects look human as well as interesting. Can I offer you supper? I imagine the pub on the corner does food? It will save you preparing a meal." He hoped to goodness there was no one else for whom she might be cooking.

She hesitated, unsure how to respond, the expression 'there's no such thing as a free lunch' clearly coming to mind.

He took a gamble. Criticising a woman's appearance was always a high-risk strategy. "Come on. You look bushed. Bad day at the office?"

She looked as though the fight had gone out of her. "OK, but it will have to be quick. I've got some ironing I must do tonight."

They walked the short distance to the pub. They found a table outside, ordering at the bar. Ham, eggs and chips for him, fish cakes for her. She opted for a large glass of Pinot Grigio, he for a Kaliber.

"Wookey's a lovely village. Have you lived here long?"

"About four years."

"Do you enjoy Wells? It's a gem of a city, isn't it? I can remember coming here as a kid. My Mum and Dad wanted to explore Glastonbury. They were into all that new age stuff at the time. It never floated my boat, I have to say."

She laughed. "I know what you mean. Wells is beautiful, but it gets too crowded in the summer. It's too small for all the tourists we get. Mind you, most of them seem to think they can do Bath and Wells in one day. Peasants."

A waitress brought their food. "There you are. Local ham. Local eggs. Local chips. Well, potatoes any rate. I can't speak for the fish." She put the plates down with a flourish and disappeared back inside the pub.

"So, Pat. Is it OK if I call you Pat?" She nodded. "James Upwood. A talented officer, I keep hearing, in our neck of the woods. Was he well thought of in Gloucestershire Constabulary?"

"Sure. He worked hard. He really didn't like not being able to close cases. And he was fair, I'll give him that. He was one of the few that we women officers were comfortable to work with. One or two were complete arseholes."

The name Muspratt sprang unbidden into Rix's mind.

"How long were you partners?"

"A couple of years. Not much more."

"What kind of cases did you work together?"

"The full range really. Burglary, assault, all sorts. We had one case where vehicles were being stolen to order. That was interesting."

He signalled to the waitress for another round of drinks. "Any amusing stories?"

"None that I could repeat. Of the ones I remember."

He toyed with his food. Sure enough she remembered something.

"Well, there was the time we had to call out the AA. He locked us out of his car. Probably the lads on the estate we were in could have opened it more quickly."

Rix made an encouraging noise and continued eating.

"And there was the man who went missing. His wife was mean faced with a temper to match. Lord, you mustn't say that. She'll sue me."

Rix chuckled. "What happened?"

"A neighbour spotted him in Weston-super-Mare. Performing a routine she'd seen him give at a children's party. He'd run off to join a circus. He was forty-eight. Hysterical."

Rix laughed dutifully. Did the incident smack of pathos or bathos? He wasn't quite sure. He found the whole idea bizarre beyond measure. "He was successful at work. Popular, too, I get the impression. But he was having a bad time personally, wasn't he Pat? He must have been devastated when their baby died."

Her face fell. "Devastated doesn't come near to describing how he felt. It changed his whole outlook on life. Certainly he wasn't as enthusiastic about work. Understandable I suppose."

"And then his wife died. Committed suicide, I heard. I can't imagine how anyone could cope with a second tragedy like that." He paused for a moment. "What was she like?"

"Never met her. He liked to keep his private and professional lives separate. That was a truly terrible tragedy."

"Were you working with him at the time?"

"Yes."

"I mean the day she died?"

Colour rose to her cheeks. "Why do you want to know?"

"It's a real human-interest story, isn't it? Handsome, capable, officer loses his infant child and soon afterwards his wife. It really tugs at the heart strings." He attended to his food again. "So were you together that day?"

"Yes." She chewed her bottom lip.

"How was he?"

"How d'you mean?"

"Anything troubling him more than usual? His wife had been quite poorly I gather."

"That came out at her inquest. Her being poorly, I mean. He was still very upset about the death of his daughter, and I think he found the inquest a bit of a strain. It must have been hard hearing about her depression, and the self-harming and stuff."

"I imagine it would. Did you have to appear?" Rix knew that she hadn't but wanted to see her reaction.

"No, thank God." She shuddered. A natural aversion to appearing on the stand? Relieved she didn't have to perjure herself? Time to explore the key issue.

He didn't look at her, but toyed with his food again. "Why did you go home early, the day his wife died?"

Colour rose to her cheeks. "What makes you say that?" She gripped the stem of her wine glass tightly.

"A couple of people I've spoken to mentioned it. A family problem, I'm guessing. Or perhaps you weren't feeling well. I'm told you got home about three o'clock."

She stared at him, eyes wide. "No, it wasn't that early…"

"Nearer four maybe?"

"Christ, I shouldn't be telling you this."

"It will come out in the story. I imagine he didn't tell anyone you'd left your post; it can only have been a few minutes away for him, surely?"

"I don't know what he said. I only wanted to get home to bed. You mustn't put this in your story. I don't want to make trouble for him."

"But it reflects well on him, Pat, don't you think? That he was prepared to risk a bit of criticism to show you compassion?"

She took a long draught of her wine. If only she hadn't been so tired, if only he hadn't been such a bloody charmer, if only she hadn't had that second glass of Pinot, she might have kept her wits about her. She'd been shafted and she knew it. Damn and blast it.

Chapter 48

The evening briefing on Wednesday was attended by the nucleus of the team, convened by Morton. He was concerned there might be little progress and was anxious news of this was contained.

Stephanie was the first to report. A short, rather untidy woman, she was nearing forty, with a rather shaggy crop and a heavy fringe. Despite her looks, low self-esteem was not one of her traits. Nor did she have any concerns about speaking in front of others.

"Alex Barron. As you probably remember, she had a British passport when she was convicted in September 2006. That gave her date of birth as 12th February 1979 and her place of birth as London. I've located a birth certificate, under the name Alexandra Baranova. Her father was given as Ivan Baranov, bookseller. Her mother's name was given as Oksana Baranova. No occupation was given for her. Alex Barron was entitled to British nationality when her father was granted indefinite leave to remain in the UK in 1985."

Morton interrupted her flow. "Do we know why the parents settled in the UK in the 1970s? Surely the Cold War would have been in full swing?"

"It's difficult to find out much about him. I wondered whether he'd fled Russia because he wanted to sell books that were banned in his home country. Maybe he was some kind of dissident."

"Maybe he was some kind of spy," someone muttered. Morton ignored the remark. If Upwood was right, Baranov was unlikely to have given an occupation that disclosed his real activities.

"Did he move into the property market in England?" he asked.

"Not that I've been able to establish. There's very little I've been able to find out except they seem to have lived in Kensington. An expensive area."

"Close to the Russian embassy," offered the same voice from the back.

Stephanie tried to regain control. She had not finished her report yet.

"It occurred to me that we aren't having much luck tracing Alex backwards, as it were. So I thought I'd try tracing her going forwards."

"Better than going round and round in circles."

Laughter erupted.

"Go on Stephanie." Morton, for one, was intrigued.

"Well, I don't know much about the habits of Russian immigrants to the UK going back that far. But I do know that these days the oligarchs like to send their offspring to good boarding schools. I did a bit of research and found that Roedean is a favourite. They have eight or so Russian pupils now. Then they had one, although her name was not Alexandra Baranova. But there was a pupil there from 1990 who was going by Alex Barron. About the same time we think her parents moved to Spain, or perhaps just after."

"How on earth did you find that out? You didn't have a warrant." Morton was impressed.

"Blind luck. I didn't even raise the idea with you in case you told me it would be a waste of time. Roedean was the first school I found with Russian pupils. I told their receptionist I would never be able to get warrants for all the schools Alex might have been to. But if she could confirm that Alex had been there, I'd ask no further questions without a warrant. I got the impression she was new to her job. I think she took pity on me."

"Very well done. I'll organise a warrant. Maybe we can find out something that will lead us to her. Anything else to report?"

"I've not attempted to follow her parents after their move. As you know, when we looked before, we were unable to find any record of Alex attending a British university. She may have done so in Russia of course, or perhaps Spain. But from the time she left school we have no official records of her here, until her conviction."

"Bookselling must have been a very lucrative business if she was at Roedean." Morton was finally able to identify the speaker as Nick Spacey, who had been drafted in from Hinchingbrooke with Stephanie some weeks ago. For someone whose main focus with his team had been CCTV, working with Joan and Dirk, he seemed to have developed some strong views about the case. Perhaps Stephanie had been discussing her findings with him.

Morton asked Stephanie if she had anything else to report.

"Not really. She may have lived in Spain with her parents during school holidays. She might have lived there for some years after leaving school. I can't tell you any more I'm afraid." Stephanie sat down, satisfied that she had at least provided some potentially useful information.

"Have you checked with the Border Agency to see if you can track her movements?"

Her laugh was brittle. "Sure. When I said I wanted information going back ten years or more you can imagine what response I got. Apart from anything else, the Border Agency as we know it now did not exist before 2008. Before that there was the Border and Immigration Agency, UKVisas and part of Customs and Revenue. I dread to think how they dealt with the systems. But the most serious problem, of course, is that she didn't renew the passport that expired in 2008. I stood no chance."

"And nothing more on her banking or housing status?"

"Correct."

Morton sighed. "Debra. You've been trying to track down Saskia Baranova. Any progress?"

"Very little. Virtually none in fact. I can't find a Saskia Baranova listed on Google's UK website anywhere. I can find no one by the name of Alexandra Baranova living or working in the UK, never mind Cambridge. I've tried various diminutive forms, but you wouldn't believe how many there are. I've found at least six which are of Russian or Slavic origin, and there are others of British origin. I've searched social media. There are plenty of Alexandra Baranovas, but almost without exception they are listed as living in Russia. She may have used the name Saskia Baranova in Spain. Or it may simply be that her mother used that diminutive form. But if she's here, I think it's under a different name entirely."

"Is she using her sister's passport?" This from Nick Spacey again.

No one laughed. Everyone there knew what had happened in their most recent high-profile case. That Alex/Saskia might have been doing the same would be a coincidence too far, and there was no evidence that she had a sister.

"I think she has changed her identity completely."

Silence greeted this final observation from Debra.

"Not encouraging," observed Morton. "Any bright ideas how we can find her?"

Nick and Joan raised their hands. Each turned to the other and grinned. Joan indicated that he should go first.

"We had a report from a member of the public that she'd seen someone like the picture we released of Alex Barron. She'd been waiting for the lights to change at a crossing on Maids Causeway. She reckons a woman cyclist stopped when she was clear to cross. She didn't get a very good look, because she didn't want the lights to turn against her before she'd reached the other side."

"How useful is the sighting do you think?"

"There's no real way of telling. But Joan and I have looked at the area and discussed it. The area is mainly residential and there are no cameras on that stretch of road. But there are on the roundabouts at each end. We're going to let Joan and Dirk loose on the footage and see if we can find her. If we do see her going through either roundabout it may be worthwhile getting someone to do some canvassing along there. Or we could set up a spurious speed trap. We might be lucky and get a handle on where she lives."

"Good thinking. Let's do it."

After the meeting Morton gave Upwood a brief update. He didn't seem hugely optimistic about the idea of trying to find Alex on camera but agreed it was worth a shot. He did think there might be some mileage in pursuing the Roedean link, although he was not wildly optimistic about that either.

"It wasn't just that I wanted to discuss, Sir. It's Margaret."

"How is she? Do we know when she'll come back to work?"

"She is back. But she's not achieving a great deal. She insists she's ready and that there's nothing she can do for Mo at the moment. His parents are still staying in Cambridge, so they're at the hospital every day. She says she feels embarrassed going when it may mean they feel the need to leave his room. But she's very subdued. Bad tempered."

"That doesn't sound like her at all. Just stress, d'you think?"

"I don't know. She seems very reluctant to talk about Mo at all. I don't know what's got into her."

"You've tried talking to her?"

"Of course. As I say, she doesn't want to discuss it and more or less told me to mind my own business last time I raised it. Did Madam Adams find out any more about her or Luuk Jansen from Herts?"

"I forgot to follow it up. Sorry."

This wasn't like Upwood and Morton was frustrated. Why did everyone seem to be distracted at the moment?

Emily Adams had clearly been distracted, too, as she admitted to Upwood that she'd forgotten to relay what she'd learnt from Herts Constabulary. And maybe that's because she hadn't learned a great deal.

"My opposite number was very reluctant to discuss it. Reading between the lines, Jansen left the service under a cloud. Whether there was a disciplinary issue, or a criminal one, involved, my contact was simply not prepared to say. He neither confirmed nor denied that Margaret was in any way involved in whatever the issue was. I was left with the impression there was some sort of cover up. Lord knows what was going on."

"Any insight into their investigation into Luuk's death?"

"Still ongoing. Apparently, he had suffered blunt force trauma to the back of his head that could not have been caused during the crash."

"How sure are they?"

"Very sure. The head bleeds easily, as you know. There was evidence of heavy bleeding from the injury site. That could not have occurred post-mortem."

"Do they know what kind of weapon caused it?"

"It may not have been a weapon. None was found there, and Jansen is unlikely to have taken it away. He may have hit his head on the doorpost."

"So unlikely to have been intentional or premeditated?"

"No. I shall be surprised if they attempt to prefer charges against Mo, but manslaughter is still a possibility."

"But if Jansen lured him there as we think, and if Jansen wielded a knife at him, then it would be self-defence, surely?"

"I hope so. But we don't have the evidence. It's not our case. And Herts are not keen to let us in as you very well know."

"Doesn't sound promising for the collaboration of Herts, Beds and Cambs does it?"

"Don't get me started on that. Let's just try to get a decent result in these cases, shall we?"

I wish, thought Upwood. He left Parkside in a very low mood. The only good feature of his conversation with Emily was that she hadn't raised the subject of Debra.

Chapter 49

It was Saturday before Rix could get down to Tirley again. He'd taken the precaution of phoning Muspratt to see if he was in, hanging up when he answered, hoping he'd still be in later. The man obviously lived on his own, was retired, unlikely to be out engaging in a bit of retail therapy at lunchtime on Saturday. More likely sitting in his mobile home with a few beers waiting for the match to start.

And so it proved to be. Muspratt was surprised, and obviously struggling to remember Rix. Then the penny dropped.

"What the hell are you doing here again? I told you all I know last time."

Rix laughed in that disarming way that came so naturally to him.

"No, George, I doubt that very much. But you did give me a good lead and I'm grateful for that. But now I need some more help. And it won't get you into any trouble. I'll make it worth your while again."

Muspratt stood aside to let Rix in. A warm fug hit him. Surely to goodness the man couldn't have the heating on again? Maybe he never opened the windows. Maybe it stayed constantly warm from lights and electrical appliances. Then he picked up on something he hadn't noticed before. A distinctly doggy smell. Another source of heat, no doubt.

"You'll want coffee again I take it?"

"If you wouldn't mind. It's a long ride."

Muspratt disappeared into what was presumably the kitchen. Rix couldn't be sure, but he thought he heard the man muttering to himself about why the journalist couldn't have stopped for a break somewhere. He came back a few minutes later with the same chipped mugs they'd used before. One had a Gloucester City logo.

"Thanks. Who d'you follow?"

"What d'yer mean?"

"Gloucester. They're an amateur club, aren't they? Don't you follow one of the league clubs?"

"Aye. Bristol City. You keen?"

"Haven't really got time to keep up with it. I'll watch the big matches when I can. But you need time to follow a club, don't you?"

"Aye, reckon you do. Well, I've got the time alright, thanks to that bastard Upwood."

Rix was keen not to send the man off on another rant, although it was of course Muspratt's hatred of Upwood that the journalist exploited.

"So the information I gave you was helpful?"

"Yes it was. I've got nearly everything I need for a good story now. I'm afraid Upwood may not come out of it too well though."

"Bloody good job. He deserves all the muck you can throw at him. But I ain't got anything else I can tell you."

"Maybe not, George. But you probably know someone who can."

The man regarded him with eyes which were not so much rheumy as bloodshot. They spoke of a distinctly unhealthy lifestyle. As Muspratt thought about what Rix had said, an old spaniel lumbered into the living area from the kitchen. He looked up at Rix with eyes almost as unhealthy as his owners, eyes encrusted with heaven knows what, only to collapse at Muspratt's feet.

"What's his name?"

"Buster."

Original. Rix simply nodded.

"So, what d'you want?"

"Name and number of someone else working close to Upwood at the time. Even if they've retired too."

"How much is it worth?"

"A couple of hundred, like before. Half now, half if they deliver."

"'S worth more'n that." The look in Muspratt's eyes now held a challenge.

Rix sighed. It wasn't just days of his life this investigation had cost, in financial terms it was racking up.

"OK. I'll double it. Two hundred now, the rest on delivery."

"All of it now."

Rix laughed out loud. "Don't be daft, mate. I don't ride around with that kind of money on me."

They settled on half now, and half later.

Muspratt went into another room, his bedroom perhaps. He came back after a minute or two with an old-fashioned address book.

"John Ferry."

"Now you're really winding me up. Stephen with a ph Gerrard was bad enough."

"John Ferry, not Terry, you prat."

"Ah. OK. Still serving?"

"Yes. 'E were a bit younger than me."

Probably still is, thought Rix.

"You have a number for him?"

Muspratt read it out.

"And he'll talk to me, you reckon?"

"That's your problem mate, not mine. Now push off. Somerset are playing Nottinghamshire."

Rix looked confused. Then he remembered, there were sports other than football.

"Cricket?"

"Aye, lad. Bugger off. I've got a pony on Somerset to win." He was to be disappointed. They drew.

Chapter 50

Margaret was at home when the doorbell rang. She had a top floor apartment in Fen Causeway, where visitors normally rang her bell at the entrance to the block. She looked through the spyhole and nearly fainted in shock. There was a knock.

"Come on sweetheart. Open up. I'm getting tired."

She opened her door. Mo was standing there with a huge bunch of flowers.

"What are you doing here?" she asked weakly.

"Let me in Mags. I've not been out of bed long."

She let him in, closed the door and leant against it.

"How did you get here?"

"Taxi. I'm not fit to drive yet."

"How did you get in?"

"The old dear on the ground floor recognised me. I told her I wanted to give you a surprise."

He held the flowers out to her. She took them wordlessly, dumped them in the kitchen and went into the sitting room. Mo was already sitting down.

"What are you doing here?"

It was finally dawning on Mo, who was still taking strong medications and whose brain was not quite as sharp as usual, that he was not welcome.

"What's the matter, sweetheart?"

She did not sit. "I'm not your sweetheart."

"What on earth do you mean?"

Colour had suffused her cheeks. Her eyes glittered.

"I've already escaped one violent man. I don't intend to spend time with another."

"Mags. For crying out loud. He attacked me."

"But you went there for a fight, didn't you?"

"What on earth are you talking about?"

"That call you got. It was about me, wasn't it? I could see it. And you've been avoiding me ever since. You went there to fight him. It was Luuk, wasn't it? Why would you do that?"

He nodded. "I think it was Luuk. He was tall, blond, very good looking. Might have had a bit of a Dutch accent. I didn't go there to fight him."

He got to his feet and immediately tumbled back down onto the sofa. He dropped his head into his hands.

"So help me, I wanted to warn him off."

"Warn him off what?"

"You. Me. I wanted him out of your life again. For good."

"And how in God's name did you think you were going to do that? You knew he was violent. You would never have warned him off unless you'd managed to beat him up pretty thoroughly. You must have known that."

"I thought I could reason with him."

Her laugh was harsh. Bitter. "Then you're more of a fool than I gave you credit for."

Silence stretched between them.

"I nearly died defending your honour, Mags."

"No. You nearly got yourself killed playing cowboys and Indians. I've had enough violence in my life. I don't want any more. I don't want to spend time with someone who thinks they can fight their way out of trouble."

"But I love you, Mags. I went for you."

"No you didn't. I've no doubt Luuk said something really nasty. What did he do? Tell you I was a prick tease? That was one of his favourites when he went off on one. You must have believed him, otherwise you would have told me about it. You didn't trust me enough to do that. Instead, you avoided me for days, made excuses for not going out on the Saturday, and went off with some half-brained idea of beating him up. I can't live with that. I don't want to see you again, Mo."

"You can't be serious. I love you." There was a look of agony on his face, both physical and emotional.

Margaret was not swayed. "Too late for that. Go. Now. Right now. Go!"

When Mo woke up he was in hospital again. How he'd got there he'd no idea. Nor did he know how long he'd been there. Morton was sitting by the bed.

"How're you feeling?"

"Like shit."

"What happened?"

"I don't know. How long have I been here?"

"A couple of hours, no more. It's about four o'clock. Sunday afternoon."

"How did I get here?"

"You collapsed outside Margaret's apartment block. Her neighbour on the ground floor heard you crash onto the pavement."

"Oh shit. Oh shit."

"Want to tell me about it?"

Mo looked at him, abject despair written on his face.

"You know it was her ex-husband I went to see?"

"Luuk Jansen. Yes. We know."

Mo turned the proposition over in his mind.

"How did you know. Did Margaret tell you?"

Morton decided there was no point in beating about the bush.

"His body was found in his car shortly after he left you. He's dead."

"Christ Almighty!" A look of terror swept his face. "I didn't kill him, did I?"

Morton was concerned that Mo had asked the question. How vicious had their fight been?

"Tell me what happened."

"Jansen called me, then sent me a really nasty text. About Margaret. I guessed it was from him. He didn't say. Told me to meet him at the pub. I asked him to tell me what he wanted me to know by phone. He said he would only tell me face to face."

"When was that?"

"I don't know. Can't remember exactly. I can tell from my phone. It was a few days before I went to see him."

"Did you tell Margaret about it?"

"No. I didn't want her to know. Do you know their background?"

"No."

Mo thought for a moment. "This is in strict confidence. She'd kill me if she thought I'd told anyone."

Morton nodded. He wasn't at all sure he'd be able to keep it confidential, but he needed to hear what Mo had to say.

"It was an abusive relationship. He raped her. She became pregnant. He raped her again. She lost the child."

He'd taken big gulps of air between each sentence. Morton passed him a mug of water and Mo drank deeply.

"I wanted to put the fear of God into him. Let him know that I'd take care of her. That there was nothing he could do to harm us."

Not a very good judgement call, it seemed.

"He was abusive as soon as he got out of his car. Then he came at me with a knife. Bright steel. It must have been six inches long."

It tallied with his injuries.

"We fought. I managed to land a few blows and then we both crashed into the back door of the pub. All hell broke loose. Lights came on. An alarm went off. And then I must have passed out."

A look of fear swept across his face again.

"I can't have killed him. He drove out of the car park. They told me that." Silence fell. "Did you find any weapons?"

An interesting question. Not 'did you find the knife?'. Had Mo taken a weapon with him? If he had, why would Jansen have taken it away with him?

"Did you find my phone? I haven't seen it since I left home that evening."

"No."

"He must have taken it. He wouldn't have wanted anyone to see his text."

"But presumably he didn't say who it was from?"

"No. But it wouldn't take a rocket scientist to work it out." Silence again. "So how did he die?"

"Drove his car into the back of a big artic on the hard shoulder near Knebworth."

"Christ. How did he manage that?"

He reached out for the water again. Morton filled his mug from the plastic jug on the wheeled table over the bed and passed it to him once more.

At that moment a nurse came into the room.

"Time to leave, Inspector. You've been here too long already. He needs to rest. We don't know yet whether he's done any damage in the fall."

Morton shrugged. "Take care, Mo. Do what they tell you. I'll come and see you again soon. Are your parents still down here or have they gone home?"

"They've gone home. Don't worry them, please."

The nurse beamed at him. "They've already been notified. Next of kin." He groaned.

Morton was frustrated. He perhaps knew a little more about what had happened at Baldock. But he didn't have a clue what had gone wrong in Fen Causeway. But he was sure something had. And badly. Should he go and see her? He couldn't face her. He'd tackle her in the week. Should he debrief Upwood tonight? He decided against it. He had a sneaky feeling Upwood was fighting a few demons of his own. Or rather Katie's. She'd be home next weekend, and no doubt manage to cause havoc as usual.

Chapter 51

Stephanie was annoyed that they would not let her follow up the Roedean lead, but there was nothing she could do about it. Debra was tasked with the responsibility. After some discussion it was agreed that she should meet Miss Amelia Shand, currently Senior Deputy Head. She had been Sixth Form Head while Alex was a pupil there.

Debra knew nothing about the school except that it was, in her words, posh. She decided to travel by train, avoiding an unpleasant car journey round London, giving her plenty of time to consider how best to conduct the interview. The approach to the main school building was impressive. It stood in a large cliff-top estate not far from Brighton. Still, Cambridge did impressive, she reminded herself, and refused to be intimidated.

Miss Shand was a tall woman, impressive in her own right, whom Debra judged to be in her early fifties. She would have been about forty, then, at the time when Alex was leaving school some fourteen years previously. Her office was just as Debra had imagined it: elegant, full of books. A bunch of flowers gave it a rather more friendly touch.

"How can I help you Detective Sergeant? I know you want to talk about Alex Barron, but I don't know why."

"I'm not at liberty to say, Miss Shand, other than it is as part of an ongoing investigation. But I do have a warrant as you know."

"May I see it please?"

Debra handed it over and Miss Shand studied it carefully. "I'll tell you what I know, of course. Where would you like to start?"

"I'd like to know firstly what you have on file about her. Then I'd like to know everything you know about her firsthand."

"There'll be some overlap Miss Graf..."

"I'm sure there will. But let's see how we go."

"Fine. She came to us in the autumn term of 1990 in Year 7 when she was eleven. Her file shows that she was brought to us by her mother, Olga Barron."

"Not both her parents?"

"No. I certainly didn't ever meet him. In fact, as it happens, I never met her mother either. Until she entered the Sixth Form, I hadn't really had any contact with Alex. My subject is music, which she did not study."

"But you have a record of the father's name presumably? And Olga's address in England?"

"Of course." She checked her file. "John Barron. 12 Markham Mews, Chelsea."

Miss Shand referred to the file again. "She was a full boarder. A good student. In the sense that learning came easily to her. But her reports remark that she was sometimes prone to be lazy. She achieved good exam results, particularly in maths."

"So she got results without having to try too hard, is that it?"

"That's a fair assessment, I think. She had good health to the extent that that is of interest to you. Her reports do, though, say that she played sport, team sports, to be precise, reluctantly. She was also reluctant to participate in other non-academic activities."

"So, she entered the sixth form. Were you already Head of that Form?"

"I was. I knew her for two years."

"Which subjects did she study?"

"Principally, maths, chemistry and physics. She achieved top grades in all three."

"You said before that she shunned team activities. But there must have been some activities she took part in."

"Well, there was drama, at which she excelled. I remember one performance she gave quite vividly. It's the scene in Lear when the king is taking shelter from a severe storm and blames himself for not having provided more assistance to the homeless. Act 3, Scene 4. She played Lear. It was a compelling performance."

"Lear was an old man, surely?"

Miss Shand laughed. "Indeed, but we do like to challenge our girls. It wasn't the only male lead she played. She could handle it better than most.

"Computing. She did spend a lot of time in our computer lab, now I come to think of it. It hadn't been open long – personal computing was still in its infancy really. We were using Amstrads at first. They'd not long taken over Sinclair if I remember correctly."

"Was the time spent in classes, or was she there unsupervised?"

"Certainly she took classes. But she showed particular aptitude, and I think she was allowed time in there unsupervised."

"Tell me about her as a person."

Miss Shand allowed herself a slight smile. "That's altogether more difficult. She was a very private person. She really only had one friend. Irina Rednikova, another Russian girl. A talented piano player. I remember her." She paused for a moment. "I say 'another' although we had been given no reason to believe that Alex was of Russian heritage. But they spoke together in Russian, which used to annoy me intensely. There was always a feeling that they did it because they did not want to be understood."

"What happened to that pupil?"

"She went back to St Petersburg to rejoin her family. Her father had been posted to Britain for a time, hence the choice of school, but was repatriated. I seem to recall that he died unexpectedly soon after."

"Was Alex involved in any activities outside school, in the community maybe?"

"Good Lord, no. The only time she left the school other than holidays was at half term in her final year. Her brother came to see her a couple of times." She laughed gently. "I can best describe their relationship as feisty. They, too, would only speak in Russian but I managed to form the impression that they were very competitive, one to another."

"Do you recall his name?"

"No I don't, sorry."

"Do you know where he went to school?"

"No. No idea. Although I want to say Dulwich, but I'm not sure on what grounds."

Interesting. But not much chance of tracking down her friend. And probably little chance of tracking down her brother either. "Where did Alex go when she left Roedean?"

"I don't know. She wasn't interested in going to a British university. Whether she went overseas I have no idea. We never saw her after the day her mother collected her. Needless to say, she did not join the Old Roedeanians."

"How would you describe her at the time she left?"

"An able student. I wouldn't say she lacked social skills as such. But I would say she had no interest in displaying them unless she had to."

"Is there anyone who might have kept in touch with her?"

"I very much doubt it."

"What about other teachers? Would anyone be able to add to your account?"

"I'd have to give you the same answer, I'm afraid. Were it not for her ability to speak Russian I doubt I would have remembered her as well as I do. It was fourteen years ago, after all. Now, I really don't think I can tell you much more, Miss Graf."

During a long and frustrating journey back to Cambridge, Debra mulled over what she had learned. She felt she had a better picture of the girl Alex had been. And that girl could well have matured into the woman they thought she now was. Were they any closer to finding her? In a word, no. Not on the strength of that interview.

Chapter 52

The atmosphere at the morning briefing was different. There was a distinct air of anticipation. Word had got round that there might have been a breakthrough. Even Upwood attended. Some of the more cynical had remarked on the fact that he'd not attended all the meetings, especially when things hadn't been going very well.

"Nick. Tell us what you've got."

"We decided the speed trap would be our best bet in trying to catch Alex on camera. And Joan and Dirk," he nodded to them, "studied footage from the two roundabouts either side of where our witness had seen her before."

Morton and Upwood looked at each other. It was encouraging to see how these newer members of the team had fitted in, even if two of them were only temporary.

Nick Spacey continued. "We caught her cycling towards town again, westbound along Maids Causeway. The speed trap clocked her. And it's definitely the same bike. We haven't picked her up on the other roundabout at all for the last week. We think she lives somewhere between that roundabout and the pedestrian crossing where our witness saw her."

"Well done. Joan. Dirk, anything to add to that?"

"We thought we'd continue to monitor the western roundabout and then see if we can track where she goes in town."

"Good. Who else has anything to report?"

Margaret spoke. Morton looked at her. She looked dreadful. Her hair was untidy. Her face was paler than usual. Her eyes looked sore. He'd have to speak to her later.

"I've been thinking about the properties along that stretch of Maids Causeway. The first apartment she lived in that we know about, the one in Brooklands Avenue, was quite expensive. So was the duplex on Riverside. Both were modern. It's possible she's trying to stay hidden and is in an old property. But I bet she's in something classy and modern again. She's been used to luxury all her life. And she's been used to keeping out of sight. I think she's arrogant enough to think she can go on doing it."

"Anna, any thoughts on that?"

It was unusual for a psychologist to remain involved. Partly because it seemed Alex Barron was an unusually complex character, and partly because they needed all the help they could get, they'd asked her to attend the briefings.

"I think it's a decent working hypothesis. It certainly wouldn't do any harm to prioritise any properties like that to canvass, assuming there are any."

Margaret responded. "I've not been out to look. But I have looked at Google Street View. I reckon there is one development that's just her style. In Queen's Walk. It's on the north side of Maids Causeway, on the right stretch. I think someone should take a photo there and see if anyone living there recognises her."

They debated the suggestion for a few minutes, but decided against it for the time being. The longer they had to collect evidence against Alex without her being aware of the interest, the better.

After the meeting Morton made it clear that he wanted Margaret to stay behind. He took her to one of the small meeting rooms. They'd passed one of the coffee machines, but she'd declined a drink.

"You don't look terribly well, Margaret. How do you feel?"

"Fine."

"But you don't look it. Did you not sleep well?"

She shook her head.

"What happened with Mo yesterday? He came to see you, didn't he?"

"Did he tell you? Bastard. I should never have trusted him." Suddenly her cheeks were suffused with colour.

Morton raised an eyebrow. "No, he didn't tell me." Morton wasn't being entirely truthful, but in the sense that he thought she meant it, he was. "He collapsed yesterday evening. He's back in hospital."

"Oh God. What happened?"

"We don't really know. He was found on the pavement outside your apartment."

She burst into tears.

Morton passed her a pocket-sized pack of tissues and let her cry.

"He went to meet my ex-husband. That's who he was fighting."

"He died. Did you know that?"

Margaret's scream was so loud, a passing officer looked in through the door. "Everything all right?"

Morton's look sent him packing.

"Mo?" The expression on her face was one of pure anguish.

"It's your ex-husband who died."

A look of profound relief spread across her face. Relief that it wasn't Mo? Or relief that Luuk had died?

"Did Mo kill him?"

Morton was shocked. "Do you think he might have?"

She started wailing again. Ought he to have someone with him? This conversation was off the record. It formed no part of an investigation. It was just man management. At least that's how Morton decided to rationalise it for the time being.

"Do you? Think he might have?"

She sobbed. "I don't know. But he didn't tell me he was going, or who he was going to meet. But I guessed who it was. He must have expected there'd be trouble." She blew her nose again. "I can't escape from violence." She sobbed again.

Morton didn't respond to that last observation. Would Margaret recall that later, and wonder why?

"Did he kill Luuk?"

"He died in a car crash."

Again, economical with the truth. It may not be a formal interview, but Morton had to tread carefully.

She looked absolutely distraught. She was in no fit state to work.

"Why don't you go home Margaret? Take some time off. Come back when you've got over the shock."

"I need to keep busy."

"I understand. But I don't think you're fit to work just now. And people will notice and start talking. You don't want that."

She sniffed. "They'll start talking anyway."

"Better they think you're just not well. We all need to let our bodies recover from time to time."

Morton went to see Upwood late in the afternoon. He explained briefly what he had learned from Mo and Margaret.

"Sounds like a bit of a lovers' tiff, Morton."

"Maybe so. Pretty serious I'd say."

"But not really our problem."

"Except it's affecting Margaret's performance. If they don't make up before Mo comes back to work the atmosphere could be toxic."

Upwood shook his head. It was for good reason that affairs between people in the same office were discouraged.

"We'll have to cross that bridge when we come to it."

Chapter 53

Debra's report of her findings at Roedean were met with some interest the following morning. Upwood was surprised at the theatrical reference to Lear, a scene he knew well. The likelihood of a Russian connection had been reinforced, too, which was useful. But when all was said and done, while Debra's findings did help them develop a fuller picture of Alex, that was pretty much all they had achieved.

The week proved a very frustrating one. Nick Spacey had taken a brief stroll down Queen's Walk, ostensibly delivering flyers from an Indian restaurant. Queen Anne's Mews was a development on the left at the far end of the cul-de-sac. There were eight modern mews style properties, two pairs of semi-detached houses fronting the road with a drive through to a courtyard at the rear. At the back of this were four slightly larger terraced houses. Each had a built-in garage. If Alex was living in one of these houses, she would have no need to leave her bicycle outside. There was a board outside advertising houses to let and judging by the lack of curtains or blinds, at least three of them were still available. The fact that all three had junk mail sticking out of their letter boxes reinforced the impression.

The cul-de-sac was short, with residential properties only on the left-hand side. On the right were hoardings with undeveloped land behind. Surveillance in Queen's Walk itself was out of the question. The only possibility was the opportunity provided by a house on Maids Causeway, on the other side of the road but close to the Queen's Walk entrance. There was a for sale board in the small front garden and the house had all the appearance of being empty.

Margaret had, albeit unwillingly, agreed with Morton that she should take time off. It was Stephanie, therefore, who researched ownership details of the mews houses. A search of the Land Registry showed that all were owned by Keresley Property Ltd. She found the letting agent to be unusually helpful. Numbers 3 and 4 (the semi-detached houses on the right-hand side of the entrance to the courtyard) were rented by Andrew David Walton and Philip Haw respectively. Both were apparently employees of Keresley and the agent had not in fact met either of them. Numbers 1 and 2 at the front left of the development were vacant, as was Number 8 (one of the four rear houses). Number 5 was rented by Charles and Mary Sullivan, Number 6 by Pierre and Isabelle Truffaut and Number 7 by Luca Favino.

Further research showed that Favino was a fifty-five year old fellow of King's College, and that the Sullivans both had profiles on LinkedIn. He was a doctor, she a retail manager. The Truffauts were both working with one of the life sciences companies near Addenbrooke's Hospital. Neither Mary nor Isabelle bore any resemblance to Alex. Stephanie was unable to discover any information about Haw and Walton, a fact which troubled her.

By Wednesday she had come to a virtual standstill. Then came the news that there had been a possible sighting of Alex. It seems that she had cycled south down Elizabeth Way, entered the roundabout closest to, and just east of, Queen's Walk, turned left onto Newmarket Road and then right into Coldhams Lane. After that they had lost her. The team were having serious doubts that she lived in the development that Margaret had identified. She was however riding the distinctive men's bike she'd been seen on before. Morton suddenly had an idea.

"Someone was going to follow up on the bike. Who was it?"

Answer came there none.

He racked his brains. "Mo. That's why we've not heard back. He probably tasked a uniformed officer to look into it for him. Debra, can you please check to see if it was actioned? There should be something in HOLMES."

When they met for the final briefing on Friday afternoon the mood was distinctly subdued. Upwood did not attend, which was again a matter for criticism by some of those present. While Morton sensed the feeling, he could not identify any individual responsible for voicing dissatisfaction. Detailed accounts were given of the efforts to find Alex and track her movements. They sounded as though those involved were trying to justify their efforts despite having very little to show for them.

The only item of real interest came from Debra. She confirmed that a PC had followed up the question of the bike and found the retailer who had sold it. They were a specialist outfit and had records of their sales. Their bikes were expensive, and customers were measured and matched to suitable bicycles. As a result, they knew that the buyer was approximately five foot ten and of average build. The bike was a Bianchi Celeste, a light-weight carbon cycle used for road racing. The customer had paid cash, unusual for something with a four-figure price tag as the retailer agreed. The PC checked the address and phone number given. The address was fictitious and the mobile no longer in service. He could find no one in Cambridge with the name given who was likely to have been the buyer.

"Maybe it's Alex's brother. Stephanie, you found her birth certificate. It's quite possible he was born in London too. Have a look, will you? It's possible his name is Felix."

Morton was about to close the meeting when Stephanie asked if she could put forward a theory she had developed.

"You know I didn't like it that I couldn't find out anything about Philip Haw and Andrew David Walton. It's like searching for Alex. Neither is on the electoral roll. Neither house has a landline installed. Council Tax and utility bills are paid by the property company and the letting agent told me that tenants pay an inclusive rent. That's usual for an HMO, a house in multiple occupation, but it's very rarely the case for houses like these. The agent told me she had not met either of them. No references were provided because they both worked for the property company owning the development."

"Is this taking us anywhere, Stephanie? Time's getting on."

"I believe so."

"OK, but keep it to the essentials."

"Fine. I started doing some research into the Keresley Properties. There are only two directors, Malcolm John Sargent, an accountant, and Nat Naseby, a solicitor. It took me a long time to remember where I'd seen Naseby's name before. It was on the website of Grey, Hamilton and Fitch who provide the registered office of the company that owned the Riverside property in which Alex lived."

"Didn't HOLMES throw out the connection?"

"No. His name wasn't entered. There was no need. When Grey, Hamilton and Fitch were entered and Edward Hamilton himself, there was no reason to suppose that any of the other partners or associates were involved with the Riverside property. I only remembered Naseby's name because I've a history degree and I made a particular study of the English Civil War."

"Right. I seem to remember that you said the firm dealt with corporate law, so it's entirely likely they have a department specialising in property companies."

"I know. But Keresley is also owned by an offshore company. And what really struck me as very odd is that Naseby is the site of one of the Civil War battles. Philiphaugh, spelt P H I L I P H A U G H, is another and so is Adwalton Moor. A D Walton. I don't think either tenant exists. I believe that we've got money laundering and a solicitor with a sense of humour."

Stephanie sat down as laughter broke out. Laughter heavy with cynicism.

"What a load of bollocks!" Other equally rude comments were muttered from the back of the room.

Morton looked hard at Stephanie. While colour had come to her cheeks her gaze remained firm.

"An interesting theory. Thank you. I'll give it some thought." He looked around the room. "In the meantime, I suggest Stephanie's theory is not discussed between you, or with anyone else until I've come to a conclusion. Let's call it a day. I want each of you to carry on with the actions you've been assigned. You know how it goes. We will get a break at some stage. We just have to keep at it."

Morton managed to find Upwood just as he was about to leave for the weekend.

"It sounds an incredible idea, Sir. But in view of your worries about links with a Russian organised crime gang, I wonder if she isn't right."

"I wonder. If she is, then we're going to have to tread very carefully. I'll need to discuss it with Emily. We'll probably need to bring in SOCA. Let's make no approach to any of the occupiers of the mews houses and tell Stephanie she is not to approach anyone associated with any of the firms involved. Can we mount covert surveillance on the development?"

"Nick says not. Well not in the cul-de-sac it's in. Although he says there is an empty house on Maids Causeway which might provide a base."

"Do it."

"Round the clock?"

"It has to be. Yes, I know it will torpedo the budget but we've had four deaths. We have to establish whether Alex does live there and either eliminate her or charge her. And quickly. If we draw a blank here, we might be right back to square one."

Chapter 54

John Ferry proved easier to find than Rix had expected. Not only was he still serving, a Detective Sergeant in Gloucester, but his photo had appeared recently in the local paper when it reported on the conviction of a man for aggravated burglary. Muspratt had given him Ferry's phone number but although he did not have his address, he thought he lived somewhere near 'that bird reserve'. Rix agonised over whether to phone him and risk rebuffal, or take a chance on finding him. 'Bird reserve' could only mean Slimbridge, surely?

It was cool and blustery again on Saturday and as Rix rode west he met increasingly low pressure and squally winds. An unpleasant journey that took longer than it should have: three and a half hours when it should have been less than three. He had decided to start his search in Shepherd's Patch, not only because it was one of the closest hamlets to Slimbridge, but its pub, the Tudor Arms, also offered bed and breakfast and evening meals. If he didn't find Ferry on Saturday, he would stay the night. He had confirmed they had a room available. They were busiest from late autumn through to early spring, when the wetlands reserve held high numbers of wintering wildfowl.

It may have been a dreadful journey, but Rix struck gold in the pub. He explained to the barman that Ferry was a friend of a friend, and that he'd been asked to look him up on his trip round the west country. Not only did Ferry live in the village but was a Saturday lunchtime regular.

Rix was nursing his second Kaliber when Ferry came in. The barman nodded to him as he drew a pint into Ferry's own pewter tankard, held in the pub for him. "Someone to see you, mate."

Ferry looked round but saw no one he knew. "Who?"

"Bloke in the corner. Reckons he's best mate of a best mate of yourn."

Ferry looked round again. "You wanted me?"

"You're John Ferry?"

"I am. What of it?"

"George Muspratt said I might find you here. Will you join me?"

Ferry, curious, nodded and sat down.

"Why d'you want to see me then? I don't know you, do I?"

"I'm Trevor Rix. George has been helping me with some research for a feature we're doing…" As Rix trotted out his well-rehearsed preamble, he sensed Ferry's wariness increasing. He paused and watched the man take several deep draughts of his beer before wiping his lips with the back of his hand and putting his tankard down on the table.

"And who is 'we'?"

"The Cambridge Herald."

"Who else have you featured?"

This was a question Rix had not anticipated. Thank God he was good at thinking on his feet. "The guy that runs Addenbrooke's Hospital. The one that runs the main homeless shelter. Master of one of the older colleges. You know the sort of thing."

"So if I look online I'll find the ones you've already published?"

Rix paused to attack his Kaliber. "We've got three in the pipeline but until we've got all six ready, we shan't publish them. It's a series, see. We don't want to publish with gaps between."

It sounded thin, even to him, but it looked as though Ferry had swallowed it. Ferry did, though, pull out his smart phone, googled the Herald, and satisfied himself that there was indeed a journalist called Rix on the team.

"Credentials?"

Rix pulled out a business card and his National Press Card.

"Why d'you want to talk to me? There's plenty of people who know him better'n I did."

"I'll be honest with you, Mr Ferry. We've got all the main career background covered. It's more the human-interest angle I'm working on now."

Ferry's laugh was bitter.

"Of course it is. His wife and baby. Why do people keep raking it up? Poor bastard's had enough to cope with without dragging it all up again."

Good. Unlike Muspratt, Ferry seemed well disposed towards Upwood. Rix winged it. "Everyone I've spoken to says he was a devoted husband who doted on his baby daughter."

"He was and he did. And he was a damn good officer."

Rix rose to his feet, reaching for Ferry's tankard. "Another? What is it?"

"A pint of best, ta. Sam knows."

Rix came back with fresh drinks and sat down.

"You say he was a good officer. His reputation is good in Cambridge, too. But he did get some serious stick recently over a series of high-profile cases."

"The wind farm murders. Wasn't the last one committed by someone else?"

"Yes. It was a very messy business altogether. Two supporters of the wind farm project were murdered. There were two people who were collateral damage. One died accidentally during an arson attack. One suffered a stroke. You might say the same man was responsible for all four. But the third person murdered was killed by someone else, hoping it would be blamed on the wind farm murderer."

Ferry shuddered. "I wouldn't want to be leading on that lot."

Rix decided not to point out that a sergeant would hardly be asked to take that responsibility.

"But he got there in the end, right?"

"He did. And our feature aims to re-establish him in our readers' minds as someone in whom they can have trust."

Ferry sipped his second pint more slowly. "So what d'you want from me?"

"There are still trolls saying Upwood may have been involved in either the death of his wife or his child. Did you know that?"

Ferry looked shaken. "No. I didn't. I've never thought that." He looked away as he said this.

"But it has been said that his alibi for his wife's death doesn't hold water."

Ferry glared at him. "Who told you that?"

"I can't say Mr Ferry. I can't reveal my sources. Can you shed any light on the question?"

"Why should I be able to do that?"

"Because you and another colleague took over at the end of Upwood's surveillance shift that afternoon. Isn't that so?"

"What if I did?"

"I'm told he was alone. That he'd taken his colleague to her home well before the shift ended."

Ferry's brow creased. Rix held his breath. Would he get the answer he needed for his story to work?

After an unnaturally long pause, Ferry sighed deeply and responded.

"There was no one else in his car when he drove off after we arrived."

"Did you tell anyone at the time?"

"No."

"Why?"

"No one asked."

"And you didn't voice any concerns to your boss?"

"No. I liked the bloke. It didn't occur to me at the time. Later I did wonder about it. But I decided to keep quiet.

He'd done me a good turn once. If I raised any doubts about him, even if he was innocent, mud would likely stick."

They stared at each other in silence.

Ferry looked ashen. "Is this on the record?"

"I'd like it to be."

"If you print this it's hardly going to help improve his reputation, is it?"

"It will if we can establish that he wasn't away from his post long enough to have driven home and murdered his wife."

Ferry laughed, a weak, mildly hysterical, laugh. "Christ, mate. And how would you do that after all this time?"

"We're good at what we do. We're thorough. Like you are."

"Do you mean me? Or the police in general?"

"The police in general."

Flattery does not always help. "Bloody hell, man. The public began to lose trust in us years ago. Think back to the miners' strikes. And the printing strikes. Never mind the Birmingham Six for Christ's sake." He laughed again. "Except you're too young to remember them. Most of us do our best. Most of us try to stay honest. I'm a few years younger than George, but I'm not that far off retiring. I'm not prepared to put my pension at risk."

"So you won't help me?"

There was a long pause. "So I won't lie."

Rix heaved a huge internal sigh of relief as he studied the man's expression. "But can I quote you?"

"That's another question. I'd rather not get involved. I shouldn't have been talking to you about this at all."

Rix pondered for a moment. He should have clarified whether the interview was on or off the record at the beginning. He hadn't done so because he did not want Ferry more on his guard than he had been. He seemed a decent bloke. "You've been very helpful, thank you. I don't have to name you."

He'd leave his name out of the article. If Anne's death were ever investigated again following its publication, his name would eventually surface. It was inevitable.

Chapter 55

Upwood collected Katie from Stansted early on Saturday evening, driving to her penthouse apartment in Glenalmond Avenue. They arrived soon after six, the continuing poor weather making it seem much later, certainly too cool to sit on the terrace.

"Do you want to fix us some drinks while I unpack? It won't take long. Most of it's going in the laundry bin."

"Sure. But do you want to eat out? You won't want to cook tonight, and I've not done any shopping for you bar the essentials."

"Why don't we slum it and have pizzas delivered? They won't be up to Papa Piero's standard, but I've eaten out so much I'm suffering from menu fatigue."

"Fine by me. What would you like?"

"Something simple. Margherita."

"Consider it done."

After they'd eaten, she curled up on the sofa. "So tell me the news. How's the case going?"

"Frankly? It's not. We've got one suspect and that's on the flimsiest of evidence. In fact it's not even evidence. It's supposition. Can I bore you by telling you about it? Emily thinks I'm barking, and half the time Morton thinks I've lost the plot. Half the time I think they're both right."

Katie grinned. "Come on, it's not that bad. Talk me through what you've got. It might make things clearer in your own mind."

"I shouldn't, but I'm past caring. OK. We have four suspicious deaths, the first occurring early in May, the last at the end of May. We believe they all died after taking drinks spiked with a very obscure poison known to be favoured by Russian assassins. We've identified someone by the name of Alex Barron as being close to the Round Church site at the time one of the spiked drinks was left. She was found guilty of causing threatening behaviour some years ago but has since dropped off the radar completely. She appears to have a decent unearned income and likes to live in modern upmarket properties. She didn't renew her passport in 2008 when it was due, and we can't find any public record of her since 2009. We do know now that she went to Roedean and a bit more about her background, but not much more.

"We issued an E-FIT showing her as we think she looks now. Frank Pell called me. She had hacked into their internal systems and said she could help them close the breach. They interviewed her, and the results of psychometric tests showed the woman to be amoral and a risk-taker. Pell was advised not to engage her. He says she then began stalking him and they had to warn her off.

"We've had two brief sightings of her since the pictures were issued, both in the vicinity of Maids Causeway, each time on an expensive men's bike. Margaret identified a smart new housing development off the Causeway where she thinks Alex lives. The development is held by a British company with an offshore parent. It has a director who's called Naseby and who works with the same firm advising the corporate owner of the last house where we know she lived. That too is owned by an offshore company. Stephanie noticed that Naseby is the name of a civil war battleground. Two of the eight Causeway properties are apparently rented by men with names very similar to two other battlegrounds. She can't find any information on either of them. She thinks they are phoney, and that the development is a money laundering operation."

He paused for a moment and sipped the last of his wine. Katie unfurled herself and went over to the kitchen and took a fresh bottle from the fridge.

"Already it sounds a credible theory, but why would she do it? Why would anyone do it?"

"We've no idea. It's been suggested she's suffering from an anti-social personality disorder."

"You mean a sociopath? Or a psychopath?"

"Maybe. Maybe not. She might be on the autism spectrum. We just don't know."

"What about the Russian connection? You haven't mentioned that at all."

"This is where Emily thinks I've lost it completely. But you found out about Oksana Baranova. My friend Paco showed me a photo on his mobile, taken by his informer, of Oksana's daughter, named Saskia Baranova, who apparently lives in Cambridge. She looks like Alex."

"And Saskia is another diminutive of Alexandra?"

"Precisely."

"Alex Barron. So what is she calling herself now?"

"No idea. My guess is that after her run in with Sandton & Pell she changed it to something completely different. If her family do have links to organised crime, getting her a new passport and ID would be no problem."

"What do you mean, run in?"

"Remember I said she started stalking Pell after they refused to engage her? They retaliated somehow, but are being somewhat coy about it. I suspect their response was, shall we say, fairly robust?"

"Crikey." Katie wasn't entirely sure she liked the sound of that. Upwood didn't seem too worried though, so she assumed he must have thought their response proportionate. And then the thought occurred to her that having a firm able to make robust responses on behalf of their own might be no bad thing. "How will you find her?"

"We shall have to keep looking. Literally. Watching camera feeds from the Causeway area and possibly even covert surveillance. If she is living in Queen Anne's Mews, it has to be in one or other of the two 'battleground' houses. All the others check out."

Katie sighed. "All I can say is good luck."

"We're going to need it."

"Will she kill again?"

"She's left no forensic evidence. Quite likely, I should say."

"People living on the streets must be very anxious."

"Poor naked wretches."

"What?"

"Poor naked wretches. It's from King Lear."

"Not one I know. Why did you say it?"

"Lear is becoming more and more deranged after the betrayal by his daughters. He is outside during a severe storm. He suddenly realises that when he was king, he gave too little consideration to the plight of the homeless.

"Poor naked wretches, whereso'er you are,
That bide the pelting of this pitiless storm,
How shall your houseless heads and unfed sides,
Your looped and windowed raggedness, defend you
From seasons such as these? Oh, I have ta'en
Too little care of this!"

"How on earth do you remember all that?"

Upwood laughed. "It was one of the texts for my A Levels. It was performed at Tolethorpe by the Stamford Shakespeare Company last year. I took June and Jeff there. While I was waiting for you in Arrivals, I looked it up again."

"Is Tolethorpe the open-air theatre?"

"Have you not been?"

"No."

"I must take you. It's magical."

"What made you think of it just now? Poor naked wretches I mean?"

"Lear was feeling absolutely powerless when he said that. It's how I feel now. Knowing that Alex could strike again and I'm powerless to defend the homeless."

"Can you not put them all into temporary housing?"

"It wouldn't work. Most wouldn't agree to go. And short of locking them up there's sod all we can do about it. We can't have officers keeping them under surveillance 24/7.

"By an odd coincidence, Alex's Sixth Form Head, as she was at the time, recalls her giving a very compelling performance of Lear in the 'poor naked wretches' scene. I can't help thinking it might be significant, but I can't for the life of me see how."

"It must be coincidence. If she played the lead in Wozzeck and worried about 'we poor people', I'd have been more impressed if that phrase had come to mind."

"So would I. She was said to be good at drama, not opera."

She laughed. "Don't be daft. You know what I mean. Lear is standard school fare. There's no reason at all why you shouldn't both know it." She sighed. "I wish I could help."

"Just being a sounding board is a help. But I did think of something while I was waiting in Arrivals. After you'd done some research on Oksana Baranova you said you thought her son was running her late husband's business. Could you have another look and see if his name is mentioned? Paco thinks it might be Felix, but I don't want to pursue it with him in case he thinks I'm interfering on his patch."

In truth there was little point in her carrying out this research, as he was confident they would soon identify him. But it would give her something to do. As soon as he'd suggested it, he realised how patronising it sounded. Fortunately, Katie did not seem worried by the request. She could access the English freesheets for the Costa del Sol easily enough.

"Of course. It shouldn't take long. Do you think he's involved?"

"I've no reason to, except there are two 'battleground' houses. And if there is money laundering going on he could be behind that. Oh, and we think he may have bought the men's bike she's been riding. Someone's trying to find a birth certificate for him."

"But you won't investigate the money laundering, will you? Madam Adams would never allow it."

"No. It would be for SOCA if it's on any scale at all. It's just a niggle. I'd like to know more about him."

"Do you think Alex is involved with the prostitute murders?"

"I don't know. And they are not my concern. But her brother might be controlling the rival pimp. Prostitution and drug-running are often connected. And the proceeds of drug-running need washing, as Paco put it."

"But you're not involved in any of that. It's the murders you have to focus on."

"I know. I know. You sound just like Emily. But my mind goes on wandering because I keep running into brick walls with my own cases. I just hope to God that the surveillance team at Queen's Walk will give us a solid lead. If they don't, I've no idea what we'll do."

Chapter 56

By the end of the following Tuesday the surveillance officers had observed the tenants of all the occupied houses come and go. Charles Sullivan at Number 5 left home by car shortly before eight each morning, returning between six and seven in the evening. His wife Mary cycled to and from the store where she worked. The Truffauts at Number 6 shared the journey to and from the biomedical campus. Favino at Number 7 walked to and from King's College, a journey of a little over a mile. Of greater interest was the driver of a car seen leaving and returning to either Number 3 or Number 4.

After that evening's briefing, Upwood was updating Emily Adams. It was not going well.

"So you're now convinced that this woman Alex Barron, possibly aka Saskia Baranova, is living in a house owned by an offshore company and that it is a money laundering operation. Is that an adequate summary?"

"The house isn't owned by an offshore company, Emily. The company that owns it is registered in England but is itself in offshore ownership."

"You're being pedantic."

Upwood didn't rise to this bait. "And I wouldn't say convinced. It is a strong line of enquiry. But the names of the tenants are suggestive of a link with one of the solicitors at the firm which provided a director of another company, also in offshore ownership, that owned the Riverside property where Alex once lived."

"This Civil War idea? It's preposterous. I've never heard anything so ludicrous in my entire career."

"I am not pursuing the money laundering issue. At the moment our priority is either to eliminate this woman from our enquiries, or charge her.

"The surveillance team have photographed the driver of a BMW that appears to be garaged at Queen Anne's Mews, although we do not know at which. It is, though, registered to Philip Haw so we assume it is at Number 4. The driver is wearing a baseball hat and sunglasses so there is only the lower half of the face visible. We've asked Joan, the super recogniser who first helped us identify Alex, to have a look and see what she can tell us.

"In the meantime, we are looking at footage from the cameras on the roundabout nearest Queen's Walk to establish which direction the car went in. We hope to learn that tomorrow."

Emily glared at him. "I'm not at all happy with the way this case is going, James. How many weeks is it now? Twelve? You've got nowhere."

Not true, thought Upwood, although he knew better than to argue with her when she was in this sort of mood. "Eleven. If it is Alex Barron who's responsible, we're up against an exceptionally intelligent woman who almost certainly has a sociopathic or psychopathic nature. One who appears to have considerable resources. And sufficiently forensically aware to have hit on a method of murder that provides no forensic evidence. And the killings are apparently random. It's about as difficult a set of circumstances as you could find." He leant back in his chair. "If you've any helpful suggestions to make I should be more than happy to hear them." He held his breath, wondering if he'd gone too far. Implicit in his last sentence was the criticism that all she'd done since the whole sorry saga started was complain.

For a moment he thought she was going to give him an almighty bollocking. He was relying on her seeing the truth of what he'd told her.

She swivelled round in her chair and gazed out of the window. Moments later she turned back. "If you're so confident, why don't you arrest her?"

He looked at her in astonishment. "We can't possibly do that. She may well suspect we are getting close if she clocked the speed camera. And even if she didn't, she would probably have been told questions were being asked about Queen Anne's Mews. I'd bet good money both Number 3 and 4 are as clean as a whistle. She'll be using a lock-up or another property to store the stuff she needs. Maybe even the bike. So you know what the outcome of an arrest would be."

Emily looked thoroughly angry, with spots of high colour in her cheeks.

"You know as well as I do, Emily. We'd end up releasing her. And then she'd assume yet another identity and, in all probability, leave the country."

Still she said nothing.

"So somehow we have to find something concrete on her."

She stood up, signalling that the meeting was at an end. "I'll give you one more week to find her."

He decided not to ask her what the penalty for failure would be.

The following day it was confirmed that the BMW had crossed straight over the roundabout and entered Newmarket Road. Officers were able to access footage from a CCTV camera outside a building society close to the junction with Coldhams Lane. The vehicle had turned into it, as they had seen Alex do on her bike some days previously. After that they could find no further sighting.

Stephanie had been marooned at Parkside for the last two days and had spent hour after hour studying the area between Queen's Walk and Coldhams Lane, as well as the area immediately surrounding it, on Google Street View and on satellite imagery. She had concentrated on the residential areas, ignoring the large retail developments. There were no rows of lockup garages to be found. But her eyes were constantly drawn back to the New Street Allotments. There were plenty of sheds, any one of which would be ideal for Alex's purposes. In Mo's absence she reported her findings to Morton, and he instructed her colleague Nick to investigate. In turn he reported his findings at the evening briefing.

"I think we're very close. I took both pictures, the original and the E-FIT, and showed them to a few people working their plots. Two said they didn't recognise her, but one man says he may do. He isn't positive, and judging by how milky his eyes are I'm not surprised. I should think his eyesight is very poor. He reckons he saw a young person, probably a woman, although he's not even certain of that, several weeks ago. He said she was anonymous looking. I think he meant androgenous."

"Sir?" A voice came from the back of the room. "Maybe Nick's jumping to conclusions because he knows Frank Pell described her as androgenous. He might just have meant the person was unmemorable."

"A fair point. Either interpretation is possible. In any event, we get the sense, I think, that she's not easy to describe. Carry on, Nick."

"It's what he said that's really interesting. Apparently, she asked him if he knew anyone who wasn't using their allotment at the moment who might be prepared to lend it to her for the summer. He only knew of one. He pointed it out to me. He had told her it belonged to Jim Saunders and that he lived somewhere on Beche Road. He'd broken a leg in a motorcycle accident so couldn't work on his allotment for the time being. I went over to look at the plot. It is overgrown but the weeds in front of the door to the shed have been trodden down and there is a conspicuously new looking padlock on it. There are also what look like cycle tread marks on the path leading to the shed. I've taken a few photos."

"Well done, Nick. Anything else?"

"Well I know I should have waited for instructions, but as it was so easy to track down Mr Saunders, I thought I'd go and see him. He was at home. He confirms that no one has asked his permission to use his allotment, or shed, and that the padlock on the door has been there for years. He says he's more than happy for us to search it."

It was the ambiguity of the gender of the person seen at the allotments that reminded Stephanie she had not reported her finding the birth certificate for Alex's brother. She relayed it now. His name was Feliks Baranov. He was a couple of years older than his sister. Now they had more solid proof of her connections to the criminal underworld. That said, Morton was furious she hadn't reported it as soon as she'd found out. It potentially made matters even more complicated than they already were. He kept these thoughts to himself, it being hard enough to keep the team motivated as it was.

Morton allocated the actions for the next day. He also confirmed that Joan believed the driver of the BMW was almost certainly Alex Barron. A long straight nose, a deep philtrum and a dimpled chin were distinctive to those with a keen eye. But was it? Might other sightings of Alex have been of her brother instead?

Upwood went to see his boss. "I need advice, Emily."

"Not like you, James. You're quite likely to ignore mine, rather than seek it." She gave him a frosty smile. He decided to ignore her criticism. That it wasn't particularly true was beside the point.

He explained about the allotment shed. "So, do we obtain a warrant and look inside, or continue surveillance on Alex? If we don't go into the shed, we're no further forward."

"And she has no reason not to continue her spree, to use your word."

"But we've every reason to believe she is forensically aware, so if we go in and find evidence clearly linked to the crimes but not to her, we've blown our cover."

"Am I right in thinking that her bike, the men's bike, is a specialist one?"

"So I believe."

"Perhaps it has unusual treads."

For the first time in the entire investigation, Emily had finally made a useful suggestion. Upwood returned home that evening in a slightly more positive frame of mind. His mood was shattered when Katie called him.

Chapter 57

There were red flushes on her cheeks when she opened the door. He kissed her lightly and passed into the main living room. There on a table was a magnificent bouquet of flowers and foliage. It was unusual, he thought. Marigolds. Yellow, orange, russet. Single and double. Not just unusual. Odd. He'd never seen a bouquet like it.

"Look at the card that came with it."

He leaned over and examined it. A standard florist's card, with rather childish writing. Probably written by the shop worker. *Welcome home, my dear. How nice to have you with us again.*

Katie was seething with rage. "How does he know I'm back? How does he know where I live?"

Upwood sighed. It had only been a matter of time before something like this happened, although he had not expected action so quickly following Katie's return. "Who knew you were coming home?"

"My senior partner, Paul Dixon, and his secretary for sure. Any number of other people at the firm probably. Members of my own team, certainly."

"So potentially a large pool of people in an accountancy firm where he may have had contacts."

"Well, the senior partner was a contact, for sure. They were in the same Lodge."

Upwood looked startled. "Were they? You never told me that."

"I overheard Dixon say so on the phone, the day after MacKay was convicted. He didn't mention him by name, but said 'It's a bad business. A very bad business'."

"He could have meant anything, surely?"

"It was the look on his face when I walked into the office, as though he'd been caught red-handed. He was very embarrassed. And there's no other explanation for that."

"Even if he were in contact, he'd never have given him your address. It's unthinkable."

"All MacKay had to do was get someone to follow me home from work, I suppose."

She was right of course. Why was it when trying to deal with her problems his critical thinking skills seemed to fly out of the window?

"Do you know what makes me really angry about this? Grief. Grief, that's what marigolds mean."

He groaned. "For heaven's sake. That's a bit fanciful, isn't it?"

"If you google the language of flowers, one of the first sites you come to says that's what they mean. I think that's what MacKay did. Or got someone to do it for him. Perhaps someone who didn't look any further, because interestingly, if you dig deeper, you find the most common associations are with much more positive emotions."

"Well, he does sound pleased to have you back..."

"Damn you, James. It's not funny."

"I don't think we should try to read too much into it. Are you sure it isn't someone at work?"

"No one there would dream of it. And why no sender's name?" She looked at the card again. "When have you ever seen a bouquet of marigolds?"

"Well, I haven't...but I don't get many bouquets sent me."

It was a further attempt to lighten the mood. She was having none of it. "But you like flowers. You told me ages ago you buy them for yourself sometimes. Not many men do that. Have you ever even seen them in a florist?"

And of course, he hadn't. At least not that he could recall. But then why would he even recall such a thing? He didn't like them, truth be told. Didn't like orange as a colour and in particular didn't like their smell. It always reminded him of the small, mean, little garden of his least favourite granny. Sticky, too, he remembered. No, didn't like them.

And liked them less now. He shook his head. Then he got out his mobile and took pictures from a number of different angles. "Can you take some, too? And a close up of the card?"

She did so. "So will you try to find out about the florist and the sender?"

"Not possible, Katie. It can't be justified. But there's nothing to stop you trying and you've still got a few days off left. You'd get a much more sympathetic response than a uniformed officer."

Her initial response was anger. But only a moment's reflection told her it was the right idea. And now of course she had the photos to help her, blast him. Even so, how difficult could it be? A bouquet like this would be memorable and not many florists would be able to provide one.

In an odd sort of way, Upwood was less worried about the flowers than he might have been. He was too used to seeing criminal activity escalate. A bouquet was a lot less threatening than a physical attack and it reinforced in his mind the idea that MacKay was simply trying to annoy and intimidate Katie. But in less sanguine moments, the idea that MacKay still intended her real harm haunted him.

The following morning, Katie phoned the major florists to ask if they could supply a bouquet of mixed marigolds. Only one sounded promising. The next day she called in and showed the shopkeeper the photos. "He didn't leave his name. I think I know who it is, but I don't want to thank him if I'm wrong. I've only been out with him twice."

The florist laughed sympathetically, although in truth she was sceptical about Katie's story. It was an odd message from someone she claimed only to have been out with a couple of times. Still, not her problem. "Not sure I've seen your man. It was a youngish lad came in to ask if I could do it. Then he came in a couple of days later to collect them."

"Please. Can you tell me his name?"

"Sorry, love. No idea. The lad paid cash. In advance."

Katie idly wondered how the florist knew what to charge for what was clearly an unusual bouquet of blooms. "Didn't you ask his name when he ordered them?"

"I was busy. Wasn't thinking. I was more concerned about whether the wholesaler could get me what he wanted. I'd got two weddings I was preparing for."

Katie left, none the wiser, but not remotely surprised. No wonder Upwood wouldn't entertain the idea of putting police resource into it.

Chapter 58

On Wednesday morning the bike retailer had confirmed to Nick that the tyre treads in his photo were unusual and similar to, if not exactly the same as, those which had been fitted to the bike in question.

There followed a long and serious debate between Upwood, Emily and, at Upwood's insistence, Morton. There was little doubt in any of their minds that they had found Alex's secret storeroom. The question, however, was when to search it.

"If we go in, she'll know soon enough. Will she then flee the country? That's my concern." The concern showed on Upwood's face.

"If she does, she'll not come back. And she might be planning to leave already for all we know. I think we have to go in as soon as possible." Morton was determined to see her brought to justice.

"If we go in too soon, we may not find enough evidence to convict her. Then we are in a worse position, even, than we are now." Emily, ever cautious. "Should we not keep up the surveillance for now?"

"Unless you are prepared to see it increased substantially, that won't help us much. Remember, at the moment we are only monitoring movements into and out of Queen's Walk. We'd have to be prepared to tail her every movement. There's a real chance she'll try to kill again. We can't let her do that. It would be unforgiveable."

"I know, James, I do accept that. If we were to up the surveillance, how would we do it?"

"At the moment we can manage it quite easily as officers go in and out of the house on Maids Causeway from the rear. There is little chance she's aware of it, unless one of them shows himself at the window at the wrong moment. But if we are to follow her, we have to be prepared to follow by car or bike – we don't know where the bike is currently."

"Or foot," said Morton. "She might simply walk into town. So either we have officers deployed three ways or we might lose her."

Upwood considered the problem for a moment. "Perhaps not. We need two cars, one west of the Mews, facing east, and one east of the Mews facing west. Each might have a bike propped up on the pavement against the nearest wall. And be prepared to abandon both vehicles if she leaves on foot. Even so, 24/7 it's a huge commitment."

"It's your call, James. You're SIO. I'll back whatever decision you take."

"Ma'am, if we go in and find material evidence, we have to arrest her immediately. We can't risk losing her. That means we have to obtain warrants in advance, for her arrest and for the search of both houses with bogus tenants."

"If that's what it means, so be it."

Upwood decided they would go ahead. In his view, further surveillance would only lead to delay with no guarantee that it would leave them in a better situation than now.

On that basis, it was decided to search the shed late morning of the following day, on the assumption that Alex was unlikely to visit while people were working their plots.

At 11.00 am the next day, having been advised that Alex was definitely at home, the team set off for the allotments. As soon as they cut off the padlock and opened the door to the shed, it was apparent that they had found her storage site. There was a man's bike, in an unusual shade of light greenish/blue, a box of latex gloves labelled 'high risk', a small tin of black enamel which had been opened, a box of syringes and other items potentially of interest. Because of space restrictions there were only two officers conducting the search and they were in full haz mat gear. Since no one knew what form the poison might take, precautions were exceptionally high.

One item was particularly intriguing: a cutting from the local paper about a conference. Held in the early part of the year, its focus had been on the promotion of inward investment into the IT and science industry parks around the city. One speaker had been Frank Pell. The nature of the article was such that Upwood was soon informed of it. He established that Pell would see him immediately and made his way to Sandton & Pell's offices, leaving Morton to supervise the team effecting the arrest and the searches. Upwood was glad of the distraction of going to see Pell. Until he knew Alex was safely in custody, he would find it very hard to settle to any constructive work.

"Mr Pell. It's very good of you to see me at such short notice."

"I'm more than happy to help."

"You spoke at a conference here in March dealing with the issues about attracting inward investment."

"I did."

"Who organised it?"

"Some outfit in London. I can't immediately think of their name. Is it important? I can easily check."

"No, don't trouble yourself yet. What I am sure you can help me with is a transcript of your talk, and a copy of the delegate list if you have one."

"No problem." Pell activated his screen. He typed rapidly on the keyboard and sent two documents to print. He handed them over.

"That's very helpful. Did your talk mention the homeless in general, or street-sleepers in particular?"

"No. Why would it?"

"But you were asked about them in the Q&A session I believe, by a reporter for the Herald."

Pell thought for a moment. "You're right, I was. He wanted to know whether the city's problem was severe enough to inhibit inward investment."

"How did you answer?"

"So far as I recall, I said that I wasn't qualified to offer a useful opinion."

"Were there any follow up questions?"

"I think he may have asked if the city was doing enough to deal with the problem."

"And your response to that?"

"That I thought they were doing what they could with limited resources. And I mentioned that there are several charities working in the area."

"And that was it?"

"I think so, yes."

"The article in the Herald quotes you as saying, 'we should do everything in our power to get these people off the streets'."

Pell shook his head. "I doubt I would have used those words."

"But did you say anything that could have been interpreted that way?"

"I don't recall. I may have done."

"What would you have meant by it?"

Pell slapped his hand on the desk. "I care about it, OK? My nephew ended up on the streets. He died on the streets. It's not something I would want widely known. My mother is still very sensitive about it. I've supported the charities here as a result of that experience."

Upwood apologised for having raised what was clearly a painful subject for the man.

"Did you see Alex Barron at the conference?"

Upwood's sudden change of tack took Pell completely by surprise. "No. I can't imagine why she would be there."

"Networking again, perhaps?" Upwood looked at the delegate list. Her name was not on it.

"Was the conference filmed?"

"Quite possibly. You'd have to ask the organisers." He tapped on his keyboard again and a copy of the agenda printed out, bearing the name of both organiser and sponsors. He passed it to Upwood.

On his return to base, Upwood asked that someone contact the conference organisers and ask about film coverage. A film had been made of proceedings and, unusually, because the event had been a public one they did not insist on a warrant. Once it arrived, it took Joan little time to recognise Alex sitting in the second row of the audience. What on earth had she been doing there? And what name had she been using? There had been one hundred and thirty-three delegates at the conference. Each one would have to be checked.

Chapter 59

Morton headed the team which at 12.15 pm began service of the warrants. He knew Upwood would have liked to lead the arrest himself, but also knew his boss had been told more than once to concentrate more on the strategic aspects of his role. For Morton, the arrest of a suspect for multiple murders would be a milestone in his career.

Morton gathered his team at the entrance to Queen's Walk for a final briefing. He scanned the road. All was quiet. It was not the kind of residential street where there might be curtain twitchers. A cat stalked towards them and sent a Blackbird up from the top of the hoarding, sounding a sharp alarm call. "Right. As per the briefing: Jack and Sam, round to the rear. Don't let her leave by the back door. The rest of you with me. When we've arrested her, Bob, take her back to Parkside and get her processed. Simon, you and Mark search Number 3. Richard and the rest of the team search Number 4." They made their way up the cul-de-sac. Morton banged loudly on the front door. "Police! Open up!" Only moments later Alex Barron opened the door. It was almost as though she had been waiting for them. A little taller than the average woman, she was slender, with a boyish figure and dressed entirely in black. Her hair was shorter than it had been at the time of her conviction. Just the right length to tuck into a baseball cap. She appraised them silently. "I am Detective Inspector Herbert Harrison. Alex Barron, I am arresting you on suspicion of the murders of Sally Bremner on 3rd May 2011, of Joseph Walters, who died on 10th May 2011, Kevin Broome on 13th May 2011, and Peter Johnson on 30th May 2011 and the attempted murder of Frederick Cornwall on 6th June 2011." As he recited the caution, a brief, sardonic smile was her only response. Two of his officers looked at each other, bemused. Neither had known that Morton was only a nickname.

Morton told her they also had warrants to execute searches of Numbers 3 and 4 together with their garages. He was interested to see if his mention of Number 3 elicited a response. It did not. Not the least sign of a reaction. Alex looked thoroughly relaxed. He had a strong suspicion that they would learn little from interviewing her. The arrest had the feel of an anti-climax, and he found the proceedings unsettling.

Alex was escorted to Parkside and processed. She confirmed her name as Alex Barron, which they were confident was not the one she was currently using, but one under which she had been known at the time of her conviction. She confirmed her address as Number 4, then asked for her London based solicitor, who proved unable to attend until late afternoon. This actually suited Morton quite well. He hoped the forensic team might be able to report something useful from the shed by then.

The first interview began at five thirty, conducted by Morton and Debra. The solicitor introduced himself as John Mortimer, a man in his fifties. He wore a dark suit of fine cloth, evidently hand-tailored, over an immaculate white shirt, with just the right length of cuff on show. Gold cufflinks, naturally. A club or regimental tie? Not a field of Morton's expertise. Then he noticed the shoes, highly polished black loafers with tassels. Perhaps not a regimental tie, then. Nonetheless, a man careful of his appearance. After the formalities were completed, Morton addressed his first question to Alex. "What is your relationship to Philip Haw?"

"There is none."

"Who is he?"

"I think he lived there before me."

"Why would the letting agents say he was still the tenant?"

"Ask them."

"Do you pay rent?"

"No."

"Does someone pay rent on your behalf?"

"There is no rent."

"Why would that be?"

"I did some work for the company that owns the property."

"You mean Keresley Property Ltd?"

"Yes."

"So they let you live there rent free?"

"Yes."

"And pay your utility charges?"

"Yes."

"How long have you lived there?"

"About ten months."

"With whom did you deal at Keresley?"

"Jack Finnegan."

"What was his role?"

"Head of Finance."

"What work did you do for the company?"

"I can't tell you."

Pulling teeth would have been less painful. "Why?"

"I am bound by a non-disclosure agreement."

Her solicitor, John Mortimer, who had not uttered a word so far, now intervened, tapping his uncapped fountain pen on the leather cover of his notebook, in which he had yet to make a single note. "DI Harrison, if you wish to pursue this line of enquiry, I suggest you do so through Keresley and avoid wasting further time here on it."

Ignoring him, Morton addressed himself to Alex again. "Where were you living before that?"

"An apartment in Riverside."

Morton consulted his notes. "Riverside, Number 38. For twelve months."

It was not a question, and she made no response. Morton recalled the advice Anna had given before the interview. It boiled down to asking simple, not compound, questions and not expecting her to volunteer information. Spot on.

"Where were you living before that?"

She smirked. "You'll have that on file, officer."

Damn her. "Was it at 42 Brooklands Avenue?"

"Yes."

"And before that?"

Mortimer leaned forward and intervened once more. "How can that be remotely relevant, DI Harrison?"

"We need as full a picture of Miss Barron as possible. These are very serious charges."

"For which you have produced not a single shred of evidence." He sat back in his chair, a faintly smug look on his face.

Morton kept his eyes fixed on Alex. "Please answer the question, Miss Barron." She smiled at him. Damn and blast her. "Where were you living before Brooklands Avenue?"

"I was travelling."

"Where?"

"Around Europe."

"For how long?"

"Several years."

"In which countries did you spend the most time?"

"I wasn't counting. I didn't stay anywhere long."

"Why?"

"Why not?"

"Can you prove it?"

"No."

This was going nowhere. "What were you doing cycling in the vicinity of Round Church on the evening of Friday 3rd June?"

"I've no idea."

"What d'you mean, you have no idea?"

Mortimer intervened again, somewhat superciliously. "I think you'll find she means she has no recollection of the event, officer."

Morton addressed Alex again. "Do you recall where you were that evening?"

"No." She was still smirking, clearly enjoying every minute. Morton had rarely found an interview such hard work.

"Do you often cycle round the streets at night?"

"Sometimes."

"Why?"

"Why not?"

At this point another officer knocked on the door and put his head round. Morton suspended the interview and went outside, leaving Debra with Alex and her lawyer. He was given a brief report on the forensic findings at the shed, which included the fact that no trace of the poison had been found. He took the opportunity to arrange that someone speak to the property company, Keresley, with a whole host of questions.

After five minutes or so Morton returned to the interview room and restarted the formalities, reminding her that she was still under caution. "What can you tell us about the shed on Allotment 19 at New Road?"

"Nothing."

"We have a witness who says you asked him if he knew of an untended allotment there."

No response.

"Did you speak to someone at the allotments about an untended site?"

"No."

"How do you account for the fact that your bike was found in the shed at Number 19?"

"I don't have a bike."

"But you have admitted riding one around the city's streets. Have you not?"

"Yes."

"We have just had confirmation that your fingerprints are all over the bike in the shed." Once more she made no response. "So whose is the bike?"

"I imagine it belonged to the previous tenant."

"How did it get into the shed?"

"I don't know. It was stolen."

Of course, she would say that, wouldn't she?

"When was this?"

"A week ago."

"Where from?"

"The Burleigh Arms."

"The Burleigh Arms on Maids Causeway?"

"Yes."

"But you could easily walk there. Why cycle?"

"Why not?"

"Did you report it?"

"Yes."

"In person?"

"Yes."

"When did you report it stolen?"

"The next day."

"Where?"

"Parkside."

"Did they give you a crime reference number?"

"No."

"Why not?"

"Because I was not the owner."

This was real *Through the Looking Glass* stuff and Morton felt as though he was losing his grip on reality. The answers to some of the questions were preposterous, yet she delivered them as though it was all entirely normal.

Soon after, Morton suspended the interview for the evening. Alex would be held in custody overnight and interviewing would resume in the morning. Debra was charged with finding out if the bike theft was reported. Morton was quietly confident that she had, and the following morning they had the proof. The officer to whom she had spoken recalled that she had not seemed unduly concerned about the theft given that the bike was an expensive one. In a city where something like fifty bikes were reported missing every week, he knew enough to recognise the manufacturer, Bianchi, as one of light-weight carbon road racing cycles. The fact that the model was a man's bike, and the fact that she said she was not the owner, was enough to make him discourage her from pursuing the matter, since she clearly could not make an insurance claim. He said she didn't seem unduly put out by that either. In fact, he thought she was trying it on. She was, of course, just not in the way he thought. Morton was fairly sure she had guessed that she'd been clocked on the speed camera in Maids Causeway.

When the interview resumed the next day, he informed Alex that, on Detective Superintendent Adams' authority, her detention was to be extended for a further twelve hours beyond the initial twenty-four-hour period due to expire at one o'clock that afternoon. He asked her about each of the suspicious items taken away from the shed for forensic evaluation. He had already been advised that, unlike the bike, there were no fingerprints on them. Alex denied all knowledge of them. When he asked her what she had done with the poison, she laughed quietly.

"Miss Barron, you have also been seen driving a BMW whose registered keeper is also Philip Haw, the previous tenant at your address. Who gave you permission to drive it?"

"I do not drive it."

"We have you on camera, leaving Queen's Walk."

Morton paused for a response, and remembered with increasing irritation that unless he posed a question, she would remain silent. "Do you deny driving that vehicle?"

"Yes."

He realised she had to deny it otherwise it was on a licence in a name she would be reluctant to disclose. Her other option, driving without a licence, was a minor offence she would be equally anxious to avoid. He turned his attention to her banking arrangements instead, a matter that also annoyed him. Stephanie had researched this and found no record of an account in her name with any of the major banks. Whether she hadn't pursued it diligently enough, or whether the building society had themselves been less than diligent, he didn't know. But when arrested, Alex had been carrying a debit card issued by Nationwide Building Society, but no others, and no store or loyalty cards. The Nationwide card had been issued in the name of Alex Baron. She had, when questioned at the time, said that she used their online banking service and gave them her log on details.

"For what reason is your account with the Nationwide in the name of Alex Baron? With only one 'r'?"

"They made a mistake."

"Did you not notice?"

"Not straight away."

"Did you not have it corrected?"

"No. It worked."

Scrutiny of the account showed that there were none of the transactions one would normally see on a current account. There were, of course, no rental or utility payments. There were virtually no card transactions except cash withdrawals. There were occasional, sizeable deposits into the account. It was the shortest paper trail any of them had ever seen. She offered no meaningful explanation for conducting her financial affairs in this way. When questioned, she claimed that she had no need to submit income tax returns since she had little or no income per se. She received occasional deposits which represented what she described as 'capital draw downs'.

Morton continued his questioning for some time, achieving absolutely nothing. "DS Graf, are there any questions you'd like to put to Miss Barron?"

"Yes. Who is your email account with?"

"I don't have one."

"How do you contact your friends?"

"What friends?"

"Are you suggesting you don't have any?"

"Why should I need friends?"

Debra could think of no sensible answer. "How do you spend your time?"

"This and that."

"Do you have any hobbies?"

Alex smiled. "Poker."

"Do you play for high stakes?"

"Sometimes."

"Do you win?"

Alex grinned. "Sometimes."

"How do you collect your winnings?"

"Bitcoin." Great. Another trail they could not follow.

Morton suspended the interview, indicating their intention to apply to the magistrate's court for a further extension to her period of detention. After conferring with his boss, Morton accepted Upwood's decision that he would handle the interview the next day. In truth he was glad to be relieved of the responsibility,

Chapter 60

"Miss Barron, I want to start this morning with questions about your family." Upwood waited, but of course she made no response. He knew he'd just fallen at the first hurdle, albeit a very small one, but it irked him that it clearly gave her satisfaction.

"Who was your mother?"

"I don't know."

"Who then is Olga Barron?"

"She was my stepmother."

"Is she dead?"

"Yes."

"When did she die?"

"Soon after I left school."

"Which was when?"

"1997."

"How did she die?"

"In a boating accident."

"Please tell us the full story Miss Barron. It will save us all a lot of time." As soon as he'd said it, he knew that's exactly what he'd get: a story.

"She was staying in Nice with a friend. They went sailing. She fell overboard and her body was never found."

"Where were you at the time?"

"At home, in London."

"At what address?"

"12 Markham Mews, Chelsea."

"Did you go out to Nice?"

"I went out immediately, but the authorities could find no trace of her."

"Where is your father?"

"He died too."

"The full story, please Miss Barron."

"I can't tell you much. I hardly knew him. I was a small child when he died. He was in Sierra Leone. Or was it Senegal? West Africa, anyway."

"How did he die?"

"Heart attack, I think. A stroke maybe. I'm not sure."

"What nationality was he?"

"American? Canadian? Don't know. Didn't care. Didn't like him."

"Your Sixth Form Head at Roedean tells us that your father was alive while you were there, and you enrolled at the age of eleven. So you were hardly an infant when he died, if he died, were you?"

"They must be mistaken."

"Your stepmother. Did you like her?"

She raised an eyebrow. "Not much."

"Who looked after you after her accident?"

"No one. I was old enough to take care of myself."

"How did you manage her affairs?"

"I didn't. Her solicitor did."

"Who was that?"

"Paul Prentice, Prentice & Co. In Chelsea."

"How did you manage for money?"

"My father had set up a trust fund before he died. My stepmother was one of the trustees. Paul Prentice was the other."

"Does Mr Prentice have control now?"

"Yes."

"Will you gain control yourself at some stage?"

"On my thirty-fifth birthday."

"DCI Upwood, on behalf of my client I must protest. In the strongest possible terms. These questions are intrusive, intolerable and can be of no conceivable relevance to your enquiry."

"I note your concern Mr Mortimer, but I shall follow whatever line of questioning I think appropriate." He turned to face Alex again. "Tell me about your brother."

"I don't have a brother."

"Your Sixth Form Head at Roedean clearly remembers his visiting you there in your final year. You spoke Russian together."

She laughed. "He wasn't my brother. He was Irina's."

"Irina Rednikova?"

"Yes."

"How was it that you spoke Russian to them both?"

"She taught me. We liked winding the teachers up."

"Where did you go to school before Roedean?"

"I didn't."

"Were you home schooled?"

"I had private tutors. One of them was Russian." She smirked again.

Upwood sighed inwardly. It was not just a story she was weaving. A lot of it was pure fantasy. But my word, didn't she tell it well? Talk about a well-rehearsed script. No wonder the Shand woman admired her acting skills. He decided to adjourn for the day. He was badly in need of some fresh air. And some serious thinking time. Meanwhile he tasked Debra with talking to Miss Shand again.

When Upwood and Debra returned to the interview room the following morning, Alex had no expression on her face. Mortimer wore a look of righteous indignation. "DCI Upwood. This is outrageous. You wasted half of yesterday with my client left languishing in a cell. You have produced not one iota of evidence against her. I demand that you release her immediately."

Upwood glanced at him briefly. "We shall hold her for as long as we see fit, in accordance with the warrant." He turned towards Alex. "Why did you lie to us about your brother Feliks?"

She stared at him. "What?"

"You told us that the young man who visited you at school was Irina's brother. She had no brother." She did not respond.

"He is your brother is he not?"

"No."

"Roedean's records clearly show that it was your brother who visited." Upwood was winging it here. The school's records of visitors did not go back that far. But Shand was adamant that Irina had no brother. She was an only child. Debra had tried prompting her recall of the boy's name, suggesting several beginning with F, but not Feliks. But it was enough. Shand volunteered the name Feliks. She remembered it because he had, she said, rather feline characteristics: moving silently, appearing alongside you without warning. She had found it rather unnerving. "Miss Shand gave us a very good description of him. Her recollection of you is very good too. Apparently, you were a very good actress. Do you remember her?"

She smirked but gave no answer.

"Do you remember Miss Shand?"

"No."

Frustrated he decided to change tack. "Why did you apply to join Sandton & Pell?"

"I didn't."

"But you were interviewed by Frank Pell and told him you could help mend security breaches. Why was that?"

"I was bored."

"You hacked into their systems. Why?"

"Because I could."

"Why them?"

"Why not?"

"What did you hope to gain?"

"Amusement."

"You know, of course, that hacking is illegal?"

"I caused no damage. I consider myself a White Hat."

Upwood glanced towards Debra, and she took the hint. "But White Hats breach a company's defences with the owner's permission. You did not have that, did you?" she asked. Alex made no response.

"Miss Barron, did you like Frank Pell?" He knew what the answer would be.

"Not much."

"Why did you stalk him?"

"DCI Upwood. Really! Who is this man Pell and what on earth does he have to do with the case?" Mortimer's attempt at righteous indignation was once again pure theatre.

"I repeat my question, Miss Barron. Why did you stalk him?"

"I did not."

"Mr Pell tells me you did. It was confirmed by one of his colleagues."

"They are mistaken, or lying."

"In my experience a stalker generally has strong feelings about the subject of their attention. Positive or negative. So did you like him or not?"

"Neither."

"So why stalk him?"

"I did not."

"Sandton & Pell can produce photographic evidence which suggests otherwise. How do you respond to that?"

"It's not difficult to manipulate digital photos."

"Why did you attend a seminar on inward investment at which Mr Pell was a speaker?"

"I don't recall it."

"We have a video recording showing you in the second row of the audience. I repeat my question. Why did you attend?"

"I must have been bored at the time."

"Why did you keep a press cutting about the seminar?"

"I did not."

"We found it in the shed. I am quite sure we shall find your DNA on it. After all, no one reads a newspaper with gloves on."

There was just the faintest flicker at last. Surprise? Alarm? Both Upwood and Debra registered it. He hoped the video recording of the interview would show it.

"That article quotes Mr Pell as saying, in relation to the city's rough sleepers, *'we should do everything in our power to get these people off the streets'*. Did you decide to support his aim by taking direct action?"

"No."

"Was it your part in King Lear at school that created your interest in homeless people?"

"I have no interest in homeless people whatsoever."

"I think you do, and it led you to kill them. And we shall prove it." Upwood knew this last remark was foolish, sheer bravado, and of course Alex did not rise to the bait. Mortimer, however, did.

"This is absolute nonsense, Mr Upwood. Why on earth would my client want to kill anyone, never mind rough sleepers whom she cannot possibly have known?"

It was Upwood's turn to smile. "Because she likes to win, perhaps. After all, her brother's one ahead of her at the moment."

"What in heaven's name is that supposed to mean?" The look of astonishment on Mortimer's face cheered Upwood hugely.

"I think we'll let Miss Barron work that one out." This time, she actually glared at Upwood. She was seething. Good. It was about time she started taking this seriously.

"Mr Upwood, I must protest. Again. You seem to have pulled together some of the flimsiest strands – I won't even grace them with the term evidence, since they are surely not – and concocted a story that is, frankly, complete bullshit. I demand that you stop this charade and release my client immediately."

"We are not finished yet, Mr Mortimer, not by a long shot."

Chapter 61

That evening, the meeting room was full. Upwood and Morton opened the briefing with a summary of the interviews so far. They gave a decent enough account, but the truth was that they had learnt practically nothing of value. He asked for feedback on the enquiries made while the interviews were underway.

Stephanie reported first. "I can find no record of Feliks Baranov following his birth. I imagine he went to Spain with his parents, although I have been unable to find a British passport for him. Presumably he assumed a different name, as did Alex. I did try looking for a male equivalent of Alex Barron, but none I found was a credible match.

"Then I investigated the father, John Barron. Conveniently, Alex tells us he's either American or Canadian, so it's no surprise I can find no trace of him. Nor can I find any trace of Olga Barron. The address she gave for her home in Chelsea is that of a hotel. It's been there for forty years. All thoroughly unhelpful, sorry."

"But it all paints a picture, does it not?"

A voice from the back of the room, carrying just a hint of sarcasm: "It makes her look guilty as hell, but it doesn't prove a thing. Sir."

"No, constable. But we press on. What have we learnt from the two house searches?"

The Scene of Crime Manager, Bill Jones, responded. "Bizarre, Sir. I've never searched a property like it. Number 4 that is. I've seen show homes that looked more lived in. Not a scrap of paper anywhere. No letters, no bills. Not even a catalogue."

From Nick: "Not even a flyer for an Indian restaurant?"

Bill chuckled. "Nope. Must have chucked it. But it's not just the lack of paperwork. There's no TV, no music system – she must use her phone for all of that. The rooms are sparsely furnished."

From the back again: "It was a rental property."

Jones conceded the point. "There were very few clothes. She seems to have several pairs of black jeans, black tops, and not much else."

"Any sign of a hooded jacket? Or a baseball cap?"

"Nope."

"Anything of interest in the bins?"

"No, we searched them all, not just those marked as No 4. Nothing of interest in any of them. As for forensic results, they are much as you'd expect. The house is as clean as a whistle. No sign of any prints except hers, apart from some on power points in the garage. I'll come back to those. We found DNA traces only of one person, presumably hers. I'd say the house has been deep cleaned recently, and very thoroughly. We've not had the results on the DNA back yet. We'll have to wait another couple of days for those. Yes, Sir. I have explained that we need the results before we have to charge or release her, but we have no leverage with the lab, you know that.

"The only potentially interesting result is that we obtained a DNA sample from the inner surface of a reflective sash in the garage. Maybe it's not Alex."

"Raising the possibility that it belongs to the mysterious Mr Haw."

"Or Feliks? Are they one and the same?"

"Good question, Morton. Let's hope to God we get those results soon. Anything else, Bill?"

"The car is still being examined. There is some DNA evidence, but it's a bit skimpy. Otherwise, nothing of interest."

"What about Number 3?"

"Empty. Again, no TV, music system or landline. Has it ever been lived in? Not sure. It doesn't look as though the oven has ever been used. There are a few prints, including some on light switches which match those in Number 4's garage. Could be the original electrician. That's about it, I'm afraid."

"What about DNA?"

"Tricky to say the least. In an unfurnished house there are no sites where DNA can generally be recovered easily, like arm rests on furniture. There are slight traces there, but all the surfaces are hard – very fine grain wood laminate flooring and so on, all of which have been thoroughly cleaned at some stage. I suspect they'll be unidentifiable – maybe just people who worked on the house."

"Thank you. That doesn't sound promising. What about the mobile phone and laptop?"

"That's me, Sir, Joe Broad."

"Of course, Joe, good to see you. What have you got?"

"The mobile is the latest iPhone, released last October. There are no contacts listed. Recent incoming calls are few – all are 'number withheld'. Outgoing calls are also few in number, to Prentice & Co, Mortimer & Ballard and a local Indian takeaway." Laughter erupted. "No, not that one. But it's one that accepts cash payment at the door, so no trail on her debit card. There's no internet browsing history, and no apps other than those which were pre-installed. Bit like her house, Sir. Clean as a whistle."

Upwood sighed. "And her laptop?"

"Worse. It's the latest Apple MacBook Pro. High spec. But virtually nothing on it. There are no data files. If she keeps them, it must be on an external hard drive. Apple don't have a consumer cloud storage facility yet, although I think it's due to be released later this year. There's no email client installed – maybe she's just using webmail. There's no browsing history and no cookies are stored. The only app other than those pre-installed is for online poker."

"Have you been able to recover deleted files?"

"Yes, but there was hardly anything there. If she was creating files she must have done so on the external hard drive rather than on her laptop. And to make matters worse, she's using an app like TOR. It's not one I've seen before. I had to consult an expert at the Met. They don't know much about it but think it's east European."

"Joe, you'd better explain. I have only a vague idea what that means." In fact, he had a pretty good idea what it meant, but thought it likely that some of his officers might not.

"Tor is an application that allows you access to the internet without leaving any record of where you've been or what you've done. It means The Onion Ring because it's as if you have to go through multiple layers to get where you want to be. Data is bounced around from one server to the next apparently randomly and generally via more than one country. You can surf the net, chat and send instant messages anonymously. TOR is used not only for licit anonymity but also for illicit purposes: the distribution of pornography, child abuse content, the facilitation of drug sales. I could go on. The term TOR is often used as a generic, a bit like hoover."

"We get the picture, Joe, thank you. So presumably we have no way of finding out what she uses it for?"

"Realistically? No. GCHQ might. But I can't see how we could get them involved."

"Quite. So, once more, no hard evidence, but a wealth of circumstantial evidence that she is involved in illegal activities. But where does she keep her passport, her external hard drive? I bet she has another phone, too. And she must have at least one current passport in order that she can make a rapid escape if necessary. Morton, arrange to have someone investigate, will you? There's too much about this woman we don't know. And we're running out of time to hold her.

"Stephanie, you went back to Keresley with more questions?"

"I did, Sir. Not that it got me very far. They say they have no knowledge of Alex Barron and if Kerrigan arranged for her to stay there it was off the books, so to speak. Kerrigan is now retired and enjoying a round the world cruise."

"And no doubt your contact has no idea which cruise line he is using?"

"No idea, Sir. Of course not. That would be too easy. And mobile reception onboard ocean-going liners is patchy to say the least, even if we knew which liner he's on."

"If he's even on a cruise," came a comment from the back.

"If he even exists," came another.

"OK, everyone. I know this is frustrating after all the hard work we've put in. I'm quite sure a lot of what we've been told is a pack of lies. Our job is to find a way through that. Now, Stephanie, what did they have to say about Philip Haw?"

"Philip Haw is apparently on secondment to an associate company based in Hong Kong, currently investigating investment opportunities in southern China."

"And no doubt just as impossible to contact." Upwood sighed. If the facts as given by Keresley were true, then the chances of their being able to contact either man before they were due to charge or release Alex were slim to non-existent. In reality, it was almost certainly another tissue of lies.

"Sir. A question. Did you ask her about her relationship to Oksana Baranova?"

"No. I thought about it. We have no proof that Alexandra Baranova is Alex Barron, although the similarity of their names is suggestive. As is the photo we've seen that appears to show Oksana's daughter Saskia taken in Cambridge. At the moment, I'd rather have her wondering just how much we do know. Whether that's the right call, I don't know. That said, she must realise that we know who Feliks is."

When Upwood discussed the case with Emily that evening, the mood was sombre.

"You'll have to release her won't you James?"

"Almost certainly. It's an absolute bugger. There's no doubt in my mind that we've identified our culprit. But proving it is almost impossible. I'm praying that we get some helpful DNA results, but I'm not holding my breath."

"I should think not, it is the weekend after all. Even though we've asked them to fast-track it, I can't see them getting anything to us before time's up. With hindsight we'd have done better to arrest her on Monday when the lab had a full week ahead of them. We'll have lost time over the weekend."

This was one criticism which Upwood was forced to concede was well-founded. "It's a fair point. We'll have to maintain full surveillance when we release her. It would be right up her street to carry out another attack."

"I don't like it, but I'm bound to agree. Thank God the Herald hasn't got wind of it."

"They have, I'm afraid. Gossip about an arrest off Maids Causeway has made it onto social media. The paper has picked it up. They asked us to confirm reports of the arrest and so far we have declined. They've put up a brief report on their Facebook page, but I don't think it gets much readership. Worryingly it does mention Alex by name, and her previous conviction. They are probably just waiting for the right opportunity to go to print."

Emily looked concerned. "How did they get her name?"

"Your guess is as good as mine. A leak or careless talk, probably. I've stressed to the team again the need to be discreet, but you know how it is."

Upwood had no choice. He released Alex without charge on the Monday morning, albeit on bail pending further enquiries. Much to his intense annoyance he later learned that Trevor Rix, accompanied by a photographer, had been outside the station, having calculated when the release was likely to take place. While neither Alex nor her solicitor answered any of his questions, Rix did at least have a good photograph. He would know that a suspect would only have been held for ninety-six hours if the potential charge was murder. It was enough for a story, if brief; one to discredit Upwood once more.

Chapter 62

DCI's dark secrets

Over a period of months, during which painstaking research has been carried out, we have learned that one of the city's most respected senior police officers has been hiding some very dark secrets.

Detective Chief Inspector James Upwood arrived in Cambridge several years ago, following a successful career in Gloucester CID. His transfer and promotion to Cambridge followed the death of his infant daughter who was only seven months old and, shortly afterwards, that of his wife. At the inquest into daughter Olivia's death, it was recorded that the autopsy had shown no obvious cause of death and the coroner concluded that the child had died as a result of sudden infant death syndrome. During the inquest, evidence was given that the child had died while in the care of her mother, Anne, who had for some time been suffering from postpartum psychosis. Questions were raised as to whether she was fit to care for the child, and while the court was told that there was no evidence to support the proposition, there are those who continue to ask whether the child had been neglected. The child's mother died three weeks after the inquest into Olivia's death. The subsequent inquest into Anne's death concluded that she had died by her own hand, while the balance of her mind was disturbed. She had been found dead in the bath, her wrists slit after ingesting a significant quantity of prescription medicine, sufficient to cause drowsiness.

Since his arrival in Cambridge, DCI Upwood has been Senior Investigating Officer on a number of high-profile cases. Most recently he and his team were able to secure prosecutions in the case of two murders and a related case of manslaughter, against one man, widely known as 'the wind farm murderer', and the murder of a man whose killer attempted to link the death to the wind farm case. The cases were complex, but it seemed for a considerable period of time that Upwood and his team made no progress. Readers may recall that during this case he was photographed enjoying lunch with an attractive female companion at a Michelin starred restaurant, which elicited some criticism. During this period, too, rumours began to circulate that he was not fit to conduct the case, and indeed, should not have remained a serving police officer after the events surrounding the deaths of his wife and daughter. Questions were raised as to whether he himself had been involved in either or both deaths. It was these questions which prompted our investigation.

Currently DCI Upwood leads the investigation into the suspicious deaths of four people who were living on the city's streets. This investigation has been underway for nearly three months with no obvious signs of progress. Having learned of recent police activity in Queen's Walk we asked Cambridge Constabulary's Press Office if it was connected to the case. They declined to comment.

Should he still be leading this major enquiry? Read the instalment which follows in our next issue for more startling revelations.

The article was accompanied by the photo of Upwood at the Olive Branch previously published by the Herald.

Detective Superintendent Adams had read the report with increasing alarm. She decided there was little to be gained by having a formal meeting with Upwood until the second article had been published. She phoned him. "You've seen the Herald's latest article I take it?"

"Yes, Ma'am."

"Is there anything you think you should tell me?"

"In response to the article? No. There's nothing there you don't already know." He held his breath.

"What will they publish next, James? You must have some idea."

He assured her that he had no idea what 'revelations' the paper might have in mind, which was by no means entirely truthful, but there was nothing to be gained by sharing his concerns with her.

Katie was shattered when she read the report. Upwood went to see her that evening. He too was troubled, probably more troubled if truth be told, than he had ever been in his professional career.

"It's that little shit, Trevor Rix. Remember I told you about him after that press conference?"

"The one who accused you of skiving off on holiday when you should have been holding the fort here?"

"The very same."

"Was he the one who wrote that poisonous piece about us at the Olive Branch?"

"I honestly don't recall. But it wouldn't surprise me. It's his style. The longer he's been with the paper the more aggressive he's become."

"Why has he got it in for you? It's vicious."

"I've no idea. I've never crossed swords with the man, apart from ignoring his question at that conference. It may not even be personal. He's probably trying to make a name for himself. Perhaps he thinks he can win himself a job on a national paper, one less likely to be reduced to an online-only format."

"But it's despicable. June and Jeff will have a fit. Will they have seen it?"

"I called them earlier to warn them. They hadn't seen it then. It's not on sale in Oundle of course. But they do sometimes look at it online,"

"What d'you imagine they are going to put in their next instalment?"

He shuddered. "I've no idea." The trouble was, he had. And the thought appalled him.

Chapter 63

The new week did not start well. Mo had supplied a doctor's certificate indicating that he should remain off work for a further four weeks when his condition would be reviewed. His decision to visit Margaret so soon after his discharge from hospital had been ill-judged and his collapse had set back his recovery. By now, everyone at Parkside knew about the article in the Herald. Already, Upwood sensed that people were taking sides, those who supported him, and those who just loved the idea of a scandal. It made for an uncomfortable working atmosphere.

Margaret returned to Parkside on Tuesday and told Morton that she wanted a transfer. She had a sister in Yorkshire and wanted to move there, away from all that would remind her of Luuk, and indeed Mo. Morton was sorry and did his best to persuade her that it was too soon to make such a decision, but she was adamant. He mentioned it to Upwood who said he would consult Emily. Emily was sympathetic to the idea that Margaret should have a fresh start. As it happened, she knew the Chief Constable in York well. It seemed as though for once, Margaret was in luck. A DC was due to start maternity leave at the start of the following month. All things being equal, Margaret could start there on maternity cover, with the possibility of a permanent posting.

Surveillance had been re-established on Maids Causeway. Morton had queried whether it was appropriate, as it was likely that Alex would be aware of it. Upwood had said that they were doing all they could. They were varying the unmarked vehicles and their positions frequently. If she left the house, they had to know where she was going.

Just as Morton was preparing to leave Parkside, Upwood was told that the body of another rough sleeper had just been found by PC Taylor. He was furious and demanded a report from the surveillance team. The officers swore blind that Alex had not set foot onto Queen's Walk, much less Maids Causeway. He despatched Debra and two uniformed officers to Alex's home to find and arrest her. He demanded that Taylor report to him immediately.

When Debra and her team arrived at Number 4, they could get no answer. She instructed them to break the door down. The house was empty. She relayed the information to Morton by phone. By now, Upwood was incandescent and told Margaret to find out how she had made her escape.

PC Taylor was anxious, to say the least, when he found himself standing in front of Upwood and Morton. His account was less than inspiring.

"I saw him about 40 minutes ago, Sir."

"About, Taylor? Not good enough. What time was it?" Upwood rarely showed anger to junior officers but his patience was at breaking point.

"16.25, I reckon. There or thereabouts. He was alright then, talking to someone on King Street. I was on the other side of the road. I didn't have a clear view of the other person because there was a pillar in the way. But I got a vague impression that he might have been given something."

"And you didn't investigate immediately?"

"No, Sir. Sorry, Sir."

"What the hell were you thinking of, man? It was you who found Sally wasn't it? We've had three more since then! It didn't strike you as suspicious that someone was giving something to a street sleeper?"

"Not at first. I didn't clock him as homeless to begin with. He was just a bit scruffy. Could have been anyone."

"And then what, for crying out loud?"

"It was about twenty minutes later. I was walking back along King Street and he was on the ground, writhing about and vomiting violently. I called an ambulance. By the time they'd come he was dead."

"Jesus wept. And what about the other person?"

"Gone. Not sure where, but instinct tells me they were heading for Milton's Walk."

"Taylor, you're a disgrace to your uniform. She might have been in custody by now if you'd used whatever passes for your brain."

Taylor gritted his teeth but did not respond. Saying sorry simply wouldn't cut it with the DCI. He was sent out to make a more detailed statement to another officer.

Upwood and Morton studied the large-scale map of the city hanging on Upwood's wall.

"She's heading for the station. She knows she can't go home. She can't take a taxi. She can't use the BMW as she knows we'd track it. She'll be walking to the station and heading for Stansted. I'd bet money on it."

"Damn and blast it, you're right. What time was it Taylor said he saw them first?"

"16.25 as near as dammit. She'd get there in about half an hour. It's almost a straight line across Christ's Pieces, down Christ's Lane, into St Andrew's Street, down Regent Street and Hills Road onto Station Road."

"So is she already on a train?"

Morton was busy on his phone. "No, but she soon will be. The first train she could catch is the 17.11 Great Anglian service, it's non-stop. Gets in at 17.41. To Platform 1."

"Call Stansted police immediately and get them to meet her. Send a photograph. It's not a long train is it?"

"No. Typically four carriages from memory." He was already waiting for a response from Stansted police. They would try, they said, but weren't hopeful they could get someone there in time. They rang back a matter of minutes later. "Sorry, Sir. Just couldn't get to the platform in time. You only gave us seven minutes. She could be anywhere now."

"CCTV. Send me the footage of passengers getting off that train, now. It's of the utmost urgency. She's killed five people. We must catch her!"

There was a knock at the door. Debra poked her head in. "Is she heading for Stansted?" They nodded. They'd all come to the same conclusion. "I think I know what name she'll be using. Sandra Lord. I was just about to tell you when I rushed over to Queen's Walk."

"Promising. How do you work that out?"

She briefly recounted the examination of the delegate list for the conference Alex had attended. Of the one hundred and thirty-three delegates, one hundred and twenty-eight had been positively identified. Of the others, one was a freelance journalist. Unless Alex was impersonating him, he could probably be eliminated. She outlined her reasons for discounting three more delegates. Upwood and Morton considered them entirely reasonable.

"My hunch is that she's going by the name Sandra Lord, or was, at least for the purpose of the conference. She, too, gave her position as freelance journalist, but I can find no accreditation for a journalist of that name. She may of course be unaccredited, but attendance at these conferences does not come cheap and I doubt a rookie would shell out unless there was a serious prospect of earning revenue from a report. And the name, Sandra, another diminutive of Alexandra, and Lord, not a million miles away from baron. I can't think why she wouldn't still be using it."

"Good work, Debra. Maybe we have a fighting chance after all."

Morton was on his phone again examining departure flight times from Stansted. "Let's assume she did arrive at Stansted at 17.41. She's probably buying her ticket there. Let's say best case she can get from the platform to her check in desk in half an hour. That takes us to 18.11. So we're looking at flights that take off two hours or so later." He moved over to a white board and began scribbling:

20:05 Krakow
20:05 Vilnius
20:10 Belfast
20:15 Dubai
21:05 Glasgow
21:10 Madrid
21:20 Dublin
21:30 Belfast
22:20 Istanbul.

"That's it."

"She won't want to be hanging around for the Istanbul flight," Debra offered.

"Cross off Dublin and the UK airports. Krakow is too far south in Poland to be of much interest to her," Upwood volunteered.

"And I can't see why Dubai would appeal." Morton crossed that off too, as Upwood nodded.

"That leaves us with Vilnius at 20.05. A good waypoint for Russia perhaps. And Madrid, at 20.10, with onward flights to Málaga. And neither flight needs her to hang around for too long at Stansted."

"Morton, get on to airport police again. Tell them to keep their eyes peeled but give a heavy focus on those two flights. I'd better go and brief Emily."

He was heading that way when Margaret intercepted him. "She got out through No 8, Sir. The house immediately behind hers. There's a door on the north side that takes her straight out to a network of footpaths, one of which leads to Midsummer Common. An easy walk across the common would bring her to Four Lamps Roundabout, a short distance from where the body was found."

Upwood went to Detective Superintendent Adams' office. It would be hard to say which of them was most angry. She was pacing around her office, her face flushed. Upwood decided to sit to keep out of her way.

She swung round to face him. "How in heaven's name did you miss this, James?"

"What conceivable reason could we have had for suspecting there might be such an escape route from the Mews? We're not psychic for God's sake! She was living in Number 4 and to all intents and purposes Number 8 was unoccupied. There's no back door shown on the original plans for the development. We've put urgent calls out to the architect and the builder to see if they can shed any light on it."

"Much good that will do. Stable doors come to mind. The press are going to have a field day with this. Never mind that cretin didn't stop her before the act. Never mind that Stansted police weren't able to establish if she was on that train. Even assuming you're right and she is going to Stansted."

"It's all very well to criticise, Ma'am, but if you've had better ideas than me on how to conduct this case you've not shared them with me. Bar your suggestion about the bicycle treads. Thank you for that." Upwood made no effort to disguise his sarcasm.

Even Emily's neck was flushed now. "It's not my job to second guess every step of the investigation, you know that. It's to supervise the process, ensure you have the right resources and so on."

"I know that perfectly well. But I'd like to think that my superior officer is more experienced and skilled than I am. It's pretty bloody demoralising if she's not. And I've seen no evidence of any support from our Acting Chief Constable. And I don't mean platitudinous statements to the effect that I have his full support. That's always an invitation to resign or a precursor to dismissal. I mean the kind of support where it looks as though we are all actually singing from the same hymn sheet. Have you ever led an investigation like this?" She gave him a stony look. "No, I thought not. Has he? I doubt it."

Emily remained silent until she was sure he'd finished his rant. "Your mind's not been on the job though, has it? Your trips to Spain. The Herald article. Katie's return."

"How the hell do you know Katie's back? And what business is it of yours? And the trips to Spain have allowed me to demonstrate the OCG links."

"In answer to your first question, it's my job to know about anything affecting your performance."

"And how has Katie's return affected my performance exactly? It's preposterous."

She made no attempt to answer his question. "As for the OCG links. They're tenuous to say the least."

"You think the fact that DNA on the cycling belt shows a clear filial link to Alex Barron, and that her brother is known to the Policía Nacional as involved in organised crime is tenuous? The fact that the latest prostitute to die was also poisoned by *Gelsemiun elegans* is a coincidence I suppose? Really? For crying out loud. You are hanging me out to dry here! I'd honestly thought better of you. Ma'am."

Emily then made a remark that was most uncharacteristic of her: "You'd never dare speak to me like that if I were a man!"

Upwood practically choked. "You are joking, aren't you? When have I ever been disrespectful to you, except perhaps when you've been having a go at me about Katie, and then you've been right out of order. Remind me who your predecessor was."

She had the grace to look embarrassed, but kept her counsel.

"Clarke, right? And you honestly don't think I'd give him a hard time in similar circumstances? Though to be fair he probably wouldn't keep banging on about personal relationships, would he?"

Emily looked thunderous but had to concede defeat. She glowered at him. "This is getting us nowhere."

Upwood sat back in his chair, knowing he'd pushed his boss to the limit and that she'd recognised it. Somehow, they had to find a solution. An olive branch was needed. "Should we hold a press conference, Ma'am?"

"And say what precisely? That we've had to release our only suspect because we can't find enough evidence to charge her and now we have another body? We'd be a laughing stock. Worse, we'd be accused of gross incompetence."

"What do you suggest then? We have to say something, and quickly."

She nodded reluctantly. "A short press release, saying that another rough sleeper has died in suspicious circumstances but until next of kin have been notified and we have the results of the post-mortem no further information will be provided."

"A finger in the dyke, at best."

"Damn it, James. Can you come up with a better idea?" He couldn't. It might give them a bit of breathing space, but not for long. "And don't ever presume to talk to me like that again, d'you understand? I'll let it go this time, because I know how much strain you've been under, but I will not tolerate such insubordination again."

Upwood rose to leave, hoping her response to his outburst had been weak because she knew she was on shaky ground.

When Upwood got back to his own office, Morton was waiting for him. We've got an ID, Sir. "A youngish man, Sir. No ID on him. But Mary Canning says he's Richard Sykes. Looks to be about thirty years of age, but, as you know, with rough sleepers they can often look older than their years. I can tell you that he has been violently sick, and had diarrhoea."

"Christ Almighty. Any sign of a can or carton?"

"Absolutely none. I've got uniformed officers searching all the litter bins nearby, but so far nothing. We did find a scattering of orange peel, though."

"And an orange would be even easier to spike than a drinks container."

"Much. Especially as she no longer has the kit we found in the shed."

"Have the peel sent to that specialist lab and ask for an urgent analysis."

His phone rang. He listened for a moment. "Damn and blast!" He slammed the phone down so hard the desk shook. Stansted police say she didn't check in for either the Vilnius or the Madrid flight. Perhaps she didn't go to Stansted after all."

"She did. I'm sure of it. I've seen the CCTV footage from Platform 1. She's doing her best to keep her head down, but I'd bet good money I saw her get off that train."

"Get the Stansted police to check the toilets in case she's hiding. Maybe she's planning on taking a flight early tomorrow. And get them to send us the passenger lists for all the flights after 20.00 this evening. Maybe she's using yet another name."

"Bloody hell! I bet she is. She's running effing rings round us!"

When the lists came through, Debra studied them. Sandra Lord did not appear on any of them. One name did catch her eye though: Aleksandra Antonova, on the Vilnius flight. The name was definitely more Russian than Lithuanian. And the forename was yet another form of Alexandra. Morton agreed that it looked promising, and called the airport police once more, asking them to send any footage they had of the queues for check in for the Vilnius flight.

It wasn't until the following morning that it came through. Debra checked the files and identified a couple of women who looked like Alex. Morton examined them and pointed at one. "That's her! She's got the same scarf she was wearing when she got off the train. And the backpack is the same. Why in heaven's name didn't they pick her up?"

The police were apologetic. Check in staff were on the look out for Sandra Lord. They had no reason to suspect that Aleksandra Antonova, who had a strong Russian accent, was the woman they were looking for.

Emily was understandably furious when she learned what had happened. The more so when Upwood confirmed that Alex's DNA had been recovered from the newspaper cutting found in the shed. Even she had to concede now that Alex was guilty. She may have been critical of Upwood during the investigation, but dammit, as usual he'd been right. There was no doubt she was linked to the organised crime group in Spain, and no doubt had all the resources she needed to escape capture. They would have to apply for a European Arrest Warrant. For now, she was in the wind.

Chapter 64

How did DCI Upwood's wife really die?
Our previous article reported on concerns surrounding the deaths of DCI James Upwood's infant daughter and wife.
Now we wish to draw attention to what appears to be his cavalier attitude to the use of his time during major investigations. We have previously reported on his lunch-time assignation with an attractive female companion at the Olive Branch in Clipsham, Rutland, during a critical phase of the investigation into what became known as the wind farm murders. Information has recently come to light that the woman in question is Katie Melhuish, a partner in one of the country's leading accountancy firms. She was also the partner of Mark Campion who was murdered in February 2007 and whose murder was investigated by DCI Upwood. Our source tells us their affair, which appears to be somewhat 'on/off' in nature, began while that investigation was underway. Was this ethical, we ask ourselves?
At the first press conference on this current wave of five murders DCI Upwood was asked why he took a holiday when a serial killer was at large. He declined to comment. We have since learnt that he was visiting Miss Melhuish in Spain. A second trip to Spain is believed to have taken place since then. Does this look like someone taking his responsibilities seriously?
On the death of Upwood's wife, the coroner concluded that she had taken her own life while the balance of her mind was disturbed. Evidence was offered to demonstrate just how disturbed she was. But would the coroner have come to the same conclusion had he all the facts?
Upwood, then a Detective Inspector, was on a surveillance operation in Gloucester, in the vicinity of Gloucester Constabulary HQ, in the company of a female officer. According to the pathologist, Anne Upwood died during the

afternoon on which this surveillance took place. Two witnesses state that Upwood and his colleague left their surveillance post that afternoon, driving four miles to the female officer's home. She was seen to enter at approximately 4.00 pm. DI Upwood drove away alone. The next confirmed sighting of Upwood is at the surveillance post when relieved by two officers at approximately 5.00 pm. One of those officers confirms that DI Upwood was alone in his car. He drove straight home. A few minutes after 5.00 pm he dialled 999 to report his wife's apparent suicide.
Upwood's home was also close to the HQ. The estimated journey time from the surveillance post to his colleague's home, on to his own home, then back to his post, would only take eleven or twelve minutes. We know from reports of the inquest into Anne's death that Upwood had been worried about his wife. Did he in fact go home before returning to his post? There is a period of approximately forty-five minutes unaccounted for. If he did go home, what did he do there? We believe these questions deserve an answer.

If Emily had been alarmed by the Herald's first article, she was appalled by this one. If the report was accurate, Gloucestershire Constabulary had not been very thorough in their investigation of Anne's death, Upwood had lied about his movements on the day in question, and there had been yet another leak, presumably from Parkside, about his trips to Spain. And how in heaven's name had they discovered that Upwood's affair with Katie began during the investigation into her lover's death? No one was going to come out of this smelling of roses, including Emily herself.

She conferred with the Acting Chief Constable, who, keen to toss the grenade as far away as possible, instructed her to email a copy of both articles to Gloucestershire's Chief Constable, Simon Pettigrew. She did so.

Someone had thoughtfully left a copy of the Herald on Upwood's desk. The article, together with another photo of Upwood was, of course, front page and above the fold. His worst fears had been realised. Emily would no doubt be calling him in short order. Until then he continued to work, albeit with his concentration badly impaired.

Sure enough, just before he was due to leave for the evening, the call came through.

"Sit down James." Her face was like thunder. "You've read the Herald I assume?"

"I have Ma'am."

"So have I. So has the Acting Chief Constable. So has The Chief Constable of Gloucestershire Constabulary. I am instructed to suspend you with immediate effect pending a decision as to what action to take."

"But you can't take action on the strength of this article, Ma'am. They have provided no substantive evidence of their allegations."

"I'm not talking about punitive action. I am talking about whether the issue is to be reviewed by Professional Standards, or referred to the IPCC. Or whether a criminal investigation will be opened into your wife's death."

"But you know most of what's in that article is prejudicial and based largely on supposition." Upwood knew there was nothing to be gained by such a response, but couldn't help himself.

"I no longer know what to believe, James. In any case it's not my decision. It's Pettigrew's. So clear your desk and leave this afternoon. You are to have no contact with anyone here at Parkside, at Quedgely, or of course, with the media. You will remain in the UK, and on call."

"Who will take over from me?"

"Morton will remain Deputy SIO. I shall become SIO pro tem, but if your suspension looks likely to last any length of time, and I'm bound to say that does seem likely, then we will bring in another DCI to replace you."

"Permanently?"

"Much too early to say. Just leave. I have called a meeting of your team in half an hour to explain what is happening. You are not to speak to them."

"Not even Morton?"

"Not even Morton."

He stood, looked at her straight in the eyes, turned and left the room.

Upwood cleared his desk of the very few items he needed and headed straight for Katie's apartment in Glenalmond Avenue. He kissed her on the cheek, put his briefcase down and headed for the kitchen. He poured two large whiskies. She looked at him strangely – they didn't normally drink whisky this early in the evening, well at least she didn't. He led her to the sofa and handed her the glass. It was obvious she was still in blissful ignorance and was horrified when he showed her the article and told her about his conversation with Emily. "I am so very sorry you've been dragged into all this." She was in tears by this time, but for him rather than herself.

"What a shit that man is! How can he live with himself when he's causing misery for so many people? You, June and Jeff, your colleagues in Gloucester…"

What could he say?

"What will happen?" Anxiety was etched on her face.

His voice was low. "I've been suspended."

"Christ, Emily doesn't believe this shit, does she?"

"It's not her call. Gloucester will decide what to do. There will be some sort of investigation."

"What d'you mean 'some sort of investigation'?"

"Professional Standards at the very least. Quite possibly they'll refer it to the Independent Police Complaints Commission. They might open a criminal investigation." He drained his glass as Katie absorbed the implications. She had, until now, hardly touched hers. Now she downed it quickly and handed it to him. He returned a minute later with refills.

"What will you do?"

"Wait. There's nothing I can do."

There was a long pause while Katie plucked up the courage to ask: "Did you leave your post early?"

Upwood stared at her. Of course she would ask that question, but he did so wish she hadn't. "I can't talk about it right now, my darling. I don't even want to think about it at the moment. I will tell you, I owe you that. Just not now. This all happened six years ago. I've had nightmares about it ever since. You've helped chase those demons away."

"And now they'll come back to haunt you. Stay here tonight please. I don't want to be on my own. I'll probably have nightmares too."

"I'd better not. Bloody Rix will have someone watching us."

"Truly, I'm past caring." In truth, so was he.

Chapter 65

Emily had told Upwood he was to have no contact with anyone at Parkside. She had imposed no ban on his speaking to the Spanish police. Even if she had thought to do it, he would have ignored the instruction. He called Paco.

"Good morning my friend. Todo bien? Cómo siempre?"

Paco laughed. "Sí, sí. All good and you?"

"Not good. Oksana Baranova's daughter. She was calling herself Alex Barron when we first met her. She has killed five homeless people. She has left England on another passport. Can you ask María to watch for her?"

"Sí, we can do this. You think she will come to España?"

"I think there's a good chance. We have applied for a European Arrest Warrant, but I don't know when it will be issued."

"I understand. I will call you, OK?"

Upwood wasn't overly optimistic, but it was worth a try.

To his astonishment, Paco called back that evening. "Is very strange. María says a woman arrive at the villa yesterday. She speak only Russian to Sra Baranova. Her hair is different. More red, she says. The señora say she is family from Russia. She have una etiqueta de equipaje. The name is Antonova. But she look like your woman. And María say she move in the house like she live there. Not like a visitor. Is a good observacíon, I think."

"It's a very good observation. She is very smart. We think Antonova is the name she used to leave England. Paco, I'll have to ask my boss to make our enquiry official. Who is the senior officer to speak to?"

"Ah, el Comisario. Comisario Juan Adolfo Sanchez. I text you a number for him."

"Excellent, Paco. A thousand thanks for all your help."

If Upwood was astonished to receive Paco's call, Emily was even more surprised to receive his.

"What do you want, James?"

"I have information for you, from Spain. My contact there, Francisco Garrido, tells me Alex has almost certainly arrived in Estepona. A woman turned up at Oksana Baranova's villa yesterday. Her luggage tag named her as Antonova. And the maid made a very astute observation. Despite the fact that the woman only spoke Russian and was apparently a family member from Russia, María said she moved around the house like she was born in it. I have the name and number of Comisario Juan Adolfo Sanchez in Estepona. I think you should phone him and ask that they maintain surveillance on the house pending the issue of the warrant."

Emily was stunned. Maybe they'd catch her after all.

Upwood had to content himself that he had done everything he could to bring her to justice. It was out of his hands. Emily had told him Mo would not face charges in Hertfordshire, one anxiety removed. Margaret's future seemed assured. Debra would not come back to her old team, whatever happened. Now all he could do was wait the outcome of his own fate. There was nothing more he could do.

Emily's optimism was short-lived. Three days later she was told that María had seen Alex leave the house, with her backpack. She got into a car and was driven away by her brother. Some two hours later he returned, alone. The clear inference was that he'd taken her to Málaga airport. And they had no idea where she was going, what identity she was using, nor how she might be found. Alex was in the wind. Again.

Notes and Acknowledgements

This book took much longer to write than planned. Sadly my beloved husband Andrew did not live to see its publication. Nor did good friend Michael McCroddan, once a member of Special Branch, who had been an avid reader of the first two books in this series, and a great encouragement to me.

As before, many people have contributed their help. In particular, I thank Dr Chris Threapleton of St George's Hospital, who helped with the passages dealing with medical issues, Barry Griffiths of Jimmy's, the Cambridge shelter for homeless people, and Dexter Petley of Jericho Writers, my editor, whose advice as ever has been invaluable. Benn Gunn, retired Chief Constable, has once again guided me on some of the higher level policy and procedural issues. Others have been steadfast in their encouragement to me to bring this book to publication. I thank you all.

If you have read my earlier books, you will know that I enjoy detailed and intricate plotting. This habit naturally creates countless opportunities for error. I take full responsibility for any errors in this book, and hope that you will forgive the artistic licence I have used from time to time in an effort to make it an enjoyable read.

If you have enjoyed it, please take a minute or two to post a review on Amazon. Your feedback will provide encouragement to me as I embark on the fourth book in this series.

Rosemary Rowntree
June 2025

Printed in Dunstable, United Kingdom